CHRIS POURTEAU

WARPATH

WAR FOR EMPIRE

2

aethonbooks.com

WARPATH
©2023 Chris Pourteau

This book is protected under the copyright laws of the United States of America. No part of this publication may be reproduced, stored in a retrieval system, or transmitted, in any form or by any means, without the prior permission in writing of the publisher, nor be otherwise circulated in any form of binding or cover other than that in which it is published and without a similar condition including this condition being imposed on the subsequent purchaser. Any reproduction or unauthorized use of the material or artwork contained herein is prohibited without the express written permission of the authors.

Aethon Books supports the right to free expression and the value of copyright. The purpose of copyright is to encourage writers and artists to produce the creative works that enrich our culture.

The scanning, uploading, and distribution of this book without permission is a theft of the author's intellectual property. If you would like to use material from the book (other than for review purposes), please contact editor@aethonbooks.com. Thank you for your support of the author's rights.

Aethon Books
www.aethonbooks.com

Print and eBook formatting by Steve Beaulieu.

Published by Aethon Books LLC.

Aethon Books is not responsible for websites (or their content) that are not owned by the publisher.

This book is a work of fiction. Names, characters, places, and incidents are the product of the author's imagination or are used fictitiously. Any resemblance to actual events, locales, or persons, living or dead is coincidental.

All rights reserved.

ALSO BY CHRIS POURTEAU FROM AETHON BOOKS

WAR FOR EMPIRE

Legacy

Warpath

Invasion

STAND ALONE NOVELS

Optional Retirement Plan

1

GET SIRIUS!

"HOW MUCH LONGER DOES THIS shit go on, Captain?"

Ben Stone ignored the question from the white-knuckled civy taking up the navigator's seat. To accommodate the mission, the pilot was pulling double duty. The jittery civilian sitting at navigation was definitely *not* a navigator.

Meteorological readings from the destroyer *Shenandoah* had identified the atmospheric storms on approach to the planet. They posed no real danger, so command had refused to delay the drop. Subspace from Earth was fat with demands. Why hadn't they landed yet? What was taking so long?

Shakespeare suggested a good start to ending humanity's problems would be to kill all the lawyers. Ben wondered if a better beginning would be purging the politicians first.

Same difference, he realized.

"What's your name again?" Ben asked.

The dropship *Banshee* bucked again, and the civy closed his eyes. In the dim interior, Ben could make out the crevices around hardened cheekbones. He wondered if the enamel on the man's teeth might crack.

"Zack!" came the clenched answer.

"That your first or last name?" Ben pressed.

"Both!"

Oh, yeah. He's one of those.

Entitled. Egocentric. Pain in the ass.

"Captain," the pilot muttered where only Ben could hear. He eyed Ben with mischief. "About thirty seconds."

Ben popped his harness loose and stood up carefully from the co-pilot's seat. He turned to find Zack, the director of President Bragg's newest morale-boosting documentary, staring up with something approaching awe at Ben's ability to keep his feet.

"About five more minutes, Zack," Ben said. Then, because he couldn't resist: "Sit tight, yeah?" The pilot turned his head so the civy wouldn't see him grin.

Ben passed Zack and through the secure fire door into the main hold. Sixty of the Alliance's finest ground-pounders, Dog Company of the 214th Battalion, First Drop Division, Alliance Ground Forces sat in two orderly rows along the ship's inner hull.

The newly promoted second lieutenant, Osira Tso, bobbed a wobbly greeting to Ben. He always seemed happy to see his captain, but then he should. Non-commissioned officer promotions were rare outside wartime. Ben's recommendation had made it happen for Tso. Wartime would be upon them soon enough. AGF Command liked to think ahead.

"How's it hanging, Cap?"

"Like a bell clapper in a windstorm," Ben answered, bracing himself against more atmo churn. "And my battlesuit's the bell."

Tso, who now commanded Devil-3 Platoon, cracked a smile wide open.

The rough ride smoothed out, the gravity compensators adjusting to the pull of Canis III. Normally, the Marines would be on their feet, ready to dive headfirst in their battlesuits for planetfall. But they wouldn't be high-diving onto Canis III. This was a command performance landing, an escort mission for Zack and his cameras.

"What's the point of this anyway?" someone complained a little too loudly.

Ben decided to make a joke of the nervous griping. "Bragg's lifting his leg on Sirius."

Snorts and guffaws answered, followed by another anonymous contribution.

"Well, he picked the right company for that."

"Dog Company dropping on the Dog Star!"

Second Lieutenant Rod Gupta, elbowing into the conversation as usual, with an attempt to ingratiate himself. It worked this time, as evidenced by a round of oo-rahs. Ben saw Gupta smile. He'd taken Devil-2 Platoon when Ben was given command of the company. Gupta sometimes acted like he was still in Officer Candidate School, still trying to make friends with men and women he should worry less about pleasing and more about leading. But he was young in his command.

Jesus, Ben thought. *Listen to me.*

He couldn't remember when he'd morphed from outcast to officer, but he knew a switch had flipped inside him after Drake's World. It was like every sermon his grandfather had ever lectured at him had suddenly solidified into a code of behavior. It was scary how hard that had set in. And a little disappointing to the playboy-maverick still squatting in his gut.

"Two minutes to planet's surface," the pilot announced.

"Vicky, why don't you take them through final checks again?" Ben said.

Victor Taikori stood up. He always seemed imminently capable of breaking out with acne, and his bulky battlesuit seemed to have swallowed him whole. But with Toma promoted, he had the tightest, most anal unit in Dog Company, which made sense, given he'd taken over Toma's old D-1 Platoon.

"Checklist!" Taikori barked, his voice breaking. Sanchez, the sergeant from Tso's command, smirked at that.

"Item three!" Taikori prompted.

"Don't forget your helmet!" Sixty pairs of heavy-gravity-trained lungs shouted it.

"Say what, Marines?" Sanchez groused.

"Don't forget your helmet!"

"Item two!" Taikori prompted.

"Don't die!"

"See also, item three," Taikori said. "And most important?"

"Don't embarrass the fucking president of the fucking Alliance!"

Taikori tossed a glance to Ben, who nodded.

"And one more time, folks," Ben said. "Practice for the cams. Get your minds right and..."

"Get Sirius, sir!"

Ben looked up and down the two benches of Marines. "That should impress the president. Helmets on." He returned to the control cabin and resecured himself in the co-pilot's seat.

"Sounds like they're eager," Zack said, his voice decidedly calmer. He was obviously looking forward to standing on a planet's surface again, even an alien one with a lot of storied lore preceding it. "Should make for great footage."

Ben grunted to himself. There'd been a time when he'd loved the idea of being the star of a presidential documentary. Then he'd become one. He couldn't take a piss without someone wanting to shake his hand. He didn't always wash first. Tiny victories.

"That's what you're here for, Zack," Ben said. "Great footage." Then, because he couldn't resist: "Might want to hold on. Landing could get bumpy."

The *Banshee* landed like the surface of Canis III was covered in velvet instead of dense iron-nickel alloy. She came to rest on a flat caprock near the old science camp location.

Ben debarked first and now stood watching the fresh activity of the engineers who'd landed three days earlier. They were the first humans to set foot on the planet in nearly eight decades. The platoons of Dog Company marched down the ramp and formed up behind him. Still aboard ship, Ben could hear Zack barking orders to his camera crew like a drill sergeant.

The discovery of Sirius C and its planets three centuries earlier had made the so-called Dog Star of the Canis Major Constellation a realistic Third Giant Leap for Mankind after colonization of Sylvan Novus in Alpha Centauri. That ambition had been snuffed out when the Arcœnum science expedition collided with Earth's own already squatting on Canis III, the only semi-viable planet orbiting Sirius C. The mercenaries protecting the Terran scientists hadn't understood the Arcœnum's insatiable curiosity about human technology because the Arcœnum lacked spoken or written language. The result had been the hundreds of thousands of deaths in the Specter War, so named for the overwhelming ability of the Arcœnum to weaponize mirage and mind-control to infect the brains of their human enemy. And it had all started here.

Somewhere among all those battlesuits in the old base camp was Major Bathsheba Toma, de facto commander, 214th Battalion, issuing what were no doubt precise orders with measurable outcomes. She and the 214th's engineering company had been sent ahead to assess the salvageability of the biodome left behind when the Alliance abandoned the planet. From what Ben could see, their work was cut out for them. The site had been the epicenter of the Specter War until it became an interstellar war destined for a fiery, costly end at Gibraltar Station in The Frontier. At this distance, the camp looked like a life-sized diorama, a museum display of the spartan architectural aesthetics of a hundred years past. Fallen into disrepair. Beaten to shit.

"This natural lighting sucks," Zack said, drawing up next to Ben. With its tinny connection, their dedicated channel made his voice sound whinier than usual. He looked awkward in his vac-suit, like a baby in a body-length diaper.

"You'll make do."

Dog Company's five platoons had finished assembling into neat blocks outside the *Banshee*. Tso, Taikori, and the other platoon leaders fronted each of their respective units. Ben turned to them.

"Orders from Battalion Command are to pup your billets in that area over there," Ben said, pointing to an area of relatively flat rock inside the perimeter of the base camp's damaged biodome. A foundation of polysteel and hexacrete sat atop the rock courtesy of the engineering company. "Major Toma also suggested I remind you about C-III's atmo—its combination of methane, nitrogen, and carbon dioxide isn't friendly to human lungs. So be prepared to live in your battlesuits for the foreseeable future."

The company channel clicked. "Captain, how long before the biodome is viable?" Gupta asked.

"A week, earliest."

"Shitting in the can it is, then," Sanchez, D-3's sergeant said.

"And everything else," someone chimed in. Followed by, more forlornly, "Almost."

Guttural laughter skipped across the company channel. Everyone sharing the same unspoken, commiserative joke.

Marine battlesuits were an unnatural wonder of human ingenuity. They contained everything a human needed to live in any environment: vacuum, heavy-g, toxic, airless, or underwater in the belly of a whale. But all that programming and airtight design couldn't account for the human psyche. No matter how hardened or macho you were, eating, drinking, pissing, shitting, and sleeping in the sealed polysteel armor twenty-four/seven felt like living in a tin can after a while. Your skin became claustrophobic and itchy. Sometimes the recycler couldn't keep up with the flop sweat. Cracks filled with it. Crannies crusted with mucous, especially in zero-g. You began to hate your own excretions. To add insult to discomfort, there was zero opportunity to relieve stress the old-fashioned way, despite the single most requested design upgrade of an inward-facing, gender-appropriate attachment. None of AGF's Engineering Design Division had ever needed it, the grousing went, and that accounted for the lack of said attachment to enable said relief.

The company went off to build its temporary housing, and Ben escorted Zack and his two assistants to Battalion Headquarters. Several hovering cases of documentary equipment followed, reminding Ben of the half-dozen floating cams that had followed him around Drake's World. The cases looked like they could carry ten times that many.

He wondered how Alice Keller was faring. He hadn't seen or heard from her since she'd been spirited away from the *Rubicon* by his grandfather and Morgan Henry. Zack's attempts at banter over comms went unrequited as Ben pondered the rewards of loyalty. Thorne was now Third Sector Fleet Commander, replacing Natasha Ferris, who'd been reassigned to the Centauri Sector. And Josiah Strickland—well, Ben thought, no man better fit the bill of an officer promoted despite incompetence. Brigadier General Bluster is how Ben named him privately. Or, after a few drinks—Brigadier General Bullshit.

"Ben!"

An armored glove waved from the entrance to the newly fabricated headquarters building. Bright over the left breast was the insignia of a full-bird colonel.

"Colonel Bradshaw," Ben said. "Good to see you."

"And you," she said. Through her plastinium visor, Ben could make out a welcoming smile. "I see you managed to land without killing the dogs." Her tone combined both tongue-in-cheek humor and a mother-bear growl.

"So far, so good, ma'am," he said.

When Josiah Strickland rose to brigadier general, he'd elevated two officers with him: Sandra Bradshaw to lieutenant colonel as his adjutant and personal liaison with and battalion commander of the 214th—now called by the media Bragg's Own Battalion. She'd recently been promoted again, in advance of this mission. It paid to have the favor of an officer with the president's favor. Bradshaw's meteoric advancement was a surprise, given her actions aboard the *Rubicon* when faced with mutiny by its commanding officer. She'd respected Nick Stone's authority as captain of the vessel and refused to intervene to stop Alice Keller's departure. But loyalty was the number one litmus test in the Bragg Administration, and somehow her adherence to strict military deference to rank had translated in Strickland's mind to an officer he could trust to defer to him, too.

Strange times, Ben thought. Who would have ever thought he'd rise to command the company who, almost to a Marine, had hated his guts? Perhaps more miraculously, he now enjoyed an amiable relationship with Bradshaw. Three years before she'd always seemed on the cusp of court-martialing him.

"Stone!"

A new battlesuit with a major's cluster on the breastplate exited HQ. Somehow, whenever Bathsheba Toma called his name, no matter the circumstances, it always sounded to Ben like "Shitbox." Strickland had promoted her, too. Truth was, the entire battalion had acquitted itself well in The Frontier flushing out pirates. Toma probably deserved the rank. She now served as operations officer and, effectively, commanding officer of the 214th whenever Strickland summoned Bradshaw.

"Major," Ben acknowledged, snapping a salute.

She returned it. "I see your people are already constructing their billets."

"Yes, ma'am," Stone said, glad to have something positive to report. Despite time, rank, and mutual advancement, he'd never shaken the feeling of being under Sheba's spyglass of disdain for his wealthy background. "We all appreciate how much you ... appreciate efficiency. Ma'am."

"I'll send a detachment of engineers over," Toma said. "Make sure your people do it right the first time."

Your *people? Don't you mean* our *people?*

"Of course, ma'am. My Marines always hate doing things twice."

Unless it's having sex, drinking to excess, gambling on credit, or...

Ben flushed the thought. Out here, there'd be little if any of those. Especially item one.

Overhead, the whine of a dropship engine came through the clouds.

"Hurry up! Unpack that equipment!" Zack waved his vacc-suited arms at his crew. One man coded a touchpad, cutting off the anti-gravs holding a case of equipment in the air. It slammed hard onto the surface of Canis III. "Careful, you idiot!"

"He's an inspirational leader," Bradshaw muttered over the private channel she shared with Toma and Ben.

"I'd say he's just the man for this particular job," Ben responded.

"Stone," Toma warned. "Remember why he's here."

Ben smirked behind the plastinium shield of his helmet. Sometimes the old him peeped through. He still liked aspects of the old him, especially the fuck-you attitude. He could almost feel the ghost of Bob Bricker leaning in to whisper into his ear.

Fucking officers.

"Jesus, this lighting *sucks*," Zack said. To his staff, "Get the cams up! We'll overdub these shitty comms later."

The dropship touched down twenty meters away, the engine spinning down quickly. Someone had an open comms mic, and the hydraulic whine of the off-loading ramp carried through the thin, toxic atmosphere of Canis III. The screech pierced Ben's armor more effectively than an enemy talon round, aiming straight for his spine.

"Confirmed, sir," Toma said over a separate command channel she also shared with Ben and Bradshaw. "Cams are hot."

Half a dozen eyes of the documentary moved into position, red and waiting. It felt like the landing on Drake's World all over again. A quick chill passed through Ben. He shook it off.

A squad of Marines marched down the ramp with the theatrical stride of a first-year drama student. They took up mirrored flanking positions at the bottom of the ramp. Their armor reflected not the colors of the 214th or any other AGF line battalion, but the newly adopted gold-and-blue design of the presidential estate on Sea Forest Island near Tokyo. The 214th might be Bragg's Own to the media, but these guys were home brewed, bred, and bought. In a different era, they would have been called Bragg's household guard. The president must have sent a detachment, or at least their armor, to put his personal brand on humanity's reclamation of Sirius for the cams. *He really is lifting his leg,* Ben thought, amused. Whenever he saw those gold-hued battlesuits, they struck him as the kind of thing a boy who liked to play with toy soldiers would design.

At the top of the ramp, another battlesuit appeared. This one wasn't current standard AGF issue, either. Its patina spoke of long use and systems retrofitted to body armor three versions older. The combined effect of the battle scars and updated external equipment created an impressive approximation of the specialization badges and service theater ribbons worn on a dress uniform. Spread out across the plates and joints of the suit, they were the wearer's battle resume.

Only not this wearer's.

Ben was pretty sure Strickland hadn't seen any real battle, at least not on the front lines, not even against the pirates in the Malvian Triangle. *Wonder where he picked up the suit. Bought from a black market, maybe. Or borrowed from a military museum.* On the upper-left of the well-worn breastplate sat the embossed silver star of a brigadier general.

"Here we go," Ben said. He'd made sure to use the private channel. "Ladies and gentlemen, the star of our show."

"Stone," Toma cautioned again.

The general strode confidently down the ramp. When he reached the bottom, he gave each of the two flanking toy soldiers a nod, then turned toward Ben and the rest of the receiving party. The cams floated all around them.

A crackle came over the comms, the general clearing his throat. He announced with a grim kind of bravado: "We ... have ... returned."

All was quiet for a few moments, save the whisper of wind over the surface of Canis III.

"Perfect, General Strickland!" Zack proclaimed. "Perfect!"

2
FORT LEYTE

"DEVIL TWO REPORTS CLEAR, sir. They're about to do a final sweep and hand the ball off."

Ben nodded to Corporal Maitland at the communications console. It was nearing the end of the duty shift, and that couldn't come soon enough. His eyes roamed the Doghouse, what Toma had dubbed Dog Company's dedicated communications building. It was small but felt luxurious compared to the closed coffin of his battlesuit. At least in here, he could take off his helmet. Though the Doghouse was vacuum-rated and reinforced, his gaze reflexively focused on the pressure door. Its hard seal indicator glowed a reassuring green. Beyond it, the anteroom for cycling between deadly indigenous atmosphere and healthy human air.

The Doghouse was windowless, and it was hard to tell planetary day from night. The low-light illumination from the bank of biomonitors displayed twenty readouts in green, capturing brainwave activity, heart rate, blood oxygen saturation levels, the works. Every member of Devil Two Platoon accounted for and healthy. With their battlesuits compensating for Canis III's gravity, twenty-five percent higher than

Earth standard, the biodata remained copacetic. Ben had briefly toyed with the idea of ordering the patrols to leave their LUVs behind and hump it across the surface to conduct their reconnaissance mission, but the daily sweeps using the light urban vehicles had already cleared out to ten klicks—a long way to hop across an alien landscape. And while the atmosphere wasn't exactly corrosive, after three days planet-side, the mechanics responsible for maintaining the battlesuits and vehicles were already getting an attitude. No sense tasking the suits more than was needed. No sense taking chances.

On the tactical display, twenty green dots organized in five clusters of four were completing their reconnaissance of grid section A-22 near the site of the original Archie landing. They'd be loading up and heading back to base shortly following a final check of the sector's perimeter. Tso and D-3 Platoon would be loading up soon to reconnoiter section A-23 next. That was a ride-along Ben wouldn't mind taking with them. There'd been a battle at that location half a century ago, so they'd at least have something interesting to look at. Maybe dig up a relic or two. In the enlistment vids, the Marine recruiters always emphasized travel, training, and testosterone. What they tended to leave out, along with the rigors of physical torture called PT, was the reality that most of a Marine's life would be spent waiting on orders or the regimentation of routine *ad nauseum*.

Ben leaned over Maitland and keyed the comms himself.

"Devil Two Actual, this is Doghouse Actual."

"Devil Two Actual," Gupta answered. *"Everything okay, Captain?"*

"I was just about to ask you that, Lieutenant."

Maitland glanced self-consciously up at Ben, no doubt thinking she'd done something wrong requiring her captain to step in.

Ben winked and shook his head. *Nothing to see here. I just need something to do.*

"All clear, Captain. This alien tech is some weird shit but nothing new. Loading up and coming home."

"Understood," he said. "Devil Three is gearing up to take the baton."

"*Solid copy.*"

"Doghouse Actual, out."

Ben turned to the woman at comms, whose face still wondered if she'd FUBAR'd something. "You're doing a great job, Corporal. Keep it up."

Maitland visibly relaxed. "Yes, sir. Thank you, sir."

The pressure door chimed. The status light flashed yellow. Someone requesting entry. The gauge showed the anteroom flushing out the planet's noxious air in favor of human-friendly oxygen-nitrogen.

"It's Zack, sir," Maitland said.

Of course it is, Ben thought. *He knows my duty schedule too.*

With some relish, Toma had made it clear to Ben that General Strickland expected the dashing young Alliance hero to be at the documentarian's beck and call. To personally escort Zack wherever he wanted to go, so far as it didn't violate military secrecy or safety protocols; to basically babysit him. It went without saying that Ben would rather be on patrol alongside one of his platoon commanders. But that wasn't his job anymore.

They waited together as the air filters completed their cleaning. The door's light cycled to green again, and the handwheel in its center spun counter-clockwise. The door opened with only a slight release of pressure, and Zack the Director stepped through in his vac-suit. The handwheel hadn't even finished spinning to resecure the door before he was unfastening his helmet.

"Thank God!" Zack took two deep breaths. "How much

longer till they finish repairing the dome over the camp? It's like walking around in a used condom!"

Ben cleared his throat to hide Maitland's scoffing.

"End of the week, in theory," Ben said.

"Thank God," Zack said again. "At least then we can get these goddamned helmets off. I've hardly shot anything besides Strickland's landing in three days. Oh, I've got tons of footage of jutting polysteel frames and engineers making hard seals, but I need faces!"

"If only life moved at the speed of media," Ben quipped.

"Wouldn't that be awesome?"

Ben was loath to admit it, but he empathized with the obnoxious man. Some brief excitement had electrified the camp when one of the overflights had rediscovered the original site of the Archie landing in A-23. Once initially cleared—there'd been no Arcœnum presence on Canis III since they'd withdrawn under the treaty agreement signed on Covenant—Strickland and his golden boy entourage had flown out to see the site for themselves. Bradshaw had gone too as Strickland's adjutant, but neither Toma nor Ben had been invited. When nothing more than grit-filled, useless, and mostly stripped alien tech was found, the 214th's enthusiasm had quickly devolved from obsessive curiosity to predictable indifference. It promised to be a long, tedious week of scouting missions and grousing.

"I have to admit, though," Zack was saying, "it's impressive watching the engineers fabricate, assemble, and complete an entire building complex like this one so quickly. Hell, it'd take me three days just to get my super to fix the plumbing back home."

"The difference is, they don't pay us by the hour," Ben said. He continued more seriously, "It's the next-generation, military-grade, 4D-printing tech. You should do a documentary on that."

Zack stared at him a moment. "Right."

"Captain?"

"Yes, Corporal?"

"General Strickland wishes to see you and Mister—uh, Zack —in the GCC."

"Now?"

"He didn't specify a time, sir." Maitland was almost apologetic.

"Now, then," Ben said to Zack. "Time to put your helmet back on, Mister Director. We've been summoned."

———

The walk wasn't far across the tight compound to the Ground Command Center, but it was long enough for Ben to appreciate the work of the engineers. Strickland had labeled the repossessed settlement Fort Leyte after the island the American general, MacArthur, had reclaimed during World War II on Earth. The half-finished, optimistically named "fort" was fast becoming a modern marvel of what the Alliance Ground Forces could accomplish given enough material and human ingenuity and just a little time.

In the eight hours he'd been in the Doghouse, they'd made measurable progress reconstituting the clear-carbon fiber-weave biodome destroyed by the Archies. The skeleton-like structure of the polysteel struts was more complete, for one thing. If not for the scaffolds and a couple dozen engineers in AGF battle-suits, Ben could almost believe it had grown on its own. The growing framework reminded him of the organic architecture in the underground valley of Drake's World. He was starting to see that hell planet in a lot of Canis III. Ben wondered not for the first time if Drake's World had wormed its way into his psyche a bit too deeply.

Though it shared its architectural DNA with the

Doghouse, the GCC was clearly the superior structure. Two stories, broader, and deeper, it reigned over the rest of the camp. A large dish pointed up from the roof, their connection to the expeditionary force fleet in orbit. In each corner of the roof, an 80-caliber fixed-gun automatic-weapon emplacement jutted out. Each of the AWEs guarded an approach, with two forty-five-degree arcs of overlapping fields of fire centered on a straight line from each weapon's respective corner of the roof. On the ground, two privates flanked the anteroom pressure door, both sporting the gold battlesuit of President Bragg's personal guard. Ben returned their salute at his approach.

"Captain Stone and Director Zack to see General Strickland," he said on the common channel.

"Yes, sir," one of the privates answered. He hesitated only a moment. Verifying their personalized suit signals in his heads-up display. *"The general's expecting you."*

They cycled through the double-locked atmosphere purifier in the anteroom to find GCC staff busy as bees in a hive. All wore battlesuits, standard protocol, but only the two golden-suited privates inside the main door wore helmets—Strickland's insurance policy in case of a breach. Logistics, tactics, comms liaising with the fleet in orbit—every aspect of military coordination on Canis III happened right here.

"Captain Stone!" Colonel Bradshaw motioned with her gloved hand from the doorway of Strickland's private office. Ben obliged, leading Zack through the hubbub of activity. The director gawked at what probably looked like chaos to him. Ben knew better. The overlapping orders, the seemingly random movement—all formed a finely tuned dance of military efficiency.

"Company manners," Bradshaw muttered before returning Ben's salute.

"Stone!" Strickland looked up from the holo-map he'd been studying with Sheba Toma. "About time."

Ben halted and offered a salute. Zack strolled lazily up to stand beside him.

"When I summon you, Captain, you snap-to," the general said.

Toma's quiet glare reinforced Bradshaw's friendlier heads up. Strickland, apparently, was in a mood today. But his attitude toward Ben had rankled of late. It was like Strickland held Ben's own celebrity status against him, was almost jealous of it. And the bastard was the one who'd orchestrated his path to stardom...

Hypocrite, thy rank is brigadier general.

"Sir, I came as—" Ben began, but the slow-motion twist of Toma's head cut the knees out from under his defense. Don't argue, just swallow. "Yes, sir."

Strickland's gaze shifted. "Zack, I'm supposed to see the dailies from the president's documentary. Why have you not been in this office reviewing dailies with me? Oh, at ease, Stone."

Ben relaxed his stance and clasped his hands behind his back. It always amused him when he observed a conversation between the general and the director—two self-crowned gods, each of his own domain. They regularly conflicted, those different religions. For his part, Strickland never failed to name the latest vid propaganda piece "the president's documentary." It was like he was determined to prove he was the alpha dog by mounting Zack from behind to establish dominance over the vid. Now *that* was a disturbing image, Ben thought, barely keeping his face neutral.

"Honestly, General? There's not much to see." Ever the performer, Zack heaved a heavy sigh for the back row of the theater. "I'm bored."

"Bored?"

"Bored."

"Man, don't you realize?" Strickland began, spinning up his own huff-and-puff. "Retaking Sirius is the next great chapter in establishing humanity's supremacy over the stars! And you're *bored?*"

"Kinda." Zack shrugged. "Don't get me wrong—your landing was great stuff."

"The lighting was horrible," Strickland said.

The director waggled his head. "Granted."

"We should reshoot it."

"Maybe," Zack said indulgently. "But to my point, that's the most exciting thing we've shot so far. The Keller vid went viral because it featured Captain Stone here, walking out of that cave with the girl in his arms."

Ben stared straight ahead. His ears began to burn. The marketing campaign with the image of him emerging from the cave network, Alice Keller cradled in his arms, had made Ben Stone instantly famous. Notoriously so in some eyes, darting a side glance at Strickland. Toma's stance had stiffened at Zack's declaration. If Strickland was annoyed by Ben's star status, Toma hated him for it. It was a holdover of hatred based on her longstanding opinion that Ben took his privileged status for granted. Bathsheba Toma had clawed her way out of the grimy slums of Mars with the help of military opportunity. She had no inheritance trust to fall back on.

Zack was pacing. "There was intrigue and mystery percolating underneath the girl's disappearance from the wreck site, a brilliant plot twist. The firefight in the caves... not to be indelicate, but two things sell to the public—death and sex. And the girl was too young for the sex angle. For most folks, I mean."

"Are you suggesting we kill a few Marines to add drama to

your lackluster footage?" Bradshaw said. Her words were controlled. Her tone, less so.

"Not at all, Colonel," Zack said. "And again, apologies if I was indelicate. I was simply stating a fact. And here's another one—the president's popularity jumped eight points after the release of *The Castaway Girl*." His cool gaze shifted back to Strickland. "Something he could use right about now, wouldn't you say?"

Strickland lifted his chin. "What do you need, Zack?"

"With your landing and the B-roll we've shot showing your Marines at work reconstructing the base, we've got maybe forty-five seconds of good footage—as long as there's a patriotic narration spoken over it and an evocative soundtrack running under, that is. Not much to show for three days' work. Or to fill a ninety-minute vid."

"Well," the general said, "fortunately for you, we've come across something that's *not* boring."

"Yeah?" Zack said eagerly.

"Yeah." Strickland turned to the 3D map. "Section A-23. One of Stone's platoons is due to scout it today. You can ride along."

"What's so special about that?" Zack asked.

Strickland turned slowly. "It's the site of the original Arcœnum science camp." He said each word slowly, suggestively.

"Really?" Zack's excited tone was trumped only by the wideness of his eyes. "I'll get my crew ready to roll!"

"General," Bradshaw intervened, "we haven't cleared that area yet. Sending civilians into it before we do could be dangerous."

"I have to agree with Colonel Bradshaw," Ben said. "If we could do some initial—"

"I'm well aware of the sweep schedule, Captain," Strickland

rumbled. "I assume you're equally familiar with the planetary sensor reports?"

Yes, Ben had reviewed them. According to the fleet's sensor analysis and the 214th's more localized readings taken on patrol, the planet was a lifeless, dense ball of rock fermenting inside a poisonous atmosphere. Without even native animal life or much flora to speak of.

"Of course, sir," Ben said carefully. "I just think we should get eyes on the area first, then—"

"There's nothing out there, Captain," Strickland said. "But seeing all that abandoned, rusting Archie tech..." There was a glimmer in his eye. Ben had no doubt he was envisioning the way it would look on video.

"It'll be emblematic," Zack enthused. "Symbolic of the Arcœnum's loss. I like it!"

Toma cleared her throat. "General, if I may—"

"You may not." Strickland stood up straighter. "Stone you'll attach yourself to Tso's platoon and personally escort Zack and his crew to the site. Give them whatever time they need there."

Ben opened his mouth, then shut it again. He traded a brief look with first Toma, then Bradshaw. He found allies there, but no one willing to charge up this particular hill with him. That's when inspiration struck.

"Sir, I believe Lieutenant Tso has already left with his platoon. I could recall them, but a second mission tomorrow might be better."

Strickland eyed him. Perhaps trying to differentiate sound tactical reasoning from insubordination. "You believe? Are you telling me you don't know if Devil Three Platoon has actually embarked on its mission, Captain?"

Crap.

"No, sir," Ben stumbled. "That is to say, sir—"

"That plan works for me," Zack interrupted. "I'd rather be

fresh from a good night's sleep. And this will give my staff time to verify the equipment's in first-class shape. Don't want a cam going down on us."

Double crap.

Though he had no doubt that Zack, clueless and self-absorbed as he was, hadn't knowingly intervened on his behalf, Ben felt a twinge of gratitude toward the man.

Strickland said, "Fine. But since you people are so worried about potential surprises, I want Tso's platoon back out there tomorrow since it's the unit conducting the initial grid survey. Attach yourself, Stone. You have your orders."

3
HUNGER AND HOPE

"I CAN'T DO IT!"

Andre Korsakov pursed his lips. "Yes, you can. But you have to *try*, child."

"Stop calling me that!"

There were things Korsakov did that got under Alice Keller's skin, but nothing irritated her more than the old fart calling her a child. Maybe she'd use the ability he was so anxious to see her demonstrate to make his head explode.

I'm seventeen!

Korsakov closed his eyes. Through the clear plastinium walls of her testing chamber—the Bell Jar is how Alice thought of it since she felt like an experiment under glass—she could see his anger building. The clenched jaw. The clipped speech. *Child.* The familiar pattern of somatic symptoms of the professor's growing frustration. It went away, but it always came back. When he got angry, when his Russian accent started to emerge, it always made him sound like a hissing snake.

Yesssss, you can. But you have to trrrrryyyyyy...

Try, try, *try*.

Lift the chair. Bend the spoon.

Fail, fail, *fail*.

"Professor, maybe we should take a break?" Ian, the professor's senior assistant said. "We've been at it a while, now."

Ian... Riding to my rescue.

Also part of the pattern. She'd come to see him like one of the heroes in the immersion vids she'd fallen in love with. Alice loved to fall asleep lost in the way the vids made her feel. They all had young women named Jessica or Anne or Meghan and suitors named Jacob or Connor or Elias.

Or Ian.

Maybe I fail just to see him mount up? Alice wondered.

Her cheeks flushed at how that particular image transformed in her mind, and the angry fire inside her seemed to bank itself, become something calmer, warmer. Her anxiety melted like gravity was pulling her failure into her feet.

"How about brunch?" Zoey, the other lab assistant, wore a hopeful expression. "Maybe some food to fuel the brain?"

"I could eat," Ian agreed. He was looking at Korsakov with a kind of wishful expression.

The professor opened his eyes and stared at Ian. Alice could see he knew exactly what his two assistants were doing—running interference for Alice. There was a chilliness trending toward coldness in his gaze.

"Very well," Korsakov said. When he smiled, he took on a distinctly reptilian quality. "Zoey, reset the subspace microsensors. We'll try again—" It was almost as if the words were having to negotiate their way out of his mouth. "—after brunch."

"Yes, Professor," Zoey said respectfully. A co-conspirator in goodwill, she tossed Alice a sneaky look of encouragement. Solidarity, even. Don't let him get to you, the look said. Ian and I know how to handle him.

Alice smiled briefly at her, then smirked at the back of

Korsakov's head. "Can I take these things off?" she asked. "My head itches."

"Do whatever you like, Alice," Korsakov said as he stalked from the lab. "You always do."

Alice blew out a breath. Korsakov had controlled his temper, at least. When the Slavic expletives began, she knew she was in trouble. But she wasn't there today, not yet anyway, thanks to Ian and Zoey.

Every time Korsakov pushed her to bring back her ability, it only seemed to make demonstrating it more difficult. It'd been so long since Alice had manifested even a sliver of what she'd done on Drake's World that she was beginning to think it would never happen again. Sometimes her power peeped through the web of microsensors he made her wear, making a needle jump or a readout ping, and that delighted him. But those rare occasions—rarer still, lately—of floating an object, or assembling blocks on a table using only her mind seemed to merely whet his appetite for more amazing examples of her ability.

They'd all seen it, the footage from the rescue. The avalanche, Ben Stone holding her in his arms, her own arms outstretched overhead, forcing the rocks raining down on them to scatter. Thousands of times they'd watched it together, and always with Korsakov asking the same questions, over and over. What were you feeling? How did you change the direction of the boulders? Tell me what you need to do that again.

And his goddamned Godwave. The complementary, synergistic blend of normal and subspace brainwaves that Korsakov was certain she'd somehow unlocked... He wanted her to do great things, he said. She had the power within her, he said, and with it, she'd unlock the universe. She had but to *try*...

A few months earlier, it'd been like a switch had flipped in the man. His insistent encouragement had devolved into exasperation and, frequently and all too quickly, furious outbursts.

The incomprehensible cursing came more and more often. And the quiet, smoldering relationship he'd shared with Morgan Henry since their arrival on Strigoth three years earlier had now become an open cold war. Korsakov, determined to push her to her limits. Morgan, dedicated to shielding her. Whenever they were in the same room together, Alice was uncomfortable.

"How you doing?" Ian asked.

Ian...

His dark hair displaced Alice's dark thoughts. And, oh my God, those brown eyes. When he smiled at her it was like he was unwrapping a gift and handing it to her. Every time.

Alice opened her mouth to respond, then closed it again. Whatever she'd been about to say would be stupid. He'd laugh at her, the little girl, the *child*. Were her vocal cords paralyzed? Or maybe they were just looking out for her. If Ian ever laughed at her... If he ever got angry with her like Korsakov. *Oh my God*, she thought. She'd kill herself. That's what she'd do. Open a hatch and let deep space suck her lungs right out of her mouth. At least then she couldn't say something stupid.

"Fine," she piped up.

God, you sound like a mouse. An anemic one!

Ian's smile broadened before he moved off to begin resetting the observation equipment. Alice felt the corners of her own mouth turning up weakly in response.

"Don't be so obvious," Zoey said, stepping into the Bell Jar.

"What?"

"With Ian," Zoey said, removing the sensor dots.

"Oh." Alice sighed. "I don't think I know how to be any other way."

Zoey winked. "Don't worry, you'll learn."

"Maybe not in time?" Alice whined. Her stomach sank. She'd never have a *real* chance with Ian. He thought of her as a child too. And who could blame him? That's what she was when they'd first met. An awkward, shy, quiet, scared little *child*. It just wasn't fair. He was so close and so far out of reach at the same time.

It's not fair!

"Just relax," Zoey said, removing the last contact from Alice's forehead. "Be yourself. It'll come naturally. Trust me."

"You sound like Korsakov. Only less like a huge dick."

"I think there was a compliment in there somewhere," Zoey grinned.

Heaving a sigh, Alice said, "I don't know what I'd do without you here. I mean, there's Ian but ... he's a boy."

"That's the rumor," Zoey said. "Hey, you've got Doctor Henry."

Alice visibly brightened at the mention of Morgan. The hopelessness she was feeling lightened a little. "Yeah, but I haven't seen him in—"

"I heard my name." The gruff, gravelly voice washed over Alice like cool water. "Explains my ears burning."

"Hi!" she said, hopping up. Brushing past Zoey, she dashed from the chamber to collide with Henry in a bear hug. His heavy *Oof!* came first, then his arms encircled her.

"Easy there, Braniac," Henry pled. "Handle with care!"

"I haven't seen you for days!" Alice said, hugging him harder. The enthusiasm was returned, if with less force.

"Seriously, kid, I can't breathe."

Alice loosened up, pulling her head from his thin chest and staring up at him. She'd been about to admonish him for calling her *kid*—a familiar, fake outrage levied regularly upon the King of Fake Outrage—but the words stopped in her throat. Not like with Ian. There, she was worried for herself, worried about looking foolish in Ian's eyes. Here, she was worried for Morgan Henry, for the look she saw in *his* eyes. And the heavy, dark circles surrounding them.

"You look tired," she said. His eyes appeared rheumier than usual. His cheeks a bit thinner. His expression, well, tired.

"I drank a hairy dog last night," Morgan replied. He gave her shoulders a squeeze when he said it.

"You shouldn't drink like that," Alice replied with the self-assurance of the all-knowing young. "You're too old."

Morgan leaned over so only she could hear. "Don't diagnose the doctor," he whispered. "And fuck you very much, by the way."

Alice laughed out loud, and any lingering tension from her testing session ebbed away. One of the things she loved most about Morgan Henry was that he didn't treat her like a "child." It's why she really didn't mind when he called her *kid*. He clearly considered it a term of affection. Another word for love.

"You're looking better today, Doctor Henry," Ian said.

Morgan gave Alice's shoulders a final, reassuring squeeze before leveling a stony expression on the young man. "And you're about as observant as a blind man during an eclipse."

He sounded angry. Somehow, she feared Morgan's bleak moods more than Korsakov's outbursts.

"Doctor?" Ian said, unsure how he'd offended.

Jerking a thumb at the corridor, Morgan said, "Go give that old coot Korsakov some good news. Make it up if you have to. Else, his face is gonna stay permanently scrunched. It's like the man eats lemons for breakfast, then pees acid."

"I think I'd rather let him—"

"Suit yourself," Morgan said in a tone Alice knew well. *Be an idiot. See if I care.*

Ian seemed to think about it, exchanging a helpless look with Zoey. "Fine. I'll bring back food for you guys. The usual?"

"Sure," Zoey and Alice said at the same time.

Putting down his datapad, Ian took his leave to find the professor.

"Don't let Korsakov the Great get to you," Morgan said to Alice. "You're doing great. You've made fantastic progress."

"Thanks," Alice said. "But not lately."

"Bah. All in its own time. Let's talk more tonight. Dinner?"

Alone time with Morgan after not seeing him for a few days sounded downright delightful. She'd have to be sure and ask him what he'd been up to. Besides drinking to excess.

"Good. Zoey—I'd invite you, but I'd like some alone time with my ward, here."

"Not a problem Doctor Admiral," Zoey said. "I have reading from the professor to catch up on anyway."

"No doubt," Morgan said. "Until tonight then, Alice." He was halfway across the lab before she thought to say goodbye. He waved lazily to her over his shoulder.

Zoe smiled at Alice. "He really loves you, you know."

"I know," Alice said, taking a seat at one of the lab tables. "I worry about him, though. He seems to be..." She struggled to find the right word. "...slowing."

"He's damned near a century old!" Zoey said. Further explanation for Morgan Henry's degrading physical state seemed unnecessary to her.

"Yeah, but..." Alice stared at the doorway to the corridor. "I think it's this place. Strigoth sucks! This lab sucks! ... it's so sterile. It's so..." She looked around at the white walls, the flashing indicators of Korsakov's test equipment, the silver-hued lights in the perfectly predictable ceiling tiles. "Dead."

"You know he won't let anyone treat him but himself. Occasionally with Ian's assistance when he needs a second pair of hands."

"I know," Alice said.

"And, speaking of Ian..."

Alice instantly became guarded. "What?"

"He was looking at you the whole time, you know," Zoey said.

Flushing, Alice said, "Of course he was! I'm the experiment!"

"Mmm," Zoey said in that way that assured Alice she wanted to say more.

"*What?*"

Why was she so defensive? Why did she always feel the need to throw up a wall anytime Zoey brought up Ian Secord?

"I think he likes you, Alice. And, I mean, you're older now. There'd be nothing wrong with—"

"Professor Pruneface would have a coronary," Alice said. "And it might be worth it, just to see that happen! But he'd also have Ian's head before he croaked."

"There is that." Zoey sighed. "Ian probably doesn't want to risk his internship."

Alice's gaze focused laser-like on the young woman across from her. "Did he tell you that? That he likes me? But he doesn't dare ask me out because Pruneface would fire him?"

Zoey turned her head slightly, considering. A grin teased the corners of her mouth. "No, not exactly..."

"Then, what exactly!"

Zoey said, "I don't think Ian knows what he wants. Hell, he's only twenty-four. Why would he know?"

Twenty-four. So much older! Of course he saw her as a child, just like Korsakov.

A cute child, maybe.

With weird abilities.

A freak.

"What do *you* want?" Zoey asked.

Alice was silent for a while, thinking about it. Why'd Zoey have to ask that question? Did Alice *have* to know what she wanted? From Ian? From anyone?

I want to find my family. I want out of this prison. I want Ian to take me far away from here.

"I don't know," she lied. Words failed her as her mind began wandering off this godforsaken planet, hand in hand with Ian, on a trail of stardust toward happily-ever-after. "With Ian, I feel..."

"Moist?"

Alice's eyes widened, snapping to Zoey's impish expression. Her neck warmed and crimson bloomed in her cheeks.

"Zoey!"

"*Well...*"

The quiet returned for a time, and Zoey didn't break it. Alice felt the heat gradually lift from her cheeks. "There's no one here my age," she said quietly. "I feel like an alien. Like I'm, literally, under observation here—whether I'm in the lab or not —all the time!" Her chin began to quiver. "I miss my family."

"Maybe..." Tentative, halting. Zoey debated within herself whether she should say what she was thinking. "Maybe *we* can be your family?"

Alice flinched. "I won't give up looking! Did Korsakov tell you to say that? Are you trying to—"

"Just until you find your real family," Zoey assured her, taking Alice's hands in her own. "A substitute family. A time-being family. You know?"

Alice calmed herself, ashamed she'd practically accused Zoey of being Korsakov's agent. Her face twisted. "Ugh. Wouldn't that make Ian my brother?"

A horrified look took over Zoey's face. "Okay. Bad idea, maybe."

"No," Alice said. "No—you are my family, Zoey. Part of my friend-family."

"And then there's the doctor admiral."

"Yes," Alice said.

"Hey, guys!" They turned to find Ian returning, a plastic tray with three plates of food precariously balanced on its too-small surface. "Anyone hungry?"

Zoey and Alice glanced at each other, and Zoey raised an eyebrow.

"*Don't you dare,*" Alice whispered.

Without looking away, Zoey said over her shoulder, "Alice is so hungry, she could eat *you!*"

"*You're such a bitch,*" Alice hissed at her.

"What?" Ian said, placing the tray on the table.

"She said she'd take the fish," Zoey said.

"Yeah, I know," Ian said, "she loves the fish. It's not like we haven't eaten together before."

A final, furtive look between the two young women confirmed that food was the last thing on either's mind.

MEMOS AND MINEFIELDS

"YOUR COFFEE, MA'AM."

Eva Park took the cup and continued her fast walk. The din of staff voices and streaming news reports proceeded unabated around her. Some people felt at home among crickets and frogs and the wind whispering through the trees. For Eva, it was the hubbub of the Citadel's political bullpen, the home office of the Sol Alliance's chief executive.

She swigged the coffee, her eyes glued to the breaking news of the capture playing on multiple wall screens. She stopped in her tracks at the taste, and the scalding liquid burned her hand as it slopped onto the floor.

"Hey!" Eva shouted. "What's your name again?"

The young intern who'd handed her the coffee halted, his shoulders slumping.

"Jarrell, ma'am."

"Jarrell, how do I take my coffee?"

"Two sugars, some cream."

Eva tipped the cup, careful not to spill again. "This is black."

"I see that, ma'am."

"Grab the wrong one again?"

"Yes, ma'am."

Several well-dressed junior staffers slipped by, doing their best to pass unnoticed. Dedicated public servants all, with a memo fetish. They flowed about her like white water around a stubborn rock.

Eva sighed. "We've had this discussion, Justin."

"It's Jarrell, ma'am."

What was that, the assertion of personal dignity? From an intern?

"Do you think I care?" she said.

"Apparently not, ma'am."

Nice. Hutzpah. That was something.

Eva pointed at the floor. "Get a towel, clean this up. And bring me *my* coffee. Two sugars, some cream, *no* spiteful spit because I hurt your feelings in public."

"Yes, ma'am."

Eva set the cup down on a desk and massaged the bridge of her nose. She'd been getting far too little sleep lately. If three years counted as *lately*, she thought. Working for Piers Bragg had been hard enough on Monolith, when the bottom line, labor disputes, and shipping quotas had been the major headaches. A fifth of good bourbon and passably competent sex had usually helped her relax back then. Now, nothing seemed to.

The good old days.

But public service was different and Piers Bragg didn't understand that. A bravado-driven, self-assured approach to the corporate board room was how he'd made his billions mining rare minerals in The Frontier. Those attributes seemed more like character flaws when it came to practical politics. Bragg expecting others to fall into line with his wishes had been sometimes problematic in the private sector. In the present crisis, they had only made a bad situation worse.

"Ma'am?"

The intern tilted a fresh cup of coffee toward her for inspection. It had a hint of caramel coloring. When she didn't bark her displeasure, he snapped the top on and handed it to her.

"Thank you, Gerald."

"It's Jarrell, ma'am."

"I know who you are, Jarrell. Lighten up. Or toughen up. Or leave politics. Pick one."

"Yes, ma'am." He moved past her, towel in hand, to mop up the spill.

She took a swig, hopping her eyes from one wall screen to the next. Miranda Marcos in custody. Finally! Dilettante, daddy's girl, rich rebel in handcuffs. News cams zipped around Marcos, capturing her sullen embarrassment from every angle. One screen showed an Alliance Central Enforcement officer leading Marcos through a gauntlet of media. The ACE agent placed a heavy palm on her head and pushed her into the back of a police cruiser. The footage was hours old but still worth a few billion eyeballs across two star systems. Three, if you counted the Expeditionary Force that had just touched down in Sirius.

Eva grabbed a passing staffer by the arm.

"President's in the Hot Seat?" she asked.

"Yes, ma'am."

Into the breach, then.

When she reached the presidential office, Eva rapped twice on the closed door to announce herself and entered.

"All I'm saying, sir, is that it could be bad optics."

She scanned the terrain as she always did when moving into the Hot Seat, the president's pet name for his working office in the Citadel. Leo Byrne, media spokesperson and head speech-writer for the administration, stood in front of the president's desk, animated in his insistence. Sol Alliance President Piers Bragg sat behind the desk, looking skeptical.

"It's a show of strength, and there's never a bad time for that." Bragg cocked his head at Eva at the door. "Ah, here's my good-looking communications director now. Welcome to the party, Eva."

She offered him a laudatory smile, then turned it on Leo, adding empathetic eyes. They'd be talking about this later. She could tell.

"No, really," Bragg clarified, "we're having a party later. Capturing Marcos requires celebration!"

"Of course, sir," Eva said, waiting as his eyes appraised her top to bottom. The price of admission to the big show. "Congrat-ulations."

"To us all!" Bragg exulted. His cheeks stretched as he turned back to his chief of staff. "You were saying, Leo?"

Eva felt Leo straighten next to her. Having her beside him always seemed to renew his strength of conviction.

"Just that many folks still see the Psyckers as a harmless club of counterculture misfits. Having ACE detain them when you came into office played heavy-handed then, but the public was willing to turn a blind eye—then—thanks to your popularity. The latest polls show public fatigue on this issue. If we overplay the Marcos incarceration..."

The president bobbed his head thoughtfully, hands laced across his belly. "First, Leo, I don't give a sloppy, limp fuck about the polls," Bragg said. "The polls are what I make them, not the other way around."

"Sir, I understand but—"

"Second, Miranda Marcos has spread sedition far beyond

Sylvan Novus and brought it right to our doorstep on Earth. Hell, even miners on Mars are sounding sympathetic. Rock miners! We need to show strength to tamp that down." Abruptly, Bragg became pensive. "Maybe a public execution..."

Leo sighed. "Sir, don't even joke about—"

"Who's joking?"

Bragg was entrenching, becoming a tick on the callous hide of don't-give-a-fuck. Eva let her eyelids come down a moment. She needed more coffee. A lot more.

"You look thoughtful, Eva," Bragg said. "Or, taking a nap?"

Eva snapped her eyes open and focused. Bragg regarded her expectantly.

Leo was right about how things looked. To Bragg and his true believers, Marcos's capture was a coup; justice finally served after months of protests against the administration's policy of suspending *habeas corpus* for Psyckers. Some of those demonstrations had even turned violent. Once Marcos was in prison, the fuel firing the protesters should drain away—or so went the conventional wisdom of most of Bragg's advisors. Leo and Eva were two of the more reasonable voices howling in that sycophantic wilderness. But to speak truth to Bragg was a bit like walking through a minefield without a map.

"Well, sir," Eva said, "let's take the temp." Stalling for time, she turned to the wall. "Feeds, on."

The multiple broadcasts she'd seen in the bullpen flickered to life, most of them culminating in the clickbait money shot of Marcos being folded into the police cruiser.

"Free Miranda! Free the Truth!" Her supporters flitted in and out of view.

Careful what you wish for.

"I agree with Leo," Eva began.

"Do you, now?"

"Hear me out, sir." She flashed a nymphic smile at her boss.

"Oh, always."

She muted the dull murmur from the feeds.

"Marcos's capture is a cause célèbre among the liberals for sure, sir." Always give him the win. Contextualize the potential pitfalls in victory. Vital experience learned from years of dealing with Bragg's monumental ego. "And also a flashpoint. We don't want to make a martyr out of her. We have to frame her incarceration as serving the law, not this office. And not some military agenda aimed at segregating the Psyckers."

"But it is those things," Bragg said. "All of them."

She felt Leo subtly step back, giving her center stage. *Thanks*, Eva thought sardonically. But she knew it was the smart move if they were to move the president toward moderation. Bragg was much more likely to accept a dissenting opinion from her. The upside of his roaming eyes.

"Of course it is, sir. And eventually part of your legacy—a *huge* part—will be how you championed the survival of humanity in a galaxy of alien antagonists. Arcœnum mind control is the scariest existential threat humanity has ever faced. Mothers put bad kids to sleep with stories of Archies coming through dimensional doorways in their closets to steal first their minds, then their souls. In a few generations, the Archies will be like snakes. Our own DNA will make us react with repulsion to them for our own protection."

"Go on," Bragg said.

"You're halfway through your first term, sir," Eva said, wondering how she'd navigate the next minefield without offending Bragg. "The AC is already looking toward the future. Keeping them on our side is more important than ever if we want to ensure your reelection in three years and set the tone of your legacy thereafter."

Bragg's gaze narrowed. "The Alliance Congress has backed

nearly every policy I've put forward, including doubling the budget for the military. Even the bleeding-heart Centaurians understand how close we came to getting ended by the mind-rapers. Why would all that change now?"

Leo chimed in. "Context, sir. The Arcœnum haven't been hostile in fifty years. When nothing external threatens a people, they tend to fall back into squabbles among their tribes. The Psycker protests, for example."

"Not a peep?" Bragg was incredulous. "I seem to remember a little documentary called *The Castaway Girl* by that brilliant ... Zed ... Zane—"

"Zack, sir," Eva supplied.

"Whatever ... that not only minted our latest hero named Stone but strongly suggested the Arcœnum were responsible for shooting down a human science vessel. The crash seen 'round the Alliance, as it were."

"*Suggested*, sir, yes," Leo said. "There was no real evidence of that."

"Polls. Evidence." It was clear from his sour-milk smile that Bragg didn't hold either in high regard. "You people think too much."

"In peacetime," Eva said, "people have the luxury of disagreeing with power."

"That's what Alliance Central Enforcement is for," Bragg responded, jerking his head toward the muted newsfeeds and their looped images of Marcos's arrest.

The door to the Hot Seat opened.

"Good morning, Mister President."

"Sam! You're just in time. I'm besieged by thinkers again."

Samson Devos, the president's chief of staff, spared a look for each of them as he entered. "Oh, sir, we all have our jobs to do."

"I suppose," Bragg said. "What news from the fringes?" Presidential code for his desire to change the subject.

Devos smiled. "The 214th has made planetfall on Canis III, sir. No problems."

"Marvelous!" Bragg stood up and took Devos's hand across the desk. "Great news! Two victories in one day!"

Eva shared a look with Leo, then they both moved in to also shake the president's hand.

"Tell me everything," Bragg said. "Do we have any of Zev's footage yet? I want to see the raw dailies. I don't care—"

"Not yet, sir, but we will soon," Devos assured him. "First steps, Mister President."

"Indeed. Indeed." Bragg said to Leo and Eva, "You two go monitor the Marcos situation. I want to talk some serious strategy with Sam here." He chuckled at the pun.

"Thank you, Mister President," Leo said before turning to go.

Following, Eva muttered,, "Feeds off." The enthusiastic banter of the two men ushered them out.

Lounging in her silk yakata, Eva peered through the expansive window of her penthouse apartment. The air was clear tonight, the moon bright. Overwhelmed by Tokyo's vibrant skyline, only a few stars peeked through from space. She ordered the window to minimal opacity, letting them shine a little stronger but squinted immediately at the rainbow of brightened, blinking city lights below. Vertigo tickled her insides.

Even five hundred floors up, it's like we're floating on a sea of neon up here.

She searched for the blue-silver light of Sirius in the night sky. First steps, Sam Devos had said. To what future? It's not that she disagreed with Bragg's desire to reengage the Arcœnum militarily. She agreed with striking first to prevent the Arcœnum from ever mustering the will to menace mankind again. Convincing the public of that ... well, there was the challenge. Though many were onboard thanks to the fantastically successful political campaign that had catapulted Bragg into power.

HUMANS FIRST!

PREPARATION, NOT REPARATION!

HOW WOULD WE KNOW?

Maybe the most effective of all, that last one. Leo's masterpiece. When a species can steal the minds of those you trust most, when aliens can make deadly enemies of your friends, of your own family ... How would you know until it was too late? The slogan that had now become the moral imperative underlying a military strategy on the cusp of execution. But the danger of failing ... of baiting the bear in its den, having underestimated its strength, resolve, and appetite for war. There was that to be considered, too.

God, she was tired.

"The city's beautiful, isn't it?" Eva turned to her lover, who knew her well enough to know the answer to his next question.

"Want a drink?" Leo asked, holding up two glasses of amber liquid. "You can only have one. Of these two, I mean."

She smiled wanly and took the Japanese whiskey. Two cubes of ice, a splash of maraschino cherry juice. She took a long swig, watching Leo's body as he moved to stand beside her at the window.

"I mean, look at all that life," he said. "All those lights."

"A veritable democracy of luminescence," she said, staring at his ass. He was never quite so sexy as when standing, facing away from her, with a drink in his hand. Dressed in his rumpled black slacks, white shirt with the collar open, tie loose around his neck—his media coordinator's uniform, as erotic as any Marine in full battle gear. A dusting of gray around his temples. The clink of ice in his glass. All the little details that, added together, turned her right the hell on.

"He's making a mistake," Leo said, still admiring the cityscape. "He's grown too confident."

Sigh. Shop talk. But at least she had his firm, policy-wonk ass to stare at.

"He was born that way, I think." She swirled the glass's contents to keep the cherry juice from settling, took another swig. "You'd think as his communications director I'd know how to talk sense into him."

"You do," Leo said, turning toward her and raising his glass in salute. His front was nice too. Something about the loose tie... "He doesn't listen to anyone, though. Never has, you know that." He paused and fixed his gaze on her. "I hate the way he looks at you. Talks to you."

"Bragg?"

"Yeah."

Eva laughed. "Oh, Leo, you really have *zero* worries there. How many times do I have to tell you that?"

"Power can be sexy," he said.

"Not as sexy as a loose tie and a glass of good Japanese whiskey in your hand."

"I'm serious."

"So am I! Trust me, Leo." She watched him drain his drink. "You *do* trust me, right?"

"Yes," he said. "It's *him* I don't trust."

"I can handle him. I have for nearly ten years now."

"Okay." He walked back to the small bar. "You believe in what he's doing though, right?"

"Why do you keep asking me that?"

Eva was annoyed. By his seeming lack of confidence in

himself? Or was it something else? The jealousy she got, but questioning her commitment to their shared political beliefs...

"Because I'm not sure I do," he said.

"You? The architect of Piers Bragg's rise to power? The man who turned existential fear into pithy catchphrases? You certainly seem to believe it when you're talking to the media."

"It's my job to *seem* to."

Two ice cubes clinked, followed by the slow, titillating pour of more whiskey.

She didn't like this conversation. The day had been too long already. Again.

She was too tired. Still.

"You know," Leo said, "maybe once the administration is done—I mean, maybe once *we're* done with *it*, one way or the other—we could try this relationship thing for real. Stop sneaking around, boss and subordinate. Have a kid or two."

Oh, Jesus.

She'd almost rather rehash Piers Bragg's power-mad short-comings than have this conversation again. It'd been less than a week since the last time. Still, she needed Leo tonight and mustered a smile.

"Thanks for reminding me you technically work for me," she said, holding up her hand and wiggling it. The ice plinked against the inside of the glass. She set it down on the windowsill. "I have a new assignment for you. Kinda personal. Hope you don't mind."

She was diverting him from the commitment question. He knew that, and Eva knew he knew it. She also knew he wouldn't care. His anticipatory smile confirmed it.

"Want me to pick up your laundry?" he teased.

"Not quite." Eva pulsed her eyebrows. Smiling, Leo plopped ice, whiskey, and cherry juice into a fresh glass.

"You know, if anyone knew about us—"

"Everyone knows. No one cares."

Leo dragged his loose tie looser. "What do you need, ma'am?"

"I need a good night's sleep," Eva said. "So come over here and fuck me."

5
GHOSTS

IT WAS ODD. Ben stood on the surface of Canis III in just his smartfatigues, without his battlesuit. He looked around, expecting to see the biodome completed to explain why he wasn't gasping for his final breath in the noxious environment.

But there was no biodome. In fact, there was no Fort Leyte. He stood alone on the flat, gray ground, a light breeze tickling his wet skin inside his fatigues, which were supposed to recycle the sweat and keep that from happening. That, more than anything else, clued him in.

Oh. I'm dreaming.

About fifty meters in front of him, a hole opened up in the rocky cliffside. Out of it poured a vibrant, violet light pulsing like a heartbeat. One dark figure emerged from the shadows, followed by another. Ben reached up to flip his tac lens in place to take a reading, then realized he didn't have a tac lens. Electric fear prickled along the length of his body. He also carried no rifle or sidearm, no equipment whatsoever. He defenseless, save for his sweat-soaked, malfunctioning fatigues.

The first figure was forty meters away and walking slowly toward him. Walking was generous—its jerky shamble seemed

45

newly learned. The light from inside the cave flared, illuminating both figures from behind. Ben saw the monstrous violation of her mouth first, as if she were yawning; but the spread of her jaws extended, became exaggerated and grotesque, like a snake preparing to swallow an egg.

DeSoto.

Ben's heart hammered against his ribs. Like it wanted out. He tried to close his eyes, to run. His body refused the command, rooting him to the spot.

The second figure entered the light. She'd had multiple mortal wounds in the back, so from the front, Baqri almost appeared alive. Except for the ill-fitting skin of decay. When she smiled at him, her withered lips stretched far enough to show gray gums, clearly visible even at this distance. Slack over corroded teeth, which shone a ghostly white in the dim light of Canis III.

The lighting here sucks, Zack said in his head.

"Hey, Shitbox," Baqri said, her voice rough and windy. "Still playing Marine?"

DeSoto came on, her hideous mouth working like she was laughing at her sister scout's joke. She'd covered half the distance to him.

One leg, at last, followed orders, and Ben backed up a step.

"Still getting Marines murdered?" Baqri pressed.

DeSoto stumbled over a rock, but only seemed to accelerate forward as she righted herself.

Ben bumped into something solid. It tapped him on the shoulder. He didn't want to look, but his body betrayed him again and turned him around. The face of Bob Bricker was inches from his own, perfect but for its weeks of decomposition. His breath—*Why do the dead need to breathe?*—was fetid with the dust of Drake's World. It rumbled in the back of his desiccated throat. His body, mangled from the cave rock that had crushed it like Quasimodo's, blocked Ben's escape. Bricker smiled that same hungry smile Baqri had.

"Tag, motherfucker."

The LUV jolted Ben in the passenger seat, rousing him from his doze. The nightmare, familiar as a bad stain, had also happened the previous night, early on so it'd kept him from sleep. In the relative quiet of his battlesuit and headed to section A-23, the nap had ambushed him.

"*I have to say, Captain,*" Zack said from the back seat, "*I'm honored to be with you on this mission.*" He'd used their private channel.

"Uh, thanks." Ben attempted to focus. "Allied Ground Forces Command appreciates what you're doing for the service," he said, reciting one of the lines the Media Relations Division had made him memorize. "Your documentaries have helped recruitment nearly double since—"

"*That's not what I meant,*" the director replied dismissively. "*I mean you, personally. You're a bona fide hero, Captain Stone.*"

Oh, that.

"*More than that, you're a* star," Zack continued. "*I could record you reading the Treaty of Covenant, and people would hand over their money just to watch it.*"

Oh, that. Not so much a hero as a star. Come to think of it, Ben wasn't sure he knew what the difference was. He'd once coveted his grandfather's fame, especially during his teen years. And for a while after Drake's World, he'd sucked as much marrow from the bones of celebrity as he could. Every man he'd met wanted to be him. Every woman he'd met wanted to fuck him. And sometimes, it was the other way around. Even superior officers, excepting the ones that knew him, rained appreciation, free booze, and promissory praise about his future in the AGF down upon him. All the trappings of being seen as a hero had served as a welcome distraction from the haunting thoughts lurking in the darker corners of his psyche: the conviction that he was responsible for the deaths on Drake's World.

Memories became accusations. Dreams became nightmares.

Even the action they'd seen in The Frontier against the pirates there hadn't distracted him. But the expeditionary recon mission to Canis III had shaken things up. Bragg was gearing up for war, that much was obvious. And in a perverse way, Ben was almost glad of it. Though still, the dreams had been here too, waiting for him.

"Captain, entering Sector A-23 perimeter," the corporal at the wheel chimed in. *"Archie camp, two mikes."*

"Former Archie camp, Corporal," Ben said.

"Ah, yes, sir."

The rest of the journey passed in relative silence. Zack spent the time informing his two assistants of his rules on the expedition: keep the cams running; don't wander off; don't disturb him unless absolutely necessary. On D-3's platoon channel, Osira Tso conducted the military equivalent, running through the three must-do's of securing helmets, staying alive, and avoiding causing Bragg embarrassment. By the time the ribbing, laughing, and crass comments were petering out, the convoy had slowed. They were approaching the Arcœnum landing site.

D-3 Platoon parked its LUVs in a circular formation, a reflexive tactic for easy defense. One of Zack's assistants pointed out how much the vehicle positioning reminded him of covered wagons in paintings from America's Old West as they prepared for an Indian attack. Ben was tempted to compliment the civy on his tactical insight until Zack reminded the man of his third rule, and the assistant fell silent.

While Tso organized his squads, Zack and Ben scanned the abandoned science camp below. It was less sexy than their expectations had promised, though the alien architecture stood starkly ethereal against the harsh, drab landscape of Canis III.

"Amazing," Zack said. *"And kinda freaky."*

"The Arcœnum have a unique style," Ben informed him. "You see it in their ships, too. Even their battle armor. A kind of elegance tempered with efficiency. Graceful lines that aren't too extravagant; yet, somehow, whatever they build—equipment or structure—is exactly the dimensions it needs to be for its designed purpose. No waste, despite the sophistication."

"I walked through one of their ships once," Zack stated, his gaze focused on the camp. When Ben turned to him, surprised, the director clarified. *"At the Fleet Museum over Earth. A captured ship, refurbished for the public."*

Ben nodded, giving Tso's D-3 squads a glance. Three squads would escort them to examine the camp, leaving two behind to guard the LUVs and man their mounted guns on overwatch. Sergeant Sanchez would be going over procedure with the grunts now. Though he'd muted the platoon channel to converse with Zack, he knew what Sanchez was saying: situational awareness ain't a goal, it's a survival strategy; stay alert and you stay alive; don't fuck up, or if you do, fix it before I find out. Instead of Sanchez's Latin-salted accent, he imagined the orders grinding out in Bob Bricker's gravelly voice. Despite the daymare he'd just suffered on the way to the site, that was somehow reassuring.

"Everything seemed too tall," Zack was saying. *"Like we were children walking through a ship designed for adults. And yet, not an inch of space wasted, like you said. Bare but just functional enough, y'know? But also artistic. Like an alien engineer had begun a second career as a sculptor and decided to design spaceships."*

Before Ben could comment, Tso cut in. *"Ready to move out, sir."*

"Acknowledged," Ben responded. They descended the slight grade of the hillside. Two sets of cams fanned out along the left and right flanks, taking longshot B-roll of the camp. The closer they got, the more like their own site the Archies' seemed, alien architecture notwithstanding. Blast marks from human ordnance were evident everywhere. Whole sides of buildings reduced to rubble. There were two main structures—quarters and the science station. The Archie expedition had been scientific in nature, Ben reminded himself. A third, smaller building connected the other two.

They passed the camp's perimeter. Now at ground level, Ben understood Zack's description of everything seeming too big in the museum ship. Stripped equipment was everywhere, gutted casings exposing unfamiliar hardware. What could either have been dehydrated blood vessels or wind-blown wiring sprouted from a score of boxy units littering the site.

"Arcanus is a low-gravity world," Ben said.

"What?" Zack asked, then pointed one of his assistants to one of the larger buildings. Tso shadowed the order to Bravo Squad, which moved out in escort of the assistant and his cams.

"The Archie homeworld," Ben said. "We never made it there, of course, but Archie autopsies and backward engineering of enemy vessels showed they're used to gravity closer to Alpha Centauri's than Earth's. It's why they're so tall and gangly. On a planet like this, their combat armor must have worked overtime."

"Makes sense, I guess." Zack stopped in his tracks. *"Hey, is that one of their battlesuits?"*

Ben followed his pointing finger. An articulated suit of atmospheric armor lay on the ground near the entrance to the smaller structure. Zack called over his second assistant and the cams he controlled. Instinctively, Ben put out a hand to restrain the civilians.

"Me first," he said.

It was clear the suit had lain in exactly the same spot for some time. Dusty with time and surface winds, the armor was camouflaged so well that it was only distinguishable from the indigenous rock of Canis III by its mechanical limbs and empty body cavity.

"Captain, let me get Charlie Squad over here," Tso suggested. *"Don't get any closer."*

"No, it's all right," Ben responded, halting next to the suit. "It's empty."

His own battlesuit's tactical sensors were working overtime, scanning the enemy armor automatically and verifying its defensive systems were nonfunctional. Desi, his familiar name for the forceful female voice reporting the data to him now, offered her appraisal in a familiar, throaty tone. But Ben didn't need her readouts to recognize the dead Archie's skull looking out from the jagged edges of a shattered faceshield.

He'd seen images of the enemy. Vids of interrogations made by the AGF during the war. Captured battle footage. The Arcœnum were often described as the lithe offspring of a jelly-fish mated to an angel and stretched to the height of a small giant. It was an old joke, and also the human mind's attempt at describing the utterly alien nature of the Arcœnum.

Even in death, their skeletons were graceful. Supple bone structure, polished by the winds of Canis III. Thinner than a human skeleton, owing to lower-g evolution. Elongated limbs inside what looked like the earliest version of Arcœnum armor Ben had ever seen outside a training vid. Made sense—the war had started here, after all. The Archies hadn't come to Canis III to fight but to conduct scientific experiments, as had their soon-to-be human enemy before them. The lack of a jointed jaw, ironically, hinted at that tragic tale. Like humans, the Archies took in sustenance through their mouths but having no vocal language, didn't speak through them. The skull's eye sockets seemed to stare at Ben accusingly.

Can't you just leave us alone? Even now? Can't you just let us rest?

He shook his head to clear it. His conscience again, over-laying the reality of the dead Archie on the ground with the morbid weight of his lingering guilt over Drake's World.

"That's one ugly motherfucker," Zack said next to him. He stood very still and regarded the dead Archie. *"When I was bad as a kid, my mother would lock me in my room at bedtime. Drop the solar shades to block out the starlight, make it pitch black. Then she'd leave. But not before telling me I'd better 'adjust my attitude' or the mind-rapers would come for me. Wigged my shit out."*

"That—" Ben began, then diverted what he'd been about to say. "—must've been hard."

"Yeah. But I've thought about it a lot, and I think maybe that's why I do what I do."

"Vid production?"

"Yeah. Storytelling, really, just with images. Kinda like the Arcœnum when you think about it. They use mind manipulation. I shoot propaganda vids for Bragg." Zack paused. *"Huh. Never really thought of it in those terms till just now. Always weirded me out that they couldn't speak, though."*

"They speak," Ben said, "just not with their mouths. Instead of the word 'ship,' they project a mental image of it into the mind. The context makes the meaning."

"Freaky," Zack said.

"Captain," Tso sent over the common channel. It was then that Ben noticed Bravo Squad standing at a respectful distance, rifles at the ready should the dead decide to rise. *"This is our*

second day here, you know. Not much left to see. A lot of the equipment is either destroyed, lost to time, or so bastardized for parts it's useless. Looks like the Archies took everything worth taking fifty years ago."

"Thank you, Lieutenant," Ben said. Several of the cams surrounded the Archie corpse, recording silently.

"This is great footage," Zack said.

Well, that's what they came here for, Ben thought. Time to escort Zack through the buildings, let him get his footage for the morbidly curious. That felt like a reason to disturb the dead, didn't it?

"Leyte Actual to Recon Actual," said Toma's clipped voice. *"Captain Stone, acknowledge."*

Stone shared a look with Tso, who as the tactical commander of the recon mission had been included in the transmission. Stone as senior officer was considered attached but separate; by rank, the 'actual' she'd called. But for Bathsheba Toma to call and interrupt the mission Strickland had ordered...

"What's up?" Zack asked, trying to read Ben and Tso. Zack, a civilian, wasn't privy to the military channel. *"Oh, it's one of those calls."*

Ben held up a hand. "Recon Actual," he answered. "D-3 Actual is with me. Go Leyte."

"Lieutenant Tso, pull your squads. Stone, get back here ASAP. There's been an incident."

Tso gave a curt nod inside his battlesuit. He keyed his platoon channel, already ordering his men to gather at their location.

"An incident?" Ben prompted. "What kind of—"

"I'd rather not say on an open channel," Toma answered. *"Just get your ass back here."*

An open channel? Comms were encrypted by default. What the hell?

"Solid copy," Ben acknowledged. "Recon Actual out." He turned to Zack.

"What's up?" the director asked again, motioning at the squads falling in around them.

"You'll have to get your footage another day. We've been recalled by command."

"Recalled? Why?"

"The quicker we get back, the quicker we find out."

"Okay."

The LUVs up the hill were firing up their engines. Zack and his assistants followed as Tso's tactical platoons humped it up the hill. Ben lingered a moment longer, his attention commanded again by the empty gaze of the Arcœnum corpse.

Why couldn't you just leave us alone?

Shaking his head, Ben cursed, annoyed again. Maybe he needed to see someone about the nightmares. Or maybe he needed the company medic to prescribe a sleep med.

And still, despite the wildfire speculation about the sudden need to return to Fort Leyte filling the comms, Ben couldn't shake the pleading thought from his mind.

Why couldn't you just leave us alone?

As if it had been planted there, and taken root.

6
SABOTAGE

THEY SAW the smoke from two klicks out. It rose in a plume over Fort Leyte, gray-black and thick.

Anxious theories went viral between vehicles. Ben ordered his lieutenants to tamp down the chatter. He understood the human desire to attach a reason to an unforeseen event, an impulse as old as mankind creating gods to explain thunder. But baseless speculation only served to stoke fear.

The smoke rose from the far side of the compound, near the hillside acting as a natural security barrier for the camp. The weapons depot? Sabotage? Marines had lost it far from home before, and fresh squaddies away from Earth for the first time were most prone to that. But stringent psychological profiling made the odds of it happening here, particularly in a storied unit like the 214th, pretty long.

Passing slowly through the main gate now doubled up with Marine guards, ancillary damage was evident. The deeper into Fort Leyte they drove, the worse it got. Cracked windows on buildings otherwise still apparently structurally sound were the most visible signs of the explosion's impact.

"Orders from Major Toma to proceed to the Doghouse," the

driver announced. *"The rest of D-3 Platoon is to help secure the fort until further notice."*

The rest of their convoy split off right toward the smoke. Ben's LUV cut left and headed for the communications building, where its occupants bailed out before the driver cut the engine.

"Roll, roll, roll!" Zack, who'd remained remarkably silent for most of the return trip, flailed his arms at his assistants. *"Get those cams in the air!"*

"There's no way you're getting close to that," Ben told him, pointing at the smoke. "Not till any danger is locked down."

"I don't want to get close to it. I want to shoot it."

"The footage will likely be confiscated."

"We'll see about that."

Ben entered the antechamber of the Doghouse to cycle out the planet's atmosphere.

Zack stuck him like glue. *"I go where you go, Captain."*

When the door finally unlocked to allow them into the Doghouse, the two Marines inside verified their identities, then motioned them through.

The tight space of the small building had too many bodies in it. Maitland was back at comms, her board alive with activity. Sheba had a headset clamped to an ear with her right hand and was talking to someone in orbit, the fleet captain by the sound of it. Signing off with a perfunctory grunt, she tossed the headset in disgust onto the comms panel. Toma turned and found Ben waiting. He was surprised to see relief flit across her face before her stoic Sheba mask reset itself.

"About time," Toma said. "Disposition of D-3?"

"Per your orders, ma'am, supporting enhanced security," Ben answered. "Ma'am, now that I'm here in person—what the hell happened?"

Toma flicked her eyes at Zack. "I'm invoking your MS clause."

Zack looked from one to the other. "Are you sure that's necessary? I mean, I'm here to document what's happening on the president's authority—"

"Corporal Evans," Toma said, looking past Zack, "kindly escort this civilian to his quarters for his own protection until such time as the—"

"All right, all right!" Zack said, stepping away from the Marine reaching to bodily remove him. "Military secrecy it is! Upon pain of death, already!"

"It's good that you understand the terms of your agreement so thoroughly," Toma said.

Zack did a double take but shut his mouth.

"We're not sure what happened," Toma said, addressing Ben. "Right now, the incident is classified as accidental."

Ben learned the source of the smoke was, in fact, the weapons depot. An explosion had rocked the camp an hour earlier, shaking the foundations of nearly every structure in camp. Proximate to the main gate and far enough away from the blast, the Doghouse and only one other building remained unscathed. That explained Toma occupying it as Command HQ. The chow hall had also avoided any damage. But others, including the newly built barracks and even the hexacrete-reinforced Command HQ building, had all been compromised. For the most part that meant cracked windows and undermined structural integrity making the facilities unsafe for humans not wearing battlesuits or vacc-suits. Only the foundation of the depot had escaped destruction at ground zero because the blast had gone up and out. Disposing of dangerous, unexploded ordnance was the current priority after triaging the wounded.

"Accidental, Major?" Ben wondered skeptically.

"No evidence to the contrary—yet. No sense spinning up the rumor mill."

Bathsheba Toma was so tightly wound that a running joke had her projecting morning coffee consumption on a spreadsheet before she poured her first cup. Until she had evidence of sabotage, Ben knew, she'd classify the incident as generically as she could. It was the prudent thing to do.

"Colonel Bradshaw is supervising on-site," she continued. "Ordnance disposal and ... body retrieval."

Ben realized something had been gnawing at the back of his mind since they'd entered the Doghouse. "Where's General Strickland?"

Toma hesitated a moment, and Ben saw the mask slip again, if only briefly. "General Strickland has been injured. He's currently being treated by Doc Wallace in the chow hall, which we've converted to a temporary hospital."

Ben took a moment to process that bit of intelligence.

"Injured? He was close to the blast?" Zack asked.

Toma held up a hand. She was listening over Maitland's shoulder. "Tell them a fresh platoon is on its way," she told Maitland. "And tell them *no one* has everything they need. Marines make do," Toma said, quoting an aphorism from basic training. "Use those words, Corporal, and sign my name to them."

"Yes, ma'am."

"You said General Strickland was injured?" Zack pressed. "How badly?"

"That's as yet undetermined, Mister Zack," Toma said.

"Okay," the director replied. "And it's just Zack."

"What happened?" Ben asked. "Why was he even there?"

"General Strickland and his staff were performing a snap inspection of the depot when the explosion happened. A dry run for a scene he'd apparently discussed with you, Mister Zack."

The director didn't correct her this time. His face had gone pale.

"Colonel Bradshaw?" Ben asked.

Toma nodded. "She was with him but took less of the brunt of the blast. They were suited, of course, but Strickland's faceplate cracked." That didn't surprise Ben, given how outmoded Strickland's battlesuit was. "The colonel is fine. She immediately took command and began recovering the wounded and securing the site."

Ben felt relieved. That the "accident" had occurred while Strickland and his senior staff were inspecting the depot was a little too much of a coincidence to be coincidental. Maybe a newly minted Marine squaddie really *had* lost their shit and aimed their ire at command. There was no small amount of grousing about Strickland among the rank-and-file. He was seen as a prima donna who'd ridden Piers Bragg's coattails to an undeserved rank. But if it really had been a malcontent that caused this ... Ben would be the first in line to court-martial the bastard and send him to The Rock on Callisto.

"Major, where do you need me?" he asked.

"Get over to the chow hall and check in with Wallace. Update me on the general's status. Now that you're inside the camp, communications should be secure but scramble the channel anyway. Until we know what we're dealing with here, Fort Leyte is in complete lockdown."

"Yes, ma'am." Ben put his helmet on and sealed it.

"And take Mister Zack here with you," Toma said, exasperated. She pointed to the heavens and the ships in orbit there. "I have enough to deal with."

"How are you feeling, General?"

Strickland's expression hardened. "Like I need to kick a few asses. Incompetence! Mister Stone, if there's one thing I cannot abide, it's incompetence!"

Zack, Ben noticed, was hanging back. At least he'd had the good sense not to bring the cams to capture Strickland's less-than-heroic state.

"Incompetence, sir?" Ben said.

"What else could it be? We're alone on this godforsaken planet, aren't we?" Noticing Zack was there, Strickland added, "My personal opinion of Canis III is off the record!"

Zack offered a nervous smile. "Of course, General. No one's recording anything here." He gestured at the empty air.

Ben took a breath and a moment to think. Strickland's assertion was far from proven, but if Sheba's assumption held, "accidental" would most likely translate to "human error" in the permanent record. That Strickland wasn't yet entertaining the notion that someone might have targeted him with sabotage reflected his own myopic sense of self-importance. But now wasn't the time to challenge that with unfounded theory.

"What'd you find out there, anyway?" Strickland asked. "At the Archie site. Zack, you get what you needed?"

The director advanced to stand nearer the general's bed. He seemed unsure how to answer. Perhaps, like Ben, he found the question trivial considering recent events.

"Uh, well, General, we had limited time. Some of that Archie tech—freaky stuff. I think we got some good B-roll, though—"

"See the skeleton in the armor?"

"Uh ... yes, sir."

"There'll be a lot more of those in the coming days," Strickland glowered. "Also off the record!—for now." He cocked his head at Zack. "Limited time, you say?"

"Yes, sir. You know..." Again, the director gestured around them, hesitant to remind Strickland of the recent events he was all too personally acquainted with.

"Captain," Strickland said, "as soon as Colonel Bradshaw agrees, get the vid team back out there. I want that Archie corpse front-and-center, Zack. Hell, I want it in the marketing teasers. We should—"

"Gentlemen, I've given the general a strict prescription of rest and recuperation." An older man in his fifties sporting the rank of a Fleet lieutenant commander approached. Colonel Bradshaw, black streaks painting her armor, dusty with gray powder, accompanied him. She greeted Ben with a subtle nod. "General, we've talked about this already," the doctor said.

"Oh, to hell with your R-and-R, Wallace," Strickland said. "I can..." As he attempted to rise from the bed, he winced, seemed to hover in mid-air, and fell back.

"Uh-huh," Doctor Wallace said, satisfied. "It's now an *order* —of medical necessity."

"General, I can brief you on the current situation," Bradshaw offered. "But could I steal Captain Stone for a moment first?"

Strickland's eyes blinked lazily, and he gave a dismissive wave of his hand. Wallace, meanwhile, inspected the blood-stained bandage covering the general's head.

"Mister Zack, if you don't mind," Bradshaw said as the director moved to follow. "I need to speak with Captain Stone alone."

"Sure." There was no demand for free access. The director seemed to have reached his limit for challenging military secrecy today. "And it's just Zack."

"Ben?" Bradshaw led him to an empty corner of the chow hall.

"How is the old man?" Ben asked when they were out of earshot. "Really?"

"I think the explosion came close to cracking his hard head," she answered. "But that's the least of his problems."

"What do you mean?"

"The initial explosion," Bradshaw said. "It pulverized the hexacrete walls of the depot, turned them into dust. The heat seared the air until the facility's oxygen burned off. The combination created a kind of concrete plaque that coats the lungs." Her voice was bitter. "Getting helmets on was too little too late in some cases."

"How many?" Ben asked.

"Two Marines dead from the blast. The general and his aide down from the dust in their lungs. Wallace says he can treat it, but ... well, let's just say Strickland won't be charging up any hills anytime soon."

Ben surveyed the room. There were far too many Marines lying on beds in the makeshift hospital. Not all of them could have been inside the depot. From what he could see, most of the injured had no visible wounds. He recalled Toma's briefing on how the blast had cracked plastinium windows across the camp.

"They're mostly recovering from oxygen-dep," Bradshaw said, reading his mind. "They'll be fine. But I'm considering implementing a new protocol—fully sealed battlesuits, all the time. Even in facilities rated for hard vacuum."

"That won't go over well," Ben noted.

"I don't really give a good hard fuck," Bradshaw answered, her anger palpable. "What do *you* think happened here, Ben?"

The voice from the Archie camp arose in Ben's mind.

Why couldn't you just leave us alone?

But now was not the time for guilt to distract him.

"The old man seems convinced somebody FUBAR'd," he said.

Bradshaw folded her armored arms and regarded the general, still under Doc Wallace's ministrations. "He's always quick to blame his own people when something goes amiss," she said. "Speaking as his second-in-command, it's one of his least likable qualities."

"Among many," Ben said.

"Among many."

"Since you asked the question," Ben said, "I take it you don't agree?"

Bradshaw sighed. "Preliminary scans indicate the presence of hypergolics. Other than the scan team and Toma, you're the only one who knows that. And it's need-to-know, Captain."

"Combustibles?"

"Combined with accelerants. A specially designed cocktail that doesn't require oxygen to burn."

Ben considered that. "Perfect for starting a fire and keeping it going on a planet without an oxygen atmosphere. One that doesn't need to last long once ordnance begins to blow."

"Keep going, Detective Stone."

"But," Ben said, "it's not like we keep the armaments lying around in the depot. Weren't they stored in sealed containers secured with bio-locks?"

"They were," Bradshaw said, "until they weren't."

What he heard in her cryptic voice seemed to suggest his earlier theory. Suspicion—of their own. Combine a Marine—Marines?—losing their shit with hatred of Strickland, and the deadly combination of motive and opportunity seemed suddenly more feasible. But Staff Sergeant Varayev, responsible for securing the depot, was neither green nor a mutineer. The thought of a veteran killing fellow Marines on some private vendetta against Strickland was anathema to the band-of-brothers blood that ran red in every Marine's veins.

Or should, Ben thought. "Are you suggesting Staff Sergeant Varayev went nuts and sabotaged his own depot?"

"I'm not suggesting anything," Bradshaw said. "I'm determining the facts as we know them. And asking your discrete opinion about those facts."

"What about the perimeter defenses? The sensor network around the depot—"

"All online and functional," Bradshaw said.

"And?"

"And *nothing*. No alarms. Nothing out of the ordinary. Just—"

"Boom," Ben said.

"Yeah."

"Archived sensor data and cam footage from the hours leading up to the blast?"

She nodded. "Reviewing those is next on our list. I've been a little busy getting the wounded situated and," she paused before trudging onward, "overseeing body retrieval. I need to get back out there."

"Ma'am, to your question, I don't want to think this could be the work of another Marine, especially one as senior as Varayev. But I also think it unlikely approaching statistically nil that this was an accident at the very moment General Strickland was touring the depot. And as for incompetence—there are just too many redundancies, too many bio-signatures required, too many safeguards in place..."

Bradshaw finished Ben's thought for him. "The AGF has gone to great lengths to factor out human error—and psychosis—when it comes to handling our weapons systems."

"Exactly, ma'am. Is Sergeant Varayev in custody?"

Bradshaw hesitated before answering, surveying the temporary medical ward again. "Sergeant Varayev is one of the two casualties."

Ben let that sink in.

Suicide bomber?

The thought was there before Ben could quash it. But no, that couldn't be it. He knew Varayev's psychological profile. He'd been an AGF lifer. An oo-rah patriot. And yet, a confluence of evidence was beginning to add up to a very ugly finding.

"I need to get back to ground zero," Bradshaw said again. "General Strickland ordered you to escort Zack back to the Archie site. I'm belaying that till tomorrow morning. I need you and D-3 Platoon here. We'll beef up security with forces from the Fleet, but not yet—I don't want any *new* down here until we know more about what happened. That means the 214th will pull double duty for a day or two. I'll rotate one platoon out for sector sweeps, but the rest will pull security and triage duty when off-shift."

"Yes, ma'am."

"And I'm making you personally responsible for keeping Zack's cams shuttered in camp. He's only authorized to shoot the Archie site. Any footage he's already taken of the camp since the explosion—confiscate it. That's an order."

"Yes, ma'am."

"And Captain?"

"Ma'am?"

"When you head back out there in the morning, be careful." Bradshaw turned away, surveying the wounded as she walked away. "Take *no* unnecessary chances, am I clear?"

"Crystal, ma'am," Ben acknowledged.

7

TRAGEDY AND TRIAL

"I THINK I'm just distracted lately," Alice said.

"Mmm." Morgan chewed thoughtfully and swallowed. He sounded exactly like Zoey earlier. Amused and holding a secret Alice didn't know. "I see you moon-eyeing over Mister Secord," he said playfully.

"Who? Ian?" Alice stabbed a piece of the delicate, broiled fish in blue wine sauce she liked so much, and it flaked into pieces around the tines of her fork. *Even the food hates me*, she thought. "You're nuts, old man."

Morgan feigned a wounded look and with a twinkle of mischief said, "More like his, I'd say."

Alice flushed scarlet and scooped up fish bits to fill her mouth. "You're just a dirty old man, you know that?"

"Hey," he said, drawing out the vowel sound, "you're seventeen—old enough to vote, enter the military, and drink legally. Who am I to judge?"

She chewed her fish that didn't really need chewing. "I think I'm just ... afraid."

"Of?"

Picking up a hushpuppy, she swabbed it around. The base

for the sauce was imported wine from the Circadian Mountains of Sylvan Novus, near where her family had lived. Stuffing the tasty distraction into her mouth kept Alice from having to answer the question.

The scrape of utensils on dinnerware filled the room.

"You know, I've never felt like just a patient with you, Morgan," Alice said. "You've always been here for me. As a friend."

His fork halted in mid-air. There was a pained expression, quickly covered.

"Ever since you and Admiral Stone brought me here, I've felt loved." Alice paused, feeling inadequate to express exactly what she was feeling. It seemed too big for words. The blue sauce blurred a bit. "Do you know—I can't remember my father's voice anymore?"

"No," Morgan said, "I didn't know that."

Also blurry, his face came into focus as her tears fell, revealing his concern. Alice wiped hard at her cheeks, leaving a red mark.

"I used to hear him all the time. His lab voice. Telling me to keep trying, that a successful experiment is repeatable. It was his voice that got me through the dungeon."

Morgan nodded. It'd been a while since she'd mentioned her harrowing experience in the underground of Drake's World.

"Now, all I hear is Korsakov," she said angrily. "In the lab. In my sleep. Everywhere!" She stabbed again at the tender fish.

"Andre cares for you too, in his way. But Alice—and I know we've talked about this before—you can't let him get to you. You have to try—"

Her expression twisted, and Morgan stopped speaking.

"Try, try, *try*! I'm so fucking sick of people telling me to try! I *am* trying!"

Morgan put down his fork. He met her anger with quiet

patience. After a moment, her fury subsided. Her bared teeth sheathed themselves again behind pinched lips.

"I'm sorry," she said, not quite contrite. "I'm sorry."

Offering a half-smile, Morgan said, "I won't be with you forever, you know."

"What?"

"I mean, look at me!" he exclaimed. "Dirty or not, I'm an old man!"

"Don't say that."

Morgan picked up a spoon and inspected his reflection. "No, it's true, I'm older than—"

"That's not what I meant!"

He put the spoon down.

"Andre is the epitome of a scientist," Morgan said. "Brilliant. Dedicated. He makes connections no one else can see." He regarded her with a sideways look. "Also, not very subtle. And socially inept beyond all repair."

The slight against their shared adversary seemed to break the dam behind Alice's anger. She felt it drain out of her.

"My father was like that, too," she said. "My mother used to say that if it weren't for his lab specimens, he'd have no social life."

Morgan chuckled, and they both resumed eating.

"I know I disappoint him," she said between bites. "But I *am* trying. I really am!"

"I know you are. And you're doing great. Your development will come in its own time. You've made amazing progress, even if Andre would like it to happen faster. But you can't rush it."

"Tell him that!"

They ate in silence again for a while.

"He promised me he'd help me find them," Alice said. "My parents and brother."

Morgan nodded understanding. "He's tried. We've all examined the records from the *Seeker* a hundred times over. And the analysis I managed to get under the table from the military. It's like your folks just vanished."

"That's not good enough," she said. Alice could feel the lava broiling again inside her. She worked hard to keep it down. She wasn't upset with Morgan Henry. He didn't deserve her vomiting her anger all over him. The room around her shimmered again. "It feels like I'll never find them."

Morgan reached over and placed his warm hand on hers. "I know. But you will. I know you will."

"How?" she demanded. She needed to know. She needed to know now. "*How?* I feel like I've failed them. All this time, I should've been looking!"

"You have been. We all have. And without Andre Korsakov ... well, I don't think we'd have gotten nearly as far in the search. It just takes time."

Time.

God, how she hated *time*. It only ever seemed to ebb by, minute by agonizing minute. It was like the universe delighted in slowing itself just to extend her torture of the moment. Until she looked up to realize how fast time had actually passed. Like when she thought about how long she'd been looking for her family to no avail. Three years!

Morgan squeezed her hand. "Hey, we need to talk about something."

Still cursing the universe, Alice was only half-listening. Her meal had grown cold. She'd lost her appetite. "What?"

"I've put this off for far too long," Morgan said. "That was me being a coward, really. And now I feel worse for springing it on you like this. I just didn't know how to—"

"*What?*"

God! What else could go wrong today? Failing with Korsakov. Zoey's nonstop teasing about Ian. And a nice dinner turned into half an argument with the only person in the whole fucking universe who really cared for her! But then it hit her. Of course. That must be it.

Morgan was just like all the rest. "You're leaving..." she said, barely more than a whisper.

"What? No. I mean—"

"I knew it! Just when I start to rely on someone, they always leave ... and now, *you're* leaving!" She stood up from the table so fast, her chair screeched on the floor.

Morgan held his hand out to her, but she turned away. "Alice—"

"Is it Nick Stone? Did they bring back the tribunal? I thought all that was done! You promised me it was all done!"

"Alice, please..."

"You promised me!"

Alice stalked away a few steps, then rounded on him, all clenched fists and blazing eyes. Her rant stopped cold when she saw Morgan's expression. His cheeks were damp. She'd never seen him cry before. Not once.

"Alice, I'm sorry," he said. "I'm dying."

Time was the true enemy. Everyone's true enemy, everywhere.

Hours had always stretched, excruciating, like days for most of Alice's time on Tarsus Station. How many times had she wished for time to hurry along, get out of the way, for her life to stop being *boring*? But the last week had passed all too quickly, marked by bouts of crying in her quarters, or calm comforting from Ian and Zoey and even Korsakov, who'd suspended testing "for now, anyway." In the past few days, time had flown by in extended visits to Morgan Henry's bedside, where Alice tried not to fall asleep—when time passed most quickly of all.

But all that crying, all that cursing at the cruel universe had forged in Alice an unexpected consequence. Her insides had switched off. She couldn't feel anything anymore. Not anger. Not desperation. Not grief. It was like her eyes leaked only from habit.

Or that's how it had been until today. This visit to Morgan's bedside had brought all those feelings rushing back. The fury; the oppressive, heavy sadness. Alice was sure this is how it would have felt had that rockfall buried her and Ben Stone. An avalanche of sorrow, crushing her. No light showing the way out. No hope.

Why me?

Her heavy heart felt sluggish, like her blood had gone cold and thick.

"Then bring me the other one!" Morgan Henry said. An order once bellowed at the top of his lungs, now uttered with barely enough air to carry the words. "Are you a nurse or just playing dress-up?"

Alice lifted her head from the sheet, soaked and salty with her tears. He was delirious again, recalling some order shouted in the middle of a battle. She held his hand tighter as Morgan triaged imaginary wounded in the sickbay of a ship called the *Manitoba*. Constantly at his bedside, she'd learned a lot about his service history. Frequently when his memories surfaced, there was a battle raging. Morgan even shook on occasion as if feeling the shock of a starship in combat. She'd pieced together the puzzle over the last few days. It always seemed to be the same battle. Or battles were so similar, maybe, that the differences between them didn't matter much in memory.

"Tell God-Admiral Bryant I've already got my hands full!"

More force. More fury of a battle long over.

Korsakov had said this might happen—that, at the end, a person who was dying often made a last, valiant attempt to hold on to life. Clawed their way back from the edge of oblivion. Rallied their memories to fight like an army for them, to prove they'd lived a life worth living, and lived still.

Morgan's body calmed. His face slackened. Eyes closed but darting in delirium, he seemed at a loss for words. Where was he now?

"I'm sorry about Amanda, Nick. I'm so sorry. I just heard."

This isn't fair. Alice screamed at the universe. *This isn't fair at all!*

She placed her forehead back onto the warm, wet sheet. Why did the universe always seem to aim its arrow straight at her? To lull her into depending on someone, caring for someone, only to snatch them away? Her family. Ben Stone. And now—

"You're older than your years, you know that?"

Alice jerked her head up. Morgan's eyes were still closed. He squeezed her hand.

"You've faced a lot. And you've overcome it. Beaten what would have killed lesser mortals," he whispered. When he'd first said those words to her, he'd been kind, supportive, with that playful note of mischief in his voice he saved for special occasions. "Keep on truckin', kid. I know you don't know what that means. Your whole generation is useless that way. But take it to heart anyway."

A smile broke open on Alice's face. After a particularly bad session with Korsakov less than a year after they'd arrived on Strigoth, Morgan had intervened with both barrels against the professor. Korsakov had stalked off following an argument that had all but come to blows. And Alice, crying, had been comforted by the warm grumblings of a man who'd done more than chosen a career when he'd become a healer. He'd answered a calling.

She wanted to say something back to him now, to answer the memory. What had she said then? Thanks, maybe. Or something equally inadequate. Maybe he would hear her. Maybe he would feel better, if only for a moment. To know she was here. To know he was loved.

Morgan's face changed, became almost petulant. "We've established what he is. Take lubricant."

Alice returned her forehead to the sheet and wished she couldn't feel anything again. How could a mind so lost to itself be so precise and vivid in its recollections? The wonders of the human brain—one of Korsakov's sayings that had wormed itself into her subconscious. *"So many mysteries remaining,"* he said in her head.

"How is he?"

Alice startled and looked up.

Korsakov, in the flesh. The door creaked behind him as it closed.

"Dying," she answered tartly. That tone had become her default mode with him. His hand touched her shoulder. If she hadn't been so tired, so washed out inside, she might have shrugged off the hand. Just to be shitty.

"I know this is hard," Korsakov said.

"Do you? Maybe it wouldn't have to be so hard if you'd worried less about my freak abilities and more about his illness."

Korsakov sighed. "I've told you, Alice, over and over. There's nothing I can do, believe me."

"I *don't* believe you. You talk about miracles all the time! You and your Godwave. Make one now, Professor God!"

His hand dropped away. "Alice, that's not fair. Doctor Henry and I have our differences, it's true, but he's been a colleague and friend to me too, especially these past few years."

"Morgan," she said because she couldn't think of anything else. "His name is Morgan."

"Morgan, yes."

There was the scrape of a chair, and then Korsakov was

sitting beside her. "There's nothing I can do," he repeated, "but…"

Her head whipped around, her eyes fastened on him. "What? Could someone else … I mean, is there a cure we could—"

"No. No, that's not what I meant."

Her insides folded in on themselves just a little more. "What, then?"

"I was thinking, maybe you…"

Alice squinted, annoyed. Another memory came into her mind's eye. The sergeant, Bricker, buried in the rockfall beneath Drake's World. And a pleading Ben Stone looking at her, begging her to make another incomprehensible miracle to save him like she'd just saved them. To heal Bricker somehow. Her unspoken, helpless response was as true then as it was now.

Everyone dies.

Not him, Alice begged, staring at Morgan. Imprinting him on her memory. *Not him!*

"Your ability," Korsakov began carefully, "seems to manifest in high-stress moments, especially situations of life and death. I was thinking, maybe with Morgan, you could…"

Andre is the epitome of a scientist. Not very subtle.

Alice stared at her sleeping mentor and friend, just to make sure he hadn't repeated those words out loud. She exhaled and wasn't aware she'd even said anything till Korsakov answered.

"What? Alice, I didn't hear—"

"I said, *please leave.*"

The room became still. Silent, but for Morgan Henry's labored breathing. Like air through tattered paper.

"Alice, I'd like to stay. I'd like to—"

"You are unsubtle," she said, pronouncing the awkward word with precision. There was a warmth building within her. A tiny fire kindling, a sun of red hate.

"What? What did you say?" His hand returned to her shoulder. This time, she pulled away.

"Get out."

Korsakov sighed. "Young lady, I think you should—"

The door to Morgan's private room reopened. She felt Korsakov turning to see who it was. She didn't need to look. But Alice knew no one was there. His gasp confirmed it.

The sun was glowing inside her now. It warmed her. It was the first thing she'd felt in days that didn't make her want to puke. It threatened to consume her, and Korsakov too.

"Do I need to make you leave?"

Korsakov stood on his own, then hesitated.

"I'm so proud of you. I knew you could—"

"*Leave!*"

The word sounded larger than itself, alive with danger. An irresistible order, reverberating off the walls and hanging in the room like a bad smell.

"So very proud of you," Korsakov muttered before walking from the room.

But Alice wasn't listening. She was already focused again on Morgan's sleeping face. Had it gotten harder for him to breathe? Maybe he'd heard her and Korsakov. Maybe he'd struggled to wake himself and step in, as he had so often before. But that's what family did, she realized. They always stuck together, no matter what.

Right up until they didn't. Right up until they left you.

Her fury at Korsakov spent, Alice sat empty of feeling. She dropped her forehead to the sheet. Her tears and purified air had made it cold. Her hitching sobs covered the quiet *snick* of the door as it closed. Once again Alice was alone with the shell of a man who'd once been Morgan Henry, kept company only by her anguish.

8

THE ENVOY

BREEZING THROUGH THE BULLPEN, Eva reflected that "The Hot Seat" was the perfect name for Piers Bragg's power broker room. Since he'd ascended to the presidency of the Sol Alliance, Bragg had courted controversy like an arrogant lover coolly confident in every future conquest.

"Good morning, Mister President."

"Eva," Bragg acknowledged. More perfunctory than usual, without so much as a leer tossed her way. He was distracted. "Close that door behind you."

Sitting in front of the president's desk, Sam Devos flashed her a cautionary glare. Eva took the chair next to him.

"Brief her," Bragg ordered.

"There's been a complication on Canis III," Devos said solemnly. "Likely nothing to worry about." His mollifying tone was meant for the president, though his mouth pointed at Eva. "An explosion in Fort Leyte. General Strickland is wounded but recovering."

Well, that explained Bragg's mood. Someone had knocked over his favorite toy soldier.

"What's the situation?" Eva asked, thinking immediately of the impact that leaked video might have on public sentiment.

"Locked down," Devos assured her. "Nothing in or out via subspace other than secured military messages. Bradshaw's on top of it till Strickland is back on his feet."

"Okay."

Eva had never thought much of Josiah Strickland. He reminded her of a pilot fish attached to Bragg's shark underbelly. She was the daughter of a Fleet officer, and Strickland's windbaggery translated for Eva as demonstrating bare competence. But he was unfailingly loyal to the president, which seemed to be the main qualification Bragg cared about, as long as things went well. Crisis could bring on a ruthless purge, though this situation hadn't apparently risen to that level—yet. That Bradshaw was in temporary command reassured Eva.

"I want you to go to Colorado," Bragg said.

The non sequitur brought Eva's thoughts to a grinding halt. "Sir?"

"It's where they're holding Marcos," Devos explained.

"Okay."

"This thing on Canis III," Bragg said. "It could blow up into something. Hell, it already has blown up."

Eva wasn't the least bit tempted to laugh at the ham-handed pun spoken in such poor taste.

"We need to dispose of the Psycker thing if at all possible," Devos said. "It's gone on too long. The president wants you to bring Marcos over."

She glanced from one man to the other. Bring her over?

"Sir?" she said to the president, hoping she'd misunderstood the metaphor.

"Everyone has a price," Bragg said. "Find hers. Bribe her. Promise her a cabinet position as some minor functionary when one's available. Hell, we'll make one available. Or create one. Whatever it takes."

Bribe her? Miranda Marcos was the black-sheep great-granddaughter of Gabriella Marcos, the woman behind the international initiative that made free trade viable across Earth, regardless of national boundaries. It'd become the blueprint for interplanetary trade with Alpha Centauri, facilitating the rapid development of Sylvan Novus. Miranda's father, Elias Marcos, was the current steward of the Marcos trillions. Bribe her with what? The family had lost more money in their couch cushions than God.

"Go talk to her as the president's envoy," Devos said. "Find out what she wants. If we can give it to her quietly, without the president taking too bruised a black eye ... we need to get this Psycker thing behind us."

Then stop rounding them up and throwing them in jail.

The best solutions are often the simplest. Eva was almost tempted to speak her mind aloud.

"Go today," Bragg said in dismissal.

Today? Leo wouldn't like that.

"Yes, Mister President," she said, standing.

"Use your imagination when negotiating—within limits, Eva. Report to Sam afterward."

"Yes, sir. Thank you, Mister President."

Suborbital flight had a way of recalibrating one's perspective on ye olde home world, especially when made aboard a private, presidential shuttle. Recalibrated one's perspective on life, for that matter. The Pacific Ocean appeared disturbingly small. Seeing the bright horizon of Earth's curvature set against an infinite, star-filled canvas had a way of making overwhelming, ground-based problems seem laughingly insignificant.

Maybe it was that feeling or the subdued hum of the launch's anti-grav engines or the fact that she was the only passenger aboard, if you didn't count the omnipresent plain-clothes ACE agents in the back of the cabin. But Eva found herself enjoying the smooth, quiet ride away from the Citadel. It was good to get away, even on a task so daunting as this one.

Bribe her with what? Eva wondered again. *A window office?*

The sun rose quickly in the east, seeming in a hurry to reach noon. The launch had traveled far enough from Tokyo that only a scattered mirage of tiny islands speckled the ocean below. The sun reflected off the sea like diamonds arranged solely for the pleasure of higher beings.

Eva reclined her seat and inhaled the calm. She hadn't realized how normal it'd become to feel tense all the time. For the first half of Bragg's presidential term, certainly, but for much longer than that, if she thought about it. Rising through the ranks of Bragg Industries. Catching his eye as a substitute from the secretary pool on Monolith. Impressing him with her people skills and her ability to read him well enough to anticipate his next request. Those qualities, no doubt, had figured into his assigning her the task to win over Marcos. In the eight years they'd been together, she'd done everything he'd ever asked of her, from bringing him tea and less virgin beverages to, now, helping shape Alliance policy.

Well, almost everything.

That way lies madness.

Leo had no cause for worry, but he had a right to be jealous. Search *Type-A Personality* and up pops an image of Piers Bragg. Winner of business wars. Cornerer of markets. A see-it-and-take-it man. To be denied his druthers, whatever form they took, wasn't something he accepted easily. But for Eva to give in to his advances? That'd be a huge mistake on every imaginable level. Piers Bragg scared her. Fending him off—and the possibility, however remote, that one day maybe she wouldn't—was the only power she held over him. The idea of surrendering the kind of mental and emotional distance a relationship with him would require was a terrifying thought. Plus, she didn't find him sexy at all. The power, yes. The man, no. And there was always that niggling concern that maybe her fear of Bragg—or worse, what his reaction might be if her officially single status ever changed—was impacting her ability to commit to Leo.

She felt herself tensing again, so Eva tried to relax. But no matter how hard she stared at the ocean, its palliative effect was gone. Zen displaced by reality. Back to business, then. Raising her seatback, she pulled up the vid file on Miranda Marcos.

Mid-twenties, just a little younger than Eva. Spanish-Persian descent, which gave her skin a dark, glamorous quality and a sharp-yet-soft cast to her features that was beyond attractive. An aroma of memory, of experimenting in college with her roommate's best friend one drunken Saturday evening attempted to rise from the grave. Focusing on the hard facts of the bio brief, Eva clucked it away. Elias Marcos, blah-blah-blah, Western Trade Association policy opening up new markets, yadda-yadda-yadda. College degree in social policy with a concentration in "political oppression through autocratic power structures." Interesting. Denounced her father at multiple dinner parties? Intriguing, not to mention humorous.

Sometime in her late teens, Miranda had begun using Elias Marcos's mover-and-shaker get-togethers to command attention for leftist political screeds. At first, she'd been deemed cute as a button by the economic elite, who dismissed her to her father with you've-raised-a-spitfire-there-Elias, backhanded compliments. But as sympathetic political groups began to co-opt Miranda's pontifications for their own agendas—with her approval or not was an open question—the corporate aristocracy began to take her more seriously. Embarrassing headlines led to family crest-topped media releases disowning her in stages and, eventually, cutting her off altogether. Public statements by Miranda suggested she reveled in her social pariah-cum-hero-ine-to-teenage-girls-everywhere, superhero status. Having been a teenage girl herself once, Eva wondered if Miranda had ever wanted to accomplish anything more than to embarrass her respected father.

Then Bragg began detaining the Psyckers. Most were just teenagers and holdovers in their twenties whose growth had been stunted by addiction. Goth dress, studded body parts, sneering faces, and fuck-you attitudes inhabiting smoking clubs and orgy dens. Somehow, Miranda had been anointed their queen. Her destiny coalesced when the media questioned Bragg's methods and Miranda rediscovered her penchant for pithy speeches sprinkled with words like "inalienable rights" and "unlawful detention." Those speeches had placed her square in the crosshairs of the current administration.

This interview was going to be interesting, all right.

"Call from the Citadel, ma'am," the co-pilot announced. "Encrypted channel."

"Thank you, Commander."

Leo's face lit up the screen. Tie secured. Smile in place. Dimples flexing.

"How's the flight?"

"Good. Peaceful. Marcos is an interesting character."

Leo nodded. "Most anarchists are."

"I think she has daddy issues."

"Most anarchists do."

"Jesus Christ," Eva said.

"Including him, yeah."

"No, I mean—I just scanned your briefing note. The president wants to give a victory lap speech?"

Leo shrugged. "Marcos was a big pain in his ass. He's feeling entitled."

"He feels that way about everything."

"Yeah, well."

"I think it's jumping the gun."

"You've just described the theme of his whole presidency, you know."

Yeah. I know.

"Can you convince him to hold off?" Eva asked. "At least until I've had a chance to meet with her? I might be able to get something he can use. Hell, maybe she'll come over to the dark side, and he can announce that."

"I can try."

"Talk to Sam first. He'll agree it's a good idea. Both of you together can maybe convince the president."

"Good idea."

"I saw your media Q&A about Sirius," Eva said, wanting to reinforce him for his talk with Devos. "Considering we can hardly say anything about what happened, you handled the barrage well."

"Thanks. And I have every confidence Sam will agree with me about delaying the speech." He gave her a look of what, *don't you think I know what you're doing?* "But I appreciate the pep talk."

She smiled at his ability to see right through her. The pitfalls of dating a man who also read people for a living.

"Right. Sorry. I didn't mean to—"

"No, no, it means you care," Leo said. "And not that you don't have confidence in my confidence in myself. That's my story and I'm sticking to it."

"Good story, media guy."

"Is there any other kind?"

"Ma'am, we're approaching the prison," the pilot broke in. "Landing in five."

"Thank you, Commander. Leo, I've gotta go. More reading to do before we land."

"Try to do that softly," he said. "Landing, I mean. You know, like when you—"

She smirked and killed the feed. It was one thing to have a relationship that was an open secret; and quite another to literally broadcast its sordid details for everyone to hear. Encrypted channel or not.

Eva's stomach lifted as the launch descended a hair too rapidly. She had less than five minutes to assimilate every scrap of info she could use in the interview. She pulled Marcos's file back up and was struck again by the woman's natural beauty. Even more so by her natural, born-leader bearing. Miranda Marcos was a formidable woman, Eva thought.

On the other hand, so am I.

Sol Alliance Penitentiary, Administrative Maximum Facility was the largest connected complex Eva had ever seen planetside. A broad, tall series of bone-white structures nestled in the Colorado mountains outside Florence in old Fremont County, SA Florence ADMAX was a supermax facility meant to lockdown society's worst offenders for as long as twenty-three hours a day. Eva suspected it was less a concern for Miranda's likelihood of escape and more how the media would report on the prison's apex-predator reputation that explained Marcos being detained there. The subtext of her danger to the Alliance was built right in.

Her immediate impression of Warden Bradley's photo in

the file was that of a walking stereotype. Middle-aged, balding, button-down. Medium height. A perennial, slightly depressed expression after a lifetime of questionable life choices. The kind of man Eva could control by simply sharing the same air. She tugged her blouse down an inch before leaving the launch.

"How do you do, Miss Park?" Bradley asked in greeting.

"Well, thank you." She accepted his offered hand.

Slightly sweaty.

Bingo.

"I trust your flight was uneventful?" the warden said, not waiting for an answer. He turned and led them away from the landing pad. Ahead, two armed guards flanked a security door, mirror images of the two ACE agents walking a respectful distance behind Eva and Bradley.

"It was."

"I must admit, I was a little surprised to hear from the Citadel," he continued. Eva could hear the tremolo in his voice, an odd counterpoint to the man's feigned gregariousness.

"Miss Marcos is a person of particular interest to the administration, as I'm sure you're aware."

"Of course, of course," Bradley said. The security door rolled open to let them enter. "Do you happen to know how long she'll be staying with us?"

Staying with us? He made Marcos's incarceration sound like a distant cousin had stopped by but he wasn't sure how long she'd want to squat on the couch. Interesting that Bradley seemed almost anxious to be rid of her.

"I would assume indefinitely," Eva replied.

"Ah."

They walked in merciful silence for a bit, passing through more security checkpoints and finally into a holding area. Eva used the time to organize the briefing facts on Marcos in her head.

"Just to prepare you," Bradley said, "we'll have to walk through a wing of general holding to get to isolation, where Miss Marcos resides for now. Most of our population is men, and—"

"It won't be the first time I've been catcalled," Eva assured him. She considered adjusting her blouse back up to show less cleavage, then dismissed the idea. Fuck 'em. "I'll be fine."

"Very well, then. Right this way."

9

MASSACRE

DESPITE MENTAL AND PHYSICAL EXHAUSTION, Ben hardly slept.

It wasn't the constant, 'round-the-clock bustle of Fort Leyte trying to restore normal operations and it wasn't the recurring nightmares. Thankfully, they'd left him alone last night. But a restless fixation had seized Ben. When he closed his eyes, the desiccated Arcœnum skull entombed within its ruined helmet haunted him. Without their skin, human skulls display a gruesome grin. By contrast, Archie skulls had a stern, determined look implying focus and concentration—as if still working to enslave the human observer, even in death.

Ben suited up quickly. Having no appetite, he skipped breakfast and reported directly to the Doghouse. His old unit, Gupta's Devil Two Platoon, should be sweeping Sector A-24, an attempt by Bradshaw to reestablish a modicum of routine while investigating the explosion. Toma's hesitation to name it sabotage had proven unnecessary. Though the perpetrator or perpetrators were still unknown, the forensic analysis so far left no room for doubt. The depot had been blown up intentionally.

Though Ben was uneasy taking civilians out to the Archie landing site, maybe it was the safest place for them, given the all-but-certainty of traitors in the fort. At least he knew whoever had fired on the depot yesterday hadn't been with them at the site. And he was mindful of the colonel's desire to minimize Zack's opportunity to record anything the AGF didn't want the public to see.

The engineers had already replaced every compromised window in every building impacted by the explosion. Only a thin wisp of smoke still rose from the depot. The remaining viable ordnance was organized and stockpiled under heavy guard outside the mangled hexacrete and polysteel. Ben noted and filed away these details as his armor carried him to the Doghouse.

The pressure door cycled to green, and the room seemed huge after the previous day. Only Maitland, Tso, and two Marines flanking the door were present. Sheba Toma and the others had reestablished their command center at Battalion HQ, once again sealed tight against the noxious vapors of Canis III.

"Widen the band," Tso told Maitland. The order had come over comms. From habit Ben's hand had reached up to unfasten his helmet; then his tired mind caught up. Bradshaw had implemented her new protocol requiring full battlesuits on-planet at all times, whether in supposedly secure facilities or not.

"I did, Lieutenant," Corporal Maitland replied.

"Well," Tso said, *"widen it further. A platoon can't just drop off the grid like that."*

"What's happening, Lieutenant?"

"Good morning, sir."

"Morning."

"We've lost contact with D-2, sir," Tso said.

"Lost contact?" Ben scanned the biomonitor panel. All were

flatlined, zeroed out. Like everyone in the platoon had simultaneously deactivated their suit uplinks. He was about to order Maitland to contact Gupta but realized she'd probably already done that. "Fill me in, Corporal."

"Bios, helmet comms, GPS locators. Everything," she said. *"Their readouts just dropped off."*

"Dropped off?" Ben said. As soon as he'd asked the question, he realized he'd fallen into a pattern of parrot-talk they used to ding officers for in Officer Candidate School. Any officer in OCS who simply repeated a subordinate's comment was seen as demonstrating his own inability to synthesize intel. Sleep or not, distractions or not, Ben was determined to snap his mind back into the groove. "How long?"

"About two minutes," Maitland said.

Ben bent over the console. He pulled up the archival feed, stored automatically, and ran it back three minutes. The data was all there as normal—bio readouts, GPS location as the platoon's convoy approached the search sector. There was even a routine progress report from Gupta to Maitland at the bottom of the hour. The data simply stopped coming in. Hails from the Doghouse began going unanswered.

"Keep trying to raise them, Corporal."

"Yes, sir."

"Ozzy, your Marines ready to go for the civy escort?"

"Of course, sir."

Ben nodded. "Load them up. We've got a new mission."

"What could have happened to twenty trained Marines?" Zack paused. "'The mystery of the missing Marines' ... ugh. Too many M's." Another pause. "'First, an explosion. Now, twenty trained Marines, missing. Is Canis III cursed?' I think we have a winner!"

Ben tried to ignore Zack, who'd been ruminating on various themes since they'd left the fort. With D-2's status unknown, he'd argued to leave the civilian and his assistants behind, and Bradshaw had reluctantly agreed. Strickland, still bedridden but cognizant, overrode her. There was no evidence D-2 had suffered anything more than tech failure, he reasoned. And the president needed his documentary, the sooner the better with the trouble back home.

So, here they were.

He tried to ignore the director but couldn't. Ben was starting to wonder if the planet really was cursed.

"Coming up on their last known position," the driver said.

Ben's LUV crested a hill behind the lead vehicle in their convoy. Comms crackled—something not quite a word but primal, like a four-letter gasp. The driver hit the brakes to avoid rear-ending the lead vehicle. Ben saw why the other had stopped so abruptly. Twenty Marines, fully suited and armed, strewn across the rocky valley below.

There were bodies everywhere, encased in their battlesuits. Incapacitated or dead, it wasn't clear. Unmoving. And still sending no bioreadings. Unlike Tso's defensive formation at the Archie site yesterday, D-2's LUVs were positioned haphazardly. One of them was overturned on its side, a huge boulder lodged against the undercarriage.

"Motherfucker," Tso whispered over the command channel from another LUV. *"Cap, you seeing this?"*

Ben was busy experiencing the most palpable sense of déjà vu he'd ever had. It was like a wet, moldy blanket wrapping around him. He could feel the cold, close air of Drake's World. Hear the empty static of interference on the commlink with DeSoto and Baqri. Only now there were more than ten times as many corpses sacrificed to an alien world. He snapped his mind back to the present.

"Yeah," he said. "Lieutenant, standard approach for a hostile situation. Keep your boots grounded." The massacre at the bottom of the ridge could induce panic in the squaddies fresh out of basic, especially on the heels of the depot explosion. The thought of just how easy it would be to join in their terror crept up on Ben. Something was wrong on Canis III. Very, very wrong. "We still have no bios, so send your medic squad to the nearest Marine and plug into their port. Assess, and if deceased..." He hated himself for being so clinical, so detached. "...move on. Proceed with caution in echelon."

"Copy that," Tso said.

"Corporal, take us down," Ben ordered. "Slowly."

"Sir," the driver acknowledged, nudging them forward. The alien rock popped beneath the LUV's tires as the vehicle crept down the slope.

"What happened here?" Zack asked, sounding scared. Sounding human.

"We'll find out," Ben said.

Each of D-3's four LUVs contained a squad of four Marines. Two fanned out to the right flank and two to the left, staggering their approach, their mounted weapons scanning the valley floor. Tso's command unit proceeded straight down the center, with Ben's vehicle shadowing and slightly behind it on the right.

By their disposition, it was obvious that some of the Marines had died in combat—with each other. More than one, like the overturned LUV, had been pinned by rolling rocks and crushed.

"Lieutenant," Ben sent to Tso on their private channel, "have your left-most vehicle keep its scanners and gun trained on the ridge at ten o'clock. Those rocks came from there, I'd stake a month's pay on it."

"*Solid copy, Captain.*"

The terrain evened out, and Tso halted his platoon. "*Alpha and Bravo squads, you've got overwatch in the vehicles,*" he said. "*Three-sixty, active sensors readings. Charlie and Delta squads, bail out, skirmish line. Advance pickets along the perimeter of the site—keep outside the radius of that rockfall! Captain Stone, if you'll wait in your vehicle, I'll reconnoiter with Charlie and Delta and we'll—*"

"I'll join you," Ben said.

"*Sir—*"

"See you outside." Ben turned to Zack. "You and your assistants stay put. I'll determine if you're allowed outside after we get eyes on this."

"Captain Stone," Zack said, "do I have to remind you that I was sent here to document exactly—"

"—or I can have the corporal here drive you back now. Your choice."

Zack swallowed whatever he'd been about to say.

"Captain, should we call the Doghouse? Let them know—" The corporal sounded like he was trying to wrap bad news with a bow. "—what we found, sir?"

Probably. But we're not sure what we've found. And the last thing I want to do is add to any morale problems.

"Let's see what that is exactly, Corporal," Ben replied, grabbing his helmet. "But I take your point. Let Corporal Maitland know we've reached the site and will report back with details shortly. But that's *all*."

"Yes, sir."

Exiting the vehicle, he took a moment to assess the terrain. It was obvious that huge boulders had rolled down from the ridge above and interdicted the convoy. An avalanche, maybe, though Canis III was a fairly stable planet, tectonically speaking. Not like Drake's World, in that way at least.

He uplinked to the Doghouse and accessed the sensor data-bank of information continuously being recorded from the surrounding sectors. Everything from hourly wind shear readings to rare precipitation measurements were stored there to help the 214th plan its reconnaissance sweeps. Ben found nothing about any quakes, major or minor.

His helmet comms keyed.

"Cap," Tso said, *"take a look at this."*

Ben approached and followed Tso's finger pointing to the dead Marine on the ground. She was someone he didn't recognize, new to the unit since he'd commanded it personally. Her faceshield was shattered. Broken inward. The déjà vu hit Ben again. In a few decades, her skin would be blasted off her skull by surface winds. She'd be the human twin to the dead Arcœnum in Sector A-23. Only, she'd be grinning.

Tso bent over and picked up a sharp, heavy stone twice the size of a man's fist. *"Here's what did it. Scanner shows microfibers of plastinium embedded in the rock."*

Someone had bashed her faceshield in. She'd died in seconds from toxic exposure. Plastinium wasn't easy to break. That's why it was used for everything from starship portholes to windows in AGF buildings.

Ben blinked. The ghosts of Baqri and DeSoto manifested, their bodies violated by the sharp end of the cave rock used to murder them in the tunnel. They stood a short distance away, watching.

"Be tough for a human to wield this," Tso was saying. *"Nearly seventy kilos, and in this heavy gravity? I mean, powered with armor sure, but..."*

Ben stared at the broken faceplate.

"I'm getting other reports, Cap," Tso said. *"There are a lot more like her."*

When Tso paused to talk to his squad leaders, Ben turned

away from the dead Marine to survey the valley. Marines had fought one another hand-to-hand. Twenty meters away, he could see the holes in one battlesuit made by talon-tipped, armor-piercing weapons fire.

"Some of this they did to themselves," Tso confirmed, his voice disbelieving. *"It's like they turned on one another."*

A mutiny fought to the death... Or had one squaddie gone nuts and somehow managed to take out the whole platoon? Crazy as that sounded, it still didn't account for the debris field of boulders.

A shiver ran up Ben's spine. A sixth sense directed his gaze upward to the ridge. He could still see signs of the avalanche. And he couldn't shake the thought of that Archie skull looking up at him. Looking down from the ridgeline at all of them.

"Lieutenant!" came the call over the common channel. *"Over here!"*

Tso crossed the fifty meters to Alpha Squad's location, Ben following. The sergeant waiting for them gestured at the ground. Ben and Tso knelt.

This Marine had died in a primitive snare. Though rare on Canis III, the few trees they'd seen planetside spawned thick clusters of heavy flora. They formed thick, hemp-like fibrous bands, and that's what was looped around the Marine's ankle. The snare had literally tripped him up. Someone—or something—had then shattered his faceshield, exactly as Ben had seen before with the other Marine.

Rocks. Ropes. Rifle fire. Marines murdering one another.

Jesus Christ. What the hell happened here?

Tso stood and moved off, motioning for Ben to join him.

"Sending you this Marine's downloaded footage by taclink," Tso said. *"For the record, it's Private Israel, sir."*

This man Ben knew. A squaddie when he'd commanded D-

2. The loss he felt deepened, as impossible as that seemed. Broadened inside him.

Tso's transmission finished transferring. Every Marine wore a body cam mounted in the top center of their helmet. It often served as first-person footage for training exercises, used to improve performance, efficiency, and tactics. In the field and paired with recorded bio-readings and suit sensor logs, it became the digital record of battle.

In Ben's heads-up display, Israel's transmission began to play. Tso scrubbed the recording forward past the banal footage of D-2 platoon's arrival at the location and Gupta's ordering the Marines to exit their vehicles and begin their visual sweep of Sector A-24. Someone noted curiously that they'd lost the comms uplink with Fort Leyte. Someone made a snarky comment about shitty AGF equipment. Someone else asked Gupta a question. Before he could answer, the image jerked once, twice, first left, then right. In the biodata, Israel's heart rate shot up. D-2's platoon channel flooded with anxious questions.

Ben and Tso watched the massacre unfold. Boulders careened down from the ridge overlooking the rocky valley, and it was all Ben could do to stay focused on the recording instead of searching for the skull looking down from the ridge. First one, then a second Marine leveled their rifles at their comrades and began firing. Gupta, screaming orders; his sergeant's cursing turning shrill. Israel began to panic, and the back-and-forth of the image as he twisted his head this way and that compounded the confusion. Israel went down, his battlesuit readouts phasing from yellow to red as they logged the penetration of talon rounds. Israel grunted, and his biodisplay showed he'd been shot twice in the left thigh. "Why? Why?" Israel demanded before calling on his suit's AI to help treat the wounds. His cam angle went sideways as Israel fell onto his side, gasping. The recording logged the chaos of the scene, registering fire from the antipersonnel gun of an LUV. *"The lieutenant's down!"* came a desperate, now dead voice over the comms log. Despite the best attempts by Israel's battlesuit to stabilize him, his vital signs began to flutter, redlining in the display. There was the flash of a silver streak, like translucent lighting dashing by his faceplate. Israel raised his hand sluggishly to ward it off before a loud *crack!* overloaded the audio. Designed to protect its owner's hearing, the AI muted. A thin line fractured across Israel's faceshield. The sharp rock came down again, and again, rapidly and with deadly force. The plastinium ruptured, and the atmosphere of Canis III finished the job begun by another Marine's rifle. The silver streak appeared again and was gone just as quickly.

"Hold that," Ben said, breathless at what he'd just witnessed. "Rewind."

Tso slow-scrubbed the recording to a point just before the first instance of the rock hitting Israel's faceshield. He adjusted a bit more to bring the silver streak into focus.

"You've got to be fucking kidding me," Tso said as the image sharpened.

Ben said nothing for a long moment. Suspended in the visual were Israel's already-failing vitals and his armored hand attempting to ward off that first blow. And there, its murderous intent clear, loomed the cause for the massacre around them in a slightly blurry but irrefutable image.

This would change everything now. Strickland would be vindicated. Bragg, ecstatic.

"Get your squad leaders to confiscate and encrypt every one of these cams," Ben said. "No one is to access anything else from them. I need to make a call."

"Yes, sir," Tso said, understanding. He knew what this meant, too. He began issuing orders to his platoon commanders to digitally secure the other nineteen cams, sight unseen.

Ben stared at his HUD a moment longer. He wondered if all humans looked alike to the Archies, the way all Arcœnum did to humans. This face, framed in a protective helmet, looked exactly like the grim ghoul he'd seen yesterday.

Only this Archie was alive.

10
THE NEST

"CONFIRMED," Bradshaw said, her voice grave. *"The depot cams didn't capture as good an image, but they caught the silver streak too."*

Ben watched the cargo carrier landing just outside the rocky valley littered with dead Marines. It carried the *Shenandoah*'s recovery teams, with orders to recover Gupta and his platoon. They'd be ferried to Fort Leyte, where a service was already being planned.

"Do we have any idea of the size of the enemy force?" Ben asked.

"The orbital fleet is scanning the entire planet, ringing outward from A-24," Toma said. *"So far, nothing."*

Tso's Devil Three Platoon ringed the perimeter of the site, each squad of four in a loose skirmish order with an LUV separating the squads. They stood, silent and steadfast, to guard the teams from the *Shenandoah* as they recovered the fallen comrades who'd given the last full measure of devotion to duty. Their formation reminded Ben of a rosary, with its smaller beads of individual Marines sectioned off by the larger glory beads of the vehicles.

"Permission to reconnoiter the ridgeline," Ben requested. Whenever his thoughts wandered away from the carnage, his eyes drifted with them, and always to the ridgeline above. "Might give us a sense of the enemy's strength in this locale."

From the direction of the fort, five new LUVs crested the rocky hill. Vicky Taikori and Devil One Platoon, coming to relieve Tso. They halted in a line, idling. Ben knew exactly what was happening inside those vehicles. Cursing. Disbelief. Anger. A cold resolve, already forming. It had, after all, been only an hour since he and Tso's Marines had cycled through the same emotions they'd experienced when viewing the minefield of horror below.

"Granted," Bradshaw sent back. *"As soon as Lieutenant Taikori takes the ball, get eyes on the ridge."*

Ben hesitated with his next question. But it had to be asked. "Ma'am, the fact that Marines killed Marines here ... do we think—"

"Captain, keep speculation to yourself for now," Toma interrupted. *"We'll know soon enough when Lieutenant Commander Wallace conducts his autopsies."*

"Ma'am," Ben acknowledged. It was Toma being circumspect again. Smart. Sensible. Others might be listening. The enemy, for one.

"Ben." Bradshaw's voice had lost some of its anger. *"Be careful on the reconnoiter. And the general is insisting you take Zack."*

"What?" Ben said. "Say again, Leyte Actual."

Now it was Bradshaw who hesitated, but only for a moment. *"He wants everything documented. Take Zack and his cams at least. If you feel the situation is too dangerous for his assistants, then—"*

"You think?" Ben said before he could stop himself. "General Strickland wants me to take a civy into a potential combat situation?"

"Captain, look around you," Toma said from fifteen klicks away. *"You're already in a combat situation."*

"I know how you feel, Ben," Bradshaw began, *"but—"*

"Anything to start a war," Ben spat. "Anything to support Bragg's—"

"Captain Stone, you're on a channel that could be under surveillance by the enemy," Sheba Toma reminded him. *"So, secure that shit."*

Ben clamped his mouth shut. D-1's command vehicle had parked, and Vicky Taikori walked toward him while the rest of Devil One deployed. Tso's Marines were pulling back to make room for them.

"Ben," Bradshaw said, a touch of sadness shading the anger now, *"the war's already started. Leyte Actual out."*

Taikori saluted, and Ben returned it. He certainly couldn't argue with Bradshaw's statement. The Arcœnum had drawn first blood here. Gallons of it. The course of future events was like a train without brakes on a downhill grade.

"Captain," Taikori keyed in. *"What a horrible thing."*

Taikori was talking about the deaths of D-2 Platoon. Feeling that loss personally for his old command, Ben also saw the bigger picture. How the horror here would magnify geometrically in a new war with the Arcœnum. First twenty, then hundreds, then tens of thousands dead.

And still, it seemed a necessary thing. Blood, paid for with blood.

Or whatever the fuck runs through mind-raper bodies.

"Find Tso," Ben said, suddenly loath for conversation. "You have the duty."

From the ridgeline, the canyon appeared bowl-shaped. Open, with no cover—tactically perfect for an ambush. Ben noted again the fresh paths where the larger boulders had careened down the hillside. That Gupta had rolled into the canyon and bailed his platoon out seemed the height of stupidity, and having that thought, while it seemed disrespectful to the dead, only bred anger in Ben. At Gupta's stupidity, but mainly at the loss of life resulting from it. In Gupta's defense, no one, from Strickland's level down, was expecting the enemy to be here. Not much of an excuse in retrospect, Ben thought. Idiocy knew no rank.

Fucking officers.

"Cap, I'm picking up a low-level power source," Tso transmitted over the common channel. He moved his short-range sweeper in an arc. *"This way."*

Zack made to move forward, his cams ringing the platoon's formation. He controlled them himself, having left his assistants behind at Ben's insistence.

Ben blocked his way with an arm. "Stay behind me."

"How do you know the danger is in front of you?" Zack asked.

"I don't. But do it anyway."

"Alpha Squad, take point and scout along this trajectory," Tso ordered, highlighting their shared tactical display. *"Bravo and Charlie, fan out in skirmish order and watch your flanks."*

The squad leaders acknowledged, and Alpha Squad, led by a pair of scouts, stepped off first. Two of Zack's cams attached themselves to the scouts and purred past Ben's head. Having their constant eyes on everything gave him the willies. It was one thing for their battlesuit recorders and the ships in low orbit to monitor their recon of the ridge at the micro and macro levels, respectively. But the cams felt foreign and somehow wrong.

Like a voyeur watching through a window as someone undressed.

"*Signal's steady,*" Tso said.

"Try infrared," Ben advised. "Scan for heat sources."

The platoon obeyed, and a small blip registered on the shared tactical grid.

"*That's it,*" Tso said. "*That's the power source. Alpha Squad, advance. Bravo watch their flanks. Cap, hang back a minute if you would.*"

Fuck that.

But before Ben could voice the sentiment, their private channel chirped. Tso's direct line to him.

"*You're babysitting, sir, remember?*"

Oh, yeah. That.

Ben's irritation didn't even have time to flower.

"*Lieutenant, found it,*" D-3's sergeant, Sanchez, said. "*It's a power converter. Older, civy model.*"

Ben, Tso, and Zack approached, the cams flittering in a circle around the sergeant to get a better view. Even if they hadn't recognized the solar converter, the SunSpot trademarked company name was still visible on its casing. Marketed to space-goers for more than a century, this one, battered and scuffed, looked old enough to be one of the first off the assembly line.

"*Cap, you don't think...*" Tso began. "*Could one of the original scientists—*"

"*No way!*" Zack said.

"You're here to observe," Ben admonished him. "Do that mouth closed."

As to Ozzy's question... A human scientist still alive after fifty-plus years? It was possible, of course. Or maybe it was their kid, a child during the original Sirian science expedition. But no. That was no human, descendant or otherwise, captured by Israel's headcam.

Tso knelt and switched off the converter. Their tactical grid came alive with heat signatures, all clustered ahead on the path about one hundred meters farther on.

"Whoa!" Zack said, tapped in through his own display. *"Freaky!"*

"Tactical alert," Tso said calmly, his demeanor a restrained contrast to Zack's amazement. *"Scouts, take the point. Sergeant, shotgun."*

Sergeant Sanchez and D-3's scouts moved up the trail, with the rest of Alpha Squad protecting their left, Bravo their right. Fanning out was a challenge on the narrow path along the ridge, but they endeavored to avoid presenting a tightknit target.

"Devil Three Actual, this is Devil One Actual." Victor Taikori's lilting voice sounded concerned.

"I'll take it," Ben said to Tso on their private channel. "Mind your platoon."

"Sir," Tso acknowledged, moving after Sanchez.

"Devil One Actual, this is Stone. D-3-A is a little busy at the moment."

"I guessed, sir," Taikori said. *"Our tactical grid just lit up."*

"Found an old-timey solar converter and switched it off. Looks like it was powering a wide-angle dampening field hiding more goodies."

There was a click and a pause on the other end. *"Explains why the Doghouse lost D-2 before the ... before the attack, sir. Would've cut off comms, GPS, the works."*

"Yep."

"Need backup?"

"Nope. But keep eyes on our tac. Just in case."

"Um ... we're a long way away, sir, should you need us."

They were. But Taikori's Marines had a more solemn duty to fulfill, and Ben wasn't about to take them away from it without good reason.

"Guard those Fleeters until they've retrieved every last member of D-2. Once they're back on their ships and in the air, head this way."

"*Solid copy, sir.*"

"Stone, out."

Zack had moved fifty meters farther along the trail. Cursing, Ben hurried to catch up. He found Tso and Sanchez standing at a hastily barricaded entrance to a hole in the hillside. A cave, covered in those thick, hemp-like ropes Canis III produced. Poor man's camouflage.

Great. Another fucking cave.

"*It's almost like they want us to come in,*" Sanchez said.

"*It is, isn't it?*" Tso agreed.

"*What does that mean?*" Zack asked.

"It means get back," Ben said. "And keep your distance this time, till I tell you otherwise."

He herded Zack back down the path while the rest of D-3 Platoon retreated fifty meters from the cavemouth and hunkered down. Their battlesuits should protect them from any blast, assuming it wasn't nuclear. Zack's civy-rated vac-suit was much more vulnerable. Sanchez pulled a grenade from his pack, paced off twenty meters from the entrance and turned back around.

Ben wrapped Zack in a bear hug, lending him the relative protection of his battle armor.

"*What are you doing?*" the director asked nervously.

"Probably something I'll regret."

"*Fire in the hole!*" Sanchez yelled, thumbing the trigger on the grenade. He underhanded it toward the cavemouth with the aid of his powered arm. Sanchez ducked and covered, presenting his back to the cave. He held up three fingers, then two, one.

The explosion obliterated the hanging hemp ropes, and a

secondary explosion made sure only strands remained. The grenade had triggered a boobytrap.

"*Alpha Squad, go!*" Tso ordered. His Marines moved. Sanchez fell in with them.

Ben released Zack.

"*How do they know it's safe now?*" Zack asked. "*What if there's another—*"

"They don't," Ben said. "But whoever or whatever is in there should be surprised from the grenade, and that's the best way to find the enemy—surprised."

The next minute of high tension proved entirely anti-climactic. With dust still hanging in the air, Alpha Squad secured the hole in the hillside. Tso entered, then Ben. After the Marines confirmed the absence of more booby traps, he allowed Zack in with his floating eyes.

"*What is this,*" the director wondered, "*a nest?*"

"Looks like it," Ben said.

"*An empty one,*" Tso groused.

Empty now, maybe, but the cave had been a home for a long time. In one corner, a bed made of the hemp-rope material, double-thick and blackened and contoured from long use. In another, a small cooking station. Ben recognized bits and pieces of Arcœnum technology similar to what he'd seen alongside the Archie remains in the armor. In fact, if he had those parts, he fancied he could piece together a jigsaw puzzle of tech from what he saw here. There was also human technology, wired and piped into the Archie stuff. The cave's resident had bastardized two species' worth of outmoded components together to survive here.

"*Cap,*" Tso sent, "*Look at this.*"

Ben crossed the short distance between them, two of Zack's omnipresent cams following.

On top of a stubby table sat an AGF field transmitter, its

green light glowing. Intended as a planetary uplink booster to cut through atmospheric interference, it was typically used to connect a force planetside to an orbiting ship. With a bit of engineering acumen, it could be hardwired together with others like it to boost a distress beacon that could reach light years distant via subspace. It was wired up now with more of the assortment of technology present elsewhere in the cave.

"What am I looking at, Lieutenant?" he asked.

"Best guess?" Tso said. *"A homing beacon."*

Ben snapped to the compact, contemporary design. Not a hundred years old, like the converter outside. "That's one of our uplinks." He was looking at a small communications station.

"Yes, sir, you're right."

"Stolen from the camp?"

"Only way it got here, I'd say."

"Maybe the attack on the depot..."

"A diversion?" Tso ventured.

A beacon. But for what purpose?

"Shit," Ben said.

"Sir?"

"What is it, Stone?" Zack said, edging forward.

Ben reached an armored hand to switch off the stolen booster signal.

From the far corner of the cave, there came a screeching, a high, keening sound of fury and fear and hatred. A figure dropped, white-silver from the shadows of the cave ceiling. Marines shouted over comms, and Ben felt the heavy shock of bodily impact. He stumbled across the cave floor, careening into Zack and past Tso. The heavy weight landed on Ben's back, forcing him to the rough ground.

The brutal scream annihilated all other sound from Ben's hearing. The attacker grabbed and yanked, flipping him onto his back with a spine-jarring thud. Above, the feral face from

Israel's cam, the armored skull come to life, opened its alien jaws. The shrieking challenge wasn't coming from there, but from a sudden flood of terror drowning Ben's brain. Louder, more powerful than any sound it chilled his skin, an irresistible force of will become action. The Arcœnum raised four articulated, angelic arms, and Ben saw a jutting piece of cave rock jutting down at his head. He knew Private Israel's terror, understood exactly the dead man's need to know *Why? Why?* Ben put up a defensive hand as Israel had, and like him too, just a moment too late. The Archie thrust its weapon down, cracking Ben's faceplate. The shock of it shuddered straight through the battlesuit to his spine.

Ben was screaming too, raging, begging as the heavy rock came down again, the too-thin plastinium of his visor splintering, ready to shatter. He tried to cry out for help over comms, issue orders, but the Archie overwhelmed his will with its savage, irresistible mental assault.

Flashes of other Marines falling on the Archie, their armored arms grappling with it, preventing a third strike meant to smash Ben's visor once and for all. They lifted the Archie off as it struggled against them. The hatred and anger flooding Ben's mind abated, as if his brain had been doused in morphine. Tso's voice filtered in through comms, insistent and reassuring.

"We didn't, sir!" Tso shouted. *"We didn't kill it!"*

An impression from Ben's short-term memory, his screaming at them not to shoot the attacker, to "Take it alive! Take it alive!"

Three powered strikes across the back of its head by Sanchez, and the alien slumped to the cave floor. It was only then Ben saw it was wearing armor like the corpse in the Archie camp. An exoskeleton-reinforced atmospheric suit.

"Sir, are you all right?" Tso said, kneeling next to Ben. Then, to one of his Marines, *"Get a patch over here!"* Tso put his

hand on Ben's chest. *"Try not to move, Cap. That crack is bad. Try not to move."*

But Ben couldn't move. He could barely think. Barely breathe. But, he realized, and surprisingly without shame, that he'd pissed himself inside his armor. His eyes fixed on the unmoving Arcœnum, its alien, armored shape splintered by his fractured visor, its segmented limbs held tightly by four of Tso's Marines. Its monstrous mind now dormant in oblivion

11

TWO QUEENS, MANEUVERING

MIRANDA MARCOS WAS EVEN MORE striking in person. You could see pampered breeding in the way she held herself— defiant, challenging, a don't-waste-my-valuable-time expression. She was taller than Eva and lithely muscled, evident even beneath her unflattering, starched-white prison fatigues. Dark eyes and darker hair but light skin, the results of her Castilian ancestry. Marcos stood, not sat, in the small, spare conference room reserved for their meeting, leaning with her back to the wall. She seemed to be a beautiful machine, cold and efficient but whose smooth, supple exterior was designed to distract you from her craftier, more dangerous qualities.

"Miss Marcos, my name is Eva Park. I'm communications director for—"

"I know who you are, Miss Park. I've seen you with Bragg."

"Good. Saves us time."

"Right."

Eva took a moment to admire the way the woman stood absolutely still when speaking. Frozen in place, expressionless, with only her lips and vocal cords seeming to move. Like a marble statue channeling some divine power deigning to speak through her.

"I know a little about you too," Eva said.

"Very little."

"Meaning?"

"You know only what your data miners told you about me. Or maybe you talked with my father, who doesn't know me at all."

So. Daddy issues on the table right up front. Well, that saved time too.

"You can hitch up your blouse," Miranda said, with a flick of her eyes to Eva's cleavage. "I don't bat left-handed."

Eva ignored the suggestion, recognizing it as an attempt to control her and, thereby, the conversation. She said, "Sit?" and gestured at the small table and chairs.

Marcos hesitated, perhaps evaluating whether sitting made her appear weak. Eva moved to her chair first, confident that she wouldn't appear that way. Marcos mirrored her movements almost exactly. To Eva it felt like chess.

Move. Counter-move.

Machine like.

"Your protest movement is over," Eva said. "We've cut off the head of the snake."

Marcos laughed out loud, her gaze never leaving her opponent. "You're familiar with the myth of the Hydra?"

Eva regarded her coolly. "Cut off one head and two more appear."

A slim smile from Marcos. "Some myths are true."

She thinks, like any well-educated, rich girl would, that her reference to obscure Greek mythology impresses me.

"ACE will round up your lieutenants," Eva said. "Including whoever's poised to take the reins of your insurrection with you gone."

"Insurrection?" Macros said dramatically. "My goodness! Now we're one synonym's leap away from 'rebels'? I knew Bragg had an instinctive dislike for the truth, given how little he speaks it. I had no idea how much he feared it." She shook her head. "Insurrection!"

Eva put on her own smile. "Words are all you have, now. Enjoy them."

"Words matter. Words change history."

"Not in here they don't."

The prisoner's expression grew cold. "Why are you here?"

"To discuss alternatives to 'here.'"

"A less notorious prison, perhaps? One where I get more than an hour a day out of my cell?"

"Something like that. But I was also speaking more generally."

Marcos lifted an eyebrow. The machine, calculating. And—Eva saw in the slight crinkles in the corners of the woman's eyes, in the barely perceptible lift of her perfect cheekbones—the kindling of hope.

"Bragg will fall," Marcos said. "Brought down by the weight of his own ego, his own disregard for the welfare of the people who elected him. Eventually, they'll see it. The people hold the real political power in the Alliance, as they ever have everywhere, not those they elect to represent them."

Eva took in a slow breath. "Finished?"

Macros leaned forward. "Those you're detaining unlawfully? Young people who joined a harmless social club. Maybe they've made a few bad decisions, but that—"

"Guess not."

"—doesn't justify treating them like fucking criminals. Insurrectionists? Not everyone bought the Alice Keller propaganda film. An excuse for war with the Arcœnum." Pulling back her passion, Marcos reset her face. "Those kids *aren't* insurrectionists."

"Maybe not. But you are. And a naïve one at that." Eva rose to her feet. She brought her wrist to her mouth. "Commander, prepare for departure. This was a wasted trip." She nodded politely. "Miss Marcos, enjoy your stay at SA Florence ADMAX. I hear Colorado is beautiful this time of year. Maybe you can see it through a window in your free ... hour." She turned to summon the guard.

"Wait!"

Eva froze, her back to Marcos, her mouth still open to call the guard. She stayed that way a moment, stock-still, the way Marcos had when Eva first entered the room.

"What alternatives?"

Eva allowed herself a quiet sigh of satisfaction, a half-smile of triumph. She wiped that away before facing Marcos again. It was enough to know she'd won the battle, if not yet the war. Lording it over the woman would only work against her long term.

Eva took her chair again. "The president wants your help."

The eyebrow again. Marcos seemed to be holding at bay the raucous laughter breaking open inside her. "Oh, do tell."

"You make a public statement disavowing the activities of the Free the Psyckers movement. Part of that is acknowledging the necessity of the detentions to ensure domestic security. You will privately call your senior movement leaders in Sol and Alpha Centauri and tell them your call to stand down is genuine, not coerced. Once all that's done and we actually see it working, you'll be released from prison."

Throughout Eva's explanation, Marcos had regarded her with increasing skepticism. "That's the deal? Betray everyone and everything I believe in? For my freedom?"

Eva's father had taught her to play poker at an early age. She knew when to show her cards and when to keep them face-down. To keep the other players wondering what else she had hidden.

"You overestimate my love of the outside air," Marcos said. "You don't think I was prepared for prison when I stood up to oppose Bragg? I'm a go big or go home kind of gal."

"There's more."

Now it was Marcos who closed her mouth and waited. This really was like chess. An opponent positioning her black pawn to directly oppose the white pawn just moved. It made Eva's insides flutter with a kind of brainy giddiness.

"Please," Marcos said, "don't stop the joke now. I want to hear the punchline."

"We have bigger fish to fry, Miss Marcos. The Arcœnum are an existential threat to humanity. President Bragg is trying to end that threat."

"By imprisoning addicts with bad fashion sense?"

"By closing possible loopholes in domestic security before..."

Damn it. One word too many.

"Before?" Marcos smiled. "Before going to war, you were about to say."

"Miss Marcos—"

"Miss Park, I've known Piers Bragg a lot longer than you have. Since I was a little girl. He used to come to parties at my father's estate on Lanais Island. The only things Piers Bragg cares about are himself and profit. He measures the first in terms of the second, with which he buys more power and influence to make more profit. But he can never make enough profit, you see, because, at the end of the day, he'll never be satisfied with him*self*. He's the simplest kind of man to figure out. For all his bluster, he's a scared little boy with sand on his face that he can never quite clean off."

Eva ignored the sudden flash of feeling Marcos had stirred

up. "He cares about preserving the species," she said. "And that's what he's doing by preparing—"

"Now who's naïve? He's no patriot. He's no hero," Marcos said. "He's an opportunist always wanting more gold to toss on top of the trove. Which, if he really is taking the Alliance into war, means there's only one reason for it—there's profit in it. He's the *real* threat to the Alliance, Miss Park, not the Arcœnum. Wake up and smell the dead *before* they die."

Their conversation had taken a decidedly unexpected turn. Miranda Marcos seemed to care about more than a few detained addicts. Eva thumbed mentally through the woman's file looking for something to use. The epiphany struck that Marcos had been right. Eva hardly knew her beyond a few quotes, slanted family media releases, and administration analyst opinions. Miranda Marcos cared about people. Or at least was convincing at seeming to.

"It doesn't matter," Eva said.

"Doesn't matter?"

"Piers Bragg is the duly elected president of the Alliance. And a majority of the people believe he's absolutely right about the threat." Eva wasn't sure whom she was trying to convince at this point, Marcos or herself. "Half a century ago—"

"The people?" Marcos snorted. "What do they know?"

Eva's brow furrowed. Another unexpected turn.

"By and large, people prefer someone else to do their thinking for them," Marcos said. "That's why slogans, not issues, win elections. That's why your boy Bragg is in office. 'Humans first?' Who says? Did God inscribe that on a tablet somewhere and I missed it? But hey, that's our tribe, so go, team, go!"

This was better than any briefing. This was an open window into Miranda Marcos's soul.

Eva said, "For someone who champions 'the people,' you certainly don't think much of them."

Marcos shrugged. Somewhere in the gesture, Eva thought she saw regret in Marcos at having shown Eva a gap in her armor. "My tribe. Go, team, go." She rapped her knuckles on the table. "And Bragg is still unlawfully detaining part of my tribe."

"Maybe the greater good will be served—"

"The ends justify the means?" Marcos said. She rapped her knuckles on the table again. "The rationale of every dictator's suspension of civil liberties throughout the meta-tribe's long, sad, history."

It was hard not to like Miranda Marcos, Eva thought. Dogmatic, sure. Dense, in a way, because of that. Myopically chained to her own viewpoint. But hard to outmaneuver for that same reason.

"You said there was more," Marcos prompted.

Eva got back on track. "Yes. Once the movement stands down, a civilian-led oversight commission will monitor the activities of Alliance Civil Enforcement as it relates to the Psyckers. The leader of the board to be appointed by the president, its members hand-selected by that leader and approved by the president's cabinet. Checks and balances."

She could see the calculations running again behind those dark eyes. "What does that have to do with me?"

Eva allowed her face to brighten a bit. Was it because she thought she'd won or because she thought the answer was a good idea? For everyone?

"President Bragg would appoint you to lead the oversight commission."

There was the slightest crack in the statue's façade. The slightest parting of the lips in genuine surprise. The involuntary betrayal of the raised eyebrow.

"You're fucking joking."

"No," Eva said. It wasn't something she'd discussed with Devos or Bragg. But the administration already exercised civilian oversight of ACE. And if Marcos thought she was doing something noble—even if it could potentially turn adversarial—she'd essentially be part of a narrative dictated by Eva and mouthpieced by Leo. Marcos's story would become the administration's story. It shouldn't be too hard a sell back home.

The dark eyes jagged left and right. Calculations at translight speed, all with one thing on the right side of the equal sign, Eva was quite sure: what would Daddy think? More to the point, how much would it piss him off? Better yet, embarrass the shit out of him?

"Oversight of ACE?"

"Yes, as far as Psycker detentions go."

"And if I find they're exceeding their authority..."

"You'd have indirect access to President Bragg through his chief of staff, Sam Devos. And full transparency with the public, assuming no issues of Alliance security are involved."

"Talk to the media, you mean?"

"Assuming no issues of Alliance security preclude it, yes." Eva stood and called to the guard. This was a power moment, exactly the right time to detach from Marcos. "Sit here and stare at the walls a while, Miranda. Think on my offer."

"I will," Marcos said to her back.

As she made her way back to the launch escorted by a babbling Warden Bradley, Eva considered the challenge of dealing with an enemy as savvy as Marcos. In war, it was easy to dehumanize the other side. Required, in fact. Makes them easier to kill. But if you sat down to talk with them, you had to make a personal connection to understand their point of view. And therein lay the great trap. Like you, they were essentially concerned with survival and needing love and wishing life was easier but, on their better days, kind of glad it wasn't. Once you realized they were just like you, you either learned to love them or hate yourself too. Either way, it made it a lot harder to treat them less-than.

Miranda Marcos had a future in power—politics or industry or somewhere—assuming any of them had a future past the coming months. Eva decided she'd like to be around to see how that future played out. For Marcos, for herself. And maybe even keep Leo around to discover that with her.

"I think we've got her, sir," Eva reported to Bragg, who was tiled with Devos on-screen.

"You think?"

So much for the good news inspiring a good mood in the president. Both men looked grim.

"She's thinking about it, sir."

"Well, isn't that big of her. Let her sit there in prison and think until her pampered sensibilities turn green. We have bigger things to worry about."

"But not to talk about over the air," Devos said, jumping in. Encryption didn't mean *absolutely* secure. "Things are getting serious."

It took less than a second for Eva to parse the code. Reclaiming the system where the Specter War began, Bragg's first step in a much larger military campaign, had become complicated. Did Bragg actually know what he was doing? The question arose in the back of her head, and not for the first time. Now, however, it was asked in the disturbingly familiar, softly seductive voice of Miranda Marcos.

Devos continued, "The capture of Marcos is dominating the narrative, and that's a good thing. Distracts from the protests, though there'll be a spike in those now, at least in the short term."

"Demanding her release," Eva said.

"Yeah."

"The media will want interviews with her," Eva said.

"Fuck the media," Bragg said.

"Mister President," Devos said, reminding him they weren't all in the same room.

Looking annoyed, Bragg said, "I need you back here, Eva. Let Marcos *think* all she likes. Let her rot as an example to the rest of the traitors."

Traitors?

The dread of the coming conflict with the Arcœnum slouching up her spine disturbed Eva almost as much. Protestors to activists to insurrections to traitors. Words matter, Marcos whispered in her mind. The evolution of labeling them had happened quickly since the Free the Psycker movement had gotten organized. In war, Eva knew, it would happen even faster. Part of the process of making the enemy less-than.

"I can be in Tokyo in a little over six hours," Eva said. "I'll come straight to—"

"No, go get some sleep," Devos said. "We'll need you at your best. Not much we can do about the other problem from here, anyway. I've got the watch for now."

Over the situation. Over Bragg. The code was veiled but not unfamiliar.

"Okay."

"Safe travels." The screen went dark.

Eva sat back in her chair. She could feel the launch's ascent in the middle of her back. Earth's gravity tugging at her body, as if the planet didn't want to let her go. The compensators would catch up, but they wouldn't help the renewed tension of muscles between her shoulder blades. Twisting ropes of antici-pated drama with Bragg. Of frustration with knowing the right answer but being unable to convince him that his answer was wrong.

She looked out the window, hoping to immerse herself again in the Pacific's beauty. But the sun was blinding in the west. The ocean shone like polished glass, and the brightness was almost painful. She drew the shutter over the window and reclined her chair, trying to hyperextend her back to relieve some of the stress. Eva took in large breaths, held them for a count of three to stretch the muscles binding her rib cage, then exhaled.

Once. Twice. Three times.

And she'd been bitching recently about how stressful the last three years had been? They felt like the easy part, now. Eva closed her eyes and tried vainly to sleep.

12

"I NEED TO RUN."

ALICE PUSHED THROUGH THE PAIN. She was pushing so hard she'd overwhelmed the smartwear designed to capture her sweat and biometric data to optimize her workout. She could feel the sweat collecting in pockets where it shouldn't be. A glance down at the counter on the treadmill showed she was approaching ten kilometers. Not enough. She had to run farther. If she ran far enough, maybe she could even outrun her sorrow.

I've let myself go.

Drake's World had taught her many lessons, including the need to maintain physical fitness in a world with higher gravity. The smaller planet of Strigoth was closer in size to her homeworld of Sylvan Novus than it was to Earth, much less demanding than the heavy-g of Drake's World. After her brutal experience in the dungeon of the Terror Planet, Alice had luxuriated in that.

Now, she just needed to run. Partly to prove to herself that she could do it, maybe even build up some endurance and tone her slack Centaurian muscles. Partly because she had to put aside the deathwatch over Morgan, if only for a little while. She needed distraction. She needed to move. She needed to make her body hurt as much as her spirit did.

Need first.

The counter chimed the ten-kilometer mark.

Her will began to falter.

Run farther.

Korsakov's voice, angry, not inspirational. She should have eaten something before coming to the rec center. To motivate herself, Alice conjured images of the shadow-spiders, pretending she could hear the tap-tap-tap of their knife-like feet in the echo chamber of the Terror Planet's underground. She thumbed up the speed setting on the treadmill. Her legs ached in protest. The shock of each step pounded from her feet to her knees and jack-hammered her hips. Sweat slung into her right eye. Alice ignored the burning.

Run farther.

A whisper, not Korsakov. From the past. Her father's voice? Could she trust herself to remember what Marcus Keller had sounded like? Maybe it was Morgan. Maybe only herself. The voice spoke again.

Keep on truckin', kid.

Definitely Morgan!

"Alice Keller, please report to the medlab."

Amplified by the empty rec center, Korsakov's request broke her stride. The belt of the treadmill jerked her backward, and Alice barely avoided smashing her chin into the machine. The conveyor belt shot her backward where she tumbled to the floor, landing with a crunch on her right knee. There was a brief moment of shock while the summons repeated.

"Alice Keller, please report to the medlab."

The pain began, throbbing from her knee through her core and up into her chest. It wasn't all physical.

"Alice!" Zoey's voice, distant. The sound of shuffling. She must have pushed Korsakov aside from the intercom. *"Hurry!"*

Alice levered herself up. Adrenaline flooded her system. With an aching lope, she rushed back to Morgan Henry's bedside.

"I'm so sorry, Alice."

Behind her, Andre Korsakov sounded genuinely sad. Standing on the other side of the bed, Zoey wept quietly. Mercifully, she reached up and switched off the flat tone of the monitoring equipment. Ian stared at the final chapter of Morgan Henry's life recorded in the medical datapad, as if it weren't too late to save his life.

With the machines turned off, the room became subdued. There was only Korsakov's quiet consolation. Zoey's sniffling. Ian's mumble as he raked through the data for the hundredth time.

In Alice's head, it was anything but quiet. Her own voice rebuked her, and was that the harsh tenor of a Russian accent beneath it? Maybe Korsakov had been right. She should have tried to do something to save Morgan. What that would have been, Alice had no idea. But she'd had no idea she could deflect tons of boulders either with her mind until that had become necessary. In times of life and death, Korsakov had said, her ability showed itself. And wasn't this—or hadn't this *been*—one of those times? Too late now. Too late. She'd done nothing in the end, and now Morgan was dead. She'd only cried for her own loss. Held his hand. Mourned in advance of his leaving her. Cursed the universe for taking one more person away from her. Exercises in meaningless self-pity. And selfish. So selfish.

Maybe if she'd studied the medical data as Ian studied it

now—back when it mattered, when it could have made a differ-ence, saved Morgan... He and Ian had analyzed his condition for months, and both had kept it secret from her. There'd be a reck-oning for Ian about that, Alice promised herself. She'd hold him to account. He should have told her!

Endogenously induced caspase-proliferative disease. A condition never before recorded in all of medical history, Morgan had told her, so they'd had to name it themselves. "I've always thought of myself as unique. Maybe they'll name it Morg's Disease," he'd quipped with a tired grin. "Truth in advertising, that."

It hadn't been funny then. It wasn't funny now.

She'd memorized the name even if she had no idea what it signified. Something about Morgan's own body turning against itself. Not exactly an auto-immune condition, where the body's immune system attacks healthy cells, and not exactly cancer. Both of those were conditions she more or less understood, at least in their effects. Morgan's illness was uniquely destructive to his specific DNA, an aberrant condition exclusive to him because it had somehow mutated from his own genomic struc-ture. It appeared viral in its expansion but left no viral trail to track. That fact combined with the geometric progression of the disease outpacing any attempted interventions precluded even the most advanced genetic tailoring from modern medicine slowing it down.

The human body—that wondrous marvel of nature designed to adapt to and conquer any external biological threat —could sometimes be too good at its job, Morgan had informed her. Because those same abilities that protected it could be turned against curative measures trying to help it, too. When a body's own system becomes corrupted, when that body begins to destroy itself, healing regimens appear as the enemy; the body attacks and kills the cure. Ian and Morgan had worked for months, at best only slowing the progression for a day or two before it leaped over their intervention like a fire jumping a fire-break. They simply hadn't been able to keep up with the accelerated pace at which it destroyed Morgan's body.

And I did nothing, Alice thought. She stared at Ian, drilled imaginary holes through him. He was still mining the datapad for a cure that no longer mattered.

"You should have told me." She sounded somehow cool and furious at the same time.

Ian looked up. "I told you before, Alice. He ordered me not to. He said he didn't want to worry you. That there was nothing you could do."

Alice wanted to answer, to curse Ian since Morgan Henry was no longer alive to endure it. And still, it took all her will to not shout at the corpse in the bed anyway—to refrain from railing at Morgan that he'd had no right to keep his illness from her...

What exactly would she have done to save Morgan from his own body? Simply willed Morgan Henry back to good health?

Something. Anything. Not nothing.

She hardly recognized the husk he'd left behind. It was like the last weeks of his illness had pricked a hole in his heel and drained him away. What was left was an empty shell of the man who'd been so dynamic, whose bile and wit could cut any target to the quick. A raucous drinker. A caring healer. A man passionate about living and life. All dead now. All of the men that had been Morgan Henry were murdered, and by his own body.

This wasn't the way she wanted to remember Morgan Henry. Paper-thin skin, slack mouth. His body so sunken into the medbed, it was hard to tell where he ended and the bed linens began. She reached out and clasped the veiny right hand of the man she'd considered her family, giving it a final squeeze.

"I'm going to my quarters," she said.

"No, wait," Korsakov said.

Alice rounded on him, ready to unleash everything she was feeling at the man.

"We'll go," the professor continued. "Zoey, Ian ... let's give Alice the room."

"But I don't want to be here," Alice said. It was almost a plea. To leave before this Morgan Henry became the only version of him she'd remember. Korsakov stayed her with a gesture until Zoey and Ian cleared the room.

"He was pronounced less than five minutes ago, just before you got here," Korsakov said.

"Thanks for reminding me I was late! I swear, you—"

"It used to be thought that brain death occurred within six minutes of the heart stopping. But my research suggests—"

"Your research!" Alice advanced on him, but Korsakov held his ground. "It's always about your goddamned research! Can't you, just once—"

"Alice, *dostatochno!*" The professor cut short his outburst in Russian. He leaned in and took her by the shoulder. "Listen to me, Alice. His brain isn't dead yet. What conventional science knows about brain death is limited, of course, by conventional means to measure it. The discovery of subspace complementary brainwave patterns—"

Your discovery you mean, she thought acidly.

"—suggests that the six-minute mark might be outmoded thinking." Korsakov stopped speaking for a moment. "For all we know about everything, we hardly know much about anything. Especially when it comes to the human mind."

Alice stared at him. "What does this have to do with—!"

"There is more to us than this easily corrupted, transient flesh," Korsakov pressed on, squeezing her shoulder. "If my theory is correct... He loved you, Alice. If he has any awareness left, if there's even the slightest possibility he could still sense you here, *stay with him*." A wave of emotion flowed through him. It was the first time Alice could ever remember seeing Korsakov vulnerable. "Don't let him feel you leave the room."

He nodded, as if reassuring himself of something, then turned and followed Zoey and Ian. She considered the possibility that Morgan might still be aware. Aware that his life was ending and of her presence and near lack of it.

Finally. Something she could do.

Alice returned to his bedside and again took his slack hand in both of hers. She held it tightly, warmed it, in case he could truly feel her there. She began to speak softly, saying whatever came into her head. Random thoughts of their lives intertwined. Stories and memories. Laughter and tears, sometimes at the same time.

"You remember that time ... couldn't believe you said that ... what a pain in the ass." All her words, in the end, translating only to one.

Love.

He looked so much more like his grandson now that he'd lost so much weight. An older, more deeply and loosely carved version of Ben.

"My God, how you've grown up!" Nick Stone said. He seemed unable to reconcile the young woman before him with the girl he'd hidden on Strigoth. "How are you holding up?"

Alice shrugged. Thinking the feed might not have picked up the gesture, said, "Okay. You?"

Stone seemed surprised for a moment, as if he'd had a plan for how this call would go and she'd just upended that plan.

"Okay," he said. There was an awkward moment, an eternity in subspace reckoning.

"I haven't talked to you since … well, since you dropped us off here," Alice said. She tried to keep her voice even, not laden with disappointment. Communication was, after all, a two-way street. She hadn't reached out to him, either.

"Morg and I discussed it. Decided it was best to keep you as low under the sensor sweep as possible. There was already so much hype around Ben and the rescue and … all that. He kept me updated on how you were doing, though."

I guess he won't be doing that anymore, Alice thought.

Brutal. In poor taste. Entirely accurate.

"I'm so glad the trial vindicated you both," she said, changing the subject. "I don't think … I don't think I could have survived here without Morgan." And just like that, they were wading right back into the middle of the heartache.

Stone smiled comfortingly. The slack skin under his neck, although partially hidden by an iron-gray and white-streaked beard, stretched up to accommodate it. She could see Ben even more in his face when he smiled. Ben in fifty years.

"Morg felt the same way," Stone said, "told me as much many times. I'm not sure he would've lived as long as he did without having you to care for. Morg had no immediate family, you know. So his passion for his patients—and his friends—filled that space in his heart. He loved you, Alice."

She felt the corners of her mouth twitch up in that perverse way your body does when confronting uncomfortable emotions. Alice clenched her fists off-camera, dug her fingernails into her palms. The pain helped her focus. *Not going to lose it. Not going to cry.* She'd done enough of that over the past few days.

"As for the trial, well," Stone continued, perhaps sensing her frailty, "that outcome was almost a foregone conclusion, in retrospect. Most of the details were classified that weren't in the media already. No great appetite on Bragg's part for publicly vilifying the Hero of Gibraltar Station." He said those last words with sarcasm. "A quiet voyage into the sunset for me, and a brace of strongly suggested retirements later and, well ... problem solved. Bragg gets a new hero named Stone in Ben, and the public victory of your rescue is the top news everywhere for weeks. Win-win."

"He was angry," Alice said.

"Angry? Ben?"

"Morgan. That he couldn't go back with you and testify in person." She half-laughed. "And tell them what he *really* thought of the president and Colonel Strickland and what happened on the Terr—on Drake's World."

Nick Stone chuckled. "He would've caused a whole new trial. Just to give himself another chance to testify and have his say."

The fondness in her eyes became melancholic. "I wish he hadn't been shot into space like that. It's so cold out there. Lonely."

"Morgan Henry was born to spend eternity among the stars." A grin stretched across Stone's lined face. "You know he once told me to recycle him?"

Her eyebrows knitted together. "What?"

"Yeah," Stone said. "Said, 'Once I kick it, burn me or churn me but put me in the stew pot of space. Eventually I'll end up back in the mix—keeping some other something alive somewhere.'"

Her heart expanded in her chest. "Always the healer."

"Always," Stone confirmed. He glanced off-screen, nodded. "Maria tells me the encrypted channel she set up is coming to the end of its secure life. You going to be okay out there on your own, Alice?"

His concern filled a hole inside her that had been achingly

empty the past few days. Alice could see why he and Morg had been such good friends. Nick Stone was so like him in disposition, only without the gruffness.

The temptation to answer something selfish was strong. *I guess I'll have to. No one else here to do the job now, is there?* Instead, she said, "Yeah," and tried her best to mean it.

"Okay-okay," Stone admonished Maria off-screen. "I'll keep in touch. Stay strong, Alice. I've never met anyone stronger. You'll survive this, too. Talk soon."

"B—"

The image disappeared before her hand could wave goodbye.

You'll survive this, too. That's what Nick Stone had said.

And then, there was Morgan's confidence from their last dinner together.

You've faced a lot. And you've overcome it. Beaten what would have killed lesser mortals.

Well, she thought. *I guess we'll see.*

Alice felt herself standing on the edge of despair again. Ready to surrender to her need to curse the universe for what it had once more taken from her. Instead, she decided to go to the rec center, see if her knee would hold up. It'd been a few days.

I need to run.

13
FIVE BY FOUR

THE FINAL LONESOME note of the trumpet lingered. A synthesized sound almost as moving as the real thing. Even over the shared comms of their battlesuits, it seemed to resist fading, as if the player had turned to walk away but played still.

The sadness hung over Fort Leyte like a dense fog on a moor.

Cold. Cruel.

"Order ... arms!"

The order came via comms from orbit to every assembled person present, military and civilian. Row after row of Fleet personnel in their dark blue vac-suits and Marines of the Alliance Ground Forces in their white battlesuits snapped to attention. Officers indistinguishable from grunts unless you looked closely enough at the rank painted over the left breast-plate. Together they formed a square around a tighter formation of twenty white headstones, ordered precisely in their own square, five columns by four rows. There was already talk of establishing a permanent memorial on the planet.

On the dais, General Strickland and his Fleet counterpart, Admiral Dayan, stood with the captains of the escort ships in orbit, along with Bradshaw and Toma and selected XOs. Set apart from the main formation, an honor guard of seven Marines raised their combat rifles. Seven shots cracked the atmosphere of Canis III. In answer, salvos of railgun tracer fire lanced out from the starships above the planet. Reclaiming Sirius was supposed to be easy, Ben reflected. A cakewalk. A photo-op mission.

A second set of shots cracked the air, followed by another salvo overhead.

Followed by a third.

Watching the final fleet volley fade, Ben caught one of Zack's cameras in his eyeline. Without turning his head he scanned the sky through the newly repaired visor of his battle-suit. Desi marked the rest of the cams on his HUD with blue dots. They were respectfully but strategically positioned to catch the ceremony from every angle. It was being streamed live via subspace, but there was a delay there, of course. Even subspace couldn't conquer the vast distance between Sirius and Sol so easily. And, of course, Bragg wanted it for his documentary.

It'll be great footage, Ben realized with harsh irony.

Strickland and Dayan descended the dais slowly, as if worried they'd lose their footing. Ben knew the deliberate pacing was for the cameras. Strickland stopped in front of him, Dayan standing solemnly beside. Ben snapped the requisite salute, which Strickland returned. In his left hand, he held the flag of the Alliance, folded into the standard rectangle emphasizing the orange star of Sol on the right, the orange and yellow of Alpha Centauri's twin stars on the left.

Appropriate, politically speaking. If humanity ever properly colonized Sirius, they'd have to change that dual-system design, Ben thought. Maybe the fold would be a triangle then, with the tri-star Sirian system in the lower corner. That'd be about right for this shitty planet. Ben immediately regretted the crass opinion, chastising himself for tainting the solemn occasion with a hatred so personal.

Strickland cleared his throat. *"On behalf of President Piers Bragg and a grateful Alliance,"* he sent over the common channel. *"Your sons and your daughters have given their last full measure of devotion. Their sacrifice will never be forgotten—"* Pause for breath and a mournful heartbeat. *"—always honored."*

"Thank you, sir," Ben acknowledged, just like they'd rehearsed. Strickland, he knew, wasn't speaking to him, but to the twenty families who'd eventually see this over subspace. "On behalf of the families of the fallen, I accept this flag."

Strickland saluted again. Holding the flag level in both hands, Ben couldn't return it. There was no need. The general wasn't saluting him, after all, but the final sacrifice of those being honored. Desi caught it all in close-up 4D glory for download later by Zack.

The general and admiral turned together and walked away. The flag resting in Ben's armored palms felt heavier than it should. The heavier-g of Canis III, perhaps. He stared ahead, waiting with the rest of the crowd while the two command officers ascended the dais again. Three figures commanded his attention from the other side of the formation. They stood behind the headstones, gray and insubstantial, a line of blue Fleeters perceptible behind them—Bricker, Baqri, and DeSoto, dressed only in the smartfatigues they'd died in on Drake's World, staring at him. Their expressions were calm. Quiet. As if they'd decided that even their solemn duty to haunt Ben Stone took second place to showing their respect for fallen comrades. They said nothing for a change. No taunts. No biting comments. They simply stood there and looked at him holding the flag of the Sol Alliance in his open palms. It struck Ben like lightning—they too were formers members of Devil Two Platoon, come to pay their final respects.

The expedition's co-commanders had returned to their marks onstage. After a few moments of dutiful silence, the chaplain from the *Shenandoah* said something profound and dismissed the gathering. The Fleet and Marine units retired in reverse order from how they'd assembled, one unit at a time. Ben found himself standing alone after a while, still holding the flag level in his hands. Even his three ghosts had taken their leave. He stood looking at the tightly assembled headstones. Symbolic, only. The bodies of Devil Two Platoon were already in cold storage aboard the *Shenandoah*, prepped for shipping to their respective final destinations—Earth, Mars, Sylvan Novus. Two of the harder grunts had even come from Callisto, Bob Bricker's hail and home. Now all were headed back to be buried, burned, or left in the sun for the buzzards, a family's choice for their mortal remains. Sealed for now like meat in lockers. Preserved from rot.

"How are you feeling, Ben?"

He snapped back to social reality and lowered his arms. Even Desi couldn't keep the ache from pinging his elbows after holding that flag level for so long. Bradshaw stood just behind him.

"Feeling?" Ben said. He'd made sure to check the comms designation first. Private. "What's that?" He immediately regretted the self-pity wrapped in smartass attitude shared with a superior officer.

She didn't seem offended. *"It's hard, I know,"* Bradshaw said. *"Harder, I imagine, it being your old unit."* She offered him an understanding smile. *"That's symbolic, you know,"* she said, nodding her helmet at his right hand holding the flag at his side. *"The families will each get their own."*

"Along with each body."

"Yes." Bradshaw let the channel breathe a moment. *"What*

will you do with yours? It'd normally go to Gupta, but ... the duty falls to you as company commander."

"The flag?" Ben lifted it, turned it over.

Burn it. Cut it to ribbons. Shit in it, wad it up, set it on fire, and leave it on Strickland's doorstep.

Sometimes he missed the luxurious privilege of being his old ill-mannered self.

"I don't know," he said. "I suppose I'll keep it."

You'd better, Shitbox, Bricker growled in his head. *Never forget.*

"Wallace's autopsies confirmed it, didn't they," he said. He'd been out of the command loop for the last day or so, granted personal time, while the Fleet surgeon finalized his report. "The reason those Marines killed each other."

"The reason they killed each other is sitting in the brig," Bradshaw said. *"Or what passes for a brig here. Strickland won't let it be transferred up."* She pointed toward the stars. *"Won't let it out of his sight."*

"They opened the door, though," Ben insisted. *So stupid. So fucking stupid. If they'd only followed orders...* "They let it in."

Bradshaw turned to inspect the final touches being put on the fort's restoration after three days. Even the depot had been largely rebuilt. An impressive recovery in so short a time. Although the planet itself still showed scars. "Yes," she said. "They did."

"I thought the no-cappers had all been weeded out. Not just out of the expedition—out of the whole damned military."

Bradshaw shrugged. "There's lots of sympathy for their position. The younger the generation, the more the sympathy, especially in the medical corps. I suspect records continue being falsified."

"Orders be damned," Ben said.

"They consider it an immoral order, another kind of body invasion as perverse as an Archie mind-rape," Bradshaw noted. He could tell she was getting irritated with him, at having to explain something she knew he already knew. She'd come over to see how he was doing after the service, and he'd turned it political. But someone had to say it out loud. "But listen to you," she continued, trying to make it an inside joke. "Who would've ever thought Ben Stone—letch with women, scourge of discipline, a legend in his own mind—would ever champion orders over whatever-the-hell-I-want-to-do, the-common-good-be-damned?"

Yeah. Who would've ever thought that?

"Walk with me, Colonel?" Ben requested.

"Sure."

The movement had grown with every generation. Bradshaw was right about that. True believers in a fundamentally flawed belief. After the Specter War—the first one; would they have to number them soon?—the principal preventative to Arcœnum mind-control was a thin polysteel plate installed in every service member's skull after signing their contract. The contract, in fact, required it. Molecularly tailored to filter out Archie telepathy, the skullcap acted as a shield, protecting humans from the influence of the enemy that had proven so debilitating during the war. After the Treaty of Covenant was signed and peace broke out, resistance rose almost immediately against the new policy of installing the caps. The war was over, the resistors argued. Keep your hands out of my head, they insisted. Generations passed and resistance became a movement, supported by medical doctors, many in the service, who went so far as to falsify records by claiming individuals had the cap installed when they didn't. Though the military policy requiring the caps remained half a century after the peace treaty, its violation hadn't been an issue vigorously pursued. It was a political third rail, even within the military, and there'd been no compelling need, giving peaceful relations with the Archies—no president who cared enough to court that kind of negative publicity. That, Ben suspected, was all about to change.

"How many?" he asked.

"Four."

A fifth of the platoon. Twenty percent compromised to Archie influence. How had humanity ever weathered an enemy that could turn a species against itself? Make it subvert its own survival?

Human ingenuity. The Hero of Gibraltar Station. His grandfather. That's how.

Ben was, at long last, beginning to understand Nicholas Stone. Had been on that road for a while now, he was surprised to discover. The man who'd saved humanity but at no small cost to himself, not to mention the lives of the thousands of service members who'd died because of his inspired intervention. Yes, the cost had been terrible, but the alternative would have been more terrible still. And that trade-off, despite its cold logic, had weighed on Nick Stone ever since. Yes, Ben was beginning to understand that weight, too.

"Bragg should be happy," he observed. They were headed for HQ, his feet following Bradshaw's lead while his mind engaged with other things.

"Yes, unfortunately. Although he's got a bit of a challenge there."

"How so?"

"These deaths, this funeral—it'll be like fuel on the fire for the coming conflict with the Arcœnum," Bradshaw allowed. "But he can't be seen as exploiting it. Not now. Besides the obvious reason it'd make him a huge prick—and more importantly, look like one—it'd be too much negativity with everything that's going on with the Psyckers, especially on Sylvan Novus."

"His support in the AC is rock solid," Ben observed.

"One might even say cult-like," Bradshaw said with sarcasm. *"But the Alliance Congress is fickle, and there are some iffy election races at the moment. He'll have his war, especially now. But he'll still have to tread carefully as its apologist. Oh..."*

Bradshaw stopped mid-stride, hesitating. Ben shortened his step and circled back to her.

"What is it, Colonel?"

"I was going to ask, but ... maybe now's not the best time."

"Sounds like the perfect time for one of *those* kinds of questions, actually," Ben said, tapping the side of his helmet with his index finger. "Dump it in with the rest of the trash."

"Did you hear about Admiral Henry?"

"No, what about—oh." What else could it be? The man must have been a hundred years old. Drinker. Carouser all his life. A man who must eat lemons for breakfast, Nick Stone had once joked. Death had probably put off taking him as long as it could.

"About a month ago."

The hollow place inside Ben seemed to expand a little. It was where he held his anger over losing both his parents, especially his mother. Morgan Henry had been an adjunct member of his family all his life. His grandfather's best friend. A crotchety, complaining confidant who'd given Ben his first real drink at fifteen because, Henry said, it was five o'clock somewhere. Even now, that incongruous joke didn't make much sense. After his mother's death, followed thereafter shortly by his father's, it'd been Morgan Henry who'd sat with him by the lake and talked about everything on Ben's mind but his parents. Ben didn't remember ever taking the time to tell the old coot how much it'd helped to center him. He wished now that he had.

"You all right?" Bradshaw asked.

Ben resumed walking. "Yeah."

The colonel fell in beside him. *"You should stop in and*

check on your grandfather when you're back home. I'm sure he'd love to see you."

Earth. Thinking about going back there felt like a fantasy. First Drake's World and now this place, and all the high-profile posts between. A dead platoon under his command, adding to his ghosts. Today's funeral, genuine in its intent to honor, half fake in its motivations. He'd be glad all right to leave Canis III—one day. The sooner, the better.

"Don't know when that will be," he said. "Things are just gearing up here."

"Strickland is sending you back to Earth. You and the 214th."

"What?"

The news hit Ben like a baseball in the side of the head.

"It's not official yet, but it's coming. The president wants your face and your unit back on Earth. He needs the good publicity."

"Good publicity?" Ben's dour mood roused itself to anger. It obliterated his sudden longing to be back home again. "What the fuck?" He quickly amended his tone. "Sorry, ma'am, but ... I can record something here if he needs a rah-rah message. From Leyte. Wouldn't it be better—"

Bradshaw held up an armored hand as they reached HQ. *"It wouldn't be the same. Maybe better, maybe not. But Bragg's ordered Strickland to send you back. I was waiting till after the funeral to tell you. You and the battalion ship out in three days."*

"But ma'am—"

The hand came up again. *"Check in with Toma at the Doghouse. After that, you should record your condolences for the families while you have time."*

That derailed him. "Condolences? ... Jesus." He'd hardly known Gupta or D-2 Platoon, despite it being his old command. Fact was, Ben hadn't gotten to know its members very well when he'd been its lieutenant, and a number of those he had known had rotated out. He'd need help from his lieutenants in the 214th, the other platoon commanders. Sanchez would've known the sergeant. Gather facts about the fallen. Something, some anecdote or personal trait to mention about each one to the twenty families in the twenty messages he was expected to record.

Ben recalled his mother's notification. How he'd watched it over and over again, analyzing every detail, willing the words to be different. Willing the solemn officer, some stranger, a colonel like Bradshaw, to suddenly smile and say it was all a bad joke. How thin and inadequate the words had sounded to Ben then. How fucking fake. And now he was expected to guide families he didn't even know through the same minefield of grief, speaking about loved ones he didn't really know, twenty times over and in short order.

Shipped out?

"I need some rack time," he said, suddenly weary with the weight of it all.

"Sure, Ben," Bradshaw said to his back. *"Get some rest."*

14

MIRROR, MIRROR

THE NIGHTMARE WAS different this time. His perceptions were different; even *how* he perceived had changed. Dreams are like that, Ben thought consciously. You could observe the conditions of your own dream state. Stand outside yourself like a spirit hovering over an operating table.

Dreams broke dimensions. They made anything possible. The dead could even live again.

He recognized the planet. Canis III again, like before. No sign of the three ghosts. Yet. They'd been replaced in his consciousness by random, incoherent thoughts. Mind pictures crafted with meaning and painted with colors like swatches of sounds. He stood on a ridge overlooking a camp. Not Fort Leyte. A civilian camp—he could tell by the lack of barrier security. The lazy, lax layout.

Ben stared at the intimately familiar that feels wondrously exotic.

Aliens. So unlike him and exactly like him at the same time.

He extended an arm. Were his reach long enough, he could touch one of the distant structures so similar to his own. Looking down at his own arm, Ben realized ... he isn't human. His hand, semi-solid. He could see his bones beneath the translucent skin. His fingers, claw-like, stretched, elongated. His arm was long and articulated.

What the fuck is this?

The masochism of a tired mind, his observer-self answered. It sort of sounded like Bricker and sort of didn't. *The self-flagellation of a guilty conscience.*

He was an Archie? A murdering mind-raper?

He tried to abandon the dream, to free himself from it. It won't release him.

The reality of it subdues his outer horror. Held fast by what he's seeing, Ben shrugged a surrender to curiosity. A morbid desire to meet the aliens so like/unlike him. Inside, a need to know what technology they have consumed him. To share it. To take it. Learn from it. Technology was something given freely to all by those who created it, after all, a gift shared for the benefit of everyone. One being's ultimate act of love for another.

He stepped down from the ridge.

The dream morphed. Reality jumped ... skewed.

In his dream-self, Ben felt it like a week's worth of pain passing through him, leaving its bitter, black memory. He was in armor. He turned to orient himself and discovered the familiar landscape of the Archie camp. But it looked like new—restored, or not yet destroyed. Across the canvas of his mind, images popped like fireworks. Other Arcœnum, excited, angry, scared, speaking through visions projected into his mind. Then, aliens armored in black drop from the sky. They're already shooting before they even hit the ground. His fellow Arcœnum in the camp scatter. A few stood, holding the meager weapons brought by their expedition, and fired back at death descending. They stood and died under the relentless fire from above. Ben's mind screamed at him in images of disbelief and incomprehension. Others, his family, trying to communicate. Visions of Arcœnum running, hiding. The projections abruptly cease. His mind-canvas went dark.

The dream morphed. Reality jumped, skewed.

He was in a building now, opened to the atmosphere by alien ordnance. His quarters? His mate lay in the middle of the broken structure, one arm outstretched toward two smaller Arcœnum bodies. Grasping but never reaching. His mind turned red. His psyche screamed.

The dream morphed. Reality jumped, skewed.

Ben peers out through a clear bubble. He brought his claws down again. The sharp rock held by them met something solid.

And again.

Again.

Each time the rock came down, he shouted a thunderous demand for explanation directly into the alien's mind. He even uses its language, which he's come to learn after decades of studying alien records, alone on an alien world.

"Why? *Why?*"

The Marine on the ground stared back in horror, one arm raised, but he fails to answer. His faceplate cracked, his eyes went dim. Frustrated and frantic, Ben stood up, still needing the answer. He's waited so long for it. He dropped the rock. Around him was chaos. Marines killing Marines. He smiled at the beautiful carnage. Already, he knows, it won't be enough.

Waking was a relief, at first. Ben hesitated, afraid of waking up at first, then looked at his right hand, then his left.

Human.

Thank God.

What the fuck was that? One of those dreams that felt more than a dream. More an alternate reality. Or maybe the three ghosts fucking with him. Were they squatting in some dark corner of his psyche, giggling amongst themselves?

The more he thought about the dream, the more Ben forgot its details. But they'd left a lingering imprint, a kind of echo of sorrow and anger and fear. Like the trumpet at the funeral. An emptiness made broader by the absence of what had filled that space before.

Ben thrust himself out of bed and dressed quickly, then assembled his battlesuit. He barely registered Desi's standard systems check. The notifications for the families would have to wait.

He quick-walked across the camp. It's an exercise in muscle memory, passing in a series of half-answered salutes. He hardly noticed the formation of headstones representing Devil Two Platoon. The acknowledgments he gave the Marine guards at the pressure door of the improvised brig were clipped, perfunctory.

"Captain?"

"Ben?"

He entered the observation room to find Toma, Bradshaw, and Tso standing in front of a one-way mirror. They weren't wearing their helmets. Strickland had rescinded Bradshaw's order, quite convinced that the only Arcœnum threat on all of Canis III was now their prisoner. He took off his own helmet and set it on the table beside the other three.

"Hey, Cap," Tso said.

Ben moved to stand beside them, his gaze never leaving the room on the other side of the mirror. Lieutenant Commander Wallace was assessing the prisoner with a medical scanner. It still wore its atmospheric suit, with each of its six limbs chained to the floor. It seemed to be kneeling. Was it breathing hard? Two Marines guarded it inside the cell.

Wallace approached the wall separating them and tapped a button.

"It can continue," he said to the mirror. From his side, he could only see himself. *"But once again I'll register my concerns about—"*

"Thank you, Doctor," Toma said. "Please come out."

Wallace offered the mirror an unfocused, harsh look. He then turned to gather up his medical kit.

"What's going on?" Ben asked.

"Interrogation," Bradshaw said. "General's orders."

"Still?"

"Yes, Captain, *still*," Toma said. "The prisoner has told us nothing of value. So far. So, we persist."

From the other side of the mirror, Ben sensed ... what? Anticipation. No, fear. Terror. No, anger. And a heavy weariness. A kaleidoscope of emotion passing through the Archie's being. Feelings as visions, colored to match their effect. Red for anger. Yellow for fear. Images instead of words for thoughts.

Wallace. The human leaves. The trial renews. Not thoughts. Visual recognition. Acceptance. Seeing the signs. Anticipating what's to come. Experience is the best teacher.

The Arcœnum stood up in its chains until they stretched taut.

Stubborn pride. Futile resistance.

"No offense, Major, but what are we hoping to learn here?" Tso's tone was less sympathetic, more practical. "The Archies have no spoken language. If it can't speak, what can it possibly tell us?"

"The general isn't satisfied that we've applied sufficient pressure. Perhaps it'll surprise us." Toma didn't sound convinced. Only committed to following orders.

The door opened and Wallace joined them in the small room. When it closed again, Toma tapped the wall comms.

"Corporal, set it to seven this time. Give it a five count, then decrease to six."

"*Yes, ma'am.*"

"I'm more convinced than ever that that creature is of advanced age," Wallace said. "I mean, we have limited knowledge of Arcœnum anatomy. But based on cellular degradation and what we can glean from its long-term diet on this godforsaken rock of a pl—"

"Thank you, Doctor," Toma said, cutting him off. "You've made your position clear enough in the last few hours."

"Now you listen to me, Major," Wallace began, incensed. "*I'm* the ultimate authority here, not Strickland. Hell, not even Bragg! Don't you presume to—"

"Lieutenant Commander Wallace," Bradshaw suggested softly, "shouldn't you check on your remaining patients in the medical ward?"

Wallace redirected his ire to her. "They're being seen to, Colonel. And I'm not going anywhere. I have a patient to observe right here."

"Very well," Bradshaw said. And do so with your mouth closed until such time as a medical opinion is called for, was the implication.

Inside the room, the Marine corporal touched a setting on the Arcœnum's armored suit. The Archie fell to its knees again. Its head fell forward. Agony washed over Ben. He put his hands against the mirror to steady himself. His joints ached. His limbs felt like they'd been injected with lead. His muscles strained to hold him up. They were using the Archie's own suit against it. Reversing its controls, normally used to offset Canis III's increased gravity. By dialing back that resistance, the wearer suffered the full effects of the planet's heavy pull. For humans, used to the slightly lighter gravity of Earth normal, it would be painful and eventually more than that. For an Arcœnum, used to the much lighter gravity of its home world in Arcanus, it was instantly excruciating.

The corporal dialed down the setting again. A scream thrust a dagger into Ben's psyche.

"We know you understand us," Toma said through the wall comms. "We will continue to motivate you until you confirm that you do."

"Ben?" Bradshaw put her hand on his shoulder.

He uttered something. Opening his eyes, he stared at the Archie chained to the floor.

You deserve it, he pushed at the alien through the pain. Somehow he was feeling what the prisoner was feeling. It almost felt good and just. *You're a murderer. You killed my Marines.*

His thoughts came back to him, as if the mirror were reflecting them.

You deserve it. Edged in red. Fat and sweating with pain. *You're a murderer. You killed my children.*

"Captain Stone, are you all right?" Bradshaw pressed.

"Stop," he whispered.

"Captain?"

"*Stop it!*" Ben turned his head, forced his clamped eyes open. "Please..."

Murderer...

Bradshaw keyed the wall comms.

Child-killer...

"Colonel—"

But Bradshaw ignored Toma. "Corporal, dial it up. Archie nominal."

"*Ma'am,*" the Marine acknowledged, adjusting the suit's gravity control.

"Let me back in there," Wallace said.

Bradshaw caught him by the arm. "You've got a patient right

here. Check out Captain Stone." To Ben, she said, "What's happening?"

The relief was profound. As if a kiloton stone had been lifted from his back. He stood up straighter, took a breath into lungs that, surprisingly, didn't ache with the effort of inhaling.

"I don't know," he said.

Wallace ran his medical scanner over him. Ben looked at each of his fellow officers in turn. Bradshaw's brow was furrowed. Tso looked equally concerned. Toma seemed annoyed, as if this might be a practical joke—yet another Ben Stone fuck-you for the hell of it.

"I..." What would he say? That he seemed to have a connection to the Archie? That wouldn't go over well. That the alien had invaded his dreams? Less well. Or had that only been Bricker and the others, adopting a new mask to torment Ben in his nightmares? "I don't know. But—"

"Heart rate is high but coming down," Wallace said. "Cortisol levels—through the roof. It's like his body just released all its adrenaline at once in response to some monstrous stressor."

"I'm fine," Ben said, not wanting more medical analysis. The doctor had described a reaction as if Ben himself had suffered what the Archie had suffered. But hadn't he? "I'm fine."

Bradshaw regarded him a moment. "What's going on here, Ben?"

"What do we know about it?" Ben asked instead of answering. "The Archie."

"We think it's a lone wolf," Toma said. "The doctor has established—as best he can—that the Arcœnum is older for its species."

"Left behind, maybe," Wallace added. "A scientist? Or a warrior? Either way, we think it could be a member from that first Archie expedition to Sirius."

"What?" Ben said, not sure he'd heard right. "From five decades ago?"

"It's a working theory," Toma said.

"Abandoned here when the Archies bugged out," Tso chimed in. "Maybe hiding in that cave the whole time. Crazy shit, huh?"

Yeah. Crazy shit.

"That solar converter powering the beacon," Tso said. "That stuff he stole from us? We think..." He looked to Toma and Bradshaw, as if for permission to continue. "We think he was sending a distress signal. Maybe calling for backup."

"Backup?" The data was coming in too fast. Ben felt over-whelmed by it.

"Or rescue, maybe," Wallace suggested. "Maybe he just wants to go home."

Ben blinked. "All this time? Stuck alone on Canis III?"

"There's precedent," Tso, the historian-in-his-spare-time said. "Japanese soldiers left behind on islands in the South Pacific in Earth's Second World War, for example. Sometimes surviving entirely on their own. Guarding their island, doing their duty, unaware the war had ended decades earlier."

His eyes wandered through the mirror to the Arcœnum. It was hunched over but standing, testing the limits of its restraints. And, despite only being able to see itself reflected by the mirrored glass, seemingly looking right at Ben.

Guarding. Duty. Protecting.

Not actual words. Impressions in images. Archies, armed and waiting with vigilance. Clarity of understanding in Ben's mind, nevertheless. Context made meaning.

I'm no anti-capper. I've got the mind-shield. How is this possible?

Revenge.

Not an answer to his question, but maybe the answer to

another that had plagued Ben. He saw the images again from his nightmare. Israel's stricken face behind the shattered faceplate. A kind of empty satisfaction in his dead expression.

Why? Why?

"I'm going to ask you one more time," Bradshaw pushed. "Are you okay?"

"I'm fine." Ben remained focused on the prisoner. His unflinching attention was reciprocated.

"Colonel, we've been at this for hours," Wallace said. "Everyone's nerves are a little frayed. Can we leave off for now? There'll be plenty of time to torture the Archie later."

"Don't use that word, Commander," Toma said. "You know better."

"Yeah," Wallace retorted, "and so should you."

Bradshaw held up her hands. "We'll stop for now. Ben, I want Wallace to give you a full going-over. Let's make sure you're all right."

"*I'm fine,*" Ben insisted.

How are you doing this? How can you communicate with me?

Images of the Arcœnum pilfering tech left behind when the humans abandoned the planet. Long, lonely hours of studying the data. Converting the symbology of human language into projections it could understand. Making meaning from lines and arcs and dots. Learning about the enemy from its own symbols.

Data. Time. Study.

Madness.

Planning the rigorous application of justice. And barring that: retribution.

Fast and furious, the visions came. The Arcœnum breaking its chains. Killing the Marine guards in the observation cell. Breaking through the mirror and murdering Toma, Bradshaw,

Tso, Wallace. Invading the fort from within. Picking up stones, pieces of equipment. Breaking faceplates. An orgy of lustful murder.

Vengeance. Retribution.

Justice.

Ben shut his eyes tightly, as if that could stop the alien thoughts inundating his consciousness. When he opened them again, the floodwaters of violence had ceased. There was only the Arcœnum standing, staring through the mirror. The two Marine guards stood at the ready. Bradshaw and the others monitored Ben, still concerned.

"I have notifications to make," he said. He had to get out of there. Recording twenty condolence messages seemed, suddenly, the easier course compared to being inside the Archie's mind. The lesser of two evils, as it were.

"Ben?—" Bradshaw began.

"Wallace can look me over after that's done. Ma'am."

He donned his helmet and exited the brig.

15
STORM

"ALICE."

Dawning awareness. She was back on the *Seeker*, her brain rebooting. Resurrecting. A burst of light. A blast of sound.

No pain this time.

But those damned birds won't leave her alone. They kept tweeting at her. Alice brushed her hand in front of her face to shoo them away. Why had her father brought them aboard the ship in the first place? To study them, like the digger-rats?

Who cares?

Shut up!

There came a numbness of touch. A hand shaking her.

Her eyelids fluttered. A sheath of sleep coating her eyeballs. Silhouettes appeared, swollen and liquid in the semi-dark. She tried to focus, but the shapes wouldn't coalesce.

"Alice!"

She recognized the voice but couldn't identify it. Her father? Mean Professor Pruneface?

Then, recognition.

Ian ordered the lights on, giving form to his face at last. The lingering haze of the dreamworld fell away, and Alice knew exactly where and when she was. In her quarters on Tarsus Station. In her bed. With Ian? An electrical charge surged through her body. Ian placed his hand lightly on her shoulder. A faster-than-light fantasy skipped hopefully across her heart.

"You slept through your alarm," Ian said, "again."

As if to put the exclamation point on it, her alarm tweeted. Ian rose to stand over her bed. Alice placed her hand on her forehead. No fantasy. Just a headache. She squinted against the bright light.

"Alarm, stop!" she shouted, instantly regretting the pain it caused.

"The professor sent me to get you," Ian said, smoothing the front of his lab smock. "He says Zoey is too lenient when he sends her."

Alice carefully lifted the covers an inch. At least she'd had the good sense to fall asleep in her clothes.

"Sorry," she said. *Not sorry.*

"This is, like, the third time this week."

"I know."

"Korsakov is losing patience."

"*I know.*"

She was tired. She was angry. She was lonely.

She missed Morgan.

Even a month out, it was like he'd passed away yesterday. His cavernous absence was just a half-thought away. It'd replaced the pain of missing her family. No, not replaced it. Expanded the well of hurt from the loss she felt inside.

Ian sat down again on the bed. Her senses came alive, on guard and hopeful by his sudden nearness.

"Listen," he said. "I know it's been hard these past few weeks." He reached out and took her hand. Her skin tingled. Her forearms flushed alive with warmth. "But he thinks..."

"What?" Alice said, anger pushing away anticipation. "What does he think?"

Ian offered what he must consider a supportive smile. "He thinks you're not even trying."

You too?

She wanted to scream. She wanted to shout till she cried. But this was Ian. He was trying to help, in his own way.

"Today will be different," she said. She hadn't thought to say it, it'd just come out. It sounded thin and excusatory, even in her own ears. "I promise."

When his thumb stroked the back of her hand, Alice could barely suppress a shiver.

"That's good. That's really good." Ian cocked an eyebrow. She thought it might be the sexiest look she'd ever seen on any human being ever. "If Korsakov doesn't yell at all today? I'll buy you dinner. How's that?"

He squeezed her hand in encouragement. Alice thought if she could just feel this plugged into life when Korsakov tasked her, she'd have passed all his tests two years ago.

"What kind of incentive is that?" she teased. "Food is free here."

Ian drew back in mock-offense. He loosened his grip, but Alice held him fast.

"Well?" Alice prodded.

"Fine," he said, "I'll synthesize your favorite food as usual and bring it to you. Good enough?"

"Just us?"

Had she said those words out loud? They'd been like a reflex. Instinctive.

A necessary thing.

Ian thought for a moment. Was he flushing red? Just a little?

What does that mean?

He squeezed her hand again, offering a friendly smile. "Sure."

Alice swore his cheeks were blooming.

What does that mean?

"Again," Korsakov said. "Concentrate, Alice. You appear distracted."

Alice sighed. Distraction was a safe word for it. Daydreaming, more like. Fantasizing.

"Reset complete," Zoey reported at the sensor panel.

Alice shot her a glance and received a covert thumbs-up from her friend. You can do this, the gesture said. Her eyes tracked to Ian. His back was to her as he monitored readouts. His body was hidden, shrouded inside his long, white lab coat. The nape of his neck was visible above the collar, though. She imagined tracing her middle finger along his skin there, twirling it in slow circles. Closing her eyes and learning every millimeter of his body by touch. Would his breath catch in his throat? Would his body respond as hers had earlier in her quarters? Would his skin ache to be closer to her as hers did for him? That's how the narrators in the romance vids described lovemaking. The desire of two bodies for one another, the heart-stopping electricity of touch, the immersion in one another as—

"Alice!"

The scowling face of Andre Korsakov bent over her. She could smell the morning vodka on his breath. There was a yellow crust at the corners of his mouth. His nearness made her hold her breath in disgust.

"The fork!"

The utensil on the small table sat where it had all morning. In her time on Tarsus Station, she'd made it move on too many occasions to remember. Korsakov considered it a warm-up exercise before moving on to bigger challenges, like moving a chair or levitating the table itself. She hadn't succeeded at a single task Korsakov set for her since Morgan's passing. Not one. Weeks of failure, piled on years of disappointment.

"Okay," Alice said, determined to end that streak now. "Okay."

Korsakov withdrew from the Bell Jar and shut her, alone, inside the transparent chamber. Alice stared hard at the fork on the table. She did her best to ignore the itchy haptic sensor net covering her head. She imagined the fork emitting a low, persistent hum to give her ears something to listen for. Raising her hand slowly from the table, she closed her eyes. Instead of light reflecting the fork to her optic nerves, Alice visualized drifting lines of energy swirling from her fingers.

Ian.

It was like stardust, reflective and absorptive at the same time, reaching out from her fingertips toward the fork. Her way of connecting to it.

Morgan.

Alice squeezed her eyes tight against the faces popping into her head. She pushed them aside, picturing the fork on the table. Its silver hue. Its handle and four tines and the empty space between them. Hearing the hum of the metal resonating in the universe. She defined the object only by itself. Not by its surroundings. Not by its purpose. Alice experienced the essence of the fork, plugged herself into it.

"He thinks you're not even trying," Ian said in her mind.

She shook her head once and sharply. The fingers of stardust in her mind's eye grew thicker and denser. She forced them to.

"Keep on truckin', kid. You've got this."

The temptation to give in to the sudden love and loss filling up her core came on quickly. But Morgan's face, craggy and smiling and mischievous as it was, was just another distraction. Alice knew this. She needed to concentrate. Needed to—

"Don't be an aberration," Marcus Keller said. A replay of his fatherly admonishment when she'd tried to move the boulders from the cavemouth. When she'd failed then, too, and found herself trapped in the bowels of the Terror Planet.

"Don't be a fluke." Her father's words but now spoken in Korsakov's voice. He loomed over her, brows narrowed in irritation. Breath reeking of sour vodka.

Alice dropped her hand. Opened her eyes.

Failure.

Again.

She slumped in her chair. All those voices inside her head, and yet she felt absolutely alone. Isolated. Trapped in the Bell Jar, her failure on display for all. Like a digger-rat in her father's lab aboard the *Seeker*.

"Please help me," she whispered.

"Again!"

She hadn't noticed Korsakov yanking open the door to the test chamber. But she saw his look of violent disappointment peering in. The end of a father's impatient indulgence. And something approaching fear.

"I've had it, Alice! It's been a month! A month!"

He stepped into the Bell Jar. Alice drew back in her chair. Korsakov seemed to grow inside his lab coat, become taller somehow, broader; his face contorted, enraged. Spittle sheened his teeth as he advanced.

"I've been more than patient with you! For three years I have fed and clothed and protected you!"

Korsakov diverted, perhaps seeing the horror on her face. He began to pace the short space of the chamber, bent like a hunchback, fists white-knuckled and shaking.

"Three years! And we've seen progress. Yes! Enough to prove my theories, even to..." Korsakov reined in his ranting. "But only *just* enough. A tease! That's what you are, Alice Keller. An intellectual tease. A scientific aperitif! A taste only promising more and—" He rounded on her, his gaze pinning her in place. Alice stared, gape-mouthed, at the professor's rage. "—never ... ever ... delivering!"

Something stirred inside her. Something primal. Buried but not forgotten. Cocooned in hurt to wall it off, now cracked open by Korsakov's fury.

"Where are they?" she said quietly.

"Do you know how much funding, how many resources I've spent on you?" Korsakov shouted. He advanced on her again. "For what? A hovering fork? A chair suspended in the air? Parlor tricks! I'll be laughed out of the halls of—"

As Korsakov loomed, Alice sat up straight. A castle wall bracing for a breach.

"Where are they?"

The close quarters of the Bell Jar amplified her anger, even above his own. Alice's voice filled the air between them.

"What? What are you whining about n—"

"My family! You promised you'd find them. You haven't! And now you tell me I can't even mourn the only family I've had since losing them! Who the fuck do you think you are?"

She stood up suddenly, forcing Korsakov back a step. He seemed confused.

"We've looked, Alice! We've examined all the data. We've followed every lead. They simply disappeared—"

"I don't believe you."

Alice took a step forward. Korsakov backed away. The Bell Jar seemed to shrink in size. The professor now appeared smaller too, an old man in a ratty lab coat. Or maybe it was Alice who'd grown larger, the swelling hurt inside her expanding outward to wrap her bones and skin like armor. The back of her neck and cheeks churned hot with blood.

"And you call me a tease..." she growled at Korsakov.

The air in the chamber began to hum. The fork began to vibrate against the table surface.

"Alice," he said, reaching out to offer a hug or, perhaps, ward off a threat, "I promise you..."

"No ... more ... promises!"

With each word, the tremolo in the air grew. The fork rattled on the table.

"Alice..." Korsakov warned, glancing around him. An odd mixture of fear and fascination painted his face.

"No!"

Korsakov ducked. Around Alice, the thrum extended into the Bell Jar itself. Fractures appeared like tiny snowflakes in its clear plastinium walls.

"Get down!" Korsakov shouted. Not to Alice. "Get down!"

The cracks in the plastinium connected. The Bell Jar shattered, exploding outward into the lab. A few quick, numb seconds of chaos, then the psychic storm passed. Alice's awareness returned, settled back into her like a spirit coming home to its host.

It seemed strange without the Bell Jar's confinement surrounding her. The wider lab seemed unnaturally huge, uncomfortably so. Blades of clear plastinium penetrated consoles, the ceiling, the walls.

Flesh?

Korsakov was kneeling on the floor, unfolding his arms from around his head. He appeared unharmed.

"Alice," he said, all his anger gone. He sounded relieved, in fact. "I knew you could do it."

She merely stared at him. Her skin still tingled. She touched her torso, felt around her body. She too was unhurt.

The explosion had been outward into the lab, away from them both.

"Zoey?" Alice turned to the console where her best friend should have been standing, monitoring data. She ripped the sensor web from her head. "Ian?"

She didn't see either of them anywhere. Only the sterile white of the lab walls, now pockmarked by jagged shards that had once formed the Bell Jar. The blinking lights of the lab equipment. No red stains, at least. No blood.

Alice stepped past Korsakov, crunching the fallout covering the floor.

"Zoey!"

A figure rose from the other side of the lab. Ian, shucking shards of plastinium from his lab coat. They clinked like ice when they hit the floor. He appeared unhurt. *Thank God.* His mouth was open. When he glanced her way, she smiled her relief that he was all right. But Ian's face was frozen in shock.

There was movement near the monitoring console. Zoey, getting to her feet, wearing the same stunned expression. Blank and wide and disbelieving.

Alice took several steps toward her. "Are you all right?"

Zoey stepped backward, staring fearfully at Alice and pressing herself into the panel. Away from her.

Alice halted. "It's okay. I'm okay."

Zoey's expression didn't change. Nor did her obvious desire to flee the room.

Alice had to turn away from that and found the same look on Ian's face. If she took a step toward him, if she reached out her hand, would he retreat from her like Zoey had?

"I'm so proud of you," Korsakov said behind her. "I knew you could do it."

Alice turned to him. She didn't want to. She hated him. She

wanted to kill—no, best not to think of that. Best not to tempt the power within her again. Best not to...

She stared at the destruction in the lab around her. Just like the sickbay on the *Rubicon*. Only much, much worse.

Zoey and Ian both began to clean up. Neither looked at her. Neither asked if she was okay. Instead, they moved mechanically. Like that doctor, Alejandro, had moved on the starship. Needing something to do. Anything other than dwelling on what had just occurred.

"Zoey, tell me you got that. Everything was working properly, yes?" Korsakov asked.

"Yes." Stifled, knee-jerk. "Yes, Professor."

Korsakov clapped his hands together, startling Alice. "Let's take a break," he said, his tone perversely jovial. When he placed his hands on her shoulders from behind, Alice was so dazed, she didn't even cringe. She could barely feel his touch. "I'm so very proud of you. So very, very proud."

She stared ahead, watching Zoey and Ian, her last two touchstones of human connection, continue their mindless clean-up. They seemed to be going to great pains to avoid looking at her.

Korsakov kissed the back of her head. "I named my discovery accurately," he whispered into her hair. "In beauty how like an angel you are, Alice. In power, how like a god."

Please help me.

The old line repeated over and over again in her head. A mantra for divine intervention. A petition for survival.

Please help me.

16
PIRATES!

EVA'S WRIST ITCHED. She and Leo sat together on a slow-sloping Floridian hill in Yellow Bluff watching the tide of the Atlantic roll in. The sea had been unrelenting and patient in its incursion, swallowing the St. Johns River whole three centuries earlier. When the tide was out, you could still see where people of means had once owned beachfront property. Staring at the old buildings felt deliciously voyeuristic, like staring at a recently deceased archeological find.

And Eva's damned wrist wouldn't stop itching. *Damn it*, she thought. *I'm dreaming again.*

She roused herself awake. The Florida coastline became a heady darkness, an interspace between real life and life as you'd like it to be, the oblivion that sometimes feels like a waking awareness of death. Eva extracted her arm from around Leo and sat up quickly, her wrist comm buzzing angrily.

"Yeah?" she said.

"Eva, where the fuck have you been? I've been ringing you for five minutes!"

She glanced at the private comm unit beside the bed, found its red message light flashing. She'd slept right through the notification chime. The haptic vibration assaulting her wrist had finally managed to wake her.

"Mister President?"

Bleary. Unfocused.

"Who the fuck else?"

"Eva." Devos's voice. More measured. "We have a situation."

Bragg scoffed at the understatement. "Get your ass in the Hot Seat! Now!"

The channel closed.

Eva scrubbed the crusty sleep away with her palms. "Lights —dim." She specified the brightness as a rushed afterthought, remembering Leo was lying beside her.

"Oh, don't mind me," he mumbled without moving. "I'm just sleeping. Or, was."

"Sorry," she said, throwing off the covers. The chrono read 3:32 a.m.

Her feet hit the chilly floor, slapped against it as she stumbled to the bathroom. Adrenaline fueled her rebellious muscles. Marcos, maybe. Rather than take the deal offered her a month earlier, Miranda Marcos had begun a hunger strike. Bradley and his prison doctor were close to sedating and force-feeding her— and how would that play once it got out? And then there was the fact that her protest against nutrition had reinvigorated the pro-Psycker sentiment. The news from Sirius was worse—a lone, leftover Archie soldier from the previous war had begun the next one early, wreaking havoc on Bragg's attempt to reclaim Canis III. Which crisis was it this time? Or maybe some new fresh hell...

Eva splashed water onto her face. The weariness, blissfully missing for ninety minutes as she'd slept, moved right back into her bones.

"What's wrong?" Leo asked.

"No fucking idea." Grabbing the brush on the vanity, she yanked tangles out of her hair.

"Need me?"

"No," she said. "Well, always. But not now."

"'kay." In the mirror, she could see him stretch to see her reflection in the mirror through half-opened eyes. "Uh-oh."

"What?"

"You're putting on a bra."

"Yeah."

"Must be serious."

"It's Bragg."

"Ah. Right."

Eva stepped into a handy set of sweats. The seal of the president's office branded her shoulder.

"Well, that completes the ensemble," Leo managed to quip despite the ungodly hour.

"I'm in a hurry," she said, dashing back into the bedroom for a pair of socks and gym shoes.

"And yet, the bra. Decorum must be maintained."

"Go back to sleep, Leo. Dream of me without one. At least one of us should get some rest."

"Deal!"

She was halfway out the door when she stopped herself, returned to the bed, and took a luxurious moment to touch Leo's forehead. He grinned, eyes closed. She bent down and kissed him lightly on the lips.

"Your top's already off," he whispered. "Now, if you can just help me with these hooks..."

Despite the tightness pulling her scapulae together, Eva smiled. "I'll be back as soon as I can."

"I might start without you!" he called after her.

The typical twenty-minute commute to the Citadel by foot was halved by virtue of the hour. No waiting at the lifts. No heavy crowds to navigate. The same stern, plain-clothed ACE agents scanned her through all the security checkpoints, but no lines.

Decorum must be maintained, Leo cracked wise.

Usually populated by energized policy wonks and interns, the bullpen's two-dozen cubicle desks stood largely empty. Only a handful of night owls worked, and those quietly. She'd seen it this way before late at night, but tonight the emptiness hit Eva as eerie, even haunted. Glancing at the muted wall of media monitors gave her no clue about whatever had prompted the president to interrupt her sleep. Marcos's hunger strike, a Martian quarterly manufacturing report, local election campaigns heating up on Sylvan Novus ... nothing new. The tragedy on Canis III hadn't broken as a story yet because the families of the dead Marines hadn't yet been notified. So, that was something.

She rapped twice on the door to the Hot Seat but didn't wait for permission to enter. Cursing from Bragg and Devos's attempts to mollify him greeted her.

"Finally!" Bragg barked as she closed the door. He stood agitated behind his desk in a sweatsuit like her own, his hair unkempt. He tended to run his fingers through it incessantly when he was nervous. Sam Devos looked up with relief as Eva entered.

"I apologize, Mister President." There was a heaviness in the room, like the air itself was sweating. "Late night."

"Whatever! You're here now."

"Eva," Devos greeted her, his tone wary.

"Sam."

Stretching his lower back made Devos wince. The wall monitors were off, more evidence that whatever this was about, it wasn't already being pimped by the media. Eva settled in a chair in front of the president's desk.

"A fucking disaster," Bragg said, flitting his eyes at her and away again. He sat down heavily at his desk. "Worst timing ever!"

"Mister President," Sam said, trying to mollify him.

Bragg shot him a look and tossed his head at Eva. "Catch her up."

"First thing," Sam said to Eva, "is that what I'm about to tell you is covered under Black Seal Protocol."

Eva nodded, though inwardly surprised. The top level of top-secret clearance, reserved for military planning and news of an economy about to crash. Punishable by death, if violated. Had the situation on Sirius gotten worse?

"Please indicate your understanding of this protocol by stating an affirmative response," Devos said formally, quoting the policy.

"I understand that the information you're about to disclose is protected under Black Seal Protocol," Eva recited the scripted response. "Disclosure of this information without express permission of the President of the Sol Alliance or his designated representative is punishable by execution."

"*Summary* execution," Bragg corrected her.

"Yes, sir," Eva acknowledged, dipping her head. "Summary execution." The nerve cluster under her right shoulder blade stabbed at her. It was like she was already on the rack with a sadistic inquisitor standing over her, demanding she divulge what she hadn't even been told yet.

"Sam, get on with it," the president said.

"Three days ago, a convoy went missing in the Malvian Triangle," Devos said. He was speaking slowly, choosing his words carefully. "Mostly composed of heavy freighters and a small escort of military vessels. Fleet Command has lost all contact, including ship transponders."

"Fucking disaster!" Bragg slapped the desk and rose again.

He began to pace, attacking his thick, graying hair with his right hand.

"What was the cargo?" Eva asked.

"Military-grade materiel," Devos said.

"I gathered that much."

"This is need-to-know," Bragg said, exchanging a look with Devos. "And you know what you need to know."

A familiar frustration ignited in Eva's stomach. This had happened before—Bragg and Devos talking around the truth in their boys' club code. She'd grown used to it after three years, but it rubbed a spot raw on her ego every time. Now it was happening under Black Seal Protocol and in the middle of the night. Becoming another half-truth requiring she leave the warmth of Leo's arms after less than two hours of sleep.

Easy, girl. They're no intern handing you the wrong cup of coffee.

"Sir," she said directly to Bragg, "I can't help you spin this if I don't know what we're really talking about. I can't advise you if I don't know what's going on."

"Spin isn't what we're looking for here, Eva." Devos gazed at Bragg expectantly. "Sir? If we're going to send her out there—"

Send her out there?

"Just tell her!" Bragg flopped onto one of the receiving couches in the center of the room and began massaging his temples with his fingers. "She knows all my secrets anyhow."

Devos nodded and sat in the chair next to Eva.

"The military escorts are disguised as civilian ships," Devos explained. "The freighters are Bragg Industries ships. They're carrying next-generation hull tech."

Fleet vessels escorting ships belonging to Bragg Industries? It was an ethical conflict of interest for a sitting president to use military assets in service of a private venture. For that matter, it violated the law. But Devos had called it a *military* convoy...

"Ever hear of a Treasure Fleet?" he asked.

"No," Eva said, her patience waning, "sir."

"I'll keep it short, then."

Thank you.

"Thank you!" Bragg laid his head back on the arm of the couch.

"Centuries ago, the Spanish assembled fleets of ships to haul home the gold and silver they'd pilfered from the New World. Huge ships riding low in the water with all that tonnage. They were considered a grand prize for political enemies like England and France. Free funding for their own agendas in the New World, including those against Spain."

Eva connected the dots quickly. "The Arcœnum?"

Devos shook his head. "We don't think so. No evidence of that."

When has that ever stopped you blaming them?

The sarcasm was silent but no less satisfying.

"Pirates!" Bragg said, bouncing back to his feet. "Can you fucking believe it? Cunt pirates!"

"That's what we think, anyway," Devos clarified.

Okay. "I still don't know what this Treasure Fleet is carrying."

"This is short?" Bragg barked at Devos. "Get on with it! Less history!"

Devos closed his eyes briefly, then said, "The president's company on Monolith has discovered a—"

"Oh, shut up, Sam, I'll do it myself." Bragg launched himself to a standing position. "They're carrying gigatons of tungsten and lonsdaleite mined from Monolith. As you know the lonsdaleite's molecular structure is a natural barrier to Archie brain waves." Talking as he walked, he reclaimed the chair behind his broad desk.

"It's the active part of the metallic polymer we use for the mind-shields the military has installed against Arcœnum influence," Sam said. "Limited supply has kept its usefulness small as a shielding agent. Until now."

Bragg huffed. "Now do you see?"

Not really. "I'm starting to, sir," is what Eva said.

"We found a major source of lonsdaleite on Monolith." Devos leaned in. "Testing shows that weaving the tungsten and lonsdaleite together not only triples the thickness of hulls against physical attack, but the amalgam also creates a natural barrier to telepathic incursions—at a starship level."

"We could have an entire fleet of nearly impenetrable ships within a year," Bragg said. Now that the floodgates were open, the secrets with death sentences attached flowed freely. "We could overwhelm the mind-rapers, once and for all."

Eva sat back, stunned. Why was she just now hearing about this? She suspected the search for extensive lonsdaleite deposits had been going on since Bragg stepped into office. But so many things could have gone wrong up to now. A disgruntled whistleblower. An intrepid reporter with a burning desire to discover what all that geological surveying was for on Monolith, where the president had made his fortune. But miracle of miracles, the secret had held up to now. The cynic in her wondered if the entire Psycker round-up initiative hadn't been a massive distraction to keep the media from looking at other things.

"Sir," she said, "if the media gets wind of this..."

"That's why you're here," Bragg said. "Besides, they're too occupied with the Marcos story."

Confirmation of her distraction theory? Was Marcos already on the payroll? Had Bragg and Devos sent her to Colorado as an actor in a private stage play?

"Sir," Eva said, "the media considers itself the conscience of power. It always has—"

"My ass—they're a ratings-driven whore factory selling snake oil between ad placements."

She closed her mouth and folded her hands in her lap.

Devos cleared his throat. "The fleet was on its way from Monolith to Mars."

"The shipyards?"

Devos nodded. "To begin construction of three new dreadnaught-class starships. We have one prototype in service, the *Monolith*."

Cleverly creative, that.

"Makes the *Eliminator* look like an ice hauler," Bragg said.

The Fleet's flagship, launched not long before the Keller rescue mission, already obsolete? If that were true, it was no wonder the loss of the so-called Treasure Fleet had caused the president's hair to be in such a chaotic state.

"Not that we shouldn't go after these pirates," Eva said, "but why not simply mine more of the minerals and use that to build—"

"No time!" exclaimed Bragg. "No time for that!"

Ah. The timetable. The puzzle pieces snapped starkly into place. Mining the lonsdaleite, hauling it to Mars, building a fleet of telepathically impenetrable starships. And then there was the pesky need to prosecute and win the war with the Arcœnum before the end of Bragg's first term, thereby ensuring a second.

"Sir," Eva said, "if Marcos hanged herself in her cell tomorrow and this story got out? No one would cover Marcos."

"It already has," Devos said.

"Sir?"

"The Treasure Fleet. The media has the story. But not the details."

Shit. In twenty-four hours, no self-respecting investigative reporter would care if Miranda Marcos lived or died. Eva looked to Bragg.

"Sir, what do you want me to do?"

"I've recalled Ben Stone and his unit from the clusterfuck that is Canis III," Bragg said. "They're on their way home now. A few photo ops, then I'm sending them back out, into the Triangle. No pirate band, no matter how big, can stand up to Bragg's Own, eh? Especially with a Fleet strike force escorting them."

Eva wasn't sure that was true. Not at all. That same "pirate band" had managed to waylay a fleet of pregnant freighters and camouflaged starships armed to the teeth. But facts never seemed to hinder Bragg or his ambitions.

"You're going with Stone," Devos said quietly.

"I'm going..." *To the Malvian Triangle? On a military mission?* "Sir, I'm a civilian without any authority to—"

"You carry the authority of this office," Bragg said, standing and stretching over his desk. He leaned across it, holding Eva's gaze. Classic Bragg. Lean and loom. Power move.

She said, "You want me to go as a babysitter." It wasn't a question. Her heart sank. Damn Leo and his warm arms. Damn her own weariness. Facing the prospect of months away—from the quiet Zen of gazing at the stars in the splendid isolation of her apartment fifteen hundred meters high; from Leo's smooth pressure to take their relationship to a deeper level. Eva realized with a sharp pang that she was already missing all of it.

Jesus, how fucked up am I?

"We want you to go as an insurance policy," Devos clarified. "You'll be our eyes and ears out there."

"What about Marcos? I'm the one who opened the deal, I should be the one to close—"

"Marcos is gaming us," Bragg said. "She'll take the deal. After she's suffered enough to satisfy the hardliners of her cause."

Eva regarded him. How certain he seemed. It could be

typical Bragg bluster or the surety of a man who'd predetermined the outcome. Was her theory right, then? Had her negotiation with Miranda Marcos merely been a charade from the beginning? Had Bragg already worked out a deal with the woman before Eva's shuttle had ever left Tokyo?

"All due respect, Mister President, how do you know that?" Eva asked, fishing.

"We don't," Devos said. "Not for sure."

"So—"

"There's no one I trust more for this mission," Bragg said. "And I need someone I can trust on this, Eva."

Eva locked eyes with him. He'd actually meant that. She could tell. But it did little to fill the longing already blooming in her core, sucking down her suddenly discovered nostalgia for home. The next thing she said came from autonomic memory, not acquiescence.

"When do I leave, sir?"

17
GRIST FOR THE MILL

"SAME," Ben said.

The bartender nodded. Grabbing Ben's empty glass, he moved back down the bar to refill it.

Neville. Ramirez. Hicks. Some of the dead from Devil Two Platoon he'd recognized, even managed to put a face to the name. It hadn't made his duty easier to half-remember them when he was trying to personalize the notifications. It'd made it harder, in fact.

The bartender returned with the refilled glass. Ben took it from him before he could set it on the bar, downed it, and handed it back.

"Same," he said again.

Ignoring the wary eye the man gave him as he moved off again, Ben glanced around the Grist Mill, Fort Leyte's improvised officer's club. No, that was a misnomer. Over Bradshaw's strenuous advice to the contrary, Strickland had authorized access to the club for all off-duty personnel, regardless of rank. His only requirement—enlisted drank with enlisted, officers with officers. Getting drunk with fellow Marines on Canis III was as scheduled and scripted as reveille and recon. The policy,

Strickland explained, was aimed at minimizing cross-tier morale issues. Neither officers nor grunts wanted to see the other in a state of drunkenness. It was like imagining your parents having sex: uncomfortable, damaging, and likely disappointing in some indefinable, existential way.

The engineer who'd designed the interior was a master of efficiency. Outside, the building looked like every other square construct of 4D-printed hexacrete in the fort. It seemed bigger on the inside. Strategic, corner-hugging triangular tables anchored the gray walls, which someone with an artistic flare had adorned with semi-nude motion holograms. Stools stood every meter along the bar, separated enough to allow bulky Marine bodies to feel insulated from socializing but close enough to facilitate friendly banter. On the floor, tables were bolted down every two meters, making the Rumor Mill—the familiar name for the place—able to accommodate two full platoons of Marines. It'd feel crowded but cordial, were it filled to capacity. Like a family Thanksgiving full of in-laws where everyone had weapons but had agreed to keep them holstered.

An adjutant, a major, from Strickland's staff sat alone at the far end of the bar. He blinked lazily at Ben's roving eye before calling the barkeep over. A couple of Fleeters sat at one of the tables in the middle of the club. Three platoon lieutenants huddled around one of the corner tables, conspiring or rumor-mongering or telling dirty jokes. Maybe all three, before their binge was over. Ben recognized two of them, though he'd come to know their names only recently.

"Be right there," the barkeep told the major as he set the bourbon down in front of Ben. "My advice, kid—drink this one slower."

"Sure," Ben said, thinking, *Nah ... Dad.*

"I'm serious. At least eat some peanuts."

The barkeep pushed the basket of synthesized protein

pellets especially DNA'd to syphon off the inebriating effects of alcohol. Ben curled his lip at them. They tasted okay, though he had no reference point to the real thing. He'd never put a real peanut in his mouth in his life. Better the clean, synthesized food that science had perfected to meet the nutritional requirements of the human body. Never trust anything that came out of the dirt fertilized with animal shit.

Ben was about to upbraid the barkeep for his unwanted advice and then remembered the man was one of the few civilians supporting the Sirian expedition. Ben's rank, therefore, was largely useless as a cudgel. So he held his tongue. The major down the bar had no such compunction.

"Barkeep!"

"I'm coming!" He gave Ben the eye, grousing, "Too used to giving orders, that one. Fucking officers."

Ben grunted as Bricker uttered hollow laughter in the back of his head. He tuned it out as best he could, glancing at the corner table with the three lieutenants. The two he recognized, barely, were Brady and Augusta. The third he didn't know. Even if he didn't know every grunt in the 214th's company under his command, he really should be more familiar with the outfit's other officers. But at least the condolences were done, now. All twenty notifications, individually recorded, encrypted, and transmitted. He'd relied heavily on the AGF's script template. The unchanging ritualistic language felt like a protective cocoon when filling in the blanks. By the time he'd recorded the last statement, though, Ben had felt like a robot reciting computer code.

Hello, [NEXT OF KIN LISTED IN DECEASED'S FILE]. My name is Captain Benjamin Stone. I'm the commanding officer of Dog Company, 214th Drop Marine Battalion of the First Drop Division, Alliance Ground Forces.

It is my solemn duty to inform you that [FULL RANK

AND NAME] gave [HIS/HER] life in service to the Sol Alliance. The entire battalion joins me in extending our deepest sympathies to you and [FIRST NAME ONLY'S] loved ones in this difficult time of loss and mourning.

The expedition to Sirius C is of vital importance to the Alliance, and [FIRST NAME ONLY] held [HIS/HER] sacred duty close to [HIS/HER] heart. Often the first to rise [OR LAST TO RETURN TO BARRACKS POST-MISSION, ADAPT AS NEEDED], [FIRST NAME ONLY] represented the best of the armed services: tough, determined, dedicated, loyal. [HE/SHE] was a first-rate Marine—a Marine's Marine—respected by comrades and favored by commanders for [HIS/HER] ability to get the job done.

[FIRST NAME ONLY] often spoke fondly of, and about how much [HE/SHE] missed, life back home. [ADD LINE ABOUT MISSING FAMILY OR FRIENDS OR THOSE THE SERVICE MEMBER LOVED IF APPROPRIATE AND VERIFIABLE VIA DECEASED'S PERSONNEL RECORD. CONSIDER ALLOWING THE BATTALION CHAPLAIN TO REVIEW FOR SENSITIVITY.] It was for you and all of humanity that [FIRST NAME ONLY] served with distinction and, without hesitation, made the ultimate sacrifice. [HE/SHE] will be missed in the 214th.

It was usually here that Ben would insert something personal about the dead loved one. He hated the rote, generic notification language, and especially those empty brackets demanding tailored information to make the notification feel individualized. To Ben, they made it feel anything but—person-alized, yes, but crafted and false, as dead as its subject. He remembered how, as a boy, he'd felt when notified of his moth-er's death. Disbelieving of his own ears, his grief numbing him in protection. Though hearing the language, unable to process it for meaning. Wondering if some old man had dressed up like a military officer and recorded a sick joke. Thinking of that man reading the news of his mother's death to [HER SON BENJAMIN] as Ben had prepared to record his own condolences had almost made him physically ill on camera. And every moment he'd been recording, he felt like a faker. A poorly rehearsed player on a cheap stage. He'd hated the officer who'd reported his mother's death, had somehow come to blame the man personally for her loss. Now, Ben just felt sorry for him.

With all that squatting in his head, Ben had put out the call to the rest of the 214th, requesting those who'd known anyone in Devil Two Platoon to come forward and give him details he could use to make the condolence message real. Or, at least, less fake. Meaningful. Consoling, if wholly inadequate to that purpose. Though the platoon had been his old command, Ben had relied on others for details beyond name-face recognition. Brady and Augusta were two who'd responded. He'd tried to inject that genuineness, those intimate details into each notification, including those for the loved ones of the no-cappers who'd prioritized belief over orders. After ten such exercises— starting and stopping, settling his stomach, starting again—Ben had felt more fatigued than any high-gravity training exercise could have made him. After recording fifteen messages, he'd felt numb, which would have been a mercy if it hadn't made him paranoid about sounding like an automaton to the grieving families. By the time he'd finished the twentieth notification— Private Israel's, which he'd put off to last—Ben hadn't felt anything at all. And somehow, that was worse.

Why? Israel's ghost pleaded through his shattered faceplate. Or was it Israel channeling the Archie, burning with the need for vengeance morphed into madness, projecting itself into Ben's mind? Why?

"Dunno," Ben said aloud.

Or—oh, what the fuck did it matter anyway?

His glass was empty again. How'd that happen?

He picked it up and *thunked* it down again. "Barkeep!"

The grim-faced civilian wandered back his way.

"Same."

"Look, Captain, it ain't for me to say, really, but I get paid whether you drink or not. Maybe you've had enough, huh?"

Ben's eyelids rose and fell. Had someone dialed up the gravity all of a sudden? His whole body felt abruptly heavy. The tips of his fingers tingled. The back of his neck felt feverish. He half-wished there was still a standing order requiring battlesuits indoors. The aid of the servos would make it easier to lift the glass. Plus, he needed to piss and could do that sitting right there on the barstool. The built-in recovery system would vacuum it away. Two birds, one stone, as it were.

Hey, I made a funny.

"Thank you for your concern, Doc Barkeep," Ben said with an exaggerated gesture of geniality. "Now get me my fucking drink."

"At least have some peanuts—"

"Fuck the fucking peanuts!"

The barkeep backed up, hands waving in surrender.

"Pipe down, Captain."

Ben squinted at the officer down the bar. It took a moment to focus. "Apologies, Major," he said with a gentleman's etiquette. "It's the bourbon talking."

"Well, shut that loudmouthed bottle up," the major said. "The rest of the bar's listening."

Reconning over his left and right shoulders, Ben saw it was true. He'd made himself the center of attention. Something he used to take a perverse pleasure in. He was suddenly back at his grandfather's retirement reception on Covenant. He could see faces around the table—Zwikker, Taikori, Old Man Mitchell.

Mitchell seemed younger than Ben remembered. More innocent. They all did.

"Stone, that's enough."

And Toma! With that judgmental, sneering disdain in her voice and—

The hand that fell on his shoulder was no memory. He turned to find Colonel Bradshaw attached to it.

Shit.

Major Toma stood beside her, that knowing look on her face: once a Shitbox, always a Shitbox.

"You called them?" Ben said, staring daggers at the bartender.

Hands up again, the man turned and refilled the major's glass.

"Don't put this on him," Toma said. "This is all Grade-A Ben Stone bull—"

"Major," Bradshaw said. "Ben, tomorrow's gonna come early. Meeting with Strickland. The 214th is shipping out. Time to pack it in."

"Sure. Absolutely, Colonel. No problem." Ben picked up his glass and tap-tap-tapped it on the bar. The bartender didn't turn around, so he tapped it again, louder. "Just one more drink and I will absolutely, positively pack it the fuck in. Ma'am."

"Stone, you insubordinate asshole—"

"*Major*," Bradshaw said again. She leaned in to whisper in Ben's ear, "That wasn't a request, Captain. We'll take you back to barracks where you can sleep it off. But my patience is wearing thin. And your behavior here, in front of these officers, is about to force my hand in a very formal way." The hand on his shoulder squeezed.

"Hey," Ben said. "I have to take a piss." He slid off the bar stool, absently aware that Bradshaw's hand had moved to his elbow to steady him. "You guys should think about re-in ... reinstat ... requiring battlesuits indoors again. Would save some time."

"Major Toma will accompany you to the head," Bradshaw said. "After that, rack time."

Ben smiled sideways at Bradshaw, then dragged his expression to the bleary-faced Toma next to her. "Come hold it for me, Sheba," he said, stumbling toward the Mill's restroom. Toma's hand had replaced Bradshaw's at his elbow, and he leaned on her to steady himself.

"If only I had my battlesuit," Toma growled where only he could hear. "I'd hold it for you then, Stone. Lock it in place."

Giggling bubbled up from somewhere. Ben thought it might have been from him. But he couldn't be sure since his ears were sitting at the bottom of a well.

In his bladder's estimation, the walk to the head took forever. Images crowded out one another in Ben's mind. Israel, on the ground with his eternal expression of horror and disbelief. The ancient battleground of the Archie camp. The prisoner's mate and children lying dead in the building blown up by orbital bombardment. The modern carnage in the open ground in the hilly valley of Sector A-23, where Marines killed Marines, directed by alien insanity. Then Ben was at the door to the head and halted so fast Toma almost collided with him. He stood swaying, his bladder near to bursting, but unable to walk in.

"What the hell, Stone?" Toma groused. "Get in there and get it done."

DeSoto and Baqri flanked the door. They'd putrefied further since the mass funeral. The skin of Baqri's face had loosened, her eyes sinking inward, a leaky, gelatinous goo. The ruin of DeSoto's mouth and its blasted teeth, splayed open from behind by the alien pike-like weapon that had split her skull, was the only thing moving. It was like her perverse, gaping smile had broken into a hundred individual smiles, each with a life of its own. The smiles were maggots, feeding on her dead flesh. Baqri lifted three bony fingers and held them up for a moment. Followed by a fourth. And a thumb. When she ran out of fingers on the other skeletal hand, DeSoto took up the count.

Ben's gut churned, bitter and threatening.

Fifteen.

Sixteen.

"Stone, if this is some kind of—" Toma began.

He broke away from her grip, racing between the ghouls and straight into the nearest stall, where he fell to his knees. The bourbon came back up, burning more harshly than when it went down. The retching came in waves, kept coming for what seemed like hours, even when there was nothing left but curdled air and muscle cramps. Able only to weather it, Ben felt Bricker standing behind him in the stall's narrow doorway. Watching him vomit.

Everyone dies, Shitbox.

Words without malice or judgment, for once. A simple statement of fact. Alice Keller's words spoken with Bob Bricker's attitude. And then it was Toma standing behind him, solid and real, patiently waiting.

"Get it out, Stone," she said. "Get it all out. Leave it as a sacrifice to the porcelain god."

18
DREAMS AND DEATH

SLEEP DIDN'T COME EASILY despite the self-medication. For one thing, Ben's small, private quarters had somehow become an independent satellite of Canis III with its own rate of spin. Likewise his internal organs, which seemed determined to observe the laws of local gravity however they damned well pleased.

Now and then, when his bed settled enough, Ben drifted into dreaming. He found himself on a beach of white sand that sparkled like diamonds in the moonlight. A desert lay behind him all the way to the horizon. Before him was an ocean of royal velvet, shades of violet and purple folding and unfolding with the tide. Flora spotted the beach, glowing with an internal, ethereal life of its own. The dreamscape was unsubtle and beautiful and set the soft teeth in Ben's drunken mouth to grinding once he realized where he was.

Drake's World.

He walked toward the ocean. His legs were more solid than he'd expected, a pleasant surprise. A part of him knew he was drunk and that this was a drunkard's dream. Sometimes the beach would fade, and he'd be back in his bunk, writhing and moaning and promising never to touch another drop of that devil's nectar, alcohol. Then his mind would calm, and he'd be back on the beach, with everything exactly as it had been before. The white sand of the plains where he and Bricker and the others had tracked Alice Keller, except instead of mountains in the distance, the slow-rolling waters of an ocean he'd never seen lapped at the sandy shore. Each step took him closer to the waterline.

On the beach, a figure squatted. Despite the bright moonlight and glowing plant life, Ben didn't recognize the person. But it was human, and in light of recent events, he'd settle for that. The person even seemed to be alive. Things were looking up in the dreamland of Ben Stone.

The squatter was doing something at the water's edge with her hands. Something mechanical and repetitious. She worked the same pattern of movement, again and again, as if on an assembly line. Hold, insert, release on the tide. *Her. She.* Well, there you go. It was a woman. She was rolling up papers and putting them in bottles, then pushing them out to drift on the lavender ocean.

Ben lost the dream, turned over in his bunk, and vomited on the floor of his quarters. Something left inside after all. He might have wiped his mouth, or he might not have. He stayed on his side, somewhere distantly aware that it made him less likely to drown in his own puke.

When he dreamt again, Ben found himself at the water's edge. Down the beach, the woman stood up and faced him. She was tall but thin. Her clothing was tattered, frayed at the wrists and ankles from long use. As if it were the only clothing she had and had worn it for years. Her hair was dirty and matted, an unkempt mane. Her face remained obscured, a blur just out of focus, even as Ben came close enough to make out other details.

Above her left breast a patch identified her ship of origin: SS *Seeker*.

Alice Keller. Of course it was Alice Keller. Who else would it be? And yet, her face refused to coalesce into the features of the girl he remembered. Funny—he hadn't thought about her in a long time. And now, here he was, drunk and dreaming and fading in and out of sweating in a bunk a long way from The Frontier; and here she was, sending messages out on a beach conjured from the deadly beauty of Drake's World he'd buried in his memory.

Blurry-Alice pointed down. He followed her index finger and knelt to pick up one of the bottles floating on the tide. Ben uncorked it and pulled out the message. When he looked up to verify that this is what she'd wanted him to do, Blurry-Alice was gone. He wasn't sure if that was a good sign or bad. If God were pleased or about to punish him.

Lightning flashed on the horizon, followed by thunder. A storm was coming. It was quickly followed by another round even more dazzling and loud than the first. He'd better hurry. If the rain came first, it would wash away the message, and then he'd never know what it said.

Ben stood up, dropping the bottle to clank in the grainy sand. He unrolled and read the note.

Please help me.

The klaxon blared like a sledgehammer made of sound. Ben's hand went to his right thigh on instinct, looking for his sidearm. Maybe if he shot the sound, it'd shut the fuck up.

Failing to find his pistol, he cracked his eyes open. It took a moment to focus. He spied the weapon hanging on the stand with his battlesuit. Odd. The visual alert over the door to his quarters was dark. The sledgehammer inside his skull became a club, then a child's toy mallet. The whoop of the fort's red alert became the chime of a comm notification. Ben rolled over and slapped it quiet.

Not a fort alert, then. And certainly not thunder on an alien planet.

"Stone," Toma's voice said over the comm. "About time."

Oh my God. Stop yelling at me.

"Report to General Strickland at Command HQ at zero-nine-thirty. And take a shower, Captain. Try to wash away some of that bourbon oozing out of your pores."

Stop ... yelling.

"Stone!"

"Yes, ma'am!" he barked, then put a hand up to massage his temple, now throbbing from the exclamation. "Oh-nine-thirty."

The channel closed.

Ben fell back on his pillow soaked with tart sweat and rubbed the crust from his eyes. There it was again, his sidearm hanging on the wall. To hell with shooting the sound. Maybe he'd just blow his own head off.

Two birds, one stone.

This morning it wasn't nearly as funny.

"If the major has no objections," Stone said, carefully forming his words, "I'd like to see the prisoner again." The coffee was working. The B12 stim cocktail was working. Now if he could just get his mind in gear. "Before we rotate out."

"That won't be possible," Toma said.

They stood in Command HQ awaiting an audience with Strickland. He and Bradshaw were conferring in his office. Ben watched them through the window. His brain finally registered what his ears had just heard.

"Ma'am? If there's some concern over what happened the last time—"

"It's dead."

He wasn't sure he'd heard her right. "Ma'am?"

"Committed suicide."

When she said it, Toma's tone was nonchalant. Weather's been nippy. Stock market's down. Archie prisoner killed itself.

"I don't understand," Ben said. But he did. He knew what had happened, and he even had an inkling as to why. But he needed to hear the official version.

"It looks like they're finishing up," Toma said instead. In the office, Bradshaw was offering Strickland a sharp salute.

"Ma'am..." Ben swallowed. "Ma'am, please."

"There's not much to tell, Captain. It somehow managed to smash the AG actuators in its suit. Not hard to do—the tech was ancient. Surprised they hadn't already broken down on their own. Without power, planetary gravity did the rest. Crushed it. Like a big bug."

"What about the guards? Couldn't they have—"

"Stone, listen to me," Toma said, turning to face him. "The only thing I regret about that Archie's death is that we didn't get any useful intel out of it before it died." She faced front again to receive Bradshaw, who was headed their way. "It's one less enemy we have to fight."

Ben felt the need to vomit again. Somewhere inside his chest, there was a new, throbbing ache. He needed another stim.

"The general will see you now," Bradshaw said, her voice cool. She acknowledged Toma's salute with one of her own, but her eyes never left Ben. "We'll discuss last night later, Ben."

Ben's lazy salute was automatic, his molasses mind slow on the uptake.

"Come in, Captain!" Strickland said, boisterous and eager. His head still sported a scar of injury but no bandage now. There was a slight wheeze beneath the general's words. Remnants of the pulverized hexacrete seared into his lungs. It lent his voice a fluty quality. Strickland's amiable attitude suggested he hadn't heard about Ben's antics from the previous night. "Heard about our guest?"

"Yes, General."

"Well, good riddance," Strickland said. "Too bad we didn't have longer to interrogate it."

Ben said nothing because nothing was required to be said.

"I hate to lose you, Stone. You and the 214th have performed with distinction on this mission. Not that we haven't had our hiccups. But overall, Bragg's Own have certainly lived up to their namesake."

Distinction? A lone Arcœnum combatant attacked the fort, killed Marines and, nearly, their commanding officer; destroyed munitions and materiel; delayed progress in beachheading Canis III and—with the help of a few selfish bastards— murdered an entire platoon. And the AGF hadn't even managed to keep that Archie responsible alive after the fact. Ben's mind spun at Strickland's ability to reframe reality, even after all that, into something that would read well Earthside.

"Thank you, General," Toma acknowledged. "It's been our honor to serve."

"The trip home will take several weeks," Bradshaw said. "I won't be going with you, so Major, you'll have operational command of the 214th until further notice."

"Yes, ma'am."

Toma sounded unsure. Not, Ben knew, of her ability to command the unit; more likely, questioning who might be her next commanding officer. Majors didn't command battalions. Maybe someone from Bragg's personal staff would be installed.

Someone without field experience, maybe, a paper-pusher more concerned about politics than Marines. Every tactical officer's worst nightmare.

Now you're getting it, Bricker told him.

"Take the time to rest and recuperate," Bradshaw said. "There will be some short downtime on Earth as well, but then the president is sending you right back out. Into The Frontier."

"The Frontier?" Ben searched his hearing memory. Had he missed something? "I thought we were rotating back to help with the Psycker problem."

"That's been resolved," Strickland said. "There are bigger fish to fry."

Toma seemed to hesitate. "Sir, if I may ask—"

"You may not," Strickland said. "I have too much to do. Zack is coming in for an interview about the dead Archie. Colonel Bradshaw will brief you before departure at thirteen-thirty."

"Today, sir?" Toma said.

So, Ben thought, she was as much in the dark as he was. The prospect of an untried officer giving Toma orders raised its head again. Whatever their differences, Ben respected Bathsheba Toma. The 214th had become a hardened battle force, united in grief and determination by the experience on Canis III. A stranger injected into that equation could be disastrous if the battalion saw action again in The Frontier.

"Today, Major." Strickland looked at her, then Ben, then Bradshaw. "As for Canis III? Mission accomplished, Marines. And now on to the next beachhead, eh? Dismissed."

"I'll join you two in a moment," Bradshaw said. "One last bit of business with the general."

Ben and Toma saluted and exited the office. Around them in Command HQ, the daily business of conquering Canis III went on. Intelligence confirmed that the Archie appeared to have been alone on the planet. The fort was complete, including the repaired biodome sealing in breathable atmosphere. Humanity had arrived and, through hard work and sacrifice, formally claimed the planet. The media release had gone out just yesterday on subspace, and that made it all true.

"Captain Stone," Bradshaw continued formally as she rejoined them, "I assume you'll be visiting your grandfather before redeployment."

"Yes, ma'am. Planning on it."

"Good. I sent Admiral Stone my condolences regarding Morg Henry."

He hesitated. "Thank you, ma'am."

The news of Henry's passing wasn't something Ben had spent a lot of time thinking about. Other, broader, deeper encounters with death had elbowed it out of his psyche. But now, as Bradshaw mentioned him, Ben's regard for the old man stepped up front-and-center.

"I only knew him in passing, during the Keller mission," Bradshaw said. "When Commander Petrović and I faced off in the *Rubicon*'s sickbay ... hell, it seemed like Admiral Henry was prepared to take us all out. Using only his mouth. And not break a sweat."

Ben smiled. "Yeah, he used words like weapons."

"Like a swordmaster," Bradshaw agreed. "Were you two close?"

"He treated me like a person," Ben said, almost to himself. "Not like a kid. That was important right after my parents died. It was the one thing no one else did."

"Sounds like a formidable man," Toma said. "I'm sorry for your loss, Stone."

He turned to regard her. Bathsheba Toma, offering genuine sympathy? To *him*? He wondered at the personal effort that must have taken for her. Or maybe it was a tribute to her character that it had taken no effort at all. Sometimes he had to remind himself that she was more than an anal-retentive hardass who only thought of him as Shitbox Stone.

"Thank you, Major," he said. "And Major ... and Colonel," he said, flashing a look at Bradshaw, "I want to apologize for last night. My conduct was unbecoming ... to say the least. You both ... you both helped me. Kept it quiet. I appreciate that."

"It wasn't for you, Stone," Toma said, her usual disdain for him showing through. "It was for the Corps. For the cams. So your behavior wouldn't taint the—"

"Thank you, Major," Bradshaw said. "I think we get it."

Ben stood before them, properly admonished. "Well, in any case," he said, "I appreciate the consideration."

"Still," Toma said, "General Strickland wasn't wrong. You and Dog Company distinguished yourselves here, Captain. Canis III is in Alliance hands. That's a win, however you look at it."

And now she was complimenting him? From Strickland, the idea that D-Company had performed admirably on Canis III had been offensive. From Toma, it was measured but well-earned appreciation for effort and sacrifice. Ben made the conscious decision to accept her sentiments in the spirit offered.

"Thank you, Major."

"Pack your gear, you two," Bradshaw said. "I wish I was going with you. Oh, I almost forgot ... Sheba, you're receiving a field promotion to lieutenant colonel, effective immediately."

Toma's mouth dropped open. Ben wasn't sure he'd heard right, either.

"Ma'am?"

"General Strickland just signed off. Wouldn't do having a major commanding a battalion. Make all the other majors jealous."

"Ma'am," Toma managed. "I ... thank you, ma'am."

"You've earned it," Bradshaw said, offering a handshake. Toma took it while the colonel pressed on. "I've transmitted the new orders to you. You'll have plenty of time to plan the upcoming mission to the Triangle on the way home."

"Yes, ma'am," Toma said. Ben could hear the anticipation in her voice. Knowing she'd have weeks to put together, take apart, reconstruct, and perfect the battalion's deployment to The Frontier. And even better—no new desk jockey commanding the battalion after all.

Ben watched as a rare, shocked look continued to hold Toma's face hostage. "Congratulations, Maj—Colonel," he said and meant it. Toma was living her best life. Climbing the ranks of the AGF, one rung at a time albeit at translight speed, and earning every new level legit. She'd come a long way from a childhood in the Martian slums trolling trash cans for scraps to feed her family. She was a woman worth admiring, he decided. Even if she was a royal pain in the ass.

"Now, both of you, finish packing," Bradshaw said. "It's a long trip home."

19

THE SHROUD

THE WHOLE of Tarsus Station now felt like another world, distant and oddly unfamiliar. Nothing about the place felt like anything close to *home* anymore to Alice.

The lab was still in shambles, though Zoey and Ian had worked for two days to return it to order. Korsakov spent his time working on something he said would prevent the havoc from happening again. Alice felt terrible, offering to help any way she could. But Korsakov suggested she rest, and neither Zoey nor Ian was eager for her company.

So she'd self-isolated in her quarters, which had grown close and stifling to her. Like a jail cell. She emerged only to eat and once to the gym. She hadn't been able to muster the will to mount the treadmill. Most of the time Alice merely slouched in her bed, cursing the power she'd been afflicted with and mindlessly gobbling down romance stories. But those stories, which she'd loved once, now seemed silly. Clichéd. They were lies. The men in them never seemed to care how flawed the women were. Or, if they did, only saw the flaws as challenges that made bestowing their unconditional love on the heroines all the more satisfying in the end.

Ian barely looked at her when she saw him in the cafeteria and didn't talk with her at all. Zoey too held herself apart and seemed just another part of the alien station—a different person who'd become foreign to Alice. Korsakov, who visited her at least once a day, had the strangest attitude of all. Upbeat, happy, almost relieved.

Alice hadn't felt this alone since staring out from the SS *Seeker* and wondering if she was the only human in the universe. Her insides rippled with the memory. She hadn't missed her family this much in a long time. She thought of Ben in the *Rubicon*'s sickbay, talking to her, soothing her. She thought of Morgan Henry's smile and roughshod manner. She missed it all, and Morgan's salty counsel most of all.

How feckless I am, Alice thought, remembering the word from one of her stories. She'd had to look it up. She rolled it around in her mouth. *Feckless*. It was one of those tactile words that signifies itself perfectly, in sound and expression. In how bitter it tasted in her mouth.

How selfish. Do I miss them only because I'm afraid of being alone? To know I have someone, somewhere, who matters because I matter to them?

Her stomach burbled. Alone. Hungry. Longing for connection. She'd experienced all these feelings before. They'd driven her out of the *Seeker* and across an alien world to begin a journey, every step of which had led her here. To this very room with its pale, silver lighting and its stifling white walls. To these broken friendships, and her frantic need to fix them.

But first, she needed a shower.

Zoey sat alone in the cafeteria, picking through a half-eaten plate of food while studying a datapad.

"Hi," Alice said.

Startled at first, Zoey's expression softened. "Hi," she answered, then returned to the pad.

Encouraged, Alice was tempted to make straight for Zoey's table. She diverted to the food synthesizer instead and took her time staring at the menu. She counted the seconds to herself while the synthesizer generated her meal, the old ritual of marking time helping to settle her insides. When her food was ready, Alice took the bowl and a glass of orange juice and, counting her steps, crossed to Zoey.

"Mind if I join you?" she asked formally.

Zoey looked up again. "Sure."

"Oh." Alice hesitated, then backed away, glancing around as if there weren't half a dozen other empty tables to choose from.

"No, I meant sure, join me." Zoey's smile was warmer now. Forgiving? "Please."

"Oh. Thanks."

She sat, placing the bowl and glass on the table, then set the tray aside. Alice added butter and honey to her oatmeal, then picked up her spoon and began to stir. She had no idea how to begin with Zoey.

"Listen, Alice," Zoey said, "I'm ... I don't really know how to say this."

"It's okay," Alice said, stirring vigorously. "You don't have to." If Zoey apologized, she'd melt through the floor in shame.

"I kind of do."

"No," Alice said, spooning oatmeal into her mouth.

"I know you feel bad," Zoey went on. "I feel bad too. I just don't know what to do with all that. I've always thought of you as a younger sister—"

"It's okay." It came out muffled.

"—but now I just feel ... scared, if I'm being honest. I mean, how many centuries of bullshit research have been devoted to uncovering 'mind powers'? And then, with the spoon and stuff, we thought, 'Well, maybe there's something to this.' But what happened the other day..."

Alice swallowed and bravely met Zoey's eyes. "We...?"

"Yeah."

Stirring her oatmeal again, Alice said, "You mean Ian. And you."

Zoey took a breath. "Yeah."

"I'm sorry," Alice whispered. She stared at the oatmeal. The patterns of butter and honey looked like a bone-colored vortex with amber wheels of cosmic light. "I'd never hurt you."

Zoey set her pad down. It made a soft click against the table surface. "You'd never mean to," she said with the formality of a near-stranger. "I know that."

Alice murmured something. A reimagining of a scene involving the distraught heroine from one of her romance stories.

"I didn't hear you," Zoey said.

Alice made herself look at Zoey again. "I hate this place," she said. "Strigoth is a dead world. And I'm dying inside too."

This was the moment in the story where the heroine's best friend reached out and took her hand, reassured her that everything was going to be okay. Zoey had that same expression of sympathy the artist had rendered on the friend's face.

"What can I do to fix this?" Alice asked.

"I don't know." Zoey sighed, picking up her datapad again. "I can't help the way I feel. I can work on it, but—"

"Ian?"

Zoey didn't answer at first, perhaps debating within herself whether to be safe with her answer, or honest. "No," she said without looking up from the pad.

Tears threatened. Alice's stomach became leaden. Her insides felt cavernous.

Her best friend now unknown to her, and perhaps unknowable again. Her hopes for something more with Ian murdered by this power she'd never wanted. Morgan, dead. She shouldn't have come to the cafeteria. She should have stayed in her quarters.

Feckless. Faithless. Failure.

Alice rose and placed the bowl and glass back on the tray. The oatmeal had grown cold.

"I think I'll go back to my room."

"Okay," Zoey replied.

Alice dumped the contents of her tray into the recycler and exited the cafeteria. When she got back to her quarters, she deleted the romance stories from her PalmPad. Every single one of them.

Alice was going stir-crazy. It'd been a day since her aborted attempt at reconnection with Zoey. When the door chime sounded, she all but leapt from her bed.

"Come!"

The door opened.

"Hello, Alice," Korsakov said. "How are you feeling?"

The same question he always asked, every day now. She was convinced he wrote whatever she said down later in a log. *The subject's current disposition suggests...*

"Bored."

"Ah," he said. "I might have a cure for that. Come to the lab. I'll show you."

"Now?" It was just past dinnertime. They hardly ever did testing in the evenings. "It's fixed? I mean, the lab is—"

"Better than ever. Your breakthrough gave me a chance to

reimagine what we're doing in there. And yes, now, child. I'm anxious to begin."

Child. After all that had happened, and still *child*.

"Come on," he said, "I'll show you."

At least, she thought, it was something to do. And Zoey and Ian would be there. Maybe things could still go back to the way they were before. Even if she had to give up the dream of Ian becoming her boyfriend. If he could just not hate her, maybe that would be enough.

"Okay."

The hum of the instruments filtered into the hallway when the door to the lab slid open. The walls still showed the scars from before, but the lab looked almost new. Zoey offered her a wan, brief smile that felt rehearsed. Ian kept prepping for the testing session without acknowledging her. The Bell Jar had been reprinted, but it looked different now. Like it had pimples.

"What'd you do to it?" she asked.

Korsakov smiled. "That's what I wanted you to see."

Though the new Bell Jar was still shaped like an inverted, oversized bottle, it now sported knob-like bumps at regular intervals over its transparent surface. Hair-thin, metallic lines connected the knobs.

"What are they?"

"Emitters," the professor said. "To help contain your power."

Alice reached out to touch one, but Korsakov lightly swept her hand aside.

"How?"

"Think of the new chamber as a shroud," Korsakov said. "The subspace emitters counter your output of the Godwave, by countering the interaction of the alpha brainwave and its omega shadow."

"The emitters produce inverse waves at the subspace level,"

Zoey clarified. "Like aiming an inverted soundwave at its opposite to produce silence."

Alice turned toward Zoey's voice to find hope in the young woman's face. Hope for continuing the experiments safely? Maybe for more than that?

"It'll block me?" Alice said.

"We think so." She look furtively at Ian, who'd spoken. "We hope so."

Alice visualized it in her head like her father had taught her. "So you don't need me anymore," she said. There was a wellspring of hope inside her, too. Hope for parole. "If you can produce the countereffect, you can produce the original, right? You don't need me anymore!"

Zoey's smile faltered. "Well—"

"We can produce the counter to your specific brainwave frequency, Alice," Korsakov explained, "the frequency that's unique to you. But we can't direct it."

"I don't understand."

"*Consciousness*," Korsakov said, and it sounded like *Eureka!* "We can't direct the effect, give it purpose."

"Oh," Alice said. So small a word for so much disappointment.

"We need human will for that." Korsakov opened the door to the Bell Jar. "Let's give it a try!"

The expectation of routine settled into her as she entered the chamber. For once, it wasn't entirely unwanted. Alice sat at the table as usual, and Korsakov placed the skull cap of sensors over her head.

They started with the spoon, which Alice lifted effortlessly. When directed to bend it, she did so. When Korsakov told her to lift a chair into the air, she obeyed. Each time Alice successfully executed a test, Zoey and Ian checked their readings, wary and fascinated at the unwarranted progress. Korsakov seemed giddy, chirping "Excellent!" a dozen times over in half an hour of testing.

What had seemed nearly impossible for so long hardly required effort now. Thinking back on those earlier failures, Alice had the sense she'd been peering at the world through a murky membrane. But now, colors looked brighter. Sounds were sharper. If she'd been merely walking through the universe before, Alice now felt plugged into it.

"It's as I suspected," Korsakov said, nodding. "The explosion of power before—it unlocked something inside you, Alice. It freed you to access your ability."

She looked at him, at his beaming face. It felt nice.

"Let's try the shroud," he said anxiously. "Ian!"

"Alice," Zoey said, reaching to stay Ian's hand, "you might feel the effect of the counterwave. We're honestly not sure what—"

"Yes, yes," Korsakov said, "but we can turn it off if there's a problem. Ian, if you would..."

"Engaged," Ian said.

It was like he'd dimmed the lights. Muted the sound. Turned the world around her down a few levels.

"How are you feeling Alice?" Zoey asked.

The professor retook his seat in the Bell Jar opposite her. "Yes, describe it please."

Alice's eyes moved slowly between them. Her brain felt anesthetized. Deadened.

"Dull," she said.

"Go on," Korsakov urged her.

"Professor, maybe we should take it slower," Zoey suggested, concerned. "We could be permanently damaging her ability to—"

"Quiet!" Korsakov shouted. "Go on, Alice."

"It's like I was swimming through water. Now the water is syrup. And the harder I try to swim, the thicker it gets."

"Good. Very good. Now, try the spoon."

Alice looked at the bent spoon on the table.

"Are you trying?"

"Yes, Professor," she said. "It's ... I've lost the link."

"The link?"

How to explain it? Alice stared at the spoon. She brought a hand up, imagining the tendrils of energy reaching out from her, lifting it. The spoon didn't move.

Why was this necessary? She'd finally learned to control her power. She'd never use it knowingly to harm anyone. She'd promised Zoey that.

"Hazy," she said. "Cloudy."

"Try harder," Korsakov said, quiet but insistent.

"I *am*," Alice replied.

This was worse than waking up on the *Seeker* when everything hurt. She'd shut her eyes to block the light. Covered her ears to stop the sound. But the spoon was an itch she couldn't scratch. A sneeze she couldn't bring. The more she tried, the more frustrating it was.

"When the environment demands it," he said, "species must adapt or die. Strain spurs development. You must try harder."

"I'm ... *trying*." If she could, she'd obliterate the spoon. Rip apart its atoms. Make the problem go away.

"*Wish* the spoon to move!"

Alice gritted her teeth. Though she stared at the spoon, Korsakov's doggedness had shifted her focus to him.

I wish you'd died! Not Morgan!

"The spoon, child! Concentrate on the spoon!"

"Professor, please," Zoey said. "Let her rest. Maybe we can dial back the—"

Korsakov glared at Zoey. "It's okay," he said, relenting. "It's okay, Alice. Perhaps we should do as Zoey suggests."

"Turn it off," Zoey told Ian. He adjusted the controls of his console.

The professor yelped, lifting from his chair and hurtling upward. He crashed against the curved ceiling of the Bell Jar, an invisible force pressing his body into the bowl shape. Korsakov grunted in pain. Zoey screamed. Freed from the dulling prison of the shroud, Alice felt alive again. Connected to everything, everywhere. And angry.

"Alice! Let him down!" Zoey ran toward the chamber.

"Careful!" Ian shouted. "Be careful, Zoey!"

Alice looked up at Korsakov, who was wincing in obvious discomfort. Had she done that? "It's okay, Alice. I'm not upset," he gasped. "But please ... let me down."

What do you think you're doing? Morgan demanded in her head.

Murderers never leave prison. Marcus Keller, lecturing.

They put them to death. Ben Stone's voice?

"Alice!" Zoey demanded, standing over her. She raised a hand, prepared to slap Alice. "Bring him down!"

Alice calmed herself. She pictured in her mind how Korsakov could float safely downward. She wished it to be so, and while he didn't move, his face relaxed as the force pressing him against the Bell Jar diminished. She brought him down to land lightly on his hands and knees on the floor. Zoey rushed to his side.

"Sorry," Alice whispered. "I didn't mean to."

As Zoey fussed over Korsakov, Alice felt the shame returning. Horrific, crushing shame. Fear cascaded over her body. No wonder Zoey and Ian shunned her. They'd understood days before what she understood now. Her power couldn't be trusted. *She* couldn't be trusted.

"I'm so sorry," she said. "Professor—"

"Part of the process, child," Korsakov said, standing with Zoey's help. "I'm not angry."

I was, Alice thought. *And look what almost happened.*

"We need to get you to the infirmary," Zoey said.

"I'm fine." He took a step and nearly fell over.

"Professor, please."

"Okay, okay."

Zoey guided him, but Korsakov stopped in front of his test subject. "This was another breakthrough, Alice. I'm so very proud of you."

Proud? A breakthrough?

I might have killed you!

"Can I help?" she asked Zoey.

"I've got it." Perfunctory. Unforgiving.

"Very proud!" Korsakov insisted as Zoey led him away.

She'd been so focused on the two of them that Alice hadn't noticed Ian approaching the chamber. He didn't come inside.

"Ian, I—" Alice wanted to say something, anything to make him not hate her. Wanted to hear anything back from him that showed he still cared for her. Or that he even still saw her as human.

"I think you should go back to your quarters," he said.

20

CUT AND RUN

DESPITE THE LATE HOUR, Alice couldn't sleep. She'd retreated from Ian's accusing tone back to the safe prison of her quarters, where her mind wouldn't stop chasing itself round and round in circles. Obsessive thoughts making imperfect stops like a slot machine programmed to lose.

Her initial joy at *finally* being able to control her ability, until she couldn't.

The encouraging ease with which she'd passed the basic tests.

Korsakov's switching on the shroud to curb her power.

His delight at her successes. *"I'm so proud of you!"*

His disappointment at her failure to push through. *"Try harder!"*

It was like Korsakov was forcing her to run a race she hadn't even trained for. Alice didn't understand it.

She kicked off the bedcovers. Her room was too warm.

"Lights." They came on at fifty percent, a programmer's respect for the body's need for predictable circadian rhythms.

Her mind took its position in the wheel again.

Zoey supporting Korsakov, hauling him out of the Bell Jar like a victim from a burning building.

Ian standing at his console, armored in data and keeping his distance. Alice could still smell the fear in his refusal to meet her gaze.

She'd hoped the session would be an opportunity to win them back. To make things like before. She'd wished for it more than anything. But wishing was dangerous. She'd wished harm to the professor, and without the shroud's protection, harm had come to him. He was lucky she hadn't killed him. Maybe there was a reason that the kind of power Korsakov was looking for from her was mythical. Maybe humans shouldn't be able to think their dreams into reality. Maybe they couldn't be trusted with that kind of power.

Morgan Henry had told her something once. Your average person, he'd said, was a selfish, self-centered animal distinguished from its four-footed brethren only by the ability to know the difference between right and wrong but, more often than not, choosing the wrong. "I think God made us like that because He was bored with perfection," Henry told her. He'd been drinking when he'd said it and apologized later. He did that a lot. "You're different, Alice," he'd backtracked, stumbling. "I didn't mean you."

Round and round her mind went. Umpteenth verse, same as the first.

But *why* should she be any different? When she'd awoken on the *Seeker*, Alice had no memory of who she was or even that she was human. Everything she'd done was dedicated to meeting one, overriding need—to find her place in the universe, her reason for *being*. Part of that required understanding what had come before.

You only know where you're headed if you know where you've been. Another pearl of Morgan's wisdom.

Alice had no memory of *before*, but she knew one thing—humans aren't born at fourteen. What if she'd merely blocked out the before, along with any significant, touchable memories of her family? What she'd done to Korsakov ... was there any better argument for the shroud? What if she'd done that to her parents? To Ollie? Gotten angry and hurt them and then blocked it all out?

The terror of that chilled her. Alice had almost accepted that they might be dead, her family, but having harmed them herself? She'd never considered it before. Maybe her search for them was her mind's way of pushing away the guilt—an endless, fruitless quest because she would never find them ... or know what had happened to them.

God, she was tired. Of feeling different and alien, under constant study like a digger-rat in her father's lab. Of feeling like a freak. Alice was tired of Zoey's detachment and Ian ignoring her altogether. Of her prison cell, she thought, scanning the four walls of her quarters.

A fingernail file sat on the small nightstand next to her bed. On impulse, Alice picked it up.

Morgan used to delight in teaching her about the history of medicine. Once, he'd talked about how ancient physicians foolishly believed that bloodletting could restore a person to health by draining out what was wrong with them. Reestablish a healthy balance in the body.

Alice stared first at the file, then at her left palm. A ghost of the old wounds was there, faded scars from her stumbling flight beneath the Terror Planet. She was tired of feeling tired. She was tired of feeling. She pressed the tip of the file into her palm, into one of the old scars, and the skin puckered with the pressure. When Alice pushed harder, the pain of the puncture felt like relief. It was simple and satisfying. Like she'd just unlocked something fundamental in the universe. Discovered a secret all her own.

She watched, fascinated, as the blood welled, minimal but vibrant. The room around her faded. The fatigue on her shoulders lifted. Staring at her bleeding palm energized Alice, helped her to focus. Distracted from her sadness. Morgan had been wrong to scoff. If a little helped a little, she reasoned, then more should help more. She pressed the point against the red hole in her hand and drew slowly, savagely down. A sob came, but it was almost joyous. The kind of sound you make seeing a loved one for the first time in a long time. After a minute or two, Alice had carved a shallow X across the lifelines in her skin. As if marking herself for deletion.

The cutting felt good, in a bad way. It felt good to focus on the pain outside for a change. To watch the red line begin to crust after a while, then flex her hand, breaking the nascent scabbing, the X growing fresh, glowing red again. But it wasn't long before she'd become used to the new ritual, and Alice grew tired of that, too.

She needed to *do* something. To make things right. She should talk to Korsakov and make sure he wasn't really mad at her. With no other ports for safe harbor, he was the one other human being who still seemed to care about her.

Alice set the file aside, wrapped her hand with a white cloth, and got out of bed.

At night, Tarsus Research Station was cold, the result of the atmospheric systems cycling to conserve heat and the energy that produced it. Unoccupied corridors remained dark until Alice stepped across a threshold when they snapped on to fifty percent illumination.

That wasn't the creepy part. Even during station day, Tarsus's dozen research staff largely confined themselves to their workspaces. But at night, as Alice wandered from one dark, chilly hallway to the next, the emptiness was deafening. Her skin prickled with somatic memory of stumbling around the rocky tunnels below Drake's World. When she saw the lab door open, its bright light and the familiar echoes of instruments filtering out, she quickened her pace. Maybe Korsakov was working late. If so, that meant he'd left the infirmary healthy enough to *be* working late. Part of her wanted to take that good news and run back to her room with it, but most of her needed to face him and say what she needed to say.

"Oh." She stopped abruptly in the doorway.

Slumped over his monitor, Ian jerked his head up in surprise. "What are you doing out of your quarters this time of night?" It sounded as curious as it did suspicious.

"Couldn't sleep."

The door didn't slide shut behind her as she stepped inside the lab. Ian had told her once how he'd often override that feature to keep the lab open when he worked alone late at night. It was just a thing he did. Some kind of phobia.

"Ian, I feel awful about what happened. I—I don't know what I'd do if I ever really hurt anyone." Her palm, throbbing against the white cloth, felt like guilt.

"You should go back to bed," he said. It wasn't cruel, but it made his preference clear.

"Yeah," she said. "But I was looking for Korsakov. I wanted to apologize."

"I doubt he needs an apology." Ian's anger didn't really seem directed toward her. "This whole station could blow up and as long as he and his data survived, Korsakov would dance a jig to celebrate."

"Probably." She tried to make the comment light.

"What happened to your hand?"

Her reassuring grin faltered. "Nothing. Just an accident at dinner." Simple. Ordinary. Believable. "I was actually headed to the infirmary to treat it. Is he still there?"

Ian shook his head. "He's in his private quarters."

"Okay, thanks."

She didn't turn to go immediately.

Ian sighed.

"We're all playing with fire here," he said. "It's a scary thing."

Alice considered how to answer. Maybe she didn't need to, but she did anyway. "My father said the main point of science is to help us better understand what we don't know yet. 'Mistakes teach us better than successes. The pain of them helps us remember. It's the only way we make things better,' he said."

"Better?" Ian said. His fury came on quickly, and this time it was tactical and targeted her. "How does having your kind of power make things better? You're a bomb waiting to explode."

Her instinct was to retreat, but Alice stood her ground. Heat crept up the back of her neck.

"I didn't ask for this power. It's not my fault I have it."

Ian seemed ready to fire again, then his lab coat wrinkled as he slumped again at his workstation. "No, I suppose you didn't. I didn't mean to hurt your feelings, Alice. I like you, actually. It's just that..."

"Just that what?" she whispered. She'd only really heard three words of what he'd said. She hated herself for hoping and dug her fingernails into the cloth wrapped around her hand.

"I don't think I have what it takes to make things better," Ian said.

"Ah. Okay." She knew what he meant but hadn't said directly. *I don't think I have what it takes to be close to you.* The last of her fascination with him guttered out inside her. Alice gathered herself and forced a grateful expression. "You said the professor was in his private lab?"

"Yeah."

"Thanks." The lights in the chilly corridor snapped on as she left him in the lab.

Alice considered ringing the chime but decided not to. What if he didn't want to see her? She'd had enough rejection for one day. And she needed to say what she needed to say. She input the see-me-anytime passcode Korsakov had given her not long after her arrival on Strigoth.

She hopped through the door when it opened, afraid she might change her mind. The anteroom to the professor's private quarters was frugal and traditional. An old-fashioned armchair sat in one corner with a reading lamp behind it. The far wall was, floor to ceiling, a bank of wooden shelves stuffed with books. Actual books, not digital archives or the recent fad of electronic publications wrapped in faux paper covers. Alice drew close enough to scan their spines. Works of literature, scientific treatises. Philosophers and poets. Demi-gods of discovery.

A voice spoke from deeper inside the suite. Korsakov, of course, talking to someone. Alice caught snippets only: *experiment, power, breakthrough*. She heard her name. He was talking about her.

She tiptoed across the anteroom, and the words began to form sentences. The conversation was heated.

"I understand," Korsakov said.

"Do you?" A different man's voice, demanding. "You must watch the media feeds. Not a lot is going right these days for the administration, Professor."

Alice peeped around the corner. Korsakov's back was to her. The man on the monitor appeared angry and impatient.

"This 'breakthrough' of yours better not be just another grant-extending excuse for more time."

Korsakov took a breath. "Alice Keller's power is nothing short of remarkable, I assure you. I've sent you the data and my analysis. You can see for yourself, Mister Devos."

Devos grunted. "We're having our people review it now. Keep in mind, Professor—space is very cold. Especially when you have no heat."

"I assume you're being metaphorical, sir."

"I wouldn't assume that at all." Devos cut the feed.

What was that all about? Alice wondered.

Korsakov cursed the blank screen. Alice considered returning to her quarters. She could try again tomorrow.

"If you think you're the scariest individual I have to talk with today..." muttered Korsakov as he pressed buttons on the console in front of him.

Then again, maybe she should get it over with. The professor would be surprised, maybe even upset at the intrusion. But once he knew why she'd come, how sorry she was, he'd understand. She prepared herself to knock.

"It's Korsakov. I've reached stage three."

Alice stayed her hand. The screen remained snowy, but there was sound, like a percussive kind of subspace interference. There was a pause followed by words forming on-screen. She was too far away to read them.

"Yes, but directing it is what we need to work on now," he said. "She's in the early stages of weaponization. But raw. Still very raw."

He was talking about her again. Weaponization? Alice pricked up her ears.

Tap-tap. Tap-tap-tap.

Her spine froze.

Words crawled across the screen.

A translation.

"She *will* be ready. I just need a little more time."

Tap-tap-tap-tap. Tap-tap-tap.

Recognition in Alice's brain caught up with her body's reaction. Korsakov was talking to *them*. The shadow-spiders.

About *her*.

She held the scream inside, but her mind blanked, wiped clean by terror. Adrenaline surged through her limbs. Her skin tingled. Once again her body did the thinking for her.

Alice ran.

"I need your help!"

Ian turned to the doorway again, scowling. "You've been running."

"I plan to run a lot farther," Alice said, forcing herself to calm down. "But I need your help to do it."

"What are you talking about?"

She moved into the lab, overrode the wall controls, and shut the door. The red lock indicator lit up.

"What are you doing?" Ian rose to his feet. He looked half ready to fight, half ready to flee.

"You don't want me here."

"No, I don't," Ian said. "You should go back to bed."

"That's not what I mean."

He understood in an instant. It wasn't that Ian didn't only want her gone from the lab. He wanted her gone from his life.

"I don't know what this is about," Ian said. "But if you're suggesting I help you leave Tarsus—that would get me fired. More than fired. Korsakov would ruin me."

Alice could hear it in his voice. The wedge between what he wanted to do and what he felt compelled to do.

"What's got you so flustered?" he asked. "Has something happened?"

She didn't answer directly. What could she say? That she'd found Korsakov talking about her with a man named Devos? And then conspiring with the shadow-spiders about her power? She'd never spoken of them since coming to Tarsus. And now facing Ian, who seemed less empathetic with each passing day— if she began babbling on about what she'd seen, he'd only think her more of a threat to his cozy internship. More dangerous. Crazier.

Well, she could work with that.

"You don't want me here," she said again.

"It's not my choice!"

"I can work with that."

The look he gave her was noxious. "What do you mean?"

"Tell Korsakov I forced you. Tell him I mind-controlled you. Tell him whatever you like."

Ian swallowed. "Would you?"

"Would I what?"

"Do that? I mean ... could you?"

Alice hated this. Hated being feared, especially by Ian. Her feelings for him lingered. But she was desperate now, and she'd do what she had to do to get away from Korsakov. To stay away from *them*.

"Want to find out?" she asked. Alice thought of the shadow-spiders when she said it. Injected her words with the threat of death and darkness.

"Not really, no."

"In that case, Ian, please, help me."

The onetime man of her dreams stared past Alice to the locked door of the lab before looking at her again.

"Okay," he said. "I know some people."

"Okay."

"You might not like them very much."

"I don't care!"

"Okay, then."

21
HOMECOMING

BRADSHAW WAS RIGHT—THE journey from Canis III was long in more ways than one. Ben had challenged himself from the moment he'd stepped aboard the *Navis Lusoria*, the troop transport carrying the 214th home—no booze. Whenever he felt the need to tip a glass, he'd run the length of the ship instead. He made it three days with his self-intervention, then fell off the wagon before climbing back aboard and falling off a second time three days after that.

When Ben was being good, the ghosts left him alone, which was motivation in itself. When he wasn't, dreams were a mash-up of grinning ghouls and lonely beaches and cracked face-plates. Daytime following a bender was worse, in its way. As he'd round a corner on his shipwide run, he'd see DeSoto or Baqri waiting for him at the next pressure door like a marathon enthusiast, urging him on.

Keep running, Shitbox.

Pop it till you drop it, Marine.

On really bad days, it was the Arcœnum prisoner that appeared, confined in its own armored exoskeleton in a ten-by-ten hexacrete cell and trapped in its grief-stricken psychosis. As

Ben passed through the pressure door, the Archie ghost would throw itself against the ship's walls, reenacting the damage it'd inflicted on the suit's regulator and collapsing to the deck, crushed to death by gravity.

Now, barely two days out from Earth, Ben hadn't had a drink in three days. He'd wandered absently into the shipboard café, ostensibly to eat. But in the back of his mind, he knew they served alcohol, too. To avoid that particular forbidden fruit he'd found an observation window and now stared outward, mesmerizing himself with the vastness of deep space.

"Hey, Stone."

Toma marched toward him on her own walkabout.

"Colonel."

"Stargazing?"

Outside the *Lusoria*, streaks of light flitted past like long-tailed fireflies. It was an optical illusion, a combination of translight travel and the human brain's need to make sense of it. Light years from the ship, well beyond the fireflies, the backdrop of stars hung seemingly fixed in their positions. More illusion.

"Something like that," he answered as she took a seat. "It's a way to pass the time."

They stared in companionable silence at the stars for a while. At first, Ben had resented Toma being made battalion commander, despite his congratulations when Bradshaw announced the promotion. He'd gotten used to Sandra Bradshaw and spoiled by her obvious regard for him following the Keller mission. It'd taken a long time to earn that, and he wasn't entirely sure he didn't owe most of it to her affection for his grandfather. And so, springboarding off his resentment for her promotion, he'd pigeon-holed Toma into the role of his babysitter, Strickland's proxy spy assigned to keep Ben Stone on a short leash.

Or maybe he deserved a babysitter, Ben thought. Toma was

a real field officer overseeing a real fighting battalion. Not a poster boy. During the weeks-long voyage home, he'd hopped back and forth over that fence, at times appreciating Toma's promotion as well deserved, at others convinced she was merely there to persecute him.

"Debating with yourself?" Toma said. "You've got that look."

"What? What, ma'am?"

"Hard to lose an argument doing that," she observed.

"I suppose." Ben recognized she was trying to be affable with the kind of distant regard expected between officers of unequal rank. She'd probably been reading up on how to become the kind of battalion commander subordinates both respected and liked. But Ben was feeling itchy today, with images of bourbon shining in a twice-tall glass invading his thoughts. Toma's attempt at cordial conversation only made him feel shittier about it.

"I could use a drink," he said, wincing when he realized he'd spoken aloud.

There was a pause, like the room was holding its breath. Toma rose to her feet. "You can't live your life inside a bottle, Stone. You can never see the world the way it really is from in there. Everything outside looks skewed."

The old snark rose up in him like a shield. He wanted to stand up and bash her with it. Goad her into impotent fury, like in the old days. But it was the new days now, and she was his CO. So instead, he said nothing. It didn't help his mood one damned bit to realize she was, of course, right. As usual.

"Mission briefing at sixteen hundred. I'm finally at liberty to disclose details. I'll notify the other company commanders."

Ben rose to his feet. "Yes, ma'am," he said saluting.

Toma returned it. She seemed like she wanted to say something else but stowed it, nodded, and left the café. It was all he could do to restrain himself from making a mad dash for the small bar. Instead, he sat back down and watched the fireflies.

Setting down on Earth felt strange. Like returning to a restaurant and ordering a favorite meal and realizing they'd changed chefs. The taste was similar but not the same.

The shuttle pilot put him down well away from his grandfather's Iowa homestead. All that running aboard the *Lusoria* had strengthened his legs, and they seemed to yearn for a long stroll on ye olde home planet. So he walked the half-klick through tall, green grass toward the farm. Not alien or potentially toxic but welcoming and smelling like grass *should* smell. The breeze was cool but not cold, the sunshine warm but not hot.

"Ruby!"

Ben heard his grandfather before he saw him. There was still the admiral's bark he'd come to dread as a teenager, but now Nick Stone's voice made Ben feel at home. Nostalgic, and glad to be around. Topping a low-sloping hill, Ben spied him standing below, gesturing away into the tall grass.

"Ruby! Come on, girl. He's this way."

A Husky-Labrador mix, Ben knew from their correspondence. The strawberry blonde fur of the dog's back rose and fell among the swaying stalks of tall grass like a benevolent sea monster breaking the waves and diving again.

Though they'd corresponded regularly over the past few years, Ben hardly recognized his grandfather. Nick Stone seemed half the size he should be. Leaner by a hundred and fifty pounds, and his movements, while stiff, appeared more animated. Retirement agreed with him.

Ruby began barking nonstop and made a beeline for Ben. The old man's eyes found him too.

"Ben!"

Nick advanced up the hill, Ruby on point and widening the distance. She squared off between them and barked at Ben descending the hill.

"It's all right, Ruby," Nick rasped as he climbed. "He's family."

"Don't kill yourself, Admiral Gramps," Ben said. It was the old insult but now said with affection.

"Can't die yet," Nick said. "You just got here."

The two men embraced while Ruby yipped. She hopped up, pressing her weight into both of them, either happy at the reunion or, jealous, determined to break it up.

"Take it easy, girl," Nick said, ruffling her head. He looked long and hard at Ben. "It's good to see you."

"You too, Granddad."

"Come on up to the house. Hungry? I've got a first-rate bourbon to toast your return."

With effort, Ben kept the smile on his face from faltering. But they had a lot to talk about. "Age before beauty," he said.

"It still blows my mind," Ben said, taking a swig of lemonade. They were sitting on the front porch of the house in lightly creaking rocking chairs, Ruby snoozing loudly next to Nick.

"What does?"

"I never would have thought they'd just let you all off like that—you and Commodore Hallett," Ben said. "And Morgan."

"It was easier than court-martialing us. That would get out in the media, no matter how they tamped it down. We were all sailing into the sunset anyway. What surprised *me* was how they treated us in the documentary."

Ben clucked something derisive. *The Castaway Girl.* His

catapult to stardom. Patriotic propaganda from start to finish, the essential facts of the rescue submerged beneath spin and innuendo alleging the Arcœnum as the likely culprit that had downed the SS *Seeker*. Also known as promotional groundwork for the AGF's return to Sirius.

"It had to be black and white, I guess," Nick said. "We were either part of the problem—"

"—or part of the solution," Ben finished. "Once the decision was made to not court-martial you, they only had one hand to play."

Nick nodded. "All part of the same big, winning, happy-family team."

The discussion petered out momentarily. Ben wondered if the old man was sorting through what it had cost him personally to let the record stand, skewed for history, as presented in *The Castaway Girl*.

"Ah, well," Nick said. "She was worth it. Doing the right thing usually is."

"I wonder how she's doing," Ben said. An image of the woman on the beach flashed into his mind, only now she had a face. But not like he'd remembered. Older, which looked odd in his mind's eyes, though it made perfect sense.

"She took Morg's death pretty hard," Nick said, solemn. "But she'll be okay."

Unexpectedly, Ben felt himself hyperfocus. "You've talked with her recently?"

"A few weeks ago," Nick said. "She's becoming a formidable young woman."

The painful memory of first meeting Alice Keller flared below Ben's right shoulder blade, where she'd stabbed him with a piece of sharp rock. "She was already that."

Nick smiled. "Right. One thing that bothers me, though."

"Yeah?"

"We hid her, Morg and I, on Strigoth to protect her from Bragg and anti-Psycker persecution."

"But..." Ben prompted.

"But it's almost like he didn't even bother looking for her," Nick mused. "And she was the real deal, with real abilities." He shook his head. "What motivates that man is a mystery sometimes."

And wasn't that the truth? Ben wasn't looking forward to the audience with the president in the morning. The man could be so mercurial.

"So, how are you doing?" he asked.

"Oh, fine," Nick answered, stretching in his rocking chair. Ruby snuffled at the movement. "Finally got a dog ... and the land is absolutely—"

"No, I mean..." Ben took another sip of lemonade. "Morg Henry's passing must have been hard."

Nick settled back in his chair. He rocked forward and back a few times. Ruby sighed beside him. "Ah, that."

"Yeah."

"I'm doing all right. We hadn't seen a lot of each other since... He was dedicated to his mission to watch over Alice. Corresponded a few times via vid. Every year, I got a top-shelf bottle of bourbon from him on the anniversary of my retirement. Always with the seal cracked. Always with two fingers missing."

Ben's eyebrows arched, asking the obvious question. An anti-grav car whirred from atop the windy hill. It skimmed low over the terrain as it approached the house.

Nick chuckled. "Morg claimed he had to taste test every bottle to make sure it was good enough to gift to me. Quality assurance, he called it." His melancholy tone brightened a bit. "I called it what it was: *stealing*."

Ben laughed.

The car glided to a stop in the front yard, kicking up dust

and leaves. Ruby was already on her feet, tail wagging. The driver's door lifted to reveal a slight but beautiful woman who'd settled into old age the way you would a comfortable chair.

"Ben!" Maria Hallett took her time getting out. "Come help me with the groceries."

He and Nick stood at the same time, and Ruby bounded off the porch to greet her mistress.

"You guys ever going to make it official?" Ben asked from the side of his mouth.

"We don't need the paper." Nick Stone shrugged. "Been together long enough now, the state considers us married anyway."

"Captain Stone!" Maria was placing boxes of supplies onto a small hover cart she'd launched from the trunk of the vehicle. "That wasn't a request. If I'm cooking, you're on depot detail."

"Yes, ma'am!" Ben acknowledged, hopping down from the porch.

After giving him a heartfelt hug, Maria occupied herself with stroking Ruby's fur in greeting while Ben finished loading up the cart.

"He's ecstatic to see you, Ben," she said. "He's missed you."

Ben smiled, securing the vehicle. "It's good to be home."

"A drink or three to Morg's memory?" Nick suggested.

There was a fire in the fireplace. The light scrape and shuffle of pots filtered in from the kitchen. Maria had insisted on preparing vegetables grown right here on the farm, and Ben hadn't argued. The smell wafting to him from the kitchen was so mouth-watering, he was tempted to rethink his unassailable devotion to synthesized food.

"I'll stick with lemonade, if it's all the same."

"Sure," Nick said. He'd poured half his own drink before, catching Ben's meaning, he stopped. "Does my drinking bother you?"

"Not at all." Ben was pretty sure he meant it. In fact, since he'd arrived, he hadn't thought of taking a slug of anything heavier than the flavored water in his glass.

"In that case, I'll have yours, too."

Ben raised an eyebrow.

"In the spirit of Morgan Henry, of course."

"Oh, of course."

"No, you won't!" called Maria from the kitchen.

Nick sighed. "Or not."

"Yeah."

"So," his grandfather said, "tell me about Sirius. All's well on Canis III?"

Ben thought about what he could share. "Can't say a lot. Classified."

"Right. I've heard rumors through old contacts that there were complications. Is it true there was a skirmish with the Archies?"

Clearing his throat, Ben said, "I can neither confirm nor deny—"

"Yeah, yeah," Nick Stone groused, but he did so grinning. "If I wanted to know, I wouldn't have retired, right?"

"I can confirm what the media has already reported. The AGF landed. Humanity is once again squatting in Sirius."

"Reclaiming the hinterlands for the emperor?" Nick said.

"Something like that."

"Five minutes!" Maria called.

With a furtive glance toward the kitchen, Nick poured himself another, shorter drink. "There's something else I wanted to discuss with you, son."

Uh-oh. When his grandfather called him *son*, things tended

to get serious. Hearing it always kindled nervousness in Ben's gut, going back to those lectures he'd earned as a teenager.

"I'm releasing your inheritance," Nick said.

Simple. Straightforward. The last thing Ben had expected to hear. He played it over again in his head to make sure he'd heard right.

"You're—"

"I'm having the attorney update the paperwork," Nick continued. It was like he'd rehearsed the spiel and needed to get it all out before he forgot the details. "The fund has grown significantly since your parents' passing. I've tried to be a good steward for you. I'd hoped to have everything finalized before you got here, but it'll be another week or two."

"Grandpa, I ... I don't know what to say."

Things had quieted down in the kitchen. The fire crackled in the hearth. Ruby's feet pumped as she chased after something in whatever dreamland dogs visit. How long had he fought his grandfather to get his hands on the estate his parents had left him? Demanded, threatened, cajoled, begged ... from his sixteenth birthday forward. And Nick Stone's response, resolute and semi-apologetic, had always been some form of *you're not ready*. But now ... apparently the old man's opinion had changed. Ben was surprised by the feeling of pride that inspired inside him.

Maria Hallett appeared in the doorway with a pot of something held between two hot pads. "Dinner is served, your majesties."

"Good!" Nick said, rising. "I'm famished."

Ben stood too, downing the last of his lemonade. Without an iota of guilt, he wished it was something stronger.

"Now you have options," Nick said, almost to himself. "You don't need the Corps. You don't need Bragg. You don't need to put yourself in danger any longer."

Ben caught his grandfather's arm as he turned toward the small dining room. "But I do have a duty. I can't just bail on my unit. Bragg, the battalion ... people are depending on me."

Nick Stone nodded. "I understand. Just know—you have options, son."

Ben slid his grip down his grandfather's arm, and the two men clasped hands.

"Thank you, sir. I won't squander it."

"It's all your folks left you, so see that you don't." There was the hint of a lecture, the legacy of their old power relationship. Nick's gaze softened. "You've earned it."

"Gentlemen! I start eating in five ... four ... three—"

"Better hurry," Nick said, "if you don't want to go hungry."

22

REVELATIONS

THE BLUE OR the light gray?

Eva examined each tunic. Both were understated, official Bragg Administration top wear that screamed well-organized and take-charge. What were they wearing in The Frontier these days? More to the point, what should *she* wear? This wasn't an official state function with dignitaries and power struggles masquerading as polite conversation. This particular engagement was part-espionage, part-military recovery, and part-hostage negotiation with gigatons of tungsten and lonsdaleite ore as the prize. In a dangerous region infested with pirates. How recognizable did she really want to be? Eva threw both tunics in her smartcase, which accepted them without judgment and vacuum-sealed them to optimize storage space.

The rest of the packing went easier because she did it distracted. As predicted, Leo hadn't taken her assignment well. He loathed the idea of Eva being gone for months. And he was downright furious at Piers Bragg for sending her into a wild region of space known for abductions and ransoms and public executions. The fact that she'd be escorted by the 214th Drop Marine Battalion provided him zero piece of mind. And so they'd engaged in a kind of cold war since she'd given him the news. What time their stressed schedules allowed them together was often passed in silence or obligatory exchanges over nothing that mattered. They'd released some steam from the boiler with hasty sex twice in the past two weeks, and more often than not afterward slept facing opposite directions, both feeling angry and justified and petulant, each too proud to admit to the other they hated the idea of being apart for so long.

"Maybe I should pack sturdy shoes," Eva announced to distract herself from the distraction. She rifled through her closet, searching for her hiking boots.

It's not like she could have said no, she'd told Leo. She served at the pleasure of the president, and if he wanted her to go, she'd go. Leo understood that in the rational part of his brain, Eva knew. Behind his breastbone, where logic mattered less, not so much.

Maybe this was her way past the cock-and-balls requirement for entering the Boys Club, she'd argued. If she did this and was successful, Bragg's gratitude would know no bounds, at least until the next major crisis. But the mission to The Frontier was an opportunity to change the president's opinion of her as a formidable brain in a pretty package. She'd already made strides in that regard by pulling Marcos in; assuming her theory was wrong about their meeting in Colorado being mere stagecraft. Either way, the woman had finally given up her hunger strike and been transported to Tokyo. Which reminded Eva, she had questions for Miranda Marcos. She'd plan to see her before leaving and determine, once and for all, what their first meeting had really been all about.

Then, there was Ben Stone. Eva had practically memorized his dossier. An entitled playboy, a hero-wannabe who might share his grandfather's genes but had little of the older Stone's natural tendency toward service or self-sacrifice. He'd lost his parents as a teenager, and sure, that could fuck up anyone. But despite Nick Stone's best efforts to parent his grandson, Ben had turned out less-than. Almost willfully so, his record argued. Though an honors student before his parents' deaths, he'd become nothing but trouble afterward. Barely admitted to OCS because of bad grades. Written up. Slapped down. Insubordinate and selfish. Stone's file showed a lot less of that lately since he'd become the face of the administration's recruitment effort. Or maybe that was just lower-downs in the food chain scrubbing the record before it reached senior staff at the Citadel—the military, handling their own, and quietly.

People don't change.

To say Ben Stone had a self-destructive streak was to point out that space was cold. Eva remembered well the drunken, brawling spectacle he'd made of himself at Admiral Stone's retirement reception and gotten thrown in the brig for it, only to be released the next day. True, on President Bragg's order, and that, maybe, was what stuck in her craw the most. Because Ben reminded her of a young version of Piers Bragg, cocksure and brazen, without regard for anyone else or concern over consequence. Stone reminded her of a character from mythology with a patron god constantly intervening on his behalf, no matter how little he deserved the consideration.

Eva grabbed and clapped her hiking boots together. Clods of earth from Mount Oku-Hotaka flaked onto the lightly carpeted floor.

Maybe that's why she'd been chosen for this mission. Sam Devos had privately praised her more than once for her ability to rein in Piers Bragg's personality. Maybe he saw her doing the same for Stone. Well, after dealing with Bragg for so long, at least she had a good idea how to do that. Appeal to Stone's narcissism. And it couldn't hurt to pull her blouse down an inch and her skirt up two before entering a room with him.

Ugh. Using her sexuality to control Ben Stone? Is that how she got the gender-free pass into the Boys Club? The notion was so ludicrously counterintuitive, so self-sabotaging, it didn't even qualify as ironic. Still, Eva Park was a practical woman. If winning were to be a moral victory, then, by ipso-facto logic, the only moral thing that mattered was winning—whatever the method for getting there. She tossed the boots into a second smartcase.

She was already feeling the fatigue of the trip with a kind of shoulder-bending weariness. The thought of spending long weeks aboard ship, fencing with and fending off Ben Stone... And she hadn't even finished packing yet.

The door to her penthouse apartment chimed once, then opened.

"Hey," Leo said.

"Hey."

"You look tired."

"Thanks."

"No, I didn't mean—"

"It's okay," Eva sighed. "I know what you meant."

They were supposed to have dinner at Sukiyabashi Jiro in an hour or so on their last night together before she left. It usually took two months to book a table. Leo had pulled strings to get them reservations. Eva was determined to make the evening special. Not spiteful or tense.

"All packed?"

It was said light-heartedly. He still wasn't happy, but she could tell he was trying.

"Not quite. But almost."

"We should be going in about half an hour," he reminded her as he always did. Usually, his habit of doing that annoyed her—like, as a professional woman who scheduled every moment of her day, she couldn't tell time all by herself. Tonight, something about it was reassuring. The familiarity of it, maybe. Even Leo's bothersome habits were something she'd miss. She cared enough about him to be bothered.

"I'll be ready," she said.

She wasn't looking at him. So when he put his arms around her from behind, it startled her. She felt her body react against him, stiffen.

"I'm sorry," he said almost formally, pulling away. "I guess—"

Eva turned around and pulled him into a fierce hug. He was still rigid, his reaction to her reaction to him, but he relaxed quickly.

"I still don't want you to go," Leo said into her hair.

She felt him breathing her in. Making a memory. "I know."

"I'll miss you."

"I'll miss you, too."

"I'm worried you're not coming back," Leo said, trying to hide the hitch in his voice.

Eva hugged him tighter. Not that he needed her permission to be sad.

"That confident in me, huh?" she teased.

"You know it's not that." Leo pulled back so he could look her in the eye. "You can't control everything, Eva. Much as you'd like to."

"Yeah," she said. "That *is* annoying as hell."

"Something could happen out there ... they're pirates, for God's sake!" Abruptly he dropped it and hugged her to him again. "It could be like this all the time," he said quietly. "When you get back, you know. We could leave all this crazy crap behind. Just go be us, together, somewhere else."

She knew it was unrealistic, but Eva was surprised by how much the thought appealed to her. She and Leo, more than just bed buddies, living alone together on a mountain somewhere, maybe even Mount Oku-Hotaka. Not a speck of high-tech in sight. A wood stove, maybe. Indoor plumbing would be nice in the winter. But no Bragg Administration crisis-du-jour. Lazy days without a schedule or reminder notifications going off for the next meeting. Less stress. It was a pleasant fantasy that smelled like breakfast cooking on a cold morning.

"We'll talk about it when I return, yeah?" Eva's voice was calm. She hoped she sounded confident because that's how she felt.

"Yeah," Leo said.

"No, really." Now, it was she who separated them to stare hard into his gold-and-green flecked eyes. "I mean it."

"Yeah. Good. Okay."

"Now come on," she said. "Help me finish packing. We don't want to be late for dinner."

The most advanced facility of its kind in the Eastern Hemisphere, the Shinya Yamanaka Medical Complex was nearly as tall as Eva's residence building. Mostly a civilian facility, there was an entire upper floor devoted to whatever the administration needed. It operated like a hospital within a hospital, with its own security-cleared staff and untouchable budget. If Bragg were ever shot in Tokyo, they'd bring him to the hundred-and-first floor of Yamanaka.

Miranda Marcos was the only patient occupying the wing. ACE agents stood outside the door. As Eva approached, Sam Devos was exiting her room. Well, that was interesting.

"Eva," he said as if running into her wasn't a surprise. "Captain Stone will be at the Citadel in a couple of hours. Ready for your pirate adventure?"

"Sure, Sam," she said, wondering what he was doing there. "How's Miss Marcos?"

"Recovering. She took it right up to the line, her little protest." Devos clapped Eva once on the shoulder. "Well, I have to prepare for the briefing with Stone. Watch out for the doc. She's a pistol."

Eva watched him walk away. Her little protest? *You mean nearly starving herself to death in devotion to her cause?* Eva wondered how it felt to believe in something so strongly, so faithfully, that you'd let your body eat itself to death rather than betray that belief. Go big or go home was how Marcos had described herself. No argument, here. Or maybe the hunger strike had only been part of the charade she still suspected Sam and the president of orchestrating?

She pushed through the door and was met with a clucking tongue and glare from the physician in attendance. "I told you ... oh. You're not Mister Devos."

"No," Eva said. "Is something wrong?" She moved into the room and read the badge on the doctor's lab coat. "I'm Eva Park, Doctor Ravani." She offered her hand.

Ravani didn't take it. "As I told Mister Devos, this woman needs rest. She's still very weak. Talking with you people is putting undue strain on her—"

"Doctor, it's okay," Marcos said from behind the physician.

Ravani moved aside to stare disapprovingly at her patient, and Eva got her first good look at Marcos. She'd seen the newsfeeds documenting Marcos's transfer from maximum security to Yamanaka, of course. Images of an emaciated and near-comatose woman, a slumping corpse still barely alive with dark circles under her eyes and bony cheekbones atop a kind of sunken beauty that hardly resembled the warrior-woman Eva had dueled in Colorado. In person, Marcos looked far worse, barely resembling the proud activist who'd refused to sit down first.

"Ten minutes," Ravani said. "I don't give a damn who you are."

Eva nodded, and the doctor exited the room.

"She reminds me of my mother," Marcos said. Her voice was thinner than it had been with the doctor.

"How are you, Miranda?" Eva asked. There was a rolling chair next to the bed, so she sat.

"Anorexic. You?"

Eva couldn't help the smile that came. She admired Marcos. Her body might be sackcloth and bone, but the woman could still flex her wit.

"About to take a trip, actually."

"Colorado again? You were right. The views are great. From the air."

"A little farther afield. Can't talk about it."

"Ah." Marcos picked at the sheets covering her. The skin of her fingers appeared slack. As if it were one size bigger than what her bones needed. "I feel like family already."

Eva asked, "Mind if I ask what Sam Devos wanted?"

"Can't talk about it."

Eva opened her mouth to say something, but Marcos cut her off.

"Kidding. Details on my future."

"And?"

"I'm to chair something called the Civilian Oversight Board for Security Enforcement."

Eva nodded. "Right. An addendum to Executive Order 9066. Establishes civilian review of ACE-ordered Psycker detentions."

"The board will oversee something called Community

Zones," Marcos said. "Psyckers in ACE custody will be relocated there."

Eva knew some of these details already. The Community Zones were a compromise between freedom and incarceration. Managed, patrolled, and comings and goings strictly enforced. A prison by any other name.

"What's the board's role, exactly?" Eva asked.

"Subpoena power to investigate any alleged wrongdoing," Marcos said. "Inhumane treatment of detained citizens and such." She took a moment to gather her strength. The conversation was taking its toll. Eva picked up the pitcher by the bedside, poured a cup of water, and handed it to Marcos. "Thanks." Marcos took her time. "We'd also monitor the graduated release of Psycker detainees once cleared as potential threats to security. We'd have representatives in the room at board reviews."

"And you'd oversee all that," Eva said, "as chair of the board."

"What Devos said, yeah."

It *sounded* good. Sure, *habeas corpus* was still suspended for Psycker detainees no matter how pretty the prison, but now there were eyes watching, ensuring humane treatment and due process. Miranda Marcos's eyes. And yet, there were no real teeth in the paper tiger. No legal recourse. Subpoena power, but Parliamentary hearings took forever and could be sidelined by procedure. Marcos could always go to the media to apply political pressure. But no legal recourse meant ultimate control over the Psyckers' fate still resided with the administration. And more to the point, with the man who'd put them in prison in the first place.

"What are you thinking?" Marcos asked. Her tone was cautious. Curious.

Eva made a slow pass with her eyes around the room. There was no obvious recording equipment, though that meant nothing. High-tech surveillance was subtle. She'd have to be too. She lowered her voice.

"I'm thinking, Sam Devos doesn't know much about the woman he's screwing with."

Marcos murmured, "Is that a compliment?"

Eva reached out and poured first one, then another cup of water, speaking as the water flowed. "They gave you no real power, but they left your greatest weapon intact."

"Which is?"

"Your mouth."

Marcos laughed a brittle sound.

Raising the cup of water to her mouth, Marcos said, "You think I don't know the limits of my new 'authority?'"

"I think Sam's underestimated you."

"I don't think that," Marcos said, and her weak gaze sharpened. "I know it."

"And yet you've accepted their deal," Eva whispered, still trying to figure Marcos out.

"'Their?' Not 'our?'" Marcos took another sip. "It's a battle, not the war. But wars are won one battle at a time."

"And you can do more out here than sitting in solitary."

Marcos let that hang in the air. Some facts didn't need confirming.

"Can I trust Sam Devos?" Marcos asked.

Eva hesitated, acutely aware again of the likely surveillance. "Sam's a straight-shooter," she shrugged, "as far as politicians go. But really, you can't trust anyone in politics when they promise you something. Unless there's something in it for them."

"Right."

"Leo Byrne," Eva said. It popped out, almost like a compulsion. "You can trust Leo."

"Your boyfriend?" Marcos's expression turned sly.

Eva tried to keep the surprise from her face. Jesus, everyone really *did* know.

"The *media coordinator*," she emphasized, ignoring the innuendo. "You can trust Leo."

"Okay." Macros leaned back in her bed, head against the pillow. She searched the ceiling before addressing Eva again. "And what about you? Can I trust you?"

Strangely, the question spoken with such timid sincerity confirmed for Eva something else she'd come here to find out. Their meeting in Colorado had indeed been genuine. Of that, she was now sure.

"I'll be off the board for a while," Eva answered without answering. "Leo's your man."

"Okay."

The door squeaked as it opened.

"Time's up," Ravani said, holding it open as an obvious suggestion for Eva to leave. "My patient needs her rest."

Eva stood. "Watch your back. We live in interesting times."

"Chinese pidgin philosophy from the administration's communications director?" Marcos said, amused.

"From a concerned citizen."

"Miss Park, visiting hours are *over*," Ravani said.

"Get healthy," Eva said to Marcos. "And stay that way. This isn't one of daddy's dinner parties. You're in the big leagues now. They play for keeps here."

Marcos regarded her as if assessing whether Eva had just given her good advice or laid a trap. She said quietly, "Thanks. I will."

23
THE HERO OF CANIS III

FROM THE AIR, it was easy to imagine Tokyo as a completely synthetic city. Everything appeared planned, constructed, maintained—nothing grown or cultivated, despite the reserves of green spaces—and diseased with brightly lit advertising. The architectural inverse of the tract of heaven nestled in the Iowan countryside that Ben had just left.

Flying vehicles crisscrossed air lanes, avoiding constant crashes by the grace of the traffic regulation sensor web. The buildings stretched so high that Ben considered it a wonder of construction science they hadn't all fallen over. Closer to the ground the densely packed neighborhoods reminded him of an infestation, built nearly on top of one another like poorly planned anthills. Something akin to the pre-jump jitters of pancaking on a planetary surface during planetfall fluttered in Ben's gut.

The transport landed in the swanky civilian sector of the Greater Tokyo Interplanetary Exchange. A short jaunt to the military dock, and he'd transfer to the presidential launch for the second leg of his trip to the Citadel. After a brief debarking process, he stood among a bustling throng and scouted signage for directions to the military terminal.

"Hey, you!"

Ben stepped aside, narrowly avoiding a woman who wasn't looking where she was going.

"Ben Stone! Hey!"

A young man, college age, was pushing his way through the crowd. "You're Ben Stone, right?"

"Um..." Ben glanced around uncertainly. "Yeah?"

"I'm Akio," the young man said. He raised his PalmPad to Ben. "This is you, right?"

The pad showed a still of Lieutenant Ben Stone, covered in gray dust and cradling an unconscious Alice Keller in his arms, emerging from the caverns beneath Drake's World. The kid had saved the promotional shot for *The Castaway Girl* as his pad's background.

"Uh..." Ben said.

"Hey! It's Ben Stone!" a woman shouted. She reached out and grabbed Ben's arm to turn him toward her and get a better look.

"Hi, ma'am, please don't—"

"Oh my God!" a younger version of the woman yelled next to her. The girl fumbled with her own pad.

"Can I get a snap?" Akio asked, ignoring them.

"Well, I—"

"Hey son, you're right. It *is* him!" A man grabbed a boy by the shoulders and shoved him at Ben. "Go shake that man's hand!"

The teenage girl jostled Akio aside. "Snap, okay?" she said to Ben. "You don't mind, right?" she said, holding up her pad.

"Hey, wait," Akio said, pushing back. "I need to scan his eyegraph or it's not authentic!"

"My son has every IAM, every toy," the father said. "He's

played every one of those adventure modules a dozen times over."

"My wife loves it when—" someone else began before being shoved aside. "Hey!"

"I feel safer knowing you're out there protecting me," said a woman in her forties with an expression equally grateful as hungry.

Children giggled shyly until they were overcome by a sea of adults. Ben tried to be gracious, but there were so many faces, voices, and hands that were angling, talking, reaching for him—it was getting hard to breathe.

"My wife will never believe this!"

"My dad was such a fan of your grandfather, you know?"

"Wait your turn!" the teenage girl shouted.

The crowd pressed closer, snapping selfies and elbowing each other out of the way to get a better shot. A switch flipped and Ben went tactical, scanning for an exit strategy.

"Guys, please, I have to get to—"

"Get off me, bitch!"

Someone slapped someone else, and the crowd roared. Ben's heart raced. Any concern with unwanted snaps was giving way to a more basic obsession with not being crushed to death.

"Break it up!" The voice was amplified, commanding, and absolute. "Everyone, move away! Break it up!" Also, entirely ineffective.

The air was hot and close, and Ben twisted, searching for escape. Any hand-to-hand training he might have used to free himself was now thirty seconds too late. He was too packed in by the crowd, which pressed closer still.

"I said move! Break it up!"

Cries and complaints. Cursing and threats. The mob around Ben surged away from the man barking orders. Ben added momentum from the opposite direction, pushing toward the man. He could see the stark, white lettering of ACE agents in smartfatigues using rifles and stunsticks to make a path to him. So far, no weapons had gone hot.

"Officers, I'm all right," Ben shouted, trying to keep things calm. "Folks, please listen to him!"

Slowly the ACE agents surrounded him, firming up a barrier against the crowd.

"I said, back up!" yelled one of the agents, the ranking officer.

"Get me out of here, Lieutenant," Ben said. "Before someone gets hurt."

"No shit, jarhead," the officer snarled back.

The presidential launch carrying him to the Citadel was the love-child of a tank and a limousine: seemingly impenetrable but luxurious. Both qualities helped to calm Ben's nerves. No one had been hurt in the crowd, and he'd gotten away with only a bad memory.

Before leaving the depot, he'd spotted the 214th loading up on military transports destined for Yokota Base for a little regulated R&R and pre-mission prep. There was a pang of guilt at his VIP treatment while his fellow Marines traveled like canned sardines. But after nearly being suffocated at the Exchange, he took the penance of his guilt in stride and managed to refuse the automated bartender's offer of a stiff drink ahead of his meeting with the president. He took the win.

On approach, he could make out the Citadel's anti-air turrets despite the effort the architects had made to camouflage them as simple guard towers. On the ground, Ben passed through multiple checkpoints after landing, his identity verified by his military ID chip and retinal scan. The civilian staff's busy disregard for him was balanced out by the sober interest of Bragg's Home Guard in their gold and blue uniforms.

And now, as he waited for his audience, Ben experienced a moment of awe in front of the president's working desk where one man's ambition and ability set the course for an entire species. The carpet was emblazoned with the seal of the Alliance, with its two halves representing the Sol and Alpha Centauri systems. Around him, the room Bragg famously called the Hot Seat was immaculately maintained. Not a speck of dust anywhere. For whatever reason, that only made Ben more nervous.

"Captain Stone, so good to see you again. How was your flight?"

He turned to find Bragg's chief of staff entering the room.

"Good, Mister Devos." Ben shook the smiling man's hand. "A little bumpy on re-entry."

"I heard about what happened at the Exchange," Devos said sympathetically. "The price of fame, I guess. Have a seat." The man gestured at one of the receiving couches in the middle of the room. "I imagine your visit to Iowa was like old-home week. Is your grandfather well?"

"Yes," Ben said, taking a seat. "Retirement's been good for him."

"And Commodore Hallett?"

"She's fine, sir."

"Excellent," Devos said. "No surprise those two got together, really. They make a lovely couple in their twilight years."

"They do, yes, sir."

"We'll be joined shortly by Eva Park, the president's communications director. And, of course, President Bragg."

Ben nodded.

"While we're waiting, I just want to say how grateful we all are at how you've stepped up to help the administration."

"Sir?"

Devos gestured broadly. "I mean your military service, first and foremost, of course. The president is never prouder than when he's hearing about the latest exploits of Bragg's Own Battalion."

"Good to hear, sir," Ben said.

"But also—and I don't know how aware you were of this on deployment in Sirius—but you've become something of a celebrity on the home front."

"I suppose I've had some inkling recently, sir."

"Right! The incident at the Exchange," Devos said. "Still, it's understandable, the regard so many have for you. And how you handled that business on Canis III? Every inch the hero, Captain. Every inch!"

Ben affected a pleasant expression but kept less gracious thoughts to himself.

"General Strickland was quite clear in his report about how vital you were to successfully recapturing the planet. How you protected lives. Captured that Archie cave dweller practically single-handed. You and your whole unit are a credit to the AGF, Captain, make no mistake."

Ben made an effort to keep his smile wide. "General Strickland is far too generous."

"I don't think so," Devos said. "I think he was exactly right. I have no doubt Zack's documentary will represent everything exactly as it should."

Ben's cheeks were beginning to ache. He'd blissfully displaced the vain director from his thoughts during the long voyage home. Now he began to imagine the commentary running between Zack's cherry-picked footage, reshaping what had actually happened into how history would prefer to remember it.

"Sir, I'm not sure what you've heard, but things didn't go as smoothly on Sirius—"

"The public needs to know what it needs to know," Devos cut in. "Not *how* the sausage gets made, Captain. Only that it tastes good."

When Ben closed his mouth, his teeth clicked.

The eastern door swished into the wall. Devos turned and rose, and Ben stood as well. "Eva! Perfect timing. You've met Captain Stone, I believe?"

"Of course. So good to see you again, Ben."

He took her extended hand and tried to place where they'd met before. Some event early on in his reign as administration mouthpiece, before he'd been promoted to captain. He'd seen her numerous times since then, but only on media feeds. She was taller than Ben remembered. It added to the impression he'd formed of her when they'd first met as a confident, intelligent woman. Easy on the eyes, too.

"Miss Park," he said.

"Eva will be accompanying your battalion for this mission," Devos said, "as President Bragg's official representative."

"Oh?" Ben said. Toma hadn't mentioned a civilian presence in the mission briefing, much less that she'd be an individual so highly placed in power. A political operative riding shotgun on a military mission? What could possibly go wrong...

"I'll try not to get in the way, Captain," Eva said, reading him easily.

"Not at all, ma'am. It should be an interesting mission."

Her expression, while outwardly positive, was strained. "That's one word for it."

"Eva," Devos said, "play nice. Captain Stone isn't used to your dry wit."

"I suppose I'll have to get used to it, then," Ben said.

"Good luck with that," Devos chided with a wink.

"I can't tell you what a help you are in getting our message out there," Eva said, switching gears. "We couldn't have asked for a better face on the administration."

On the heels of what Devos had said before she'd entered, Park's comment sounded slick and rehearsed. A talking point generated by committee. Ben wondered if they saw him only as a blockheaded Marine too dense to notice how obvious they were in their attempts to flatter him. Well, that was a consideration worth filing away.

"Ladies and gentlemen!"

The broad, bombastic voice was unmistakable.

"Mister President," Devos said.

Like the accomplished politician he was, Bragg locked eyes with and nodded to each of them as he entered the Hot Seat before halting in front of Ben. The president had grown an academic's well-tailored goatee since they'd last met.

"Captain Stone!" Bragg offered his hand. "Welcome to the Citadel."

Ben stood there, hand pumping up and down in the president's too-animated grip. If he'd been swimming earlier in the history this room had witnessed, he was now sucked down by the undertow of Piers Bragg's personality.

"Eva's right. Your pretty face dresses up this ugly mug of mine in the media. One thing I do well is pick talented people and inspire them to make my agenda their own. What you did in subduing that bastard mind-raper that attacked Fort Leyte... You, sir, are a hero! The Hero of Canis III!"

Ben opened his mouth with a response he hadn't yet formulated.

"Eva, get Leo on that," Bragg said, saving him the trouble.

"Sir?" Park said.

"Branding," Bragg said. "Don't push it too hard at first, let the media pick it up." He spread his hands toward the ceiling as if unfurling a banner. "'The Hero of Canis III.'"

Uh, Ben thought.

"'Hero of Sirius,' sir?" Devos ventured. "Shorter. Punchier."

Bragg considered a moment, then dismissed the suggestion. "Too prone to punchlines. 'A hero who's serious?' 'A serious hero?' Etcetera."

"Right," Leo agreed.

"Eva, get Leo on it before you leave. If he can come up with something better than 'The Hero of Canis III,' I'm open to it."

"Yes, sir."

"Sit," Bragg said, waving at the receiving couches. "Everyone, sit."

Bragg took his place at the head of the gathering in an ornate chair strategically facing the two couches.

"You've been briefed?" Bragg asked Ben.

"Yes, Mister President."

"Excellent."

"You're aware," Devos said, "that this entire mission is covered under Black Seal Protocol."

"Colonel Toma said as much, yes, sir," Ben said.

"I don't have to tell you how important recovery of what Sam calls the Treasure Fleet is," Bragg said, all business. "That materiel is vital to the coming ... conflict. Without it, we cannot ensure victory over the Arcœnum. And victory we must have, once and for all, Captain Stone. Don't you agree?"

"Er, yes, sir," he said. The words had been pulled out of his mouth like Bragg had cast a hook in and grabbed them. In truth, Ben wasn't at all sure a second war with the Archies was a good idea, especially after what he'd seen only one of them do against a fort full of Drop Marines.

"Excellent. Have you been keeping up with the Psycker situation here at home?"

Ben was thrown by the topic change, but course corrected to meet it. "Yes, sir. It seems by bringing Marcos into the administration, things have calmed down?"

"Just so," Bragg said.

"Technically, she's not part of the administration," Devos said. "But effectively—"

"Skip the details," Bragg admonished, "they're unimportant. My point in bringing it up is that you're sitting next to the architect of that solution."

Ben turned obliquely to Eva, who'd placed her hands in her lap.

"It was a team effort, Mister President," she demurred.

"Bullshit," Bragg insisted. "All you, Eva. All you."

That was interesting, Ben thought. Eva Park was either a humble person at heart—unusual in a political type—or she was canny enough to spread responsibility in case it metastasized later into blame. Either way, she'd confirmed his instinct to keep an eye on her.

"You've got a dealmaker at your side, Captain," Bragg was saying. "She knows just what to say and how to say it to get what she wants. Her counsel is invaluable to me. And that's why she's going with you on this mission."

Ben's internal tactical alert triggered. Making "deals" wasn't in the scope of most military missions. Kill the enemy, take the tactical objective—both in the service of achieving larger strategic goals. Dealmaking hardly ever figured into that rather simple equation.

"To be clear, Captain," Devos said, "it will be your job to not only deal with the pirates but to protect Eva. Consider her an embed with the 214th. I'll say the same to Lieutenant Colonel Toma."

Oh, I bet she'll love that. If anything set Bathsheba Toma's teeth on edge, it was an unpredictable factor like Eva Park and the muddy waters she'd bring to the chain of command. Well, this mission was getting more and more fun by the minute. Ben glanced at Eva to find her looking down at her hands.

"Sirius was only the first step," Bragg said. "And we can't go farther without that shipment. Understood?"

"Sir," Ben said, "yes, sir."

"The future of humanity depends on it. As does *your* future, Captain Stone."

Bragg's tone was solemn, his implication clear. Fail to recover Bragg's Treasure Fleet, and Ben's own career would take a precipitous dive off a cliff. Subtle, the man wasn't. Even accomplished politicians like Piers Bragg seemed to believe that all Marines needed things explained with small words spoken in smaller syllables. The others' blatant attempts to stroke his ego earlier, and now this? But hey, that was fine. Let them continue to underestimate his ability to see through them. Advantage: Stone.

"Yes, sir," Ben said. "I understand completely."

"Excellent." A feral smile stretched Bragg's neatly crafted beard.

24

CONFLICTING AGENDAS

STARING at the vastness of space through the ship's observation window was a test. More like a trial. Eva concentrated on the low thrum, a poor man's foot massage, coming up through the deck plates of the *L'Esprit de la Terre*. The ship's military call-sign was *Citadel Two*, but the more innocuous *Spirit of Earth* served as camouflage. Only yesterday, the vibration from the engines might have soured her stomach. Today, she found it soothing.

How the hell had she lost her space legs so easily? Raised as a planet hopper by a Fleeter father and a xenoarchivist mother, Eva had grown up more comfortable with artificial gravity than the natural kind. Three years on Earth had ruined that for her, and it'd taken her two weeks to get over being space sick on the voyage. It'd been fucking embarrassing, making excuses to staff and especially to the *Terre*'s captain, Mattei, who'd invited her more than once to dine with him and his officers.

Thinking of food was still a dicey prospect, so Eva focused on the stars instead. She found herself hoping to see Monolith again while they were in The Frontier, only a week away by translight drive. She hadn't been within sight of the planet since

Piers Bragg's presidential campaign. Monolith, the seat of his industrial power. A planet so rich in rare metals and ore that a rush on claim staking two centuries earlier had damn near sparked an Alliance civil war. It was somehow appropriate, then, that Monolith had lent itself as the nom du guerre of the mammoth new starship leading their tiny fleet to retrieve the stolen freighters.

Monolith had also been the closest thing to a home Eva had ever known. Not so much the planet, maybe, as the Bragg Industries megastation in orbit above it, but still... When you're a planet hopper, anywhere you land for more than a night or three inspires both hope and fear. Fear because you don't want to become reliant on the stability of living in one place; hope because the place holds the potential for that very permanence.

But when Eva thought about that notion now, she experienced an epiphany. No matter where her dad was stationed, no matter what alien ecosystem her mother had just returned from documenting, it was seeing *them*—not the comfortable apartment she holed up in to study or the station it was part of—that felt safe, warm, secure. It'd been people and not places, Eva realized, that had always felt like home to her.

That revelation surprised her. She'd always been a closed-off person, someone with a vast interior world that she protected and that protected her. A home within herself that nothing, save dementia or death, could ever take away. As a hopper with often-absent parents and local relationships so transient she sometimes didn't learn last names, Eva had come to depend only on herself for connection. Which seemed odd, now that she thought about it, given her chosen profession of manipulating opinion for a living. Or, maybe it wasn't odd at all. Forced by circumstance, she'd learned to read others quickly based on gestures, word choice, personal appearance—the little things most people don't even notice they notice. Maybe Eva was so good at her job because she'd never really been close to anyone growing up.

If it'd taught her nothing else, being in politics had shown her that irony seemed to be God's chosen language for connecting with lesser beings. It was certainly ubiquitous enough to, like gravity and the speed of light, be reliable and frustratingly consistent.

And then came Leo. His quest for closer connection had, until very recently, elicited only a kneejerk reaction from Eva to pull away—her defense mechanism against the potential for betrayal and hurt. *Never try, never cry, head up high.* Her battle hymn recited a thousand times as a loner teenager moving from station to station. There'd been sex partners in college. Itches needed scratching. Companions for dinner, entertainment, and the occasional hiking trip. Combinations of both, on rare occasions when she was acutely lonely. Until Leo, though, Eva had never met anyone she'd ever feared losing.

The sonofabitch tricked me, she thought, only half joking. *Like Earth, that bitch, and her constant, perfectly natural gravity.*

Reflection-Eva in the window smiled back at her. There was a hint of secret knowledge in her eyes, too. She'd had more conversations with Leo from the *Terre* in the past two weeks than in person over the last year. Small talk, at first, and almost formal. *How's the weather back on Earth? ... Sure, the voyage is smooth enough, just don't ask my stomach. ... I miss you, too.* Almost like they were dating again and trying to fill the uncomfortable quiet between forks scraping plates. When Leo pointed the obvious out, they'd both laughed, inexplicably embarrassed with a person who'd seen them naked and vulnerable too many times to count.

Ice, broken.

And with that, their discussions slipped back into the old, familiar groove. Leo's reports on the administration's latest goings-on amounted to summarizing media briefings spiced with safe if salty personal commentary. In return, Eva confessed her queasy travel log but spared him her expert critique of the inside of her cabin's toilet bowl.

It wasn't long before their conversation migrated to Leo's notion of a life together beyond politics. It'd been Eva, in fact, who first guided them there. At first, Leo had become solemn and defensive, thinking she was teasing him. But Eva reassured him, observing that often the people who help get an administration into power leave it once that work is done. By that standard, she noted, they were two years late in their thinking. Maybe, she said, it was time they thought seriously about bowing out. Leo was so delighted he started a list of things to do together once they left public life. Hiking every single trail on Mount Oku-Hotaka for no less than two weeks straight topped the list.

Reflection-Eva was smiling at the memory of that conversation. Leo's list—and how happy it made him, and how important his happiness turned out to be to her—was worth a toast or two. Her stomach felt settled, finally, and she wondered what quality of liquor a starship bar stocked for the President of the Sol Alliance. Like a child stepping away from a dream, Eva fluttered her fingers in goodbye to her reflection and went to find out.

The bar's designer had certainly hit all the right notes.

Soft lighting that created dark corners for intimacy. The distant tinkling of piano music piped in, re-interpreting some pop tune as if filtered through a grandmother. A murmuring of quiet conversations, sometimes smiling, sometimes slurred, sometimes both among the patrons, a mix of administration staff and ship's crew. All housed within the dimensions of an oversized shipboard suite with perfect acoustics. Every glass that clinked was like someone playing crystal in a jazz symphony.

Mars Shinshu's Iwai 25, Leo's favorite Japanese whiskey, was good at its job. Breathing after taking a sip conjured butterscotch and vanilla in Eva's nose, which reminded her of an ice cream shop on Covenant, where she'd lived for six months as a tween. The whiskey was full of far-past and recent-past memories intertwined in the present.

"What's the smile for?"

Eva turned, her eyes adjusting a little slower than her neck moved. The nostalgia curdled.

"Captain Stone." She settled back into herself, thinking, *Game face, girl.*

"Mind if I sit here?" he asked.

"Not at all." *Might as well get this over with now.* She took another swig of the 25. Her history of fending off unwanted advances from men had begun not long after becoming a teenager. Since then, she'd had plenty of practice.

"What'll I get you?" the bartender asked.

Stone seemed to hesitate. Or maybe her ears, like her eyes, were slowing.

"Club soda. Twist of lemon."

"On duty?" she asked.

"In theory, always," Stone said. "Colonel Toma sent me to say hello."

"To babysit the political officer, you mean?"

Her sarcasm seemed to push him back a bit. The bartender set a small, square napkin down, then the club soda on top of it.

"Is that what you are?" Stone asked watching the man walk away.

Shit. I said game face, *not transparency.*

"Don't mind me, Captain. I haven't been out of my cage in a while. I'm a little on edge."

"Okay," he said, sipping his soda.

But she hadn't been on edge. Just the opposite, in fact. Then Piers Bragg Junior sat down next to her and she'd glanced at the upper button of her blouse to make sure she wasn't advertising. This is why she preferred her interior life to the one out here. *That* she could control absolutely.

"What brings you to the *Terre*?" Eva asked.

"Now that we're almost to The Frontier, Colonel Toma wants a permanent military presence aboard. So here I am, with a platoon of Drop Marines commanded by Lieutenant Osira Tso. We're to be billeted here for the remainder of the mission. The rest of the battalion will remain aboard the military transport."

"Not enough staterooms on the *Terre*?"

"Right."

"Okay." The whiskey sang inside Eva's nose with its lingering suggestion of an ice cream sundae. "So, tell me what's new. I've been indisposed these last couple of weeks."

"I wouldn't know," Stone said. "Toma's kept us busy. PT. Daily mission briefings. Oo-rah, team-building exercises."

"Sounds fun."

"It's not, particularly."

"I was being sarcastic."

"Big surprise, that."

Something made her smile return. Blame the whiskey.

"Political officer, huh?" he probed. "Like those ancient empires that didn't trust their own militaries, so they sent someone along to keep a coup from happening?"

"Nothing like that," Eva replied. "We live in a representative democracy, after all."

"So I've heard."

"But kinda."

"Yeah," he said. "Figured."

Eva stared at her half-glass of 25. She was losing the aroma. She wanted it back and took a swig.

That isn't helping, said Leo's voice in her head. *You get talky when you get toasty*. Something he'd told her once at a party, a warning. She considered heeding his advice but took another drink instead. To warm her interior world.

"What are we doing out here, Miss Park?" Stone asked. "Really."

The question put Eva on her guard. Leo stood in the back of her head, arms crossed, tapping his toe and eyeing the whiskey still in her hand. She set the glass down.

"You know why, probably better than I do," she said.

"Okay. Let me rephrase—why are *you* here?"

There was a part of her tempted to bark back. Pull rank. Be Bragg for a second. Slap at the insolence she'd heard in his question.

"As a military man, Captain Stone, you should appreciate President Bragg's initiative," she said instead. "The tungsten-lonsdaleite amalgam is a game-changer."

"Lower your voice, Miss Park," Stone said as the bartender approached.

"Need a refill?"

"I'm good," they both said at the same time.

The man nodded and moved away.

"I apologize," Eva said. She pushed the whiskey away from her. "Thank you for ... catching me."

Stone nodded beside her. The prospect of breaking Black Seal Protocol and its ultimate consequences—over something as stupid as whiskey loosening her lips?

"President Bragg hasn't dealt with the pirates effectively in his three years in office," Stone said in a near-whisper. "And now he sends one battalion and a small fleet to do it?"

He was skating dangerously close to criticizing the boss, Eva thought. Or just being typically insubordinate, if his record was accurate. Either way, his attitude annoyed her.

"We're not here to fight, Captain, unless we have to. We're here to secure that—the prize—however we can."

"See, and that's what I'm talking about. You don't send an attack dog to make a deal. And you don't make deals with pirates. This is my problem with this mission. Conflicting agendas."

"How's your grandfather?" Eva asked, suddenly casual. She needed to get off the other topic before her private thoughts stormed the gates of her mouth again.

Stone sighed but took the hint. "He's good. He and Commodore Hallett are very happy together. Beautiful place. Nice dog."

"That's good," she said. "He gave his life to the service. He deserves his happiness."

Stone took a drink. "We talked about that, actually."

"Yeah?"

"Why he was allowed that. Happiness, I mean."

"I don't know what you mean."

"I'm sure you do, actually."

Goddamnit. Couldn't he just let her drink in peace? Did every topic they covered require she sift her thoughts before speaking?

"Hypothetically?" Eva said.

"Is there any other way to discuss this?"

"Not really," she said. "If I had to guess, I'd say it was just easier. Less public drama. And whatever happened on that last mission, what I said stands—your grandfather, Hallett, Henry; they all gave their lives to the service."

"Prosecuting heroes of the Specter War was more trouble than it was worth," Stone said.

"Something like that."

"Others more loyal to Bragg got theirs, too."

"You'll have to explain—"

"General Strickland, for example," he said. "And Captain Thorne—sorry, Rear Admiral Thorne—now commands Third Fleet in The Frontier. Replaced Ferris, who's now stuck commanding the Alpha Centauri Sector."

"I'd consider that a step up for her," Eva said. "A home base with amenities, not a badlands like The Frontier."

Stone grunted. "Out with the old, in with the new?"

"Sure. Administrations do it all the time. Pretty much every time."

He took another swig. Something in Eva's brain had begun counting the beats of their conversation. It was feeling more like a dance. Or a chess game. Friendlier, though, than the one she'd played in Colorado.

"I've done some research on you," he said.

She side-eyed him. "Really?"

"You know what they say: Keep your friends close and..."

"You consider me the enemy, Captain Stone?"

"I consider you a mission asset."

"What'd you call me?"

"A sense of humor." He drained his club soda, set down the glass, and made invisible scribbles on a nonexistent datapad. "Research ongoing."

"And what else have you learned, Captain?" Eva asked, intrigued. "Do tell."

"You've climbed high in a short amount of time," he said.

"A life path we share."

He inclined his head, acknowledging the point. "You're extremely good at your job. Smart. Coy. Articulate. Funny, as I said. All excellent characteristics in a communications director. And when you're not shaping the message or spinning it, you're distracting from it with how attractive you are."

In Eva's lizard brain, Leo clucked a jealous tongue. She felt the blood rushing upward and eyed the whiskey, sorely tempted. Picking it up, she knew, would make her look weak. Or worse, let Stone know he'd gotten to her. Now, how the hell had a ground-pounder troublemaker like Ben Stone managed to take control of their conversation? That was her fucking job, and she was goddamned good at it.

The whiskey called again.

Oh. That's how.

"I already have a boyfriend, Captain Stone," Eva said, raising Leo like a shield. She looked directly at him to prove she was unaffected by his compliment. Her lips curled slyly. It felt good to say that out loud to a near-stranger. Make the public declaration that she was off the market.

"You also care," Ben said.

"What?"

"About what you do. No, not just that. About the people impacted by what you do."

"And just how do you know that?" Eva asked.

"The way you talk about the Psyckers in the media briefings," Ben said. "I went back and watched a number of them from the archives. Even when you're pushing administration policy, you talk about the Psyckers like they're human beings."

"They *are* human beings," Eva said.

"I'm not sure your boss agrees."

"He's your boss, too."

"Yeah."

The bartender returned eyeing Ben Stone's empty glass, but the captain shooed him away.

"Captain Mattei has invited Lieutenant Tso and me to dine

with him and his officers at eighteen hundred. That's six o'clock civy time."

"I know military reckoning, Captain," Eva said. "My father was Fleet."

"Ah, right. I knew that from my research." He looked like he might wink at her for a moment but didn't. "The captain suggested I pass along the invitation. Can I tell him you'll join us?"

"Sure," Eva said, feeling confident in her stomach. It'd held the 25 just fine. So far. "I'd be delighted."

Stone grinned.

"What?"

"There's that sarcasm Devos warned me about." He climbed off the barstool. "See you at eighteen hundred, Miss Park."

25

BLIND PASSAGE

WAKING WAS little different from sleeping for Alice. Except, being aware of time's passing, for the plodding boredom. She had little to do in the pilot's cabin of the *Archimedes* except be grateful she'd escaped Korsakov. For most of the first day of the journey, that had been enough. But as she traveled farther from Tarsus Station, the high-burn fuel mixture of fear of shadow-spiders and fury at mad scientists had succumbed to the tedium of sub-light travel. Human nature was beginning to assert itself, making her less than content with what she had.

The small starsloop Ian had commandeered technically belonged to Korsakov. It was his personal ship, which he'd never used in all the time Alice had known him. It'd been paid for by patent royalties earned earlier in his career, when he'd been less a pariah among his peers. Korsakov had been very proud of the ship like you would be a sports trophy won in youth. Now, it was Alice's means of escape, and that particular irony tasted delicious.

But as the empty hours passed aboard the *Archimedes*, she'd come to realize that escape was not the same as freedom. Korsakov would, within hours, know that she'd fled and how.

He'd conduct a systemwide search for the sloop's drive signature, as unique to a starship as a retinal scan to a person. That effort wouldn't be trivial, Ian had warned her. Korsakov had close ties to Alliance higher-ups, not to mention long-standing relationships with merchants and suppliers all over The Frontier. The more Ian talked, the more Alice worried, but he'd assured her he could at least give her a fighting chance to get away. He explained that tweaking the drive mix just a little and altering the ship's transponder code, which registered the vessel on the flight network, would mislead searchers, at least for a while. The *Archimedes* wasn't as hidden as a needle in a haystack, but Ian had at least made the haystack a little harder to sift through.

For any auto-inquiries pinging the ship passively, Alice was listed as Anne Macy traveling aboard her father's personal yacht *Shelley's Fever Dream* registered out of Covenant. The flight manifest indicated the *Dream* was on its way to Ionia. The listed destination was the one accurate fact in the ship's profile. Odd to be sailing in a sector haunted by pirates, maybe, but less suspicious than a stolen sloop harboring a known refugee. It would, Ian told her, buy Alice enough time to get to the waypoint he'd set for her before continuing on to Sylvan Novus in Alpha Centauri. Or such was the plan.

Alice had been effusive in her gratitude as they took leave of one another, but Ian hadn't softened any. He was only too happy to have Alice gone, that much was clear. He hadn't said it out loud, but he had, really, with body language and attitude. He hadn't been cruel, but he hadn't been kind either. Alice hoped the cover story they'd agreed upon, that she'd forced Ian's cooperation, would sell to Korsakov. She thought it should. The professor's personal experience with her power, combined with Ian's own visceral fear of her, would make a strong case to explain his complicity in her escape, anyway. Their last bit of business together was for Ian to pre-program the course into the navigational console since Alice had no idea how to pilot a ship. He hadn't returned her final goodbye.

Like Strigoth, Ionia was one of the six habitable planets of The Frontier. When she'd woken from her first restless slumber aboard ship, Alice decided to do a little research. She was delighted, at first, to find Ionia to be as different a world from the craggy, desolate Strigoth as she could imagine. She smiled when she read that Ionia was advertised as a "pleasure planet" that "served every need of our valiant military." That sounded interesting. Even patriotic! She admired the military, or more to the point Ben Stone, since he'd saved her from the tunnels under the Terror Planet. Men in uniform made her feel safe.

When Alice drilled down to learn more about the pleasures mentioned in the advertising, her blushes came quickly. The descriptions alone were more risqué than anything she'd ever experienced in one of her immersive romances. Dimensions, durations, and denominations were noted for each service or product, compounding her embarrassment with details. And yet, she couldn't look away; and anyway, no one else was here, right? The taste of knowledge titillated her curiosity. When even that turned boring, Alice forced her attention to move on to playing games or watching vids from the ship's library.

Eventually, she fell into the habit of sitting and staring at the ruddy-stained cloth wrapped around her left hand. The sloop's engines sounded like a river flowing, and for the most part covered the blood pounding in her ears. She'd sit with the mechanical sound humming within the walls around her and think about cutting again to freshen the stain. Dried blood seemed dirty somehow.

Sometimes Alice wondered if it was even possible for her to *be* happy—to let herself feel content about anything. But what had her life been to this point but one trial after another? Her father had once told her about animals that suffer abuse and how, eventually, they come to expect it. Once they were conditioned to anticipate pain, the sweetest person in the world could raise a hand in love to a dog, and expecting a blow, the dog would shy away. Alice wondered if that was to be *her* life—constantly preparing herself for the next blow. Hunkering down in a corner, hiding from the light, hoping not to be noticed. And terrified that, if she were pushed like Korsakov had pushed her, she might hurt someone else—even kill them.

Or was that, 'kill again'?

Mom. Dad. Ollie.

Alice unsnapped the locket hanging around her neck. Whenever she thought she might have forgotten their faces, she'd open it and stare at the four of them, gathered as a family, happy and close. People so unaware of their own future and the danger it held, they were too ignorant to hide from it. Even sailed toward it in the *Seeker*, all the way to Drake's World.

"We'll get you back home," Ian had said as he worked, and in that moment, it'd been a comforting thought for Alice. Anyplace that wasn't Tarsus Station, ruled by Andre Korsakov and threatened by shadow-spiders. Now, in the quiet solitude of the ship's cabin with her thoughts wandering and often dark, Alice wondered what *home* really meant. The only home she'd known not aboard a ship was Sylvan Novus, but with her family gone... Their only extended family—her father's brother, his wife, and their two children—she'd barely known before boarding the *Seeker*. Marcus Keller's obsession with science and exploration, with uncovering the secrets of the universe, had been at odds with his brother Isaiah's back-to-the-land, technophobic pioneerism. Her mother and father hadn't spoken much about the rift to her or Ollie, but as Alice grew older, it'd become all too apparent. Holidays, birthdays, celebrations of any kind didn't include anyone from outside their own close foursome.

Sometimes her father's colleagues from the institute or her mother's academic friends would come to a dinner party, and Ollie and Alice would be shuffled off to amuse themselves elsewhere in the house. The rare occasion when Alice ever saw her Uncle Isaiah or his family usually involved a funeral both brothers were obligated to attend. Even then, the two families never sat together.

Had any of her extended family even looked for her? How would she know, hidden as she'd been all this time? And if they had, it was her own fault they hadn't found her, wasn't it? Morgan had emphasized, over and over again, how important it was to stay hidden with Korsakov. The documentary had carefully avoided mentioning her telekinetic ability, and all the better from Morgan's perspective. He'd warned Alice how untrustworthy he considered President Bragg and that, if the man found her, he'd likely put her in jail beside the Psyckers. So, Alice had stayed hidden—from everyone. Now she needed a new hiding place as far away from Korsakov as possible, and Sylvan Novus fit the bill. Though she had no expectation of a warm welcome from her uncle, he couldn't turn her away, right?

At least the *Archimedes* knew the way to Ionia, and that was a start. Alice squeezed her fingers into the cloth and was comforted by the dull ache in her palm. Her reflection in the window appeared very different from the clueless girl who'd stared up at the stars from the *Seeker*, wondering if she was alone in the universe. Though she felt that way now too, at least in one way. After three years of enduring Korsakov's theories and tests, Alice understood how rare her telekinetic ability was in a human. Wherever she ended up, she'd have to hide that ability. It was too easy to lose control of it. And if her estrangement from Zoey and Ian had proven anything, it was how easily others could be ruled by fear. And *they'd* started out as friends!

Imagine if people didn't even like her, then found out about her power?

Maybe they'd *want to kill* me.

The red light on the navigation panel blinked three times. Ian had warned her it would. She was approaching a broad area of space dust and heavy rock called the Shallows, where ships sometimes traveled to avoid detection. Part of the Malvian Triangle, a region popular among pirates, according to Ian. They'd leap out from the edges of the Shallows and shanghai merchant vessels traveling the more traditional shipping lanes. It had all sounded very exciting then, but as the way ahead grew more obscure, Alice found the notion of pirates leaping out to take a ship's crew unawares less and less appealing.

She distracted herself with other details Ian had passed along. Since the hazy debris of the Shallows interfered with both navigational and tracking sensors, it was known as the Blind Passage among navigators. Kind of confusing, a region with two different names. While challenging for a trained navigator, Ian had assured Alice that the autopilot could carry her safely through and the Shallows would help further obfuscate her trail.

Outside the ship, the pink-sandy dust of the region parted before the bows of the *Archimedes*. The sloop's autopilot reduced speed, as Ian had warned her it would, to reduce the potential for damaging impacts against the hull.

The *Archimedes* crawled through the stellar backwash. After staring at pinpoints of dead starlight thousands of light years distant, seeing that space had real substance was somehow comforting. The particulate matter washing over the sloop began to thicken, reflecting the ship's running lights back at her. Alice adjusted in the pilot's seat, trying to get a better view. No starlight from beyond the Shallows was visible, now. Only dimly lit dust and, too near for comfort now, the odd space rock passing by.

Thump.

Alice jumped in her seat. Another dull impact thudded against the outer hull from the rear of the ship.

"You'll hear it sometimes, too, the rocks skimming the hull," Ian said while programming the course. "They're just grazing the hull, and the deflectors are redirecting most of the impact. The autopilot will slow you down if needed. Just don't touch anything, and you'll be fine."

"Okay," she said aloud, as if he were sitting beside her. Hearing her own voice, a human voice, helped her nerves.

Thump.

This one sounded closer and came from below. She'd even felt it, through her feet on the deck. Alice scanned the console. Looking for—what?—she wasn't quite sure. A blinking red light. The calm recitation of a flight computer suggesting a breach in the hull and counting down the seconds to her imminent death. Isn't that how it happened in Ollie's adventure vids? She remembered what the doomed pilot always said in the critical scene. Alice repeated it now.

"Computer, report on hull integrity."

A woman's face, digitally rendered and smiling deferentially, appeared on the blank screen center console.

"Hello, Miss Macy!" Oh, God. She was perky. And her hair blew in loose strands around her smiling face. Some programmer's fantasy of a sexy ship's computer. "Hull integrity is one hundred percent."

"Thanks," Alice said reflexively.

"You are very welcome. Hope your day is going well!"

Alice smirked as the broad, smiling female face disappeared. She sat for a moment staring at the empty screen, then realized she too was smiling. That had almost been fun, engaging with the ship's computer. A pert, disarmingly annoying, and fake veneer who hadn't looked much older than Alice herself. Learning to hate her could be a fun pastime all its own.

Thunk.

A slightly different sound. Thicker. Like that particular rock had hit the *Archimedes* with purpose.

A red light appeared on the navigation console.

Trust the autopilot, Ian said in her head.

"Okay," Alice answered him. Part of her wished Ian really was sitting beside her, even if he hated her. When you're scared, companionship of any kind is better than none at all.

Thunk.

A second space rock with purpose. A second location. From the first point of impact, a humming began. By the time she identified the sound, a second object hit the hull in a different location.

What was happening? Ian hadn't mentioned anything about any humming.

Trust the autopilot.

It was becoming a mantra for Alice. A prayer.

The humming went on for two or three minutes. When the perky ship's computer brought itself back to life, Alice shouted in surprise.

"Hull breach," the computer reported. Her frothy enthusiasm had morphed into serious concern. "Aft section, main cabin."

"What?"

"Hull breach," the perky informant said again. "Aft section, main cabin."

Trust the autopilot.

The humming sounded more like drilling now.

"Fuck the autopilot!" Alice shouted.

Ian hadn't said anything about...

The drilling stopped. A whir came from behind her head. Alice turned to find a media drone hovering in the doorway between the pilot cabin and the main section of the ship. The cam hung in the air, scanning with its red eye until it found Alice.

"Who are you?" she whispered.

But the camera merely held its position.

Watching.

26
A BAD IDEA

"IT'S STILL A BAD IDEA," Ben said.

Sheba Toma's breath released over their private channel. It came across as a leaky hiss. Not everything about the latest short-range comms tech was an improvement. Embedded under the skin behind his right ear, the near-field communication interface had recently replaced the more easily damaged wrist-worn device. Tied into the ship's communications array, the NFC enabled them to converse over an encrypted channel without needing a battlesuit's longer-range capability.

"Of course, it's a bad idea," Toma said. *"'Here we are. Come and get us.'"*

Despite being crewed by Fleet personnel, *L'Esprit de la Terre*'s bridge hadn't been designed for military operation. There were communications and navigation stations, with the navigator doing double duty as tactical officer. The captain's chair seemed small and more likely to bruise shins than inspire confidence. To Ben, the conflicted design aesthetic was yet another sign the *Terre* should never have been designated the command ship for a mission involving pirates. But Eva Park had made it clear that she was in charge, and Commodore Crawley, designated fleet admiral of the flotilla, hadn't argued.

"So why's Crawley allowing it?" he said. Since the *Terre* and her escort fleet of six starships had entered The Frontier, Park had insisted on broadcasting a broad, local message to the pirates offering to negotiate the release of the stolen freighters. Her overtures had thus far been answered only by the background radiation of the cosmos. Her mood grew darker the longer that went on.

"Fleet Admiral *Crawley*," Toma replied, emphasizing his taskforce rank, "*is taking his direction from Rear Admiral Thorne, Commander of Third Fleet. And his boss a few rungs up the ladder is—*"

"Bragg, yeah, I know," Ben finished for her. "Still, fucking stupid."

"*Careful, Captain, you never know who's listening.*" Toma was a few hundred thousand klicks away aboard the *Navis Lusoria* with most of the 214th, but her tone added still more distance between them. "*I think the term you were looking for is 'tactically dubious.'*"

"Thanks, Colonel. I appreciate your having my six." His wry wit demanded a clapback from Toma, but there was only silence. "Colonel?"

"*Hold, Captain,*" Toma said, distracted. "*We're getting some news.*"

A gasp from the other side of the bridge pulled Ben's attention to the *Terre*'s comm officer. She'd put one hand to her ear, turning to look toward Captain Mattei's command chair. "Captain..."

"*Jesus, Stone,*" Toma said in his ear. "*Oh, man.*"

"What's happened?" he asked, still interpreting the comm officer's body language. She and Toma, he realized, must be getting the same news at the same time. And it wasn't good.

"Lieutenant?" prompted Mattei.

"It's Sirius," Toma said.

Her mouth open, the officer at communications seemed to have a hard time speaking. "It's Canis III, sir."

"What about it?" Mattei said.

"It's fallen, Stone," Toma growled. *"Fort Leyte has fallen."*

The light cruiser, *Ford of the Yalu,* and three destroyers —*Nanchang, Irkutsk,* and *Shenandoah*—came to a stop in space surrounding their flagship, the *Monolith.* On-screen they seemed to Ben like nervous children hovering around a distraught mother. The troop transport *Navis Lusoria* and the *Terre* looked the odd men out among the bigger, bristling warships. Park had agreed to cease transmitting her overtures to the pirates out of respect for the moment.

Ben found himself conflicted with a bitter mix of guilt and relief at the fall of Fort Leyte. Guilt that he, Dog Company, and the rest of the 214th hadn't been there to help defend Canis III. And relief that they hadn't been there to suffer more casualties after the massacre in the rocky valley.

Stone gathered with Tso and his platoon in the ship's galley, one of the few spaces in the *Terre* large enough to hold twenty Drop Marines. To Ben's chagrin, Eva Park elected to join them there. The three monitors in the galley snapped on, piping Fleet Admiral Crawley's image to them and all other personnel in the small fleet.

"This is Commodore Martin Crawley." His face was suitably grim. *"You have all heard by now what happened on Canis III. Let me set any rumors straight with the facts we know.*

"Approximately three weeks ago, the Arcænum attacked Fort Leyte, our foothold in the Sirius C system. The attack occurred

without provocation or warning. Although our forces fought valiantly, they were ultimately driven out of the system. We lost several corvettes and numerous transports, not to mention hundreds of Fleet and AGF personnel—an exact casualty count is not yet public knowledge. The dreadnaught Eliminator *and her remaining escorts were able to conduct an ordered retreat from Sirius C. The mind-rapers seemed content to kick us out and squat on the planet. There was no follow-up harassment of the retreating vessels."*

Strickland? Ben wondered. *What about Bradshaw?* He knew Crawley wouldn't provide specific names here, even if he knew them.

"Ladies and gentlemen," Crawley continued, *"we are now in a formal state of war with the Arcanus Collective."* He laced his fingers together and leaned back in his chair to let that sink in. Around Ben, Tso's Marines—*his* Marines—promised retribution for their new-old enemy. The Archies, every Marine pledged, would live to regret their actions. But not for long. Ben felt the same righteous fury blazing within himself.

Across the room, Eva Park looked like a stranger to him. Ben realized why—she was clearly scared—not a look he was used to seeing on her. He thought, at first, it was by the prospect of the war already upon them. But her eyes were darting back and forth like a rabbit's, assessing the tightness of the galley now broiling with unrestrained hatred. Ben tamped down his own anger and did his best to project reassurance when she caught his gaze.

This is who we are. This is what we do.

That, she sent in return, is what worries me.

"It is now more imperative than ever that we successfully complete this mission," Crawley said. *"We're going to need every advantage over the Arcænum to win this fight. So, take an hour to process this new reality we all now find ourselves in. Talk to*

your comrades. Talk to your chaplains and counselors. Hell, talk to your bartenders. Do whatever you have to do to get your minds right. Harden your hearts. In one hour, let there be no equivoca-tion, no hesitation regarding what must be done. We are one fighting force. With one mission, and only one mission, ahead of us. Crawley out."

The signal hadn't fully faded before the galley erupted. A shared look with Tso confirmed agreement—they should let the steam from their Marines boil off. Ben made his way calmly toward Eva through the rough language and chest-beating.

"Don't worry about this. We need it. They're getting their minds right, like the commodore said."

"I know," she said. "I told you before—my father was Fleet."

"Right."

"That's not what I'm concerned about," Eva said. "It's that we're not ready for this fight."

Ben took her by the elbow and lightly turned her away from the oo-rahing Marines. "Keep that sentiment to a minimum," he said, his voice low.

"What? Why?"

"Because you're in a position of power here. Your insistence on hailing the pirates non-stop, for example. That Crawley agreed to that against Colonel Toma's recommendation put you at the top of the perceived chain of command, whether that's strictly true militarily or not."

"Civilian oversight of the military is part of the balance between—"

"You're not hearing me, Miss Park."

"Eva, please," she said.

"See? That's what I mean. To the Marines in this room and all the military personnel in this fleet, you're their commander—President Bragg's right hand in country, so to speak. They might not like it, but they'll respect it as long as Crawley and Toma allow it."

"Allow it? You sound like I'm some rich daddy's girl ordering the help around—"

"That's not my intent," Ben said. "But having you in charge is an uncomfortable thing for them. It's unfamiliar. They're watching you closely. Everything you do makes an impression."

"Okay." The thought seemed to sober her. Being watched by seven ships' worth of military personnel wasn't something she'd likely considered when asserting her authority to transmit parlay messages to the pirates.

"So," he said, getting closer, "you can't go around saying things like 'we're not ready for this fight.' These folks can't hear their commander—actual or perceived—voicing defeatisms. Sometimes morale is more important than anything else in winning wars, Miss Park."

"I understand. Until now, though, that was an abstract concept for me." She paused, then said, "You know, you're not what I expected. You're not what your record reflects."

"Few people are," he said, sliding some wit back into his tone. "The rep on you is that you're an elitist, pushy ladder-climber."

"Oh, well," she said wryly, "that happens to be true."

Ben shrugged. "Sometimes the rumors are right."

"I'll keep that in mind. It's good to know how the cheap seats see you."

"Anytime you feel the need to be humbled, just let me know." His private comm channel pinged. "Colonel Toma is calling. I have to take this."

"Of course. I need to speak with Captain Mattei on the bridge anyway."

Ben engaged his NFC, pushing a path through the still-blustering Marines for Eva to follow. "One moment, Colonel. Let me get somewhere I can talk." They'd get their minds right soon enough, he thought. Afterward came the hardening of the hearts, as Crawley had said. And doing what must be done. Without conscience or mercy.

As Eva called the lift for the bridge, Ben held himself away from the raucous galley. "What do you hear, Colonel?"

"The commodore's account is accurate, as far as it goes," Toma said. *"We've been booted from the system, and it's now claimed—reclaimed, depending how you look at it—by the Arcœnum."*

"Strickland?" asked Ben. "Bradshaw?"

"Unclear. Reports of a last stand in the fort supposedly relieved by a big push from Eliminator *and her support ships. Evacuating the survivors is how we suffered most of our casualties in the engagement."*

Ben made a disgusted noise. "Why do I think Strickland was already safely in orbit and it was Bradshaw who led the fight planetside?"

There was a slow sigh on the other end. *"Not the time, Captain. We need a united front, now."*

"Understood, ma'am. I was just saying the same thing to Miss Park. I'll watch my mouth from here on out."

"That'll be a refreshing change," Toma said. But it was ribbing, not a reproach.

"It was the beacon, wasn't it? The one the Archie rigged up with the stolen tech from the fort."

Silence from Toma, as if she were debating going there. *"That's speculation at this point, but it's reasonable speculation."*

"Maybe if we'd gotten to it sooner..."

"*Unproductive, Captain. We couldn't know there was an Archie on-planet from a war ended fifty years ago. Or that he'd called for help, until we found the equipment. Remember the dampening field he had over the area.*"

"I suppose."

"*Don't suppose,*" Toma said. "*Internalize it as fact. Hang on...*"

Ben heard the click of Toma's muting the channel. A passing crewman offered him a salute, and Ben returned it.

Toma keyed back in. "*Do you believe in coincidences, Captain?*"

"Not usually."

"*The Treasure Fleet just popped up on long-range sensors. It's just sitting there, several light years away. And on the heels of the news about Sirius...*"

"Sitting there?"

"*Stationary in space.*"

Ben thought about it. "Technically, not a coincidence though, Colonel."

"*Explain.*"

"Canis III happened weeks ago. Even communications via subspace suffer from light delay at that distance. The Treasure Fleet showing up is weird as hell, but I wouldn't call it a coincidence."

"*Awfully suspect timing, at the very least,*" Toma said. "*And the battle might have happened weeks ago, but the news is just now making the military rounds. I wouldn't put it past the pirates to have moles.*"

"Point taken," Ben said. "So we're back to your point of unlikely coincidences."

"*Makes me think the Archies might be working with the pirates,*" Toma said.

That was something that had never occurred to him. The

thought of humans, any humans, working with enemy aliens was simply outside his realm of consideration. That Toma, who usually waited till sunrise before assuming a new day would start, had suggested it was as eerie as it was intriguing.

"Sure you're not just being paranoid, Colonel?"

Sure you're not just rationalizing, Captain? Ben jibed at himself.

"Maybe," she answered. "Doesn't mean it's not true."

His comm pinged, announcing another incoming request. It was Eva Park.

"Her highness is calling. Where do you want me, Colonel?"

"Right where you are," Toma said. *"I'll consult with Commodore Crawley and get back to you. And make sure Tso keeps his Marines under control. Turn that testosterone to fighting the Archies."*

"Solid copy. Stone, out."

"—poses no real threat to the *Terre*."

Exiting the lift to the bridge, Ben caught the tail end of the commodore's proclamation. Eva Park stood next to Captain Mattei. The forward screen showed a split image, the left half with Crawley's face, the right showing a small, dingy, rather featureless ship hanging off the *Terre*'s starboard bow.

"Commodore, I agree," Eva Park said. "The first priority, especially now as you said in your fleetwide address, must be securing those freighters."

"What's going on?" Ben whispered to Mattei's comm officer.

"It's the pirates," she said, nodding at the screen. "They've responded to Park's hail. That little ship out there, the *Junkyard Dog*, is their white flag."

"Is it now."

"Yeah."

"Huh." Just another convenient coincidence of timing? The defeat at Sirius, the unexpected appearance of the stolen freighters, and the sudden arrival of the criminals who took them to "negotiate." Maybe Sheba wasn't so paranoid after all. Ben moved to Mattei's other side.

"Commodore, apologies for my tardiness," he said. "I was helping Lieutenant Tso get his Marines squared away. Could I get caught up?"

"Colonel?" Crawley prompted.

Toma advanced a half step on-screen. "The freighters are at extreme range, about three light years, cloaked under RAM. *Our* assumption"—and Toma's emphasis made it clear to Ben that it wasn't *her* assumption—"is that the pirates put them there thinking they were out of standard sensor range—which they are. But not out of range of the *Monolith*'s newest generation sensor tech. No sign of any escort vessels."

"Really," Ben said. So, the prize without the muscle for protection? Ballsy. Or just the pirates' lack of awareness that the *Monolith* was the latest and greatest Fleet had to offer?

"What's RAM?" Eva asked.

"Radiation-absorbent material," Mattei supplied. "It's a bit archaic. In the old days of so-called stealth tech, planes and ships were built out of polymers that absorbed radar or other radiation trying to detect them. So, they'd seem invisible. That theory was adapted during the Specter War to use drone satellites to throw up a detection-bending web around a ship or fleet to hide it. Made it undetectable to ship sensors."

"You're making my case for me, Captain," Crawley said. "That broken-down pinnace off your starboard bow—the *Junkyard Dog*, is it?"—poses no threat to the *Terre* whatsoever, as I've said. Boasts minimal armament. We're only ten minutes away from the freighters by translight drive. And you've got a full platoon of AGF Marines aboard should they try anything especially stupid, like boarding. Miss Park, you can have your parlay while we secure the freighters. The pirates likely don't even know we've discovered them. The *Monolith* is the most advanced starship ever built. The technology they're using to hide the freighters? Nearly a century old. This is a no-brainer."

Toma shifted nervously on-screen next to the commodore. Few others would have noticed the subtlety of her body language, but Ben did. She was not in agreement with the ranking officer, and Ben knew why. Crawley was taking a lot for granted, namely the superiority of Fleet technology in the face of pirate-scavenged, outmoded tech. Likely, he was right. But add the confluence of recent circumstances into the mix, and Toma's uneasiness was understandable. But she was usually as stoic as a weathered rock, and her nervousness now infected Ben, too.

"This communication is encrypted, right?" he asked the comm officer.

"Of course," she said, half offended at the question.

"I agree, Commodore," Park said. "Secure the freighters while we talk terms here."

"This is a bad idea," Ben said. Park and Mattei regarded him, and Toma and Crawley on-screen also shifted their attention to him. Toma did not seem happy, and for once, he wasn't the reason for her lack of joy.

"Thank you for your input, Captain," Crawley said. "But I have absolute confidence in our ability to deal with a few pirates who have no idea of the advancements in modern warfare their facing here today." He cleared his throat. "Captain Mattei, make arrangements for Miss Park's negotiation. I'll take the fleet, secure the freighters, and update you once we know their drives are online. At that point, we can decide whether to blow the *Junkyard Dog*"—he spat the name out—"straight back to the junkyard."

Fucking, Ben mouthed to Toma.

Stupid, she answered on-screen.

"Aye, Commodore," Mattei acknowledged. "Lieutenant, hail the pinnace."

"Finally," Eva Park said. "Progress!"

27

POSITIONS OF POWER

EVA HAD HOPED to host the pirate representative aboard the *Terre* for face-to-face talks. Especially after she learned her opposite was a woman. That intrigued her, perhaps because she'd expected a historical cliché to sit down at the table with her. Maybe he'd even thump his pegleg dramatically to make his point.

The desire to have the pirate envoy on the *Terre* had been less about courtesy and more about home turf—to start talks aboard a vessel strange to her, to have her distracted by its unfamiliarity and the ever-present specter of capture. But Sayyida al-Hurra had refused the invitation, not even bothering to snub Eva herself. She'd sent her regrets via subspace, text only, relayed through an intermediary.

So, Eva settled for rearranging the small ready room near the bridge. Ben Stone was amused when Eva asked him to lower the lighting by ten percent and adjust the camera lens to ensure the background behind her included the widest window angle possible showing the stars. She wanted to project power, Eva explained, and she'd learned from dealing with the media that success in doing so required a bit of stage management.

"Is there any way to lower the camera's position so I'm looking down into it?" Eva asked.

"Well," Ben replied, rubbing his chin, "I suppose I could rip the computer console off the desk and put the comm panel on the floor. Or we could find you a highchair."

"Hilarious."

"I thought so. Want me to—?"

"Never mind, Captain."

"Whatever you say, ma'am."

Truth was, Eva was nervous, and self-aware enough to know that all her efforts at optimizing her environment reflected that. Ben's obvious delight in chiding her brought that home. Excited, but nervous. The stakes were much higher here than they had been in Colorado, and yet that encounter was on her mind as she prepped for al-Hurra. The Alliance was in a formal state of war. She wondered if the pirates knew about that yet and, if they did, how it might affect the talks. President Bragg hadn't yet taken to subspace to address the situation with the public, but rumors of war traveled fast. Leo was no doubt pouring over a speech at this very moment, worrying over every syllable, the rhythm, how the takeaways would land with listeners. Staff writers would suggest a word or phrase, and it fell to Leo to choose the precise language that would give the people hope. *That morale thing*, Eva thought, remembering Ben's lecture in the galley. She didn't envy Leo. He'd be walking a tightrope of rhetoric to capture the significance of the moment for posterity without making Bragg appear too focused on his political legacy. Leo must be in his own private purgatory-heaven right about now.

The comm panel chimed on the desk.

"She's early," Ben said.

Eva seated herself at the desk, yanked down her blouse to

smooth it, made sure she wasn't showing too much cleavage, and then pushed a lock of hair out of the way. "How do I look?"

"Anxious. Take a breath."

She did, and then a second time. The comm chimed again. A final exhale, and Eva accepted the call.

"Hail from the *Junkyard Dog*," the comm officer relayed.

"Lieutenant? There's about five minutes left before—"

"Yes, ma'am, but Miss al-Hurra is insisting on speaking with you now," the young officer said. "She sounds ... upset."

"Well," mumbled Ben, "this is starting well."

Eva shot him a look. *Remember, you're on my side.*

Without further comment, Ben sat down beside her. She'd be the face of the dealmaking, but she'd invited him to sit with her in the shot. Having a decorated Marine captain and humanity's current flagbearer beside her could only help reinforce the strength she intended to project. Maybe his rugged good looks would even distract the woman on the other side of the virtual table. Now, wouldn't that be nice for a change? Having the man sit quiet and look pretty while the women talked.

"Just keep your mouth shut," she murmured, "and everything will be fine."

The screen flashed to life.

"Greetings, Miss al-Hurra," Eva said, hoping she'd pronounced the name right. Dark eyes reminiscent of Marcos. But unlike her lighter Castilian skin tone, Sayyida al-Hurra's features had a burnished look. Mediterranean? "It's good to finally meet you."

"Why has your fleet left the area?" al-Hurra demanded without prelude. *"What's going on here?"*

The outburst surprised Eva with its vigor. She put on a look of puzzlement to buy time while she gauged her opponent's tone and expression. Eva exchanged an innocent look with Ben to sell it.

"I'm sure I don't know what you mean."

Al-Hurra's eyes narrowed. *"I'm sure that you do."*

Ben leaned in, directing his mouth away from the cam's mic. "The cat jumped over the moon," he whispered. "The dish ran away with the spoon."

Now Eva really was confused.

"I'm informing you the fleet departed a while ago," he said patiently. "You're on."

Ah.

"Miss al-Hurra, Captain Stone here has just informed me that our fleet has jumped away briefly. The details, of course, are classified—even from me, if you can believe it!" That's it. Build a sisterly bond. No deception here. You're both out of the loop. "I'm sure it's nothing to worry about."

The signal fritzed. She could see al-Hurra speaking but couldn't hear what she said.

"Weird," Ben said.

"I'm sorry, could you repeat?" Eva requested. "There was interference."

"I said, I don't believe you."

Eva felt herself growing irritated. The discussions had begun rocky and seemed headed for rockier shores still. She'd scripted an entire dialogue to keep the pirates occupied while Crawley and Toma secured the freighters. In retrospect, that plan was doomed to fail. The absence of their escort was hardly a detail to go unnoticed.

"I don't really care what you believe," Eva said. "We came out here to negotiate in good faith for the release of our ships and materiel."

"Good faith?" spat al-Hurra. *"From Piers Bragg? From the Alliance military?"*

If the original plan wasn't going to work, maybe it was time to call an audible. Eva cocked her head. "Personal insults are beneath the demands of the moment, Miss al-Hurra."

"And what the hell does that mean?"

Affecting a grave expression, Eva said, "I assume you've heard about the attack in the Sirius system?"

al-Hurra hesitated, considering her next words carefully. Calculating, perhaps, if she should admit to knowing a war had just broken out.

"I have."

"Then you should also know how important it is for the Alliance—for humanity—that we secure those freighters."

"Vital to the war effort, eh?" al-Hurra probed. *"Tell me more."*

Ben cleared his throat.

"Nice try," Eva said without acknowledging him. "But know this—every hiccup in commerce, every disruption in the supply chain will benefit the Arcanus Collective. And undermines your own chances for survival."

A snowy signal clouded al-Hurra's response, but not the facetious look she gave Eva.

"Say again?" Eva prompted.

"I said you have a flare for the dramatic, Miss Park."

Eva sat back away from the camera. Was this woman so self-centered that she couldn't see how helping the enemy, even inadvertently, could lead to the extinction of her own species?

Ben reached forward to mute their mic.

"What are you doing?" Eva said.

"I don't think she's here."

"What?"

"al-Hurra. I don't think she's aboard that ship."

On-screen, al-Hurra threw up her hands. *"Now, I can't hear you!"*

Eva held up a just-a-second finger. To Ben, she said, "What are you talking about?"

"The comm interference. Happens in subspace sometimes, usually the result of radiation or ionization along the signal's path."

"Yeah, so?" Eva said.

"She's supposed to be in the ship right next door," Ben said.

Eva regarded him a moment. The repeating signal she'd broadcast since entering The Frontier had specifically requested a personal meeting for parlay. The pirates, when they appeared, had agreed. Now, this.

Reengaging comms, Eva said, "Let's talk about good faith, then."

"What now, drama queen?" al-Hurra said. From off-screen there was mumbling, but al-Hurra waved it to silence.

"Your hail promised an in-person meeting," Eva said bluntly. "And you're not even in the same region of space."

On the comm console, a notification from the bridge chimed. Eva ignored it.

"Well, there it is then," al-Hurra said, sitting back. A thin smile formed on her lips. *"Our little ruse discovered."* She turned to the person off-screen, asking, *"They're engaged with the freighters?"*

Nodding acknowledgment of the answer, al-Hurra returned her attention to Eva. *"Negotiations are over."* She leaned forward and cut the feed.

"What the hell?" Eva said.

The console chimed again, and Ben accepted the call from the bridge. Mattei's face appeared. "We've got a problem. The fleet's been attacked."

"Attacked?" Ben said.

"Are they crazy?" whispered Eva. "I'm calling her back!"

"Don't bother," Ben said as he stood. "I'm on my way,

Captain." Feeling suddenly alone and unprotected, Eva sighed out her exasperation and sprang after him.

"What's going on, Captain?" Ben asked as he led Eva onto the bridge.

"The freighters were bait," he said, not sparing them a glance. Mattei sat at a station normally empty for presidential ferrying. He was staring at a screen displaying red and blue symbols. Eva hadn't seen a tactical map in at least a decade, not since living with her parents. She and Ben peered over Mattei's shoulder.

"What do you mean 'bait?'" she said, her spine tingling at the word.

"Just what I said." Mattei sighed. "The escort fleet took up position around the freighters. Colonel Toma and the 214th launched in shuttles to board and secure them through force of arms." He addressed Ben, saying, "The pirates launched embers —from the freighters, if you can believe it!"

"Embers?" Eva asked.

"Electromagnetic burst bombs," Ben said. "Used to disable ship's systems, short them out. They make a starship dead in space until the engineer reboots systems and replaces any shorted circuitry. It's a very old tactic that..." He paused to think it through, then said to Mattei, "You're telling me it was success-ful? It should have been easy enough for the PDCs to neutralize them beyond their effective range."

At least that was something she wouldn't have to ask about, Eva thought. Point-defense cannons, the shield of slugs rapid-fired from a starship to neutralize inbound threats, like nuclear weapons.

"And they would have," Mattei said, "if they hadn't been so tight on the freighters to secure them."

"They were too close?" Ben ventured. Understanding dawned. "Crawley was too cocky."

"Yeah," confirmed the *Terre*'s captain.

"Even the *Monolith* with all its latest-greatest tech?"

"Even the *Monolith*," Mattei said.

"Explain." To Eva, it was beginning to smell like testosterone around her again. And she was stressing too much to be patient. "And please speak civilian!"

Ben regarded Eva a moment without amusement. "The fleet moved in close to board the freighters, which apparently is what the pirates were waiting on. Drones launched and got embers inside the commodore's defense perimeter—sorry, the effective range of his point-defense cannons. But I'm still confused, Captain. If they detonated the EMBBs, wouldn't the pirates be disabled too? And our hulls are shielded now—designed to protect against embers. It doesn't make any sense."

"Not if you think conventionally, no. But that's the really bad news here," Mattei said. "The pirates used clampers."

Eva looked from Mattei to Stone, expecting a quick explanation. Ben's eyes widened in shock.

"Clampers?" he whispered.

"Clampers," Mattei confirmed grimly.

Blowing out her breath, Eva demanded, "What the hell is a clamper?"

"Clampers, Miss Park," Mattei explained, "are Archie tech used in the last war to drill through hulls. Once the hole is there, the Archies would drop psychic enhancers inside the ships to facilitate mind-control of the crew."

Ben muttered, "Only this time, the pirates dropped embers instead. Maybe Toma was right."

"Archie tech?" Eva said to Mattei. "How can that be?"

"Maybe the pirates and the Arcœnum *are* working together," Ben said.

Eva and Mattei stared at him. "That's not possible," Eva said, though with each word conviction waned. Maybe al-Hurra's uncaring attitude about hampering the Alliance war effort had been more than merely self-centered. Maybe it'd been strategic.

"Lieutenant," Ben said to the comm officer, "hail Colonel Toma. Priority, tightbeam."

She looked to Mattei for permission to do so. He nodded.

"If the pirates and the Archies are working together..." Ben said.

Eva didn't need to hear the rest to know what such a coalition would mean. If outdated tech could so easily disable the Alliance's latest prototype warship, what chance did their less sophisticated vessels have against the Arcœnum? Add to that a fifth column of human traitors—masters of space-based guerilla warfare, mind you—in their own backyard... Eva swallowed into a throat gone dry as a desert.

"Are you telling me," she whispered, "we're defenseless?" And was she referring to the *Terre* or the whole of the Alliance?

Ben Stone moved off to talk to Toma. The comm officer said, "Captain Mattei, it's a hail from the *Junkyard Dog*. It's...um..."

"Play it, Lieutenant."

"Um, but sir—"

"Play it!"

She complied, and the bridge filled with mean-girl laughter.

"*This is Cinnamon Gauss aboard the* Junkyard Dog! *I just wanted you to know who's about to kick your ass!*"

"Who the—" Eva began, but the feed dropped.

"Sir!" The navigator gasped. "Incoming drones!"

Mattei stood up so swiftly that Eva was almost knocked flat.

"Stone! Deploy your Marines. Tell your man Tso to get squads to engineering, environmental, and the weapons locker. And get a squad up here to defend the bridge."

Ben dropped Toma and called Tso to carry out the captain's order.

"Navigator," Mattei said, "secure the ship. Boarding protocol."

"Boarding proto...? Sir, we haven't even practiced that since—"

"Now! Prepare to repel boarders!"

Above their heads, there was a metallic thump from outside the ship. It tolled like a deadened bell. The sound reminded Eva of the breach exercises she'd endured on space stations as a kid. *How fast can you get into your vacc-suit?* She could still hear the teacher's quiet urgency. When the grinding of the drill began overhead, her skin grew clammy and cold.

"They're landing all over the hull, Captain," the navigator reported.

"Oh, hell," Mattei said, eyes cast upward. "Lieutenant, send shipwide—power blackout likely imminent."

"Sir," she said, her voice barely perceptible, "aye, sir."

The look on the young lieutenant's face reflected Eva's own feeling of being at the mercy of circumstances beyond her control. In times of crisis, civilians naturally looked to leadership to feel secure. To know that someone was in charge. Someone who knew what to do. Mattei's apparent surprise fell far short of demonstrating competence.

"Captain, pull the plug on the emergency backups," Ben suggested. "Crash the system."

"What? Why?"

"Can't short out what isn't operational, sir. If they fire off embers to crash the primary systems, restart the emergency systems after the burst. At least we'll have lights and atmo."

Mattei hesitated to employ the tactic. Or maybe he was just thinking it through.

"Captain, we don't have much time," Ben said.

Nodding, Mattei said, "Lieutenant, get engineering on the horn. Hard crash the emergency backups if they have to, but get them offline."

"Aye, sir."

Eva hated herself for being so scared. She thought of her ludicrous stage preparations for the parlay. Lighting and setting and camera angles. What a joke. Sayyida al-Hurra had prepared for a real fight. And all of them—Eva, Crawley, Mattei, all of them—had been lured straight into the mousetrap by their own egos.

She saw Mattei looking at her. "Captain?" she said, fishing for some of that reassurance from the *Terre*'s commander. And doing so unashamedly. "What do we do?"

"We do what we have to, Miss Park," Mattei said. "That's all we can ever do."

Ben grabbed her by the elbow. "Come with me," he said.

28

MADWOMAN PIRATE

BEN DRAGGED Eva to the lift.

"Where are we going?"

Grunting, Ben said, "Someplace less a target than the bridge."

"And where—"

"Miss Park, please shut the hell up." Ben patted his sidearm as the door swiped shut. "*This* is how we'll be negotiating now." The lift began its descent, and he keyed his NFC to establish a private commlink. "Tso, report."

She looked at him open-mouthed, anger blooming inside her. The lift began its descent. While he talked to Tso, Eva felt something else too, something solid. It took a moment to recognize what she'd been looking for on the bridge—feeling protected. She kind of hated Ben for being the one providing that comfort. Or maybe it was herself she hated for needing it.

"I'm taking the package to the cargo hold," Ben was saying. "Send a squad to rendezvous as soon as you've secured the vital areas of the ship per Captain Mattei." He paused to listen to the reply. The lift's hydraulics sounded like a slow heartbeat as they passed decks on the way to the small ship's underbelly. But the soothing rhythm of the lift helped calm Eva's nerves. "Coordinate as best you can, and if he gives you any guff, tell Mattei those are *my* orders. Once those embers fire off, comms will be—"

The lights snapped off. The emergency brakes screeched, and the lift ground to a halt. The sudden stop threw Eva against Ben with a small squeak of alarm. Ben's body pressed her against the lift wall for a moment before she felt the heaviness leaving her body. The soles of her boots released their grip on the floor.

"Uhhh..." she whispered, then understood what was happening. The electromagnetic pulse had knocked out ship's gravity. Like all other systems aboard, the AG was powered by the *Terre*'s reactor.

"Tso!" Ben barked. "Tso, come in."

She could smell his sweat. Her hands came up between them to push him off her, but he held her fast.

"Ben, please."

"Quiet! Tso, respond."

The reinforced smartfatigues he wore felt bulky against her thinner business suit. They were rising, slowly and together, in the pitch black of the lift.

"Well, shit," Ben said, "I hope he got all that. Tso's on his own until comms are restored." He maintained his grip on her arms but opened some space between them. "You all right?"

"Yes," she said. She smelled her own sweat now, and it was different from his. Hers smelled like liquid fear. Jesus, was she really so easily rattled when shit got real?

"Stop pushing me away," he said. "The more you move, the more dangerous it'll be when the AG comes back. Try to stay still."

He let her go but only to reach around her to get purchase on the wall. "Hold on to me," he said. "Try to keep your back against the wall, soles of your feet pointing down, if you can. I'll do my best to keep us anchored."

"How long till the lift comes back online?" she asked, complying. Her fists bunched the rigid material covering his chest. Ben cautiously paced his hands down the wall, recovering the half-meter or so they'd floated upward in the zero-g. When Eva's feet found the deck again, it felt like a trapdoor ready to spring open any moment.

"Depends on how fried the systems are," Ben answered. "If Mattei got the emergency systems offline in time, they should be rebooting now. Couple minutes, maybe."

"Will that help us?"

"Sure. AG and lifts are priority systems needed for damage control."

"Right."

The mundane soundtrack of a ship's systems was something you got used to traveling in space. The quiet vibration of the engines resonating in the deck, the soft flow of the environmental system recycling air and regulating temperature. In the close blackout of the stalled lift, all that was missing. In its place, Ben's breathing and Eva's own rapid heartbeat thudding in her ears. When the lift creaked, it sounded unnaturally loud. An answer seemed to come from deeper within the *Terre*, a sympathetic groaning of the ship's superstructure as the pressure inside the ship resisted the vacuum of space beyond the hull.

The emergency lights kicked in overhead, bathing them in a crimson glow. Her eyes adjusted, and Eva found herself staring up into the scruff of Ben Stone's five o'clock shadow. The floor became solid, reliable again beneath her feet. The lift's controls came online and they began to move.

"Good job, Mattei," Ben murmured.

"Captain Stone..." Eva said, releasing his fatigues.

"Yeah? Oh." He stepped back, his sudden awkwardness amusing Eva. And here she'd thought their closeness had only made her uncomfortable.

The lift once again slowed to a stop.

"We're here," Ben said.

The doors opened to a red-lit deck. Ben drew his sidearm and motioned for Eva to stay behind him while he scouted the corridor.

"Follow me," he said. "Stay close."

Ben slid along the wall, heading aft near as Eva could reckon. She followed, flattened against the wall behind him.

"Where are we going?" she whispered.

"Storage Bay. Big space, a few places to hide. Not a strategic location they'll target, I think."

"You think?" she said.

From somewhere above and behind them, a loud *clang!* sounded.

"On a ship like this, it's the people who are important. Not ship's stores or passenger luggage."

His reasoning was sound. They passed a wide door marked Storage Bay 1. It was double-sealed against a potential hull breach from without.

"We're not going in?" Eva asked.

"Never choose door number one," Ben said lightly, reaching the controls on the pressure door of Storage Bay 2. "You did well back there, by the way."

"What?"

"In the lift," Ben said before cursing the door's stubborn security lock. "You kept your head. That's always half the battle."

Huh.

And here she'd been feeling scared to death. Maybe life in

politics had taught her something. Like how to look brave, even when you didn't feel that way. Maybe especially then.

The pressure door unsealed with a motorized sigh. He reconnoitered the bay, then motioned her inside. "Come on."

The space was small and largely empty save for cargo secured to the deck. Logos Eva recognized emblazoned the sides of the containers. The door to the corridor slid closed.

"Find a comfortable spot over there," Ben said, indicating she should hide behind the largest container. "I'm gonna see if I can figure out what's happening."

She made her way to a position around a corner of the larger of the three containers, which belonged to Mao-Wierzbowski Conglomerated Foods. The biggest food manufacturer in the Sol System and a longtime provider of daily meal kits to the tens of thousands of employees working for Bragg Industries and its subsidiaries. And now, the prime holder of the contract to supply the Alliance military—their reward for generous contributions to Bragg's presidential campaign. Sometimes Eva's head swam with how random the vast universe could be, recent events included. But political payoffs were one constant never failing in their predictability.

"Tso, respond," Ben said, engaging his NFC.

"I thought comms were out."

Ben waved Eva to silence. From the half she could hear, Eva learned that multiple fire teams had breached the *Terre*, aiming exactly for the same vital sections Captain Mattei had told Ben to protect with his Marines.

"They're pirates, Osira," Ben said. "Your guys should be able to ... no, I get it. Did you get a squad to the bridge?" She watched Ben's reactions to what he was hearing. It didn't look good. "I have the package secured and will maintain position. Ping my location—and get that squad down here ASAP! Stone, out."

He began trying several command combinations on the wall comms, each resulting in a negative chime.

"What are you doing?" she asked.

"Trying to contact the bridge."

"Your Marines—it sounds like a tough fight," she said.

Ben grunted. "You could say that. How the hell these guys can go toe-to-toe with AGF Marines ... they always run, the pirates. Scurry like cockroaches from the light."

Eva glanced at the storage bay around them. "If you haven't noticed, there's not much light at the moment."

"Funny."

"Hey," she said, "yeah, I *was* trying to be funny. Lessen the tension a little. How about you lighten up? You're supposed to be the one who's cool under fire, Hero of Canis III."

Ben ceased his efforts at the panel and shot a harsh look at Eva. "Don't call me that."

She'd thrown the name at him to make herself feel better. She hadn't considered how it might land following Fort Leyte's loss. "Sorry. I wasn't thinking."

"Yeah, well...try doing more of that and speaking less."

Ben was angry, but he sounded tired, too. He was punching the panel controls like they could launch missiles at the pirate ship—or maybe the Arcœnum back on Canis III. Eva sighed, trying to think of something profound and supportive to say.

The blaring of the ship's klaxon saved her the trouble.

"*Breach, deck four,*" the *Terre*'s computer announced shipwide.

Ben pressed another series of buttons, and the audible alert ceased howling in the storage bay.

"What's happened?" Eva asked. "Besides the obvious."

"The pirates just boarded the ship a couple decks above us." He drew his sidearm again. She started to say something, but

Ben held up his hand. "Go, Tso." He listened to his commlink as the other man reported in.

"Let me hear, Captain," Eva said. All this being out of control was getting to her. "Please." Without breaking his conversation with Tso, Ben complied, patching into the wall comm panel.

"*—pressed hard in engineering,*" Tso was saying. "*They've hit every major target on the ship, and now there's a breach two decks above you.*"

"We heard," Ben said.

"How could there be so many of them?" Eva wondered. "All from that one little ship?"

Ben ignored her. "Ozzy, any word from Mattei?"

As if conjured by his question, a bosun's whistle sounded, a herald announcing that shipwide communications was about to slave all wall comm units.

"*Attention all personnel. This is Captain Mattei. I'm ordering all ship's personnel and AGF Marines to stand down. I repeat: all personnel, lay down your arms. L'Esprit de la Terre has surrendered.*"

"My ass!" Ben shouted.

"Captain?" Eva couldn't believe it either. Her fish-flopping-on-land fear was back.

But he'd already muted the wall speaker and was calling Tso on his NFC again. "Tso, ignore that bastard. Your Marines are *not* to stand down." There was a pause, and Ben's face hardened. "Tso, acknowledge!" He paused for reply, then jerked his head left and turned off the embedded comm unit. "Jammed!"

The pressure door cracked a few millimeters. Someone was overriding the door's lock with manual controls.

"Hello in there!"

"Get back!" Ben hissed at Eva. The gap in the door

widened. Ben brought up his pistol, backing toward Eva and the container. "Stay in cover!"

With a screech, the door slammed open. Ben slipped behind the container, pushing Eva farther back. She could just make out four blurry figures dashing into the bay and finding cover behind the smaller containers. Ben squeezed off two rounds. They echoed like cannon fire in the bay, the ricochets pinging off the wall.

"Nice try, jackass!" A woman's voice, young. And sounding half-crazed. "Didn't you hear the captain?"

"I heard him!" Ben yelled.

"Then for ole Eva's sake there, you'd best put down that pistol, buckaroo."

"It's down." Ben taunted. "Come on out!"

"Ha! Good one!"

Eva did a double-take. The woman with the mad voice had referred to her by name.

"Only one way this ends, poster boy," the woman said.

Now it was Ben who scoffed. "Our escort fleet will be back anytime now. We'll see how it turns out then. I'd dust off while you still can."

"You've got a million of 'em, huh? But I wouldn't count on your Fleeter friends! They're a little busy right now not freezing to death."

Eva could hear movement, but it bounced around the walls of the near-empty bay, making it impossible to track. Her eyes didn't help much. The deep red hue of the emergency lighting infected every inch of the room, creating odd shadows.

"I see a pirate, I shoot a pirate!" Ben promised.

"Aw, that's not nice."

More shuffling. Ben squeezed off two more shots in the madwoman's direction.

"Keep wasting your ammo! We've got all day!" she said.

"Like hell you do," Ben replied. He began dividing his attention between the main door, which now stood open, and the bay's whispering dark corners behind Eva.

"Hey, I've got an idea! I'm gonna put my weapon away. Let's parlay!" the woman said. "Isn't that why you came all this way, Eva-baby?"

Ben spared Eva a glance, and she could tell he had the same question she did—why was the crazy woman calling her by name? "Probably accessed the passenger manifest," he said. "She's just trying to get inside our heads."

It's working, Eva thought.

She felt a presence behind her before she heard the heavy boots. Eva turned in time to see a massive shape come around the back side of the container. "Ben!"

Before he could swing his pistol around, Eva was grabbed up by the neck and swung around to face Ben. The pirate held her up as a shield.

"Drop it," the pirate said. Another woman, Eva realized. A rather large, muscular woman. Eva struggled in her grasp, but the pirate held her off the floor in a vise-like grip.

From behind Ben, a second woman appeared. Spiky hair, slight form, much shorter than the giant holding Eva. The smaller woman cocked her left hip out, holding her pistol on Ben almost lazily.

"I see you've met Torque," the madwoman said. "Hello, Eva Park." Too busy trying to breathe, Eva didn't respond. "You heard my friend there, poster boy. Drop it."

"Go to hell," Ben said.

The muscle-bound Torque wrenched Eva's arm up behind her back. She cried out. Her eyes welled up with pain.

"There's a reason she's got that name," the madwoman said. Her other hand stabilized her pistol, and now she held it on Ben more steadily than needed from a meter away. "She specializes in broken arms. But don't worry, Eva. Torque's in a good mood today. Nothing worse than a dislocation, promise."

"Ben..." Eva whispered. "It's over."

He still seemed unwilling to give up. "My Marines will—"

"Your Marines are locked down," the madwoman assured him. The flippant attitude had vanished, replaced by the surety of the victorious. "Drop it or I drop you, Captain Stone."

Ben still hesitated. "You pirates put a lot of stock in your word," he said. "Promise of safe passage for Miss Park. No harm will come to her?"

"Oh, agreed!" The glibness was back. "We wouldn't think of harming her ... much."

Ben looked at the woman who, despite her slight build, was clearly the leader of the band of four that now had them surrounded. All women, all holding their weapons trained on Ben. Except the one holding Eva off the ground.

He lowered his pistol and flipped it around butt-first. The madwoman took it.

"Who the hell are you, anyway?" Ben asked.

"I'm Cinnamon Gauss, poster boy. And I always keep my word. Like that promise I made earlier."

The large woman, Torque, released Eva and set her lightly back on the deck. She even brushed the back of Eva's suit off. Eva stood there, happy to be able to breathe freely again and massaging her freed arm.

The *Terre*'s normal lighting snapped back on.

"What promise?" Ben asked.

Gauss flashed him a sideways smile that spread out the brownish freckles on her cheeks. "To kick your ass, of course! Keep up with current events, man!" She motioned toward the corridor. "Let's go, Captain Hero."

Ben and Eva followed the other two pirates from the storage bay. Gauss and Torque brought up the rear.

"And no funny business, okay?" Gauss said. "Ha-ha or otherwise. No one's allowed to be funnier than me, that's just the rules. And as for the other kind of funny business, just remember that Miss Park here will foot that bill. Got it?"

"You're crazy," Ben said as they were herded toward the lift.

"Best you remember that," Gauss said. "Now, move! We're burning starlight!"

THE *JUNKYARD DOG* WAS A PATCHED-TOGETHER, Grade-A, piece-of-shit pinnace. Blackened blast lines along her hull, a main hatch reinforced with recycled bolts redrilled too many times. Weaponry that looked like, if fired, they might implode the ship with their recoil. If Gauss's fire team hadn't been poking them in the back with weapons, Ben would have refused to board on principle.

"Where are my Marines?" he demanded, sitting next to Eva. Captain Mattei, also a prisoner with his hands bound, took the seat opposite in the cramped ship. Gauss's four-woman crew had dispersed to duty stations. The short, spiky-haired woman with the attitude was, against all reason, their acknowledged leader.

"They're fine, hotshot," Gauss said. "We don't kill those who serve unless we have to."

"How considerate of you," Eva said.

"It is, actually," Gauss snapped back, "since you don't extend the same courtesy to us. This won't be a long trip, but it won't be a planet hop either. Pipe down and enjoy the ride."

"In this thing?" Ben snarked.

"Watch your mouth, pretty boy!" Gauss said. "That's my baby you're talking about!"

"Ugly baby..."

"She'll do the job!"

Ben's grunt was dubious. "Speaking of doing the job, you don't have enough people here."

"What?"

"You locked down five Marine squads and trained Fleet personnel and used the people I see here taking us hostage. How'd you pull that off with four poorly trained—"

"Pirate magic!" Gauss exclaimed, splaying her fingers wide. "Look out the porthole, Einstein. And like I said, no funny business. Torque especially doesn't like funny business."

She offered Ben a smirk of triumph before heading forward. Torque folded her thick forearms and briefly loomed over them with a menacing look, then followed her captain.

Ben peered through the small window. Three ships stood off the *Dog* to starboard. The graffiti painting the bow on the nearest vessel named it the *Sorcerer's Apprentice*. The names of the other two ships were too far away to read.

"It smells in here," Eva said. "Like a brothel wiped down with dirty socks soaked in machine oil."

"That's probably pretty accurate," Ben said. "Brothel expert, are you?"

She flashed him a get-stuffed look.

Ben looked around carefully, determined to make the trip worthwhile and at least gather some intelligence on the pirates. First impressions were appalling. The *Junkyard Dog* was a dark, close workhorse of a ship—built for speed and maneuverability and rated for both, say, a century earlier, when it'd seen better days. The sublight engine spun up like a braying donkey caught in a bear trap. The hull shook, the walls shook, and unsecured equipment rattled against the deck. Outside, the

Sorcerer's Apprentice and her sister ships also fired up their drives.

Where the hell is the fleet? Ben wondered. *Where's Toma?*

"Is this thing safe?" Eva whispered.

Ben turned skeptical eyes her way. "You're joking, right?"

He thought he'd pieced together what had happened: al-Hurra and the pirates had lain an elaborate trap. Taking advantage of Eva Park's request for in-person negotiations, they'd used the freighters to lure the *Monolith* and her escorts away from the *Terre* so they could take high-profile hostages. But the freighters had been far beyond conventional sensor range—distant enough so only the *Monolith*'s latest-generation sensors could spot them. Somehow, the pirates had known that and used it to their advantage. The question was, *how* had they known? How had *pirates* gained access to intelligence detailed and accurate enough to know the *Monolith*'s capabilities? The ship had just been built! Crawley, disdainful of his enemy and too confident in his new ship's invulnerability, had fallen for it. There was a smell about it, and it wasn't just coming from the rotting interior of the *Junkyard Dog*. The pirates must have moles in the Alliance military, and more than that, moles with access to Fleet's most precious military secrets. The implications were frightening.

The *Dog* whined as its TLD engaged. She lurched and shook but entered translight space in one piece. From somewhere forward, there came a whoop like a diver rappelling from an ice cliff on Titan. Gauss, celebrating the fact she was still alive, no doubt. Across from Ben, Mattei held on with shackled hands to the bulkhead between his legs. He looked ill.

"Why'd you surrender your ship?" Ben asked. He tried to avoid sounding judgmental, though not because he cared for Mattei's feelings. Ben considered him a coward for having so easily forfeited the *Terre*. But it might be a long ride to wherever

Gauss and her squad of Amazons were taking them. "My Marines would have held until Crawley returned."

Mattei didn't answer. He didn't even look at Ben. He merely sat with shoulders slumped. Ben refrained from pressing him. Mattei's career was over. No matter the circumstances of his decision to surrender his ship, Fleet in the finest of naval traditions would hold her captain completely responsible. He'd face court-martial and quite possibly criminal prosecution before a Fleet court. Someone had to be held to account.

"I don't understand how they bested Crawley," Eva said. "They don't have anything that can match the *Monolith*. I mean ... do they?"

"No," Ben said, though he felt less sure than he tried to sound. "But they might not be working alone."

"Your theory that maybe they're working with the Arcœnum," Eva ventured. "I still can't believe that. I can't believe a human being, no matter how criminal, would sell out their own species."

"See that duct up there?" Ben said, pointing. "The silver one that looks like it's made from banded intestine?"

"Yes."

"I saw similar, organic conduits on Canis III—in the Archie camp. Look around. This ship is patched together from new tech, old tech, and yes, alien tech."

"My God," Eva said. "If that's true..."

"The good news is, that conduit looks old. Maybe it's just something they picked up as salvage and spliced in."

"We can hope, I suppose." Eva sighed, putting a palm to her forehead. "I'm tired."

"It's been a long day," Ben said.

"No, I mean..." She leaned her head against the wall and closed her eyes. "I'm tired of being scared. I'm not used to not being in control. I'm usually the one who scares other people."

Ben chuckled to himself. "That I can see."

"I'm serious."

"So am I."

She held out her hand in front of her, and they both watched it quiver. After a few seconds of concentrating, she made it stop.

"When they were boarding—I was scared, Ben. Scared to death. I've lived in space most of my life, but when the gravity failed and the lights went out, I thought I was going to die."

Ben listened to the ship rattling around them, trying to think of something to say. "But you were brave, too. You did what needed doing."

"Do? What'd I do? I did what you told me to do."

"Which is what you needed to do," Ben said. He wanted to comfort her but was unsure how to go about it. *Go with what you know.* "Courage isn't the absence of fear," he said. "They teach you that in OCS. Courage is conquering fear, at least long enough so you can act."

He assessed her from the corner of his eye to see how it'd landed. Eva's smile was tight, but it was there.

"My father told me something like that once," she said. "He told me, 'Being brave means going forward, even when that's where they're shooting at you from.'"

"Yeah," Ben said, "that's exactly right."

"I just wish I felt braver."

He made a curt, wistful sound in the back of his throat. "Everyone does," he said.

The *Dog*'s drop into normal space was nearly as rough as its jump to translight. By the time they came to rest on a landing pad, Mattei was turning green. Odd for a Fleet veteran much less a starship's captain, Ben thought. He offered to help the man off Gauss's ship, but Mattei shrugged him away. Ben didn't offer a second time.

The *Dog's* sister ships had also landed, and he could read their names now: the *Emasculator* and the *Shrieking Ex*. Along with the *Sorcerer's Apprentice*, now seen close up, they made the *Dog* appear well maintained. Gauss and her entourage led the captives down the exit ramp and into a port facility unlike any Ben had seen before. He was used to the efficient lines of military ports of call, where every rivet shined, every line served a useful purpose, and waste wasn't tolerated. Civilian ports were fat and indulgent by comparison, with cushioned seating and too many leisure shops tempting passersby every few meters.

This port was neither. It was the *Junkyard Dog* writ large, a structural collage of mismatched metal and clashing architectural styles. Ben looked up at the massive plastinium habitat dome above them. Must be reinforced, he surmised, to stand up to random strikes from the asteroid field. Or maybe they used an overlapping, redundant series of deflector fields to divert the hits. Either way, it was an impressive feat of engineering. Like everything else he'd seen regarding the pirates, the high-tech atmospheric shield contrasted with the junkman's bargain appearance of the port around him. Ben was so fascinated by the grimy, run-down eyesore of the docks around him that Eva had to grab his arm to alert him to the woman coming to meet them: Sayyida al-Hurra.

"Welcome back, Captain," she said.

"What do you mean?" Ben said. "I've never been here."

Mattei advanced stiffly and came to attention. "Thank you, ma'am."

"You look a little out of sorts," al-Hurra said, reaching forward to release his handcuffs.

"The cost of doing business, ma'am," Mattei said with a stiff upper lip.

"You did what was necessary," she assured him.

Eva stepped forward. "What the hell is going on here?"

"He's a traitor," Ben said, the light dawning.

"What?" Eva turned to the *Terre*'s commander. "Captain?"

He had that sickly look about him still. Ben guessed now he knew what prompted it.

"Captain Stone's right," Mattei acknowledged, "from his perspective."

"What other perspective is there?" Ben said, taking a step toward the man. "You sent my Marines away from where they were really needed, namely guarding Miss Park; then gave my location to these bastards."

Torque and another of Gauss's crew moved to answer Ben physically. Al-Hurra stopped them. Clasping his hands behind his back, Mattei didn't give ground as Ben's nose came within inches of his own.

He thinks he's in the right here, Ben thought, incredulous.

Something shimmered behind Mattei, but Ben barely spared them a glance. Bricker, DeSoto, and Baqri—a Greek Chorus of witnesses, observing from the netherworld. Bricker, whose slack mask of death never seemed to decay like the others' did. DeSoto and Baqri merely stood by, greasy skeletons with badly painted bones, one distinguished from the other only by DeSoto's jaw hanging by a thin strand of sinew.

"What about your duty to the Alliance?" Ben said to Mattei. "What about the oath you swore?"

"Don't speak to me of duty, Captain Stone," Mattei said coldly. "You've spent most of your career shitting on the AGF. You have no idea what *duty* really means."

Bricker's apparition lifted his ghost-rifle to point at the flat of Mattei's back. Ben watched the dead sergeant's lips work silently, but he didn't have to hear him to know what he'd said.

"Captain Mattei, go get some food and some rest," al-Hurra said. "My father wants to see you as soon as possible."

"Yes, ma'am." Mattei turned smartly on his heel and marched away, Bricker's ghost barrel tracking him every step.

"As for you two," al-Hurra said, "my father wants to see *you* right away." She brushed past Eva, whose mouth had opened to ask a question.

"Don't keep King Hadrian waiting," Gauss said, smirking. "He doesn't like that."

"He also doesn't like it when you call him that," al-Hurra said without breaking stride.

Torque motioned after al-Hurra with her weapon. Maintenance personnel and other ne'er do wells stopped what they were doing as al-Hurra led them from the docks. It felt like a perp walk of two prisoners on parade.

They passed through a large archway Ben recognized as the pressure door from a starship cargo bay. The narrow corridor was lined with vacuum-rated umbilical material characteristic of docking bridges for transferring personnel between ships in space. More of the organic conduit material he'd seen aboard the *Junkyard Dog* lined its walls, patched into military-grade piping. As aboard ship, the network of system connectors married Archie and human tech. Again Toma's theory of collusion between the pirates and Arcœnum knocked on the front door of his mind. He shivered with the thought.

The tight passageway opened into an expansive cavern. More residents stood and stared as they marched by. Some began to chant Gauss's name, and she and her crew ate up the adulation. Gauss pumped her fist and threw her arms wide toward Ben and Eva, displaying her prizes for all to see. Ben ignored the cheering, studying instead the remarkable melding of natural rock and manmade architecture. Anchored to the asteroid, a symmetrical metal superstructure extended upward for at least a dozen stories. It took Ben a moment to understand that what he was seeing wasn't a single design but yet another amalgamation—partial decks from starships welded together and secured to the rockface. The result was a series of stacked apartments overlooking the hollowed-out interior of the cavern. Smartglass and plastinium windows formed an open wall facing them. Some were dark, while others were lit and providing a voyeur's look inside what Ben assumed to be the homelife of the colony's residents. The side-on cutaway appeared as a full-scale version of the three-dimensional cross-sections of starships he'd studied in OCS. Only these weren't deck plans but patch-worked decks adapted as permanent living quarters. It was like looking at a human-sized ant farm, with only shadeable smart-glass protecting the occupants' privacy. As they drew nearer to the adapted structure, Ben recognized old-style ship designations and serial numbers—and even a partial name, *Revenge*—from the era of the Specter War.

"You carved this out?" he said, indicating the cavern around them.

"We claim-staked the asteroid," al-Hurra explained. "The rest..."

Well, Ben thought, 'the rest' spoke for itself. Recycling the wrecks for housing must have taken decades—*generations*. Talk about a salvage operation! It made his onetime dream of mining a fortune from recovered ships seem a childish fantasy.

"Impressive, eh?" Gauss said. "King Hadrian's father was a great engineer. Outlined the plans for everything you see here."

"Stop calling him that," al-Hurra said. Another pressure door opened before them with a *phish* of air. "After you, Captain; Miss Park."

They entered an octagonal room. Ben wasn't sure what he'd

expected to find—maybe a dilapidated bar or brothel peopled with pirates straight from the storybooks. Greasy men dressed in rags, drinking and blustering, with whores wriggling on their laps. Instead, the room they entered better resembled the bridge of a starship. Or, more accurately, the command-and-control center of a starbase. Sector maps adorned the walls, displaying space bodies in motion and active ship movements across the stellar landscape of the Malvian Triangle. The individuals manning the various stations appeared as indigent as Gauss and her crew, but their dutiful chatter was pure Fleet lingo.

"Father," said Sayyida al-Hurra, "I've brought our guests as ordered."

A man in his mid-fifties nodded to her, finished his explanation to one of his crew, and turned to meet them. He was tall, just over two meters, which Ben ascribed to living a lifetime in light gravity.

"Well, well," the man said, "at last I get to meet the Hero of Canis III. Miss Park, please pass along my compliments on the recent promotional campaign to Mister Byrne. He's quite the salesman." His face was lined, but his smile was broad and welcoming. It almost made up for the chiding tone of the compliment. "I'm Hadrian al-Hurra."

"The Pirate King!" Gauss exclaimed with a flourish and a bow.

Both al-Hurras, father and daughter, flashed her an impatient look. "How many times have I asked you not to call me that?" the elder al-Hurra said.

"But it's fun!"

He stepped forward and offered his hand to Eva. Leaning close, he said, "Please don't encourage her."

"Oh, I wouldn't think of it," Eva replied.

"Since we're getting titles straight, don't call me that," Ben said, refraining to take the man's offered hand. To al-Hurra's raised eyebrow: "That hero thing."

Al-Hurra appraised him. He had the look of a man presented with something he hadn't expected. "Don't use 'king' when addressing me, and I agree. Commander al-Hurra will do."

"Deal."

Hadrian al-Hurra nodded and stepped back. Opening his arms to take in the whole of the busy room and beyond, he proclaimed, "Miss Park, Captain Stone—welcome to New Nassau."

30
THE SEPARATED

"NEW NASSAU?" Eva said.

"You've been given a rare privilege," Hadrian al-Hurra said. "Few strangers get to see our home."

"And *live*..." Gauss supplied with a sinister tone.

"Cinnamon, please," al-Hurra warned.

"Yeah, about that," Ben said. "Why did you take us hostage? For a bargaining chip with Fleet to get the freighters back?"

"Ha!" Gauss laughed. "Heroes aren't the cleanest code in the program, are they?"

"Cinnamon, please," al-Hurra said, his exasperation showing. "Captain Stone's confusion is understandable."

"I'm confused too," Eva said.

"Commander," one of the techs said, "Crawley's fleet is powering back up. They've put Marines and prize crews aboard the freighters."

"Prize crews?"

"Pardon our jargon, Miss Park," al-Hurra said. "It seems your Fleet personnel have taken control of the freighters and are preparing to depart." He said it like he was ticking a box.

Acknowledging the next step in a process he'd already mapped out to its conclusion.

"You're wrong," Ben said. "Once they have those freighters secured, they'll scour this region for us."

Al-Hurra offered a baleful look. His posture had a sad, generous quality to it. "They'll make a token attempt, no doubt, for the historical record. They won't find you."

"Commander," the tech interrupted again, "the freighters are spinning up their TLDs. *Monolith*, too."

"Colonel Toma—my unit—would never leave me here," Ben insisted.

Al-Hurra nodded, like part of him wanted that to be true. "Unfortunately, your colonel isn't in charge of the operation. Commodore Crawley is. And he's achieved his primary strategic objective in recovering the freighters."

Before Ben could speak, the tech interrupted again. "Sir, they've left *Nanchang*, *Irkutsk*, and the *Navis Lusoria* behind. All other Fleet vessels have jumped away with the freighters."

Eva gasped.

Ben cursed.

Al-Hurra seemed sympathetic. "That feeling that's sinking into your stomachs right now? I've lived with it—all of us here have—for generations."

"What feeling?" Eva whispered.

"Abandonment."

She met his eyes and exhaled.

"Who the hell are you?" Ben asked.

Instead of answering, al-Hurra addressed his staff overseeing the sector's tactical displays. "Continue monitoring the destroyers and troop transport. Sayyida, Cinnamon, please join me and our guests in my office." He indicated a doorway, and his daughter led them through it.

They moved into what, Ben guessed, had once been a shipboard conference room. From back in the day when starships were designed to make their human passengers feel comfortable, at home during extended voyages between star systems. Unlike the more utilitarian designs of current Fleet vessels, it felt indulgent, even luxurious by comparison. A round conference table dominated the middle of the room.

"Coffee?" al-Hurra offered as they entered. Gauss closed the door, shutting out the constant buzz from the command center.

"Please," Eva said at the same time Ben said, "No, thanks."

Al-Hurra's grin was a reflex. "It's not poisoned, Captain. There are easier ways to kill you. And I'd never waste coffee like that."

"No ... thanks."

Shrugging, al-Hurra said, "Have it your way. How do you take it, Miss Park?"

"Two sugars, some cream."

Their host dressed a cup for Eva and handed the carafe to Gauss, who poured herself a cup, black.

"Rocket fuel!" she enthused.

Al-Hurra gestured toward the circular table, and the five of them sat. They exchanged us-and-them glances over the tops of recycled cups. Cinnamon Gauss waggled her eyebrows at Ben. Eva assessed al-Hurra, then his daughter, while she blew steam off her coffee. "You never wanted the freighters," she said, taking a tentative sip.

Al-Hurra nodded. "Correct."

"You wanted us," Ben said.

"Mostly correct. We wanted Miss Park. You were a bonus, Captain Stone."

Ben exchanged a glance with Eva. "Crawley and the fleet will come after us," he said, not sure if he believed it anymore. "It's only a matter of time."

Toma, he had no doubt of. But as al-Hurra had stated, the 214th's newly minted colonel didn't command the mission. The technician in the command center, however, had made the mistake of betraying intel, including the fact that the *Navis Lusoria* was still in the Triangle. That gave him hope that Toma was actively searching for them.

Al-Hurra shrugged. "Perhaps. But they have what they came for—the freighters and the ore. If I know Piers Bragg, he'll play up your losses as a terrible tragedy and move on."

"He'll probably blame the Arcœnum for your disappearance," Sayyida said. "Use it to fuel the propaganda engine ginning up public support for the war."

The war.

Ben tried to keep his agreement from showing. Bragg had bigger concerns now that precluded spending military assets in a search for Eva Park. And al-Hurra was right—the outrage and sympathy Ben's capture would generate would be helpful against the Arcœnum, if Bragg spun it that way. *When* Bragg spun it that way.

"You took the freighters and their escorts only to give them back. You kept the escorts and returned the freighters—why?" Eva asked. "I get why you kept the escorts—a bigger fleet for you —but pirates aren't known for abandoning treasure."

"It's only treasure when it's valuable," Sayyida said. "What would we do with all that ore? Did you see any advanced ship-building capacity walking in from the docks? Notice any refineries to manufacture metal for hulls?"

"Why do you think we kept the freighter escorts?" Gauss said. The joking loudmouth had left the room, like a banished black-sheep personality. "We can't build our own ships. So we take what we need."

"What happened to the crews?" Ben asked.

"We released them," al-Hurra stated, "those who wanted to

go. Unharmed. Repatriated them to The Frontier near Alliance bases where they'd be picked up. Didn't you hear about that through briefings, or perhaps in the media?"

"No," Eva said, her tone suggesting she didn't really believe it.

"What a surprise," Gauss deadpanned.

"You said, 'those who wanted to go,'" Ben said. "Are you telling me there were other traitors like Mattei who chose to stay?"

"You use that word a lot," Sayyida said. "*Traitors.*"

"If the label fits..." Ben shot back.

"Ladies and gentlemen, please," al-Hurra said. "Let's keep this civil. We have a great divide to cross here, and little time to cross it. Yes, Captain Stone, some chose to stay. After we explained who we are."

"You're pirates," Ben said. "What else is there to know?"

Eva placed a hand on his arm. "You still haven't answered the captain's question. Why us? What value do we have as hostages? Administration policy is to not negotiate with—"

"That's not it, Miss Park," al-Hurra answered. "We took you and Captain Stone because we need your help. And now there's a second reason: Bragg is leading us all toward extinction with his war-mongering. We thought we'd have more time to convince you of this. But Sirius happened."

"Convince us?" Eva said.

There were half-formed ideas in the back of Ben's head. They were beginning to vibrate like magnetic puzzle pieces wanting to come together but not yet able to connect: the kidnapping, New Nassau, the military bearing of al-Hurra and his pirates. Painting the portrait of what was happening here was as frustrating as attempting to recall a faded memory.

"Who are you?" he asked again.

Al-Hurra glanced at his daughter.

Sayyida shrugged. "They're here."

"We can send them back," Gauss suggested. Whatever silent agreement might be solidifying between father and daughter, the spiky-haired loudmouth wasn't entirely onboard.

"We had the vote of the Captains Council," al-Hurra said to Gauss. "We have a responsibility to try." He sat up straighter. "We call ourselves the Separated, Captain Stone."

How dramatic, Ben thought but didn't say.

"After the Specter War, many serving in the military decided they'd had enough. Seen too much. And the *way* it ended..." Al-Hurra gathered his thoughts. "Your grandfather's strategy at Gibraltar Station was inspired. Saved the species. But it cost tens of thousands of lives. Many of them loyal, dutiful personnel doomed below decks on those compromised ships."

"I'm lost," Eva said. "What does this have to do with—"

Ben said, "The Great Separation?" Those puzzle pieces were more than agitated, now.

Al-Hurra met his gaze. "You begin to see, then? The Specter War exacted a heavy toll on those who fought. Beyond the pressures of battle, I mean. Those are to be expected. But the *psychological* cost... Sustained warfare against a foe who turns your own brother into the enemy by mind-control? The constant threat of Containment Protocol? And then, ultimate victory won by sacrificing so many patriots trapped on ships taken over by the true enemy? A necessary evil for humanity to survive, perhaps, but it proved too much for too many."

"Containment Protocol?" Eva asked.

"A standing order that, once invoked, couldn't be rescinded," Ben said, meeting her gaze. "Technically, it's still on the books. At the first sign a comrade was compromised—if you suspected a fellow service member of being mind-controlled by the Arcœnum—your orders were to kill the individual for the good of the whole. Regardless of rank. Regardless of relationship. It's why the service requires the mind-shield, now, and forcefully prosecutes any who refuse to get it."

"Your own grandfather shot his captain I believe, Captain Stone," Sayyida said.

"Yes," Ben said, "he did."

"Once the Archies were defeated," al-Hurra explained, "humanity began turning inward again. It seemed like the whole species decided in that one moment to reassess itself— what matters, and why."

"Near-extinction events tend to make you thoughtful," Gauss said in a salty tone.

"Despite regulations and service contracts, tens of thousands of service members resigned," Ben told Eva. "Those who qualified took early retirement."

"I know something about it," she said. "My father is in the generation that came after. He..." She glanced at al-Hurra. "No offense, but he didn't much care for those who 'walked away from their posts.' His words, Commander al-Hurra."

"No offense taken. Later generations can't appreciate the sacrifices of those who've come before, much less their motivations. They have no concept because they have no context for understanding." This last al-Hurra said looking at Sayyida, whose expression remained carefully neutral. Something was going on there. al-Hurra sighed. "But that's the way of things, I suppose."

"I still don't understand—" Eva began, but al-Hurra held up his hand. "Why do you call yourselves the Separated?"

"When a service member leaves the service, it's called 'separating,'" Ben said.

"Exactly so," al-Hurra nodded. "We are the descendants of those who walked away. As you know, their desertion was not taken well by the military at the time. The Alliance Congress voted to cut off all benefits and backpay for anyone leaving without proper authorization, even those with a deferment for disabilities received in combat, physical or otherwise. The Treaty of Covenant was too fresh. The public too scared. No one trusted the peace to hold, and the mass separations were seen as an absolute betrayal of trust—not just of an oath sworn but of the entire species. Initially, those who left were hunted and court-martialed and jailed until the military determined it was spending too many resources bringing so-called deserters to so-called justice."

"They weren't 'so-called deserters,' they *were* deserters," Ben said with Bricker's gravel in his voice. "And the concern that the peace wouldn't last—all the more reason they should have sucked it up and fulfilled their commitment." Al-Hurra bristled and seemed ready to argue the point. But that would achieve nothing, so Ben softened and spoke first. "But, as you suggested, arresting and detaining all those people wasn't practical. And so, in most cases, most were simply allowed to leave with dishonorable discharges blotting their records. It took the military a full generation to recover, with everyone on pins and needles the Archies would take advantage and launch a new offensive."

Sayyida said, "But they didn't."

"Why not?" Eva asked.

"Because the Arcœnum aren't warlike by nature," al-Hurra said, "whatever the current administration would have you believe. Unless provoked, they're a peaceful species."

"That's changed, apparently," Ben said. The conduct of one lone, grief-crazed squatter on Canis III was paramount in his mind. Maybe the Archie's extreme version of the kind of psychological damage al-Hurra was describing in the veterans of the Specter War. Ben dared not look away from the commander for fear of seeing the Archie in a corner of the room succumbing to the gravity on Sirius.

Al-Hurra dodged the debate. "The Separated were allowed to leave, yes, but with no prospects, no way of providing for their families," he said. "So, they gathered their loved ones—"

"—and came here," Eva said. "To the Triangle."

Ben grunted. "No wonder you're so good at waylaying merchants and avoiding Fleet. All that military training."

"Passed down, yes," al-Hurra said. "My great grandfather was a young engineer aboard the fighter carrier *Shōkaku*. He and his entire engineering crew were part of the exodus. They brought their families out here and built New Nassau."

"And you've been Robin Hooding it ever since." Though part of Ben was disgusted by al-Hurra's excuses for desertion, it was hard not to be impressed by what the Separated had built out of scrapped ships and rock. "Taking vessels, stealing cargo."

"We take what we need to survive," Gauss said again with a growl.

Al-Hurra tapped on the conference table. "Did you ever wonder why there were so few casualties when the Alliance sent your expedition to root us out last year, Captain?" he asked. "We run, we dodge, we hide. It's the government and the military establishment we hold in contempt, not those called to service on the front line. Quite the contrary in fact."

"But there have been deaths," Eva said. "I've seen the reports—"

"Yes," Sayyida said, "unfortunately so. To survive, as a last resort, we fight. Sometimes, we kill."

"Consider our most recent action." Her father brought up a tactical map of the Malvian Triangle. Red icons represented the two destroyers and the *Navis Lusoria*. "Not a single pod of your Marines sent to secure the freighters was harmed, Captain. Merely disabled, and temporarily at that. The same for the fleet escorting them. The same for your ship, Miss Park. And we lost three of our own people in the boarding action fought to bring you here."

Ben was tempted to remark on the just fate of the dead pirates but stayed the impulse.

"You mentioned a vote earlier," Eva said. "What vote?"

"We want to come home." As one, Ben and Eva looked to Sayyida, who'd spoken. "We have a few of the first generation still with us, though fewer every day. The fervor that drove the Great Separation—it's dying with them. Those of my generation and younger ... we're tired of living hand-to-mouth."

Hadrian al-Hurra's face showed conflict. Gauging the terrain, Ben shifted his gaze between the older man and his daughter. The desire to 'come home' appeared generational, as Sayyida had intimated.

"How did you ever get agreement to chance it?" he asked. "Most must be relatively content here."

"Military types like to tout that the service isn't a democracy. It's a top-down, order-driven hierarchy," Sayyida answered. "Our founders turned that on its head. Here, it's one person, one vote. Each group is represented by a ship's captain they've voted into that position—and can vote out again with a simple majority."

"A pirate republic?" Eva said.

Sayyida nodded. "Represented by the Captains Council. Which voted to go home."

"You voted to what," Eva said, "reintegrate with society?"

"Yes," Sayyida said.

Eva scoffed. "Maybe you should've checked with society first. I can't imagine—"

"That's why you're here, Miss Park," Sayyida said. "You will represent us."

Eva Park's expression began with surprise, then dashed quickly to disbelief. She seemed at a loss for words.

"I can see we have a lot to discuss," al-Hurra said. "Captain Stone, at this point, I'd like to talk solely with Miss Park. It's time at last for our parlay, and the discussion is a political one. Your presence is not required."

Ben balked at being dismissed. The holster on his right hip felt suddenly, conspicuously empty. "I'm not going anywhere," he said, making no effort to rise. "Miss Park is under my protection."

Cinnamon Gauss stood up. She put one hand on her sidearm. Her eyebrows jotted up and down at Ben.

"Cinn, please," al-Hurra said. "There's no need for that."

"I'm just stretching," she said, her gaze with its promise of violence never wavering from Ben.

"Ben," Eva said, "it's okay. I'll be fine."

"Eva, you can't stay—"

She gripped his forearm. "I'll be fine."

The room fell silent. Gauss tapped her sidearm with an impatient rhythm.

"You'll be held in the brig, Captain Stone," al-Hurra said. "I'm sure you understand why. But no harm will come to you or Miss Park."

Ben read the room. Eva nodded again to reassure him. Finally, he stood up. "After you," he said to Gauss.

"Oh, no," she said, still tapping the pistol butt. "Age before beauty, poster boy."

31

REUNION

WALKING BACK through the command-and-control center, Ben took his time. He'd been preoccupied with meeting al-Hurra earlier and assessing the likelihood of the man's intent to do Eva harm. Now, he let himself see the room. The half-dozen staff, each performing duties he'd expect to see in any C&C. Tactical, fire control, communications. A burble of tech-talk revealed a current exchange with the station's power plant. Everything about al-Hurra's operation screamed military, not catch-as-catch-can piracy.

"Hurry up, poster boy," Gauss ordered him as she waited by the door.

"I've never in my life hurried toward a brig," Ben replied. He made a point of stopping to look around. "Nice place. I like the retro-thief motif."

Cinnamon Gauss crossed her arms, tapping each index finger on either elbow, and cocked her gun hip out. Ben was starting to recognize the posture for the challenge it was.

Someone stepped up behind him, and Ben turned to find Torque glowering.

"Do I need to reintroduce you two?" Gauss said.

The tall, thick woman grinned hungrily at him. One amenity New Nassau did not have, evidently, was a proficient dentist.

"On the other hand," Ben said, "I could use some me time."

Six stations, standard duty distribution, and a sector map that somehow tracked starships, both friendly and not, despite roaming ion storms that played havoc with sensors. He knew more about al-Hurra's command than when he'd walked in here. Mission accomplished.

Gauss led the way and Ben followed, his bulky feminine shadow close behind. They headed back the way they'd come from the docks, but rather than turn toward the impressive condominiums, Gauss went left. Ben sketched a map in his mind, counting steps and noting a burn mark on the corridor floor at one turn, an abrasion on the wall at another. They came to a long hallway with armored cams bolted to the ceiling at each end, and Ben recognized the kind of facility he'd become intimately acquainted with in his service life. Starship or starbase, planetside or in orbit, a brig was a brig.

"Welcome home," Gauss said.

"Not for long," Ben retorted before Torque pushed him into the cell.

"Well," Gauss replied, "I guess that depends on Eva Park's open-mindedness."

He was used to higher-tech accommodations. A forcefield for a security gate, cameras in all four corners of the cell. The design was medieval and reminded him of Fort Leyte's blocky, architectural simplicity. Four walls of molecularly compacted hexacrete, and a door of bars fashioned from the titanium-reinforced metal of a starship's hull. The pirates must use every bit of their salvaged prizes not traded away, he thought. Nick Stone had described once how the natives of the North American continent had used every piece of the buffalo they'd killed, from hide to tongue to testicles, rather than let anything go to waste. Whatever a buffalo was. The waste-not-want-not of the cell's construction reminded Ben of that.

"My grandfather designed it."

He looked to Gauss, angled in her roguish pose again. Torque closed the barred door and locked it with the touch of a finger.

"Engineer?" Ben ventured.

"Marshal."

"Cinn's grandfather leads the law in New Nassau."

It wasn't the first time he'd ever heard Torque speak, but it was the first time he took notice. Her voice was like a bear's after finally snagging the honey without breaking its neck.

"I guess apples don't always land close, then," he said.

"What's that supposed to mean?" Gauss demanded.

"You don't act like a marshal's granddaughter."

Torque laughed a little. Before Gauss could respond, two new faces appeared outside the cell, both male.

"Stone, meet your new guards," the marshal's grand-daughter said. "They'll keep you company until the king finishes his talks with Eva Park."

"You needn't have troubled yourself."

Torque laughed again. It sounded unforced, even appreciative of Ben's sarcasm.

Cinnamon Gauss's smile showcased a lot of teeth. "Don't *make* any trouble, jackass, and there won't be any." She gave him her back and leaned in to speak privately to the two men.

"I like you, Stone," the honey-bear said. "You're more than just another pretty face."

"Wow," Ben said, taking a seat on the bed-bench, the lone piece of furniture in the cell except for the toilet. "That means so much, coming from a pirate."

Torque's grin dropped into disappointment. "Maybe both of us are more than our clichés, eh?"

He didn't respond, arching his ears toward Gauss and the guards. Too late.

"Come on, T," Gauss said. "Cool your heels, Stone. Enjoy your me time." Before following her leader Torque offered Ben a wink and a dainty wave, which was ludicrous as presented by such meaty fingers.

Save for the low mumblings of the two guards outside, the cell grew quiet. Ben leaned his head back against the cool hexacrete wall and closed his eyes. It was the first time since Crawley discovered the missing freighters that he'd found a quiet moment for himself. Me time, indeed. Ben let himself sink into it. Felt some of the tension flow out of his limbs like excess energy bleeding off an overclocked reactor.

Park could take care of herself. If al-Hurra had wanted to harm her, he needn't have kidnapped her to do it. Maybe his story of the Separated was true. Maybe after decades of piracy in deep space, they simply wanted to live in natural gravity again. Truth was, Ben didn't much care if they were lying or not. He didn't trust al-Hurra or his story or his motives. First chance he got, he was getting Park the hell out of here. Toma was surely scouring the Triangle looking for them, the *Junkyard Dog's* drive signature, *something*. Anything to recover Ben and accomplish their shared mission of protecting Park. Not because Sheba had suddenly developed a fast affection for Ben, but because he was one of her officers and, by God, Drop Marines didn't leave their own behind.

"Hey, poon magnet, that true?"

Ben felt himself dragged back from semi-consciousness. He'd almost managed to slip into a doze. Grudgingly, he cracked his eyes open. "You talking to me?"

One of the guards, the larger of the two, leaned on the wall outside. "Yeah, poon magnet. He was talking to you."

"What was the question?"

"You the Stone who rescued that girl? From the planet? Like in the vid? You look like the guy in the vid."

"You mean Alice Keller?"

"Yeah," said the smaller, younger guard. What he said next sounded slick. "I call her Sweet Alice."

"Do you."

"I do."

"Anyway," the bigger guard said, losing patience, "did you rescue her, or was that just more Braggaganda?"

Ben weighed whether or not to answer. Name, rank, hexadecimal code. That's all he was supposed to give them as a prisoner of war. But, he reminded himself, there was technically no formal state of war with the pirates. The Alliance military had ever only declared a perennial police action. Besides, he might be sitting here for hours, maybe longer. A little conversation would pass the time.

"I was part of the Marine unit that pulled her out of a hole on Drake's World, yeah."

"I *knew* it!" the smaller guard said. "You owe me a hundred!"

The bigger guard cursed. "He could be lying."

Ben shrugged. "I'm not."

"I knew it!" The smaller guard gripped the bars, ignoring for the moment the need to collect his winnings. He looked no older than nineteen. "So, how was she?"

"What?"

"You know," he said. "Grateful for rescue. A hull-line jaw like yours. How was she? How many times did you—"

"She was fourteen," Ben said. The annoyance of being wrested from sleep returned with a vengeance.

"Hey," mused the teenaged pirate, "old enough to bleed, old enough to—"

"Shut up."

Ben's eyes target-locked the kid's, whose mouth hung open like its mechanism had jammed.

"Careful, pretty boy," the big guard said. "Or we could interdict your ill-advised escape attempt."

Ben shifted his gaze to the older man. "Well now, that could be fun." He flexed the fist draped lazily over one knee. "Wonder if you people have kept perfecting personal combat training like we have in the AGF..."

The bigger pirate appeared tempted, then sneered and turned his back. He offered the younger guard his pad. "Take your win and shut up."

The teen grabbed the pad. "I knew it was him!"

"Yeah, yeah."

Ben reclined against the wall again. He stared up at the ceiling, also dense hexacrete, and its total absence of a man-sized point of egress from the cell. The air vent was tiny. Marshal Gauss, if that was his name, had certainly done his due diligence in fortifying the space. Its security owed to its simplicity. High-tech cells could be hacked. Force fields shorted out. Without heavy ordnance, he'd never get through one of these walls. The only way out was through that barred door and the two morons guarding it. He considered ways to lure the guards, especially the young one, but dismissed every scenario as too risky. He'd be no good to Eva Park dead. *And little good alive, apparently.* Ben tried again to relax, but his senses were too heightened now, his moron radar pinging too loudly in proximity.

So much for me time.

A dreamless doze found him after all, and the only reason Ben knew it had was by feeling himself tugged back to full wakefulness. He didn't know if he'd been out for two minutes or two hours.

"You've got a visitor, Stone."

Through a crusty blur, he found Cinnamon Gauss beyond the bars. Moron and Moron's Little Brother were nowhere in sight. As his vision cleared, a second young woman appeared beside Gauss. He mistook her for another of Gauss's crew at first, but she seemed too clean for that lot, too tidy. His heart lurched suddenly. His brain sharpened in recognition as she smiled at him. Ben rubbed his eyes to make sure he hadn't been dreaming after all, or wasn't still.

But there's no beach here.

"Hi, Ben."

Alice looked so much different. Her features leaner. The light behind her eyes, brighter. The girl he'd last seen in the *Rubicon*'s medbed, hyperaware and afraid of everything, had been replaced by a young woman with posture slightly bent as if burdened by a light field back. That smile of hers was intimately familiar, though. It shone brightly from somewhere deep within.

"Alice?"

He didn't remember standing or advancing toward the bars.

"Hold on, Stone," Gauss said, putting her hand on her sidearm. "Keep your distance."

"Can I go in?" Alice asked. "I'd like to visit with B—Captain Stone. If I may."

Cinnamon Gauss eyed her suspiciously. "That's not what we discussed."

"I know, Cinn. But it's been so long."

Gauss looked at Ben. "I let her in there, you'd best mind your manners."

The initial shock of seeing Alice again was ebbing. "That's funny, coming from you," Ben quipped.

Gauss smirked but released the e-lock. She opened the barred door wide enough for Alice to enter. Once she was in, Gauss locked it again and stood, observing them.

"A little privacy, please?" Alice said.

Exhaling, Gauss tapped her sidearm. "I'll just be down here, then." She moved up the corridor, whistling something that sounded like an animal caught in a trap. Ben could still hear it after her footsteps stopped, the pirate's way of letting him know she was only seconds away should Alice need her. Interesting, that. Alice launched herself into his arms.

"Ben!" The force of her hug tested his reinforced smartfatigues. "I'm so glad to see you!"

"Same here, kid," he said. Her hug became fiercer, and he returned it tentatively. She was a young woman now, all right. Ben flushed with the realization as she pressed firmly against him. He asked lamely, "How are you?"

"Better now!" she exclaimed. "When Cinn told me you were here, I just had to see you!"

Alice hadn't released the hug, its ferocity strong as ever. Ben gave her a little squeeze of stage direction. Reluctantly, she pulled away.

"I've missed you," she said, beaming up at him like a sun.

A sentiment he hadn't expected. And he was surprised to find the same held for him.

"Me too, kid."

"Let's sit. I have so much to tell you!" Alice took his hand, and they sat on the bed-bench facing one another. She'd grown up so much in so many ways, but little-girl energy still seemed to fuel her.

"Where do I start?" she asked. "So much has happened..."

The whistling filtered to them from down the corridor.

"Keep your voice down," Ben said. "These people don't need to know more than they need to know. You know?"

"Oh, they're fine," Alice said dismissively. "They've been very kind to me."

That answer begged a new question. "Why are you here? How did you get here, Alice?"

"I escaped," she said. "And they took me in."

"Escaped?" Ben swiftly assembled the information Nick Stone had shared with him. "From Strigoth?"

"Yeah."

"What do you mean, 'escaped?' I thought Doctor Korsakov..."

Alice's expression hardened, and he stopped speaking.

"I have a lot to tell you," she said.

Ben sat, caught up in her story, as Alice related the past three years of her life to him. She seemed at pains to speak well of two techs, Zoey and Ian, but when mentioning Korsakov, her voice swelled with anger and disappointment. Ben found himself brushing up against his own grief when she cried over losing Morgan Henry. But then the unbelievable stuff came. The charges that Korsakov had been working not only with Bragg—which Ben deduced when Alice named the man Korsakov had talked to via subspace as "someone named Devos" —but some unknown alien species as well, Ben was tempted to write it off to teenage drama. Alice's story was almost too wild to believe. But elements of it rang true, especially when she talked about the creatures she called "shadow-spiders." Her descriptions of them dovetailed with how DeSoto and Baqri had died; details never released from the military. Ben remained focused on Alice throughout her tale, half-expecting the molting corpses of DeSoto and Baqri to appear and offer silent witness to her testimony.

"It got worse when Morgan died," Alice said.

"Korsakov, you mean?"

"Yeah." She was fidgeting with her hands. Staring at her half-hidden palms. "I thought Korsakov cared about me, Ben. I guess I needed to think that. But he only wanted to draw out my —whatever it is. I mean—he kept pushing and pushing. And after Morgan died, it was like..."

"Like any restraint had been taken off."

"Yes! Exactly!"

He wanted to bring her back around again to the shadow-spiders, but talking about them made her even more emotional than discussing Korsakov. So he decided to go for the low-hanging fruit instead. "Why would Korsakov be working with Samson Devos? For Bragg? They've been incarcerating Psyckers since he came into office. Why would they want Korsakov to develop your ... your talent?"

The doomed-spirit whistling from outside the cell got louder. How long had they been talking?

"Have you told any of this to them?" Ben asked quickly, cutting off her answer.

Alice wavered. "Not really. We've talked about the deal Ian worked with them to help me get back to Alpha Centauri. He—"

"Good. Keep it that way."

Footsteps drew closer, adding a rhythm to Gauss's tone-deaf tune.

"They said I needed to stay here a while because of the war. It's been weeks! Cinn's been so nice, but—"

"Oh, that's good to hear," Gauss said, reappearing at the cell door. "Come on, little sister, time's up."

"Can't I stay a little longer?"

Gauss raised an eyebrow and cocked her hip. For once, she didn't fondle her sidearm.

"That means no," Ben said, getting the sense of an older sister enforcing a curfew on a younger one.

"Yeah, I know." Alice got to her feet. When Ben stood, she embraced him again. Less fierce, more assurance of more hugs to come. "I'll see you again. Soon!"

Ben hugged her back and stared straight at Gauss. "Count on it."

32

BRAIN IN A BLENDER

"HE'S SOMETHING OF A FIREBRAND, isn't he?" al-Hurra said after Ben had left them.

"You should read his record."

Al-Hurra gave Eva a sly look. "What makes you think I haven't?"

She picked up her coffee and took a sip. There it was again, that chasm-like yawning in the pit of her stomach. The one from the subspace parlay with the daughter, the one from the ship's storage bay. An awareness that she wasn't in control here. Knowledge that Hadrian al-Hurra could shoot her in the head if he so chose and none who cared for her would be any the wiser.

"People like Mattei," she said, "you have them throughout the Alliance. To feed you information regularly." Speculation, not a question. "Sounds more like a fifth column, or a pirate rebellion."

"Fifth column?" al-Hurra's eyes narrowed. "Rebellion? Have you heard anything at all I've said to you, Miss Park?"

"Earlier," she said, deliberately turning to Sayyida, "I sensed some disagreement between you and King Hadrian here. What's that about?"

al-Hurra cleared his throat. "I'd prefer you didn't call me that."

I know, Eva thought while staring expectantly at the daughter.

"There is no disagreement," Sayyida al-Hurra claimed, adding, "None that matters, anyway."

An opening.

Eva said, "If I'm to even consider proffering reconciliation to President Bragg, I need to know what cards I have in my hand. Not just what the dealer tells me I have."

The father and daughter conversed without speaking for a moment.

"As I said, enthusiasm for the idea is generational," Sayyida said. "Those few of the Separated still with us who made the initial decision to leave the Alliance, they're the most reluctant to return. Their children, like my father— they've been taught to not trust those in power. It's why we have one person, one vote to elect captains. My generation and those younger, we see the Alliance growing. Alpha Centauri is ripe with promise and governed more to our liking. Less authoritarian, being so far away from Sol's seat of power. Certainly, it's less corrupt than Sol. Alpha-C holds the potential for a future beyond the Triangle, where we live in constant fear of being nuked or hanged from the spar of a space station."

Finally, Eva thought, she was getting somewhere. "There are many Alliance citizens, not just service members, who would reject you outright. Some are the same people you'd have to live beside every day. You might feel betrayed as a result of what you deem to be past wrongs, but it's your ancestors who'd be seen by your new neighbors as betrayers who shirked their duty."

"We understand that position," the elder al-Hurra said.

"Maybe intellectually," Eva allowed, returning her focus to him. "Emotionally? I doubt you'd accept it."

"You might be right," Sayyida said. "But don't presume to know us, Miss Park."

"This vote of yours," Eva pressed, still fishing, "how binding is it? How likely is it that your people are willing to weather what such a transition would demand of them? I'm not talking about the obvious—like the difficulties of uprooting your colony and establishing a new life on a new world—I'm talking about the potential for armed resistance in some communities."

Sayyida sighed. "There will be problems. We know this. We'll work through them."

"This could work to your advantage," al-Hurra suggested. "You haven't thought it through."

"My advantage?" Eva was intrigued. "Do tell, Commander."

"Humanity is once again in a state of war with the Arcœnum. Bringing her lost children home will have a positive impact on morale within the Alliance."

"That's debatable," Eva said.

"Why do you resist?" Sayyida asked, annoyed. "Why is every positive possibility met with such scorn?"

"I'm in politics," Eva said. "I'm paid to be jaded." She took a breath and tried to set her own feelings aside. Al-Hurra's mention of a potential political upside got her thinking. The war had likely already shot public tension through the roof. The loss of Sirius was a devastating blow, particularly since the Bragg Administration had hung so much of its political prestige on recapturing the system. Bringing these people home would be difficult logistically, if it were possible at all. But the emotional boost ... Al-Hurra wasn't wrong. Families reunited, new generations of descendants discovered. Humanity's estranged tribe returning home ... Eva could already see the headlines, and they were powerful. Maybe there was opportunity here. Maybe al-Hurra was right about that, too.

"How many of you are there?" she asked.

"Men, women, and children, approximately thirty-eight thousand," Sayyida said. Her face softened when she said, "You're beginning to believe, Miss Park, aren't you... in the possibility. In the potential for what reconciliation could mean. For everyone."

She didn't answer aloud but Eva figured the sparkle in her eyes spoke for her.

Maybe.

"There's something else," al-Hurra said.

"Father, now is not the time," Sayyida rushed to say. "We're just beginning to make headway—"

"If not now, when?" he said. "Time is the problem!"

Eva watched the exchange with avid interest. In their disagreement, she sensed weakness again.

Al-Hurra said, "You have a knack for reconciling those who fundamentally disagree with your president."

Stumbling at first over the change in topic, Eva clued in quickly. "You mean Marcos?"

He nodded. "I was very impressed by that. And Bragg's willingness to extend the olive branch."

"Marcos was a matter of political expediency, a clearing of decks to focus on more important things," Eva said. She didn't add that Bragg's promise to Miranda Marcos had been a hollow one, a title without real authority beyond a bully pulpit with the media. Marcos had only taken the deal, she reasoned, because the alternative of rotting in prison had been worse. "I'll tell you one thing—if you truly want to go home again, you should stop thinking of Piers Bragg as *my* president. Put aside your 'us and them' mentality. He's your president, too."

Al-Hurra winced. "The price you pay, I suppose. Is that what you told Miranda Marcos?"

"Her, I didn't need to tell."

"Father, can we hold off—"

"I sent Captain Stone out for another reason," al-Hurra pressed on.

"Okay."

He thumbed the comm in front of him. "Send in Louie."

Eva exchanged looks with Sayyida, searching for a clue to the mystery squatting in the room like a fragrant gorilla. What she found was anxiety spiking on the young woman's face.

The door to al-Hurra's office slid open. Through it walked—no, glided, like a spirit—the first Arcœnum Eva had ever seen in person.

"This is Light Without Shadow," al-Hurra said. "We call him Louie."

Eva's reaction was immediate and instinctive. She leapt backward out of her seat, as if she'd suddenly discovered a snake slithering up her pant leg.

"What the fuck!"

"Please, Miss Park—"

Sayyida's entreaty was drowned out by Eva's total immersion in the creature walking toward her. Its movements were elegant, despite the armored exoskeleton it wore. Its multiple appendages lifted like a human swings their arms when walking, but more gracefully. Its transparent head was elongated and complex in its interior biology, the skin luminescent with a silvery hue.

"Stay away from me!" Eva screamed.

She looked around in terror, frantic for escape. But the Arcœnum stood, halted now, between her and the exit.

"Louie, please keep your distance," al-Hurra said.

The alien retreated a step.

"What the fuck," Eva said again, though her malice drained away as she spoke.

She was thinking of a waterfall, its cascade a reassuring rush. Birds twittered, like the ones in the garden outside the Citadel, where she sometimes roamed among the perfectly manicured hedgerows after especially stressful meetings. Then Leo's face appeared, smiling, as he held up two drinks, the amber liquid sparkling with Tokyo's city lights below and the stars above, shining through her apartment window.

These weren't her thoughts. Hers were murderous and desperate and being laid down flat, subdued by these placid, anesthetizing images injected directly into her mind. By that ... that *thing*.

"Get out of my head!" she whispered. It became a shouted demand. "Get out of my head!"

"Louie," al-Hurra said, still calm. "I know what you're trying to do, but it's not helping."

The placid scenes evaporated, replaced by the red, rapid pace of her heartbeat and the terror of her lizard brain calculating the odds of sprinting past the monster for the door. Eva's skin crawled with its nearness, with the violation she'd just endured, and the sure knowledge she was helpless to stop it happening to her again. Every story she'd ever been told as a child about Archies coming to steal bad children in the night gnawed at her from the creeping shadows of little-girl memory.

"I'm sorry to spring this on you," al-Hurra said, "but as I said, time is running out."

"Please, Eva," Sayyida said, "sit down."

The Arcœnum opened its arms, all four of them. Had it been human, it might be a gesture offering peace. To Eva, it felt like a trap waiting to be sprung. The alien backed away another step and approximated a sitting position, using its exoskeleton for support.

"Please." al-Hurra gestured to her chair.

Mechanically, Eva sat back down. The Arcœnum remained motionless. Didn't appear even to breathe.

"I'll explain," al-Hurra said quietly. "Captain Stone sees us as thieves, and while we may be that too, we're primarily traders. We've survived by trading what we take for what we need."

Eva's rational mind tried to right itself. "What does that—"

"The Frontier," Sayyida said, "is the principal trade hub for the Alliance. It also borders Arcœnum space. Merchants from both sides pursue profit there. And administrations, regardless of party, have encouraged that since the war."

It was too many words. Crowding them out, one thought kept repeating in Eva's mind: *I need to get out of here...* But the alien, frightening as it was, made no overt threat. And her efforts to calm her rapid pulse were, at least, her own.

"The first thing it did was try to control my mind," Eva spat.

"Louie didn't mean you any harm," Sayyida insisted. "To placate the fear response in humans is instinctive for the Arcœnum. He thought he was helping you, calming you down."

"He?"

"Yes," Sayyida said. "They have gender. They have families. They live, eat, love, breathe—"

"Stop," Eva said, rubbing her forehead, "just stop."

Al-Hurra held up his hand to stay his daughter's monologue. "Trade in The Frontier has kept us alive. The Arcœnum, like the Alliance, have profited greatly from the Covenant Peace Accords. Louie is their trade representative in New Nassau. He lives here with us."

"*With* you?" It was beginning to feel like her brain had been dropped in a blender set to purée. "How is that even possible?"

"Mutual profit is a powerful salve for old wounds," argued al-Hurra. "Makes for strange bedfellows, I admit—"

"Strange bedfellows! More like sleeping with the enemy!"

She'd thought Ben's theory of pirates conspiring with the Arcœnum ludicrous when he'd first brought it up. But they'd been doing exactly that, and for a long time apparently. The fear that had assailed her then came back now, fueled with certainty. What chance did humanity have against such unholy allies?

"You're traitors," Eva said. "Just like Ben said. You have been all along. Coming back is just a way to infiltrate and eat away at us from the inside."

"'Us?'" growled al-Hurra. "Now who needs to put aside their us-and-them mentality?"

"We're at war!" Eva shouted.

"Not with Louie," he insisted.

The comm's hail sounded.

"Commander, we have a situation."

"I'll be right there," al-Hurra said. "Louie—we will get this sorted. Please return to your Customs House Embassy."

The Arcœnum stood but otherwise didn't move. Instead, he stared at Hadrian al-Hurra.

"I know it. And I agree. Trust is a fragile thing." He looked to Sayyida as he said it. "But we will not abandon you."

She too nodded to the alien. "As my father says."

Opening all four of his arms again, Light Without Shadow ducked his head in obeisance and backed from the room. Eva Park gaped, watching him leave.

"Follow me, Miss Park," al-Hurra said.

"Status report," al-Hurra said, peering closely at the sector map as he entered the C&C.

Sayyida closely escorted Eva, who found the woman's nearness less intrusive than she might otherwise have. It was nothing compared to Louie the Shadow—or whatever the hell its ... *his* ... name was filling her mind with false images to sedate her emotional response.

"Sir, Third Fleet has entered the Triangle in force."

"What?" al-Hurra sounded caught off-guard.

The sector map was populated by a dozen new, red icons just over the borderline from normal space and moving deeper into the Malvian Triangle. Blue icons—pirate forces, Eva guessed—dotted the map in strategic locations. Offset from center, toward the lower right corner of the Triangle, hovered a hexagon labeled New Nassau.

"What's happening?" Eva demanded.

"Third Fleet is out of Covenant," Sayyida said soberly beside her. "Commanded by Rear Admiral Malcolm Thorne. He has no love of pirates."

"Your father seems surprised they're here," Eva said. "I don't know why. Captain Stone warned you they'd come looking for us."

Sayyida muttered something Eva couldn't parse, so Eva focused on the father. Like her, Hadrian al-Hurra was a planner. Used to being in charge and in control and ready for every contingency. His demeanor now was calm but agitated. That he hadn't seen this coming seemed to rattle his daughter, too.

"Countermeasures," al-Hurra ordered. "Standard procedure, people. Drop the lures across the Triangle, try to lead them away. No need to panic just yet."

"What's going on?" Eva asked again and louder.

"Come closer, Miss Park," said al-Hurra. "I'll show you."

Sayyida followed her into the heart of the C&C.

"Admiral Thorne pioneered tech that's very good at penetrating spatial anomalies like ion storms and nebulae to find ships. He calls it Pathfinder. Our spies tell us it's a combination of traditional sounding tech, like infrared sensors, and predictive astrophysics." He must have noticed her expression because he simplified his explanation. "In other words, it's good at sounding out our hiding places."

"Okay."

"We're also good at fooling the tech," he stated, then addressed his communications officer. "Get Captain Stone up here. I want all of our assets in this room."

"Aye-aye, Commander."

"Why are you showing me this?" Eva asked. "More to the point, why would you summon Ben here while conducting counter operations? Aren't you afraid you'll give away all your secrets?"

A faint smile parted his lips. "Like I told our local representative from Arcanus, Miss Park—trust is built over time."

"Translation, Eva," Sayyida said, "adding together what you know now about our relationship with the Arcœnum, the wider war, and our own vote to go home—our life here is likely over, one way or another. It's time for a leap of faith."

Or you could just kill me, Eva thought. But she knew, somehow, that wasn't in the cards.

Minutes passed as al-Hurra issued orders. On the tactical map, Thorne's Third Fleet sailed deeper, if slowly, into the Triangle. Flitting around the edges of its sensors at a snail's pace, green icons slowly teased the Alliance fleet away from New Nassau's hexagon on the map. The arc of the misdirection was subtle but consistent. The sinking feeling in Eva's gut arced more sharply, and downward. Hope of rescue faded as al-Hurra's countermeasures appeared to be working.

The door to the C&C swept aside. Cinnamon Gauss led Ben in. Surprised at how glad she was to see him, Eva had to consciously restrain herself from taking a step in his direction. More of Gauss's crew followed, and then, of all people...

"My God, what's *she* doing here?" Eva blurted out.

It was Alice Keller, except older and leaner than she'd been in *The Castaway Girl.*

"She's our guest," Sayyida said.

Ben made the introductions automatically. He seemed enthralled by the drama unfolding on the tactical map. Eva shook Alice's hand limply.

"Looks like you were right, Captain," al-Hurra said. "I might have miscalculated your value. Or Miss Park's."

"You were right about something else, too," Eva said. "The pirates are working with—"

"No."

Alice said it quietly but with authority, capturing everyone's attention. The C&C staff went about their duties, but everyone else, including Gauss and her crew, regarded Alice Keller, who in turn stared at the tactical map and the red Alliance fleet represented there.

"I don't think they're here for either of you." The young woman swallowed hard. "I think they're here for me."

33
LIES AND ALIBIS

"YOU'RE GOING to need to explain that," Sayyida said.

But Alice knew she'd said too much already. Cinnamon Gauss slid toward her protectively. But Alice waved her away with a furtive hand, so the pirate captain diverted to stand next to Ben Stone. Her hand rested on her sidearm as if guarding him had been Cinnamon's intent all along.

"I can't, really," Alice said. "But ... I think I'm putting you all in danger by being here."

"Can't or won't?" Sayyida said with suspicious eyes.

"Sayyida, please," al-Hurra said. "Alice is our guest, not a prisoner to be interrogated."

Sayyida regarded him with an expression somewhere between skeptical and rebellious. "Father, we're at the tipping point for the colony. We've put all our cards on the table with these people. Third Fleet appears for the first time in a year... One small thing going wrong can wreck everything. One very large thing going wrong will surely do so!"

Hadrian al-Hurra let his daughter's anxious anger flow over him. Alice observed how different he was from Adrian

Korsakov. Al-Hurra was a measured man. Controlled in the midst of crisis.

"Alice, please tell us what you mean," he said. "Why do you think they're after you?"

"Alice..." Ben warned.

"What the hell is going on?" Eva Park demanded. "I'll ask again, what's she doing here?"

Alice took a breath. That, at least, was an easier question to answer. But those details, too, would have to be few.

"A friend, Ian, is helping me get back home to Alpha Centauri. He reached out to his friend—" And here she looked to Cinnamon Gauss. "—and she was helping make sure I got to Ionia safely, and then from there to Sylvan Novus. But the war came and—"

"We know all this!" Sayyida said. "A deal with Tarsus to ferry you home in exchange for tech. That doesn't explain the incursion of Third Fleet. Or are you making up their interest in you? I swear, Alice, if this is some teenage drama—"

"I, for one, didn't know about any deal," Park said. "Tarsus Research Station? Korsakov's research?" Her eyes narrowed. "Alice, did Doctor Korsakov discover something? Has his work yielded..." Ben flashed Eva a warning glance and she stopped speaking.

Sayyida looked first to Park and then Alice, who attempted to avoid eye contact. "And the mystery deepens! What the hell is so special about Alice Keller?"

She advanced on Alice. Ben and Cinnamon moved to cut her off. Sayyida halted, staring in surprise at the young pirate. "If you know something, Cinnamon," Sayyida said, "you'd better speak up now."

Alice hadn't been entirely truthful with Ben before. She *had* told one other person more of her story. Cinnamon Gauss pursed her lips together against Sayyida's request for information. Alice loved her for it even as she struggled with the secret herself. On the one hand, her hosts deserved to know how she'd endangered them. They'd been so kind, pulling her out of the Shallows and housing her in New Nassau till safe passage could be secured to Ionia. But all she could think about was Zoey and Ian turning against her the moment they'd begun to fear her. And how Korsakov, whom she'd relied on to keep her safe second only to Morgan, had betrayed her. Could she trust these people to accept her once they knew? To not betray her too?

"I'll ask you one more time, Alice," Sayyida said. "Why is the Alliance sending its sector strike force to find you?"

"I ..." she began. "I have—"

"Sir!" An officer pointed to the tactical map. "They're altering course."

The red icons representing Third Fleet had been pursuing the pirate vessels redirecting them away from the colony. Now their flight paths had begun curving back toward New Nassau. Someone uttered a curse.

From Eva Park, there was a gasp that sounded like hope. "Time's running out," she said. "Commander al-Hurra, if you offer me your unconditional surrender now, I can intervene on your behalf for leniency. I can't promise similar treatment for the Arcœnum I saw here, but—"

"What?" Ben said. "What did you just say?"

At the same time, Cinnamon Gauss exploded, "Fat chance!"

"Commander," the tactical officer said, "what are your orders? Should we begin evacuation—"

Sayyida al-Hurra stepped toward her father. "We must continue with our plan—"

"Quiet! Everyone!"

A frustrated al-Hurra placed his hands on the railing in front of him and leaned into it. He watched the Alliance fleet creep forward on the map. The hornet-like harassment by multiple pirate vessels seemed entirely ignored by the red fleet. It now appeared headed straight for New Nassau.

"Father, if they really are here for her," Sayyida said, moving nearer to him, "we can start reconciliation out on good terms. Let's just hand her over."

Cinnamon inhaled sharply.

Ben said, "You can't do that."

"This isn't your decision, Captain!" Sayyida said. "Our whole future is at stake, and if giving them this one girl can make the difference—"

"No," al-Hurra said, watching Third Fleet draw nearer. "Even if Alice is right, they're too close now. Thorne will never take her and leave us in peace. Maybe before but not now, with the war. They'll take this opportunity to clean us out. And trading her for leniency ... that wouldn't be right."

"Right? Father!"

"What kind of pirates are you people?" Park asked.

"That's a question we've debated for generations, Miss Park," al-Hurra said. "But pretty soon, the reason Thorne is coming in force won't matter."

"I'll renew my offer to intervene with them," Park said.

"With Thorne?" al-Hurra scoffed. "Do you know our name for him, Miss Park? The Hangman. He executes the Separated publicly after sham military trials. As a warning to other pirates."

"There's a priority message coming through on subspace," the communications officer interjected. "Slaving all channels."

"What does that mean?" Alice asked.

"It means an Alliance-wide emergency," Park said. "Or a presidential communiqué."

"It's the latter," the comms officer confirmed.

Al-Hurra and his daughter shared a look. On the tactical map, Thorne's fleet continued its advance on the colony.

"Let's hear it," al-Hurra said.

Piers Bragg's solemn baritone filled the C&C.

"—taking such drastic action, but austere times call for the resolve to do what must be done," the president said. On-screen, his expression was set, determined. "Therefore, under the Presidential Wartime Powers Act, I'm implementing multiple directives, each one necessary not just to achieve victory in this war, but to ensure the survival of our species."

"Listen to him," Cinnamon said. "He's growling like a hungry wolf."

"Item one," Bragg said. "The Civilian Oversight Board for Security Enforcement is hereby suspended for the duration of the conflict. All individuals who self-identify as Psyckers or who are known to have close ties to Psyckers will be detained, questioned, and, if necessary, interred in the Community Zones without freedom of egress. This is not something I want to do—"

"Yeah, right," Cinnamon snarled.

"Cinn, please," al-Hurra admonished.

"—required of the moment. Of course, I informed Chairperson Marcos of this decision before announcing it here. While I understand why she reacted the way she did—"

"Oh, no," Park muttered.

"—militant response left me no choice but to reinter her after she violated the conditions of her release from prison. I leave open the possibility—and this is in Miss Marcos's hands—that she can reenter service to my administration in some form, perhaps in a modified capacity to monitor confinements in the Community Zones. However, until I'm convinced of her *loyalty*, this will not be possible. We simply cannot brook dissension in wartime."

"Sonofabitch," Park said.

"Item two: Current parliamentary elections both here in Sol and in Alpha Centauri are delayed indefinitely."

"What?" Sayyida said. "He can't do that!"

"He can," whispered Park.

"He has," said al-Hurra.

"Those currently serving in each parliamentary body will continue to do so. I have reason to believe there are Arcœnum sympathizers who are one vote away from taking power. In the interests of Alliance security, I am not at liberty to reveal the intelligence behind that assertion. But to allow them to sow the seeds of doubt now would be tantamount to treason. As your president—of all the people!—it is my sacred responsibility to prevent that."

"I don't understand," Alice said. "What's happening?"

"Our party—his party," Park said, "currently has a majority in each system. He's just codified that into law—temporarily, at least."

"Maybe he really believes it's necessary," Ben said. "For the good of the—"

Cinnamon Gauss sneered.

"Item three: You might have seen the recent reports of atrocities committed against Arcœnum in the integrated communities of The Frontier," Bragg said. "While these reports are likely exaggerated by special interests sympathetic to the enemy in the media, I cannot turn a blind eye to the likelihood that, even if such incidents are not yet occurring, they could happen in the future. Emotions are running high. I am, therefore, imposing martial law in The Frontier with the express purpose of keeping the peace. Any Arcœnum living within our borders should consider themselves under house arrest, save for essential travel such as medical treatment. We'll show the enemy that we protect *their* rights too within our own borders, even during wartime. Because I cannot spare Alliance resources, I've vested local authorities in each community with the right of enforcement—"

"What a joke!" Cinnamon said. "He doesn't give a shit about the Arcœnum."

"It's a justification," Park said, voicing an inner thought. "An excuse for closing his fist."

"Quiet," al-Hurra said. "He's past the flag-waving part. Listen."

"—four: I'm issuing a writ of *habeas corpus* for Alice Keller."

Alice gasped. "What—what does that mean?"

Bragg, as if speaking directly to her, provided the answer. "Miss Keller is a dangerous individual. I know," he admonished, raising a hand, "to all of you she's 'the castaway girl,' and I too was taken in by her tragic story. But recent intelligence has proven that she's much more than that. Rather than a victim of the Arcœnum along with the rest of her family, I've come to believe she was working with the Arcœnum and was, ultimately, responsible for the downing of the SS *Seeker* on Drake's World. That's all I'm able to reveal at this time."

"Is he kidding with this crap?" Cinnamon said.

Alice realized her mouth had dropped open. Sayyida al-Hurra turned to stare at her, hard.

"That explains Third Fleet," al-Hurra theorized over Bragg's rationalizing. He turned almost sadly to Alice. "It seems you were right, Miss Keller."

"I'm therefore offering a bounty for Alice Keller," Bragg continued. "Anyone who turns her in—*alive*—will receive ten million credits, no questions asked. But she must be *unharmed*."

"Why?" Sayyida demanded again. "What's so special about you, Alice?"

But Bragg grabbed their attention again with his dénouement. He expressed regrets at such draconian measures. He shared his hopes that martial law would only be necessary for a short period of time. He assured listeners of his ironclad belief that humanity would triumph over the extinction event threatened by Arcœnum aggression. All the public had to do was believe in Piers Bragg. He'd navigate them through to the other side of survival.

"Turn it off," al-Hurra said, disgusted. Addressing his daughter, he said, "These are the people you wish to reconcile with?"

"Father," Sayyida said, "we're out of options. We have to hand her over now. There's a greater good to consider, for all our people. She's practically a stranger!"

Al-Hurra regarded her, his expression turning sad. His face reminded Alice of Morgan's when, at times, she'd somehow disappointed him.

"I thought I'd taught you better than that," al-Hurra said. "To *be* better than that."

"Commander," the tactical officer said, "what are your orders? Third Fleet will be here in a few hours." She gestured at the map. Alice was surprised to see how much closer the red icons seemed after so short a time.

Al-Hurra sighed. "Sound evacuation. I'm activating Operation Exodus. All personnel will embark for the coves."

"Father!" Sayyida shouted.

"It's done! Comms, start transferring data and spiking the drives. All records indicating Miss Keller was ever here. I want you to not only delete the data but also to reformat the storage sectors where it resided. Cinnamon, I want you to..."

Al-Hurra ceased speaking when his daughter leveled her pistol at him. Alice gasped. Everyone in the room froze. Only the mumblings of the C&C staff continued, head-down in executing al-Hurra's orders. That too ceased when Sayyida commanded them to stop.

"Sayyida, don't do this," al-Hurra said.

"I have no choice! The captains voted for their crews. We barely achieved a majority, and now you'd throw it all away for someone we hardly even know?"

"I'm not throwing anything away," al-Hurra said. "In fact, I'm holding sacred what your grandfather and his generation stood for. It's you who seems to have forgotten those values."

Eva Park slid to one side. Sayyida backed away from her father toward a bare wall. She swung her weapon toward Eva.

"Sayyida, I'll make my same offer to you," Park said. "I can speak to Admiral Thorne. Minimize the potential for conflict."

"Yes, please," Sayyida said, abruptly moving the pistol off her. "Interceding on our behalf is why we brought you here."

"To hell with that." Cinnamon Gauss stepped in front of Alice. "King Hadrian has spoken." Ben sidestepped to Sayyida's left.

"Shut up! Stop calling him that!"

Cinnamon took a step forward, hand outstretched. "Give me the gun, Say."

Sayyida adjusted her grip. "No."

The rogue took another step toward her. "Last chance..."

Sayyida aimed the pistol at her. She was clearly conflicted but also determined.

"Sayyida, don't!" al-Hurra implored.

Alice pushed Cinnamon Gauss aside and stepped between the two women. "Don't hurt her!"

"Alice!" Cinnamon shouted at the same moment Sayyida pulled the trigger.

Someone screamed.

Everything stopped, as if time itself had been shocked to stillness.

In the air between them hung the bullet from the pistol. Sayyida's face showed disbelief. Alice extended her left hand and turned it slightly, the bullet mirroring her movement. With a beckoning finger, she summoned it, and the slug crossed the space and came to rest in her scarred palm.

Sayyida dropped the pistol. Cinnamon and Ben jumped forward together to restrain her.

"I don't believe it," Eva Park said. "Did I just see what I think I did?"

"We all saw it, Miss Park," al-Hurra breathed. "And now I think we have our answer to why the president is so keen to recover Miss Keller."

Ben shoved Sayyida into Cinnamon and bent quickly to the floor to recover the pistol. The rogue's foot was faster, and she trapped the weapon against the deck. Ben looked up to find Cinnamon's sidearm trained on him.

"Not so fast, poster boy." She squatted, never losing her aim, and picked up the second pistol. "What do you want me to do?" she asked al-Hurra without taking her eyes off Ben.

"Funny you should ask," he replied. His voice was so odd in the moment, so light and out of place, that everyone turned to look at him. "I want you to evacuate Miss Keller and Captain Stone to Tower's Fall."

"Sir?"

Alice had never seen Cinnamon flummoxed before. She was unflappable, someone who specialized in stirring up everyone else. But for once she seemed at a loss.

"Get them out of here, Cinn, aboard the *Dog*. And be quick about it, before Thorne's fleet cuts you off. Keep her out of Bragg's hands."

"But sir, I can't leave you—"

"Do it," he said. "That's an order."

"If I'm going somewhere," Ben said, indicating Eva, "she's coming too."

"I'm afraid that won't be possible," al-Hurra said. "My daughter is right. We need her now more than ever."

Ben turned to Alice. "I can't go with you," he said, his tone heavy. "I have a mission—"

"Go," Park said. "I'll be fine."

Ben was tempted. "I appreciate the gesture, but—"

"*Go*," she said again. "She needs protecting more than I do." And then, almost as an afterthought, "From Bragg, especially."

Ben's eyes seemed to look past Alice for a moment, focus on something beyond her.

"Come on," Cinnamon Gauss said, brushing past him despite Sayyida's renewed protests. "We're burning starlight."

"Thank you," Alice said to al-Hurra. "For everything." To Sayyida, who was approaching hysteria, she said, "I'm so sorry." She followed Cinnamon out, and Ben, after a moment's hesitation, followed them both.

34

THERE'S NO WHINING IN WAR

AFTER THEIR DEPARTURE, Eva retreated somewhere deep inside herself. Sayyida al-Hurra's stubborn insistence that the pirates hand over Alice Keller. Her father's grating silence in response. Thorne's steady progress toward the colony. She walked away from the drama to think.

Bragg's speech had hit her hard. The need for his edicts she could understand. In times of war egregious actions, unthinkable in the luxury of peacetime, were often swallowed whole by the public without the slightest hiccup. During the Specter War, austerity had been commonplace. Citizens asked to sacrifice for the good of the whole. Corporations pressed into service to mass-manufacturer materiel from toilet seats to translight drives. What would have been damned in peacetime as the fascistic takeover of industry was hailed as patriotic. Your job, public sentiment said to its elected representatives, is to protect us—no matter the cost.

But in all that time of hard choices, not once had elections been suspended. Not once had a group of people—even that minority of dissenters pleading for peace from the very government doing its best to protect their right to do so by defending them militarily—been segregated into communities in the name of Alliance security. No bounties had been levied on individuals. No writs of *habeas corpus* issued.

And now all of that had happened, and in a matter of moments. Time would tell if there would be dissent beyond a few raised voices. If, say, the planetary parliaments of Sol and Alpha Centauri would attempt to curtail the executive orders. Not likely, given they shared the president's party affiliation. So for now, Piers Bragg's decrees had become law under the Presidential Wartime Powers Act. Bragg was now the most powerful man in human history.

Marcos reincarcerated. Alice Keller—once the darling of the president's First Hundred Days honeymoon—now essentially an outlaw? Eva recalled her introduction to the girl during a half-heard negotiation between the newly elected Bragg and Andre Korsakov. My God, had that really been three years ago? She'd only been the president's personal assistant then, someone who brought him tea and coffee and otherwise organized his social calendar—a habit from his CEO days that didn't survive long among the multi-tiered demands of his young, ambitious presidency. Within six months she'd vaulted over scowling campaign hangers-on to become his communications director. And she'd come to know Alice Keller intimately—at least the Alice Keller portrayed in the dailies from *The Castaway Girl*. Her expressions, her moods, her obvious crush on Ben Stone. When the documentary became the most popular feature across two star systems, she and Leo had milked it for all the positive press they could, and Eva had found herself glad that Alice was tucked quietly away with Andre Korsakov "under evaluation." How could the girl in that documentary now be Public Enemy No. 1? Even with what Eva had seen in this room, even knowing Bragg's pathological hatred for the Arcœnum...

Alice Keller? Really?

What Eva wouldn't give for a two-minute, encrypted confab with Leo. He'd no doubt been the lead writer on Bragg's address; she'd recognized his prosaic lust for metaphor and too-fond affinity for alliteration. But it was hard to imagine him outlining the geometric expansion of presidential powers represented by that speech. It would have gone against every ethical grain in Leo's being to empower Bragg that way, even during wartime. Eva could still remember what Leo had said to her when he'd first expressed doubts about the president during his second year in office: even villains see themselves as a hero in their own stories. Bragg's problem, Leo speculated, was that he wanted to be the hero in everyone else's stories, too. He needed that approbation to see *himself* that way. That made him not only needful of outside acceptance, but dangerous.

What Eva now realized was that, for her, Bragg had become the anti-hero in a number of stories: Miranda Marcos's and now Alice Keller's. And her own, for that matter. Eva's faith in Bragg's vision to protect humanity had been failing for months, and the rate of erosion ramped up the more he persecuted the Psyckers. The public embracing that policy had only emboldened the man. And now Bragg had reimprisoned Marcos ... It was getting hard to differentiate political maneuvering from personal animus. In his speech, he'd alluded to Miranda's resistance to his latest anti-Psycker initiative to revoke paroles from internment.

I'll bet *she resisted.* Eva smirked. *I'll bet she threatened him with anarchy across two star systems. Go big or go home, right?*

So Bragg had used whatever pushback Marcos gave him to justify stripping her of what little power she'd had. Was she sitting in her newest prison cell cursing Eva for betraying her from day one as the president's representative? The thought soured Eva's stomach.

I wish I'd been there, Miranda, to warn you. Our dear leader doesn't take kindly to being reprimanded, especially by women.

"You have to stop them, Father!"

Sayyida al-Hurra's passion pulled Eva from the quicksand of her self-recrimination. "There's still time!"

Eva mined her short-term memory to catch up on the drama. The commander was losing patience with his daughter. Sayyida's angry insistence reminded Eva of a saying from the previous war that had even become a headline—a rallying cry for those prosecuting the war. A tactic for shaming nay-sayers into silence.

No whining. There's no whining in war.

"Listen to you," Eva said. Both father and daughter turned their attention to her. "You talk about being mistreated after the Specter War, about being forced by circumstance and an uncaring government into the life you lead now. And yet here you stand, willing to sacrifice a young woman—who's done nothing to you—for your own ends. I'd say you've slid a ways down the slope of your moral high ground, Miss al-Hurra."

Sayyida regarded her, eyes smoldering.

"Commander, Marshal Gauss is hailing," the officer at comms announced.

"Speakers," al-Hurra said. "Go, Joseph."

"Things are getting bad down here, Cap." Around the man voices were raised, some in anger, many clearly scared. "We don't have enough ships to get people out. Some folks are asking why we aren't fighting instead of running."

"For one thing, we're too dispersed across the Triangle at the moment." It was obvious al-Hurra was tired of explaining himself. "And even if we weren't, this has always been the plan. We can't stand toe-to-toe against massed Alliance firepower."

"Hey, you don't have to convince me," Gauss grumbled, his

voice ancient and leathery. Old and stiff, but less likely to bend for that. "I'm just reporting status."

Al-Hurra exhaled. "Right, Joe, I know. Follow the plan. Families dispersed to the coves. Everyone's been pre-assigned. But have the captains prepare for a ground assault. We know Thorne is bringing at least one battalion of Marines. I'm counting on him having bigger fish to fry than filling his cargo holds with our people and weighing his personnel down with guard duty. And he won't want to spend the bodies on a ground assault if he doesn't have to."

"About that, Cap," Gauss said. "We've already lost some to panic. Including a kid killed when a crowd surged in the Havens. Knocked the kid right out of his mother's hands."

Al-Hurra closed his eyes. Sayyida looked stricken. Eva kept silent.

"But making preparations has the added bonus of giving the croakers something to do," Gauss said, pushing on. "Besides stir up trouble."

"Yeah," al-Hurra allowed. "Maybe if they're prepping to fight it'll make it easier to let their loved ones go, too." He opened his eyes. "Joe, how are *your* people doing with all this?"

A grunt from the other end of the line. "They're doing their jobs. Like I taught 'em."

"Trained by you, I'd expect no less."

"Me either," Gauss said, side-stepping the compliment. "And they know it."

"Keep order as long as you can," al-Hurra said. He added sarcastically, "Pretty soon, you'll have help."

"Glad to see you haven't lost your gallows humor, Cap. Strange how it's so important when there's so little to laugh about."

Very little, Eva thought. She couldn't get the image out of her head: a crowd of panicking citizens, pirates or not, racing down the stories of the stacked apartments she'd seen as they came in from the docks. Pushing, a mother screaming at them to give her room, and the child wrenched from her arms. And then, only more screaming...

"As for Cinnamon..." al-Hurra left the thought unfinished.

"I've got no worries for her," breathed Gauss. "She can take care of herself." Eva, though she didn't know the man beyond a minute of snowy comms traffic, didn't believe his bravado.

"I'm counting on it," al-Hurra said.

"Me too."

"I'll let you know before the landings start."

"I would hope so," Gauss said, and it was almost angry. "Hey! Put that down! Gotta go, Cap."

"Take care."

The low mumble of the C&C's steadfast personnel filled the room. Even Sayyida was quiet. After a moment, Eva said, "Cap? Why does he call you that?"

Al-Hurra was too distracted to answer.

"Back in the day, when Father was a ship's captain, Joseph Gauss was his quartermaster," Sayyida explained. Her voice was mollified and sounded almost nostalgic. Maybe tinged with just a little bit of grief. "But that was a long time ago."

"I'm more concerned with the future," al-Hurra said. His face appeared graver than ever. "And Thorne is hailing."

Eva took a deep breath to center herself. Not an easy task, considering how unmoored she felt inside. Things were about to get very real very fast. For one mother, they already had.

"Once again, Commander," she said, affecting formality and as much sincerity as she could, "I'll offer to mediate. As you said, we don't want more casualties. One unnecessary death is one too many."

"Commander?" the comms officer said. "Should I acknowledge—"

Al-Hurra stayed her with his hand. "We're down to the nut-cutting here, Miss Park. No more deaths would be nice, yes."

"On either side," she clarified.

The leader of the Separated nodded. "Why should I trust you? If I was dubious about your willingness to help before, your reaction to Louie earlier..."

"I'm still terrified," Eva said without hesitation. It came easily because it was true. "You said it yourself—you sprung him —it—him... whatever! ... on me. I..."

She did vacillate now, and the hesitation came from the old negotiator's instinct. How transparent—another word for *naïve* in politics—should she be? She wasn't sure that reconciling these people to the larger Alliance was a good idea, whatever the political upside might be. Especially given their too-close relationship with the Arcœnum. But now seemed not the time for either posturing or circumspection. al-Hurra wasn't just the leader of his people, he was an experienced ship's captain used to negotiating with scared merchants and self-assured Fleet captains like Thorne. She had to decide whose side she was on, and if she were being honest with herself, selling them out felt more wrong than not.

"The truth, Commander?" Eva said. "The president's speech disturbed me. When I transitioned to his campaign from corporate, I did so because I thought he was the best man for the job. I believed—and I still believe—the Arcœnum are an existential threat. But about Bragg being the best man to deal with that threat? Of that, I'm no longer sure."

"How conveniently conflicted," Sayyida said with apparent contempt.

"At the moment," Eva went on, "my concern for Alice Keller outweighs my disgust for your association with the Arcœnum. I don't have all the facts there, I acknowledge that. But Piers Bragg—him I know."

"You also know Miss Keller's destination," al-Hurra said. "I should drop you in the deepest hole we have until Thorne eventually finds you. Give Cinnamon Gauss as big a head start as I can."

"I know they went to someplace called Tower's Fall," Eva said. "First, I have no idea where that is. But I give you my word, I won't even tell Thorne that much. For Alice's sake."

"Don't believe her, Father" Sayyida warned. "And if he gets the information from her, it'll do *us* no good. Let *me* talk to him first. By handing the girl over, we can minimize bloodshed, maybe avoid it altogether!"

"No." al-Hurra's judgment was final. "Didn't you hear Joe? It's too late for that already."

Sayyida clenched a fist at her side. "In that case, I have people I need to attend to. Captain Mattei and others to evacuate while there's still time. Else, Thorne will surely execute them for treason. They don't deserve—"

"See to it," her father said curtly.

Sayyida made a stiff bow to his dismissal and whirled on her heel. Al-Hurra, his face falling into regret, watched her exit the C&C.

"Commander," the comms officer reminded him, "Admiral Thorne is hailing again. They could interpret further delay as implicitly hostile."

Al-Hurra steeled himself. He stared hard at Eva, drilling down through her eyes, determined to find the deception he was sure was there somewhere. She returned his assessment, unflinching. Somewhere in the short distance between them, understanding was born.

"Very well, Miss Park," he said. "At this point, I'm not sure I have much choice but to trust you. But until I call on you, remain silent. Comms, acknowledge the hail."

35
DEPARTURE DELAYS

BEN DIDN'T TRUST Sayyida al-Hurra as far as he could throw her. He didn't trust any of these deserter-pirates, but her willingness to sell out Alice pushed his instinctive dislike of the woman toward personal hatred.

He followed grimly as Gauss led them through the agitated corridors of New Nassau's command HQ. Residents brushed past them or bumped into them in confusion or fear or disbelief over Third Fleet's imminent arrival. Ben blocked and elbowed them aside, running interference for Alice, who seemed shut down from what was happening around her. Her feet moved, but like Ben, her mind was elsewhere. Somewhere along the line, the virus of duty, honor, and country had infected him. While conflicted over leaving Eva alone in al-Hurra's hands, something inside told Ben to prioritize Alice first. As if it were a higher, more fundamental calling than his sworn duty to the Alliance. That he was disobeying President Bragg, his superior —specifically, Bragg's order to take Alice into custody—only added to Ben's moral confusion. For once he wouldn't have minded an appearance by Bob Bricker's sneering specter, so long as the dead man offered him a little useful advice. Or even the molting corpses of Baqri and DeSoto, so long as they lifted their bony fingers and pointed him in the right direction. So far, none had shown.

Gauss had them glued to the right wall lined with more of that human-Arcœnum bastardized tech. Seeing it reminded Ben of a detail he'd somehow failed to follow up on amid the conflict in the C&C—Eva Park's suggestion that the pirates were working with the Archies. The possibility—probability now?—that al-Hurra's den of thieves was in bed with the Arcanus Collective disturbed Ben even more than Bragg's speech had.

"Hold up!" Gauss yanked a closed fist up next to her ear. They were near the end of the access corridor connecting the command center to the main colony. Once through the doorway, they'd be just four more people floundering among the throng of panicky residents.

Torque, who brought up the rear, placed a light hand on Ben's shoulder. He whirled sharply anticipating an attack but found merely with a half-smile. "I'm not getting fresh, pretty man," she assured him. "Back against the wall. Unless, y'know, you'd prefer to turn the other direction." She quirked an eyebrow suggestively.

Ben swallowed his irritation and guided Alice forward. "Back flat, side profile," he told her. "Smaller target."

"Target?" Alice said. "Is someone shooting at us?"

"Not yet," Gauss grumbled.

"What do you see?" Ben asked.

"More a feeling than a sighting," murmured Gauss, straining to see through the busy throng with her tactician's eye. After a moment, she nodded definitively. "Over there."

It took Ben a moment to pierce the flow and counter-flow of New Nassauers before he spied what she'd seen. Across the common area between their position and the stacked condos were several islands of unmoving individuals, two or three to a group, each stationed with good sightlines on the end of the corridor Ben's group now occupied. They seemed innocuous enough, as if they were merely social clubs hanging out for afternoon conversation. Except for the residents swirling around them. And the fact that they were looking for someone.

"You think they're looking for us?" Ben said.

The rogue leader clucked. "Who else?"

"Maybe they're your grandfather's," Torque suggested. "Sent to keep order. People are pretty scared."

Gauss gave that its due diligence. "Maybe. But I don't recognize them."

"Deputized?" mused Ben. "Needs of the hour?"

Gauss made an unconvinced noise. She seemed in no hurry to vacate the safety of their covert position, despite people cursing at them to get out of the way.

"Assuming they're not friendlies, any other way to the docks?" Ben asked.

"Longer ways," Torque said. "But maybe safer."

"Usually not the case in combat," Ben said. "Those myths about serpentining under fire to avoid getting shot? Complete bullshit. Two points, straight line, fastest route."

"We're not in combat. Yet," Gauss said. "Torque, keep eyes on our friends." She nestled closer to the wall to engage her embedded comms. "Gal, you there?" A moment later, "Then where the hell are—never mind! Get back to the ship and get her prepped for dust off. Tout de suite!"

"Who's she talking to?" Ben asked.

"Our navigator," Torque said. "You'll like her. She's small. Like you."

"What's going on?" Alice said.

"We're trying to get you out of here, little sister," Torque said. Ben noted again the nickname that sounded more like a term of endearment.

"Catch Gal with her pants down again?" Torque said.

"I knew I should have called earlier," Gauss muttered, pulling them into a huddle for privacy. "She's getting her priorities straight as we speak."

"And her pants on," Torque said.

"The longer we stand here," Ben said, jerking his head toward the commons, "the more of those folks will show up."

"Yeah, yeah," Gauss said.

"Give me a gun," Ben said. "I can be useful."

"Nice try, jackass," Gauss said under her breath.

"You're already useful," Torque said. "Just walk out front. They'll be so starstruck, they'll drop their jaws *and* their weapons."

Alice preempted Ben's angry retort with one of her own. "Don't talk to him like that."

Her tone was even, but the strength behind it captured everyone's attention.

"Ben saved my life," Alice said. "You should talk to him with more respect."

"Torque didn't mean anything by it," Gauss assured her. "She was just having a little joke at his expense."

"It's okay, Alice," Ben chipped in. "Big Bertha here's got nothing on me in the snark department."

Alice eyed him protectively but didn't speak again.

"Well, well," Gauss said as if she'd just unlocked a troublesome mystery. "Knowing the high regard little sister here has for you, Stone, I like you more now. By which, I mean, I hate your guts less."

"You say the sweetest things," he said. To Alice, "See? I can take care of myself."

Alice tried to smile.

"Stay in the same order," Gauss said, gesturing. "Guns stay holstered, Torque. And no, Stone, you can't have one. We're just four more scared residents trying to save our skins. Alice, keep your pretty face aimed at the ground. Stone, you do the same. If we're stopped, I'll do the talking. Keep quiet."

"I have a pretty face?" he baited her.

"Did you hear the part about keeping quiet?"

Gauss strode forward, followed by Alice, Ben, and Torque bringing up the rear. After the close quarters of the corridor with its humid press of fear sweat, the wide-open space of the commons felt liberating but disorienting. Above them, the igloo-like reinforced plastinium of the habitat dome was a window on the Triangle's beauty, though Ben hardly had time to appreciate it. One of the teams of two was looking their way.

"We've been made," Ben said loud enough for Gauss to hear. She was moving way too slow for his liking.

"I see them," she tossed back.

One of the men of the duo said something to his partner. The second man nodded and turned slightly away. Ben knew someone issuing a comms alert when he saw them.

"Can't we move any faster?" he said.

"Too late," Torque said.

All three teams were moving now. Converging on the first twosome's position, about as inconspicuously as a stripper walking down the aisle in church. The beehive activity of the citizenry hindered them.

"Shit," Gauss said.

They'd made it halfway across the common area and were in the most exposed place for an ambush. Open, without cover, and surrounded by clueless civilians.

"I got this, boss," Torque said.

Ben felt Torque's bulk approaching before he saw her. She quick-walked past him with long, purposeful strides of her powerful legs. She looked like a warehouse jockey wearing one of those heavy exoskeletons for unloading cargo. Only hers was inside and made of bone and sinew.

Before Gauss could stop her, Torque was well on her way to confronting the twosome. She waved one meaty hand like a tourist spotting family. "Hi, boys!"

The duo drew their weapons. Ben checked the other two groups. They'd been standing apart to cover multiple access points and now were having trouble getting to the twosome as more panicky civilians spilled into the commons from the stacked condos.

"Break right," Gauss said. Alice followed, which meant Ben followed too.

"Didn't you hear what I said about serpentining?"

Ignoring him, Gauss led them off at a forty-five-degree angle. At Ben's ten o'clock, Torque had almost reached the twosome. The group of three from the far right were now closing the distance toward Ben's party, refusing Torque's bait.

"This is better?" he growled, fumbling from instinct with his holster. He swore when he found it empty. Gauss hadn't yet drawn her pistol.

Torque's hands were in the air. She appeared downright jovial to see her two fellows, despite them pointing their weapons at her.

"Make way!" Gauss said to the crowd thickening around them. "Make way, I said!"

The other group, the threesome angling toward them, still hadn't drawn their weapons.

A shot rang out from Torque's direction. Someone shouted in alarm. Ben upped his gait to a quick-step, his peripheral vision scouting Torque's position. The crowd was making way over there, all right. They dived, jumped, and ran, avoiding the source of the shot however they could. Torque stood solid as an oak tree, one vise-like hand wrapped around the first man's gun hand, his weapon pointed at the plastinium dome overhead. The second man leveled his pistol, and Torque grabbed the belt of the first pirate with her free hand, pulling him close and twisting him around as a shield and forcing his pistol from his grip. The second man hesitated, and that was enough. Torque lifted the pirate and physically threw him into his advancing partner. Both went down.

Remind me never to piss her off, Ben thought.

The third group advancing from the other side of the commons was almost on top of her. Torque turned, spotted them, and leapt over the twosome attempting to disentangle themselves. She made a beeline for Gauss.

"You folks don't want to do this," Gauss said to the trio that had cut them off. They gave ground to her slow, methodical advance but still blocked her, spreading out to surround Ben's group as best they could.

The civilians nearby gave the scene a wide berth. Alice's eyes darted from the first pirate to the second to the third. Ben moved past her, making sure to stay in her sightline and between them.

When the leader of the trio stopped retreating, Gauss halted too. They were in a standoff that Ben knew his group could only lose. The bad guys had backup coming. They didn't.

"It's okay, Alice," he said to comfort her, and maybe himself. "She knows what she's doing."

I hope.

Alice pressed into him, wrapping her arm around him before he could react. He almost pushed her away because she'd just nixed his options for helping Gauss. He held her and watched, trying hard to trust the *Dog*'s captain.

"You boys need to clear out," the pirate captain said, trying to sound nonchalant. She still hadn't drawn her pistol. "King's orders."

"We have different orders," the leader said. He was the man who'd lost the bet to the horny teenager outside the brig. "Now give me the gun, Cinn, and we'll write this off as an unfortunate misunderstanding."

She drew her pistol so fast that Ben had to blink to make sure he wasn't just wishing it so.

"I'll give you one end of it," said Gauss. "Clear the way, I said!"

Ben attempted to disengage from Alice so he could back Gauss up, but she only held him tighter. He turned to look for Torque but didn't see her.

"We don't kill our own," Gauss said.

"Not till today," answered the older pirate.

A roar erupted from behind Ben's shoulder. The few brave civilians close to the action scattered. The member of the trio at Ben's eight o'clock lifted into the air like his personal square of artificial gravity had failed. Ben spotted Torque's thick legs beneath and behind the man, spread straight for leverage.

He grabbed Alice by the shoulders, demanding, "Let go, Alice! Let me help them!" She released her grip on him as Gauss batted her opponent's weapon aside with her own. Gauss dropped her head like a bull and plowed her full bodyweight into him, orange spikes and all, crashing her skull hard under his jaw. The third of the pirate trio advanced on Gauss, aiming her pistol but hesitating to fire. Ben darted in from her blindside, twisting to sweep his shin against the back of her knees. She landed hard on her back on the deck, the air *whooshing* from her lungs. A report from her pistol brought civilian screams again. Ben righted himself and pinned her shooting arm to the ground, yanking the pistol from her weakened grasp as she struggled to fill deflated lungs. She eyed him in shock, and Ben clocked her one sweeping hook to the jaw.

"Lights out," he said, rising over her unconscious form. He secured her pistol in his belt. "Alice, come on."

The older pirate had recovered, and Gauss was pinned on her back by his bulk. Torque's man was down and unmoving, and she launched herself at the older pirate about to pistol-whip her captain. Her bodyweight knocked him off, and the impact with the floor forced the gun from his hand. Together, the two women made short work of him.

"Hey!" came a call from across the commons.

The two Torque had taken down earlier were back on their feet and running with the other trio toward them, weapons drawn, unhindered now by anyone in their path.

"Through there!" Gauss barked, leaping into the corridor that led to the docks and the *Junkyard Dog*.

They kept their order, with Alice following Gauss, and Ben behind her. Torque paused her flight to work the controls of the pressure door separating the corridor from the commons. A screech and slide of metal on metal, and the door crashed shut.

"Out of the way! Out of the way!"

Gauss's command parted half a dozen citizens, who pressed themselves into the walls. Alice tripped and nearly fell to her knees, but Ben grabbed her arm, and she kept her feet.

They traversed the corridor quickly and came out onto the docks. If the commons had been chaotic, then the docks—with every berth containing a ship in some stage of preflight—were pandemonium. Engines of every make and model churned in preflight, each in a different, percussive key. The cacophony of evacuation panic overloaded Ben's ears and set his teeth on edge.

It could have been worse. He'd expected another welcoming committee to hinder their escape but found everyone at the docks dedicated to the same task of getting the hell out of New Nassau. A woman with dark stains on her face stood at the base of the entry ramp to the *Dog* motioning to them to hurry up.

"Moze!" Gauss shouted to be heard over the thunderous roar. "Prepped?"

"Yeah, boss," said a woman at the top of the ramp. "But a couple of things—"

"Great!" Gauss proclaimed, darting past her and into the ship.

The woman, Moze, watched as first Alice, then Ben mounted the ramp. "Uh, welcome aboard?" she shouted to them as they entered the ship.

36
THE GIRL'S THE MISSION

BEN NODDED at the woman as he passed, giving her the once-over. He'd seen her before, one of Gauss's crew who'd abducted him and Park from the *Terre*. Socially awkward, stained clothes, and with a perpetually curious look on her lined face. Gauss had called her Moze, and she must be the engineer, he surmised as she exchanged jibing greetings with Torque.

"Close up, close up!" Gauss shouted. "Chop-chop!"

Ben and Alice quick-stepped into the middle compartment where less than a day before he'd been held prisoner with Eva Park and Mattei. "First things first," he said to Alice. "Let's get you strapped—"

He stopped speaking when he saw her petrified expression. Her eyes were fixated behind him, and for half a moment, he thought she must be seeing Bricker and the scouts.

"Alice?"

The hydraulic lifters made a shrill grind as they pulled up the ramp.

Ben snatched the pistol from his belt and spun. At first what he saw confirmed his suspicion that his ghosts had become visible to others. Here was the left-behind Archie from Canis

III, ready to reenact its bone-crushing suicide. But Alice could see it too...

The exoskeleton was different. Modern. And the Arcœnum only sat on its haunches, if "sitting" was the right word, and stared passively. The image of a waterfall began flowing in Ben's mind. And what the hell were twittering birds doing inside the piece-of-shit pinnace?

He brought his pistol up, cradling its grip for stability in his off hand. "What the—"

"Whoa!" Torque exclaimed, nearly bowling him over. "Pistol down, partner! That's Louie!" She stepped between them.

The Arcœnum remained motionless. But the peaceful images of nature in Ben's head faded. He grasped how they'd gotten there, and he could almost smell the brig on Canis III. The sensory memory was that strong. He moved back a step but didn't lower his weapon.

The woman named Moze appeared, glancing timidly around Torque's shoulder. The ramp shunked tight, and the seal indicator switched from red to green. The *Dog*'s engines rose in pitch, their power shaking the ship. It was all Ben could do to maintain trigger discipline. If Torque weren't standing between him and the Archie... One thing for sure—it was no hallucination.

"Stone, give me the pistol!" Torque said, opening a hand to receive it. Ben retreated another half-step in Alice's direction, his eyes never leaving the Arcœnum.

"What the hell is that thing doing here?" he yelled. And how had it projected those tranquil thoughts through his mindshield? *The same way the marooned Archie did in the brig.* An answer explaining nothing.

Moze thumbed the comms panel. "Boss, you best get back here!"

Snarky invectives erupted over shipwide followed by a clumsy shuffling of safety straps.

Torque's hand hung in the air, awaiting the pistol. Ben had no intention of handing it over. The Archie remained still as a statue.

In his head Ben heard Eva Park whisper, *You were right about something else, too.*

Cinnamon Gauss burst into the hold. "Louie?"

"Boss, that's what I was trying to tell you," Moze said. "Your grandpappy called, asked us to—"

"Stone, put down that weapon," Gauss ordered, slowly drawing her own but with its muzzle facing the floor. "We don't have time for this."

"What's it doing here!" Ben demanded again. His pistol was shaking, whether in resonance with the ship's engines gearing up or his own nerves, he wasn't sure. At this range, to the Archie, it wouldn't much matter.

"I'll explain later," Gauss said, her voice surprisingly mild. "But right now, we need to get out of here."

As if to make the point, small arms fire peppered the outer hull.

"You'll explain now," Ben said.

"Stone, look at me!" Gauss said, moving beside Torque. "Look at me!"

"Don't think I'll fall for—"

But before Ben could finish, Torque leapt in, batting his pistol aside and grabbing its barrel. A single shot rang out, ricocheting once inside the compartment and dying in a wall.

"Sonofabitch!" Torque exclaimed, wrenching the pistol away from him. Her hand flexed open but the weapon hung in the air, pinching the web of skin between her thumb and forefinger. "Ow! Moze, get this off me!"

The engineer came forward, touching the pistol gingerly, the big woman's splayed hand still attached.

"Hurry up!" Torque implored.

"Safety first," Moze said, "literally." Once she'd engaged the gun's safety, Moze opened the slide, releasing Torque.

"Ow!"

"You're welcome."

Torque whirled on Ben. "I oughta pound you into paste, you stupid jarhead—"

"Pound him later," Gauss said. "Everybody, strap in. Stone, get your ass up front with me." When he didn't move, she finally leveled her pistol at him. "Or I can crack that ramp and chum you to our friends out there as a diversion."

The motivating sound of small-arms fire popped again along the outer hull.

"They'll have bigger guns than that soon enough," Gauss said. "Follow me, damn it."

"I can't leave her here with that thing," Ben breathed, indicating Alice. She seemed to have calmed down. Was that thing in *her* head now?

"She'll be fine," Torque growled, putting her hand to her mouth and sucking on the wound. "Louie'll keep his thoughts to himself. And I'll be here."

"*Cap,*" came a new voice over shipwide, "*we got other problems up here. Are we leaving or not?*"

"Moze, crack that ramp—" Gauss began and took a half-step toward Ben. She hadn't lowered her pistol.

"Fine," Ben said. To Alice: "I'm one shout away, kid, okay?"

Alice eyed him. "I'm okay. I've never seen one up close. I was just surprised is all."

"Me, too," he said. Squeezing her shoulder in solidarity, Ben followed Gauss to the cockpit.

The pilot's cabin was as jerry-rigged as the rest of the ship.

Loose conduits, a touchpad that was entirely dead, and seats with tape barely holding the padding in. The whole cabin appeared salvaged from a scrapyard.

Very likely, Ben thought.

Gauss said, "Strap in to tactical."

Ben crawled into the third officer's chair at tactical. It positioned him behind and at ninety degrees to the two pilot chairs facing the forward window. One of the restraint buckles attached to the seat was busted. "This thing's broken."

"Tie it off!" Gauss barked as she strapped into the co-pilot's station. There was another, younger woman already in the pilot's seat. "Marines make do, right? What are you, stupid?"

Ben mumbled something unsavory but settled into the tactical officer's seat.

"Launch, Gal, launch," Gauss ordered.

"Flight control has a bunch of balls in the air," the pilot reported. "They've assigned us—"

"Boss," Torque yelled from aft, "they're bringing up those bigger guns!"

Gauss leaned over the console to Gal. "The only balls I care about are mine. Punch it!"

Sighing, the pilot shrugged. "You're the captain, Captain."

The *Junkyard Dog* grumbled, like its namesake shaken awake too early in the morning. The pinnace slowly lifted off the pad leaving in its wake, Ben hoped, a number of seared, shocked pirates. There was always a brief window as the artificial gravity converted from the more stable field exerted by a base to the less-sophisticated shipboard AG, and Ben felt his stomach surf the transition. He tightened the broken straps of the tactician's seat and held on.

Angry voices hailed the *Dog* from dockside over comms, demanding she power down her engines. Gauss switched the dockmaster off instead. "Turn off the transponder, too," she said to Gal. "Run silent, run deep."

"Acknowledged," Gal said.

As the *Dog* rose, the lights of New Nassau were obscured by the prickly stellar rock of the asteroid sheltering it. The grainy, magenta swirl of the Triangle awaited.

"Course plotted for the Fall?" Gauss asked.

"Well, about that..." Gal said.

Ben could hear the air physically leave Cinnamon Gauss's lungs. "What? *What?*"

Moze stuck her head in from the hold, bracing herself with all four limbs in the cockpit's vibrating doorway. "That's the second thing I wanted to tell you," she said sheepishly. "Translight drive no-workie."

Pulling at her safety belts, Gauss turned in her seat. She appeared speechless.

One good thing, Ben thought, closing his eyes. *One good thing today after all.*

"I can fix it!" Moze insisted. "You caught us off-guard needing to launch so soon."

"Translation," Gauss said, "I caught you in the brothel instead of taking care of ship's business first."

"Bobby's working," Moze said. "You know I can't resist his—"

"Fix it!" shouted Gauss.

"Boss!" Moze acknowledged, tossing off a quick salute and ducking sternward.

"That's not all, Cap," Gal said.

"What? *What?*"

"Fleet fighters." It was Ben who spoke. He indicated the tactical screen and the icons just appearing at the edge of sensor range. One, two, then four red triangles. "Thorne's advance fighter cloud," he said. "He uses them to extend the range of his Pathfinder—"

"Great!" Gauss flipped a switch, engaging shipwide comms. "Moze, mind on the work!" After a deep, sedating breath, she said, "Torque, double-check that everyone is strapped in back there. It's liable to get real bumpy real soon." She thumbed off the intercom and leaned her orange spikes back against her chair's cockeyed headrest.

"If they catch us with that thing on board," Ben said, "we'll be in deep—"

"Best way to keep your captain happy," Gauss interrupted, patience straining at the end of its leash, "is to shut up. Unless you see a flashing red light. That's the time to speak up, yeah?"

A ripple shuddered along the *Dog*'s superstructure as she overcame the last of New Nassau's gravity well. Ben's stomach stabilized as his body finally acclimated to the ship's antiquated AG compensators. Gauss was already out of her chair and leaning over him to observe the fighters, now numbering six.

"Want to help little sister?" she asked. "Well?"

"Of course," Ben snapped.

"Then keep Gal here informed of tactical."

The navigator leaned back in the co-pilot's seat. "Mango Galatz at your service, sir," she said with a warm smile inappropriate to dire circumstance. "Cinn and the sisters call me Galileo cuz, y'know, 'pilot to the stars.' Gal, for short."

Curious, Ben said, "Mango?"

"My parents loved perversely flavored margaritas. Disgusting!" Gal's pruned expression emphasized the point. Abruptly, her face brightened. "Speaking of loving things, I loved your vid! *Castaway Girl*? Very heroic. Rugged. Nice jaw. Does the package match the wrappage?"

Ben stared at her a moment, not understanding. Until he did.

"I swear, you and Moze, one-track minds," Gauss said, "Keep your straps tight, Gal. Stone, supply her with tactical info. *Only* tactical info. I'm gonna see if I can help Moze and speed up repairs." The *Dog*'s captain exited the cockpit.

"Right," Ben said.

After a moment, he felt the gaze of Mango Galileo "Gal" Galatz still fixated on him. Her eyebrows jumped up and down three times. "Well?"

"Well, what?"

"Package, matchage, wrappage?"

"Shouldn't you be watching where you're going?"

Her lips curled up at the corners. "Auto-pilot."

Ben turned deliberately to the tac display, searching for rescue. "Well, I don't think *they're* on auto-pilot." The fighters extended their semi-circular perimeter as they advanced on New Nassau. A seventh and eighth triangle had appeared.

Gal frowned. "Yeah." She turned back to her controls. In the lower-right corner of Ben's display, a blue triangle labeled "JD" followed a deliberate arc to starboard along a sharp tangent away from the approaching fighter wing. Maybe they hadn't yet noticed the pinnace. Not far behind them, Ben knew, would be Thorne aboard *Monolith* and the rest of Third Fleet. And Toma and the rest of the 214th on the *Navis Lusoria*.

That same tension he'd felt at leaving Eva with al-Hurra tug-of-warred inside Ben once more. Every meter he traveled away from the pirate colony was, technically, a meter farther into treason. And yet the thought of handing Alice over to Bragg repulsed him. His loyalty to her was an imperative, his duty to the Alliance more a conditioned compulsion. When the two conflicted, as they did now, there was only one choice Ben knew he could live with later. Maybe Toma would under-stand, and maybe she wouldn't. Maybe it didn't matter to Ben if she did. Life had been so much simpler a few years ago, when the only thing that mattered to Ben Stone was Ben Stone.

The girl's the mission.

A whisper of memory. Bricker's admonition to him beneath Drake's World prickled the hair at the back of his neck—a moment of legacy passed along before the weight of alien rock had crushed the life out of the sergeant.

Ben glanced over his shoulder to the empty space between Galatz's co-pilot seat and his own, half-expecting to see Bricker and the others standing and staring in the claustrophobic space. Hell, even the dead Archie crumbling in agony to the *Dog's* deck would be welcome at this point. Whenever they appeared, things seemed to clarify, giving Ben direction. Not this time. The only other presence in the cockpit was the navigator with the overclocked libido. *That's about my luck,* he thought.

Fucking ghosts.

From the back of his mind came a rumbling chortle of amusement. The need for a drink always came on Ben suddenly. When he heard Bricker laughing, that monkey jumped on his back with the weight of a gorilla. The angry desperation of a man having stumbled through a desert toward an oasis, only to find it an illusion.

"Hey!" Gal was peering at him again over her shoulder. She seemed frightened. "I can see a mirror of your tac screen on my nav panel but with less detail. Do I see what I think I see?"

Ben focused on the display in front of him. It took a second for his brain to register what his eyes saw. "Oh, shit."

"I'll take that as a yes." Gal engaged comms. "Cap, Moze— y'all about ready to hit start on that thing?"

Gauss's animated voice came on, panting. "A few more minutes. We rush, we risk cracking the chamber."

On Ben's screen, the closest fighters of the thirteen now visible had begun to skew their flight paths toward the *Dog.* Gal altered the ship's course more acutely away from their advance, but the fighters were already adjusting to match the new trajectory.

"We've attracted some fireflies," Gal answered. "Check the guns."

Was she talking to him?

"What?"

"You're a Marine, right? You know what guns are?"

"We're going to shoot at them?"

"That's what guns are for!" Galatz made a clucking sound and popped her straps loose, then crawled over her seat. She reached past Ben and touched the screen, bringing up fire control. A two-dimensional rendering of the pinnace appeared, with dorsal and ventral turrets on top and bottom, respectively. They were red, but the grind of hydraulics told Ben they were levering guns into place at the top and bottom of the ship. When the grinding ceased, their icons on the display turned green.

"Well, at least those are working!" Gal gave Ben a peck on the cheek. "For luck!"

From the front of the *Dog*'s side-on profile in the fire control display, a lone, low-grade auto-cannon appeared. Its icon too changed from red to green.

"See? It worked!" she said. "Say, you have something of a reputation with the ladies. Right? I mean, a face like yours..."

Ben could feel her body hovering close, her breath caressing his ear.

"I suppose," he said.

"Well," Gal purred, "I'm no lady."

From the corner of his eye, Ben spied her lecherous grin.

"Lucky for me, then," he said. In his head, it'd been laced with sarcasm. In the pilot's tight cabin, it sounded unnervingly earnest. And curled up at the end like a question.

Gal leaned in closer. She'd had onions at her last meal. "Damned right."

Hopping away like a jackrabbit, she vaulted back into the co-pilot's seat. "Don't report me to the captain for the kiss," she said as she strapped in. "Like I said, it was just for luck. Y'know —mostly."

But Ben wasn't listening. Four of the red triangles had broken formation and were definitely headed for them.

"I can't fire on them," he stated. "I *can't*."

"Maybe it won't come to that," Gal said. "More kisses, more luck?"

Ben didn't answer. He was too busy watching the four fighters on his tac screen. Because now they weren't just tracking the *Dog*. They were closing the gap.

37

AN ACCORD

"YOU'LL HAVE to be more specific, Admiral," Hadrian al-Hurra said. "We have a lot of ships leaving port today. Bad weather coming. Not all are taking the time to file flight plans."

On-screen, Rear Admiral Malcolm Thorne did not appear amused. He appeared ill-inclined to ask about the *Junkyard Dog*'s destination again. He seemed more disposed to rain hellfire down on New Nassau.

Eva stood apart, out of sight of the camera aimed at al-Hurra. Thorne sat in the captain's chair of the *Monolith*, his crew working diligently behind him at their bright, smooth duty stations. The scene exuded power. By contrast, al-Hurra stood alone in front of a blank wall marked only by exposed conduits and old welding wounds. Both men knew the reality of the situation—Thorne held the high cards here. Except for one very important one: knowledge of where the *Dog* was headed.

The admiral considered his next words carefully.

"Commander," Thorne said, pronouncing al-Hurra's rank like it tasted bad, *"I've already dispatched fighters to intercept Captain Gauss's ship, which I'm aware led the assault on the* L'Esprit de la Terre. *The fighters can intercept them peacefully*

... or not. Produce Alice Keller, and I'll know she's not aboard. I might even be inclined to let Gauss go."

After the attack on the Terre? Eva thought. *Not bloody likely.* Such obvious lies made Thorne sound desperate. Maybe he was.

"I don't know any Alice Keller," al-Hurra said. He darted an index finger into the air, became contemplative, eyes widening as if he'd just snapped to the name. "Wait, *the* Alice Keller? The-castaway-girl-from-the-vid-of-the-same-name Alice Keller? *That* Alice Keller?"

Thorne leaned forward in his chair.

Power move.

"Al-Hurra, stop wasting my time. Your grandfather served aboard the *Shōkaku*, I believe," he said. "During the Specter War. Engineer, was it?"

"Chief engineer, in fact," al-Hurra replied.

"And what would he say, knowing you're disobeying a presidential order? And obstructing a fleet admiral in carrying out that order?"

Al-Hurra spread his hands wide. "Oh, you mean turning over this Keller girl? Again, I wish I could help you. But to your question, I don't think he'd say much of anything, being dead and all. You've heard the old pirate saying, I'm sure."

Al-Hurra rocked back on his heels with a smile. A decidedly different expression painted Thorne's face. Enough was enough.

"I have a battalion of Marines preparing to drop on New Nassau the moment we're in orbit. I will take you and your senior staff into custody, and we'll dump every data core you've got until we find what we're looking for."

"That could take a while," al-Hurra observed. "Especially if we don't simply hand them over."

Thorne scoffed. *"You'd offer armed resistance against three hundred armored Marines? You wouldn't last five minutes. And that particular bloodbath will be on your hands ... Commander."*

Colonel Toma's Marines mowing down the residents of New Nassau seemed unlikely to Eva but not impossible, if Thorne gave the order. Al-Hurra darted his gaze her way, and she recognized the summons for what it was. Stepping forward, Eva took up position beside the commander.

"Let's avoid that if we can, Admiral," she said.

Thorne showed the briefest hint of surprise before his mask of command settled back into place. *"Eva Park? It's good to see you alive. President Bragg will be pleased."*

"I've been treated well here, Admiral. And if you both are through comparing penile lengths, perhaps we can reach an agreement that doesn't involve hundreds of civilian deaths," Eva said. She'd learned a long time ago that getting the upper hand when negotiating with men often required little more than implying that their manhood needed measuring. "I'd like to act as mediator. If that's acceptable to you, Admiral."

Thorne studied her. Deciding, perhaps, why she was making the offer. *"I'm amenable to mediation. However, once we're in orbit, that's done. I start laying waste to your den of thieves, Commander. And the Marines land."*

Al-Hurra released a breath. Before he could speak, Eva said, "Admiral, we've already had unneeded deaths here, a result of the panic caused by the appearance of your armada."

"Frankly, Miss Park, I couldn't care less about a few dead pirates. The fewer we have to—"

"One casualty was an infant child," she interrupted him. Thorne had no immediate reaction to that. "Think it through, Admiral. Think of the consequences of bombing and invading here. And not just to the families. I grant you, a few more dead pirates might actually play well with the public, but when those dead include women and children?"

She could see his poker face falter a bit. Thorne was jumping weeks and months ahead in his mind. Conjuring questions by his superiors and the president's office about his tactical choices. Maybe even contemplating his own court-martial.

"We're at war with the Arcœnum," she continued, looking first at al-Hurra, then back to Thorne. "The last thing we need is humans making their job easier by killing other humans."

Thorne pointed his jaw at her like it might be loaded. *"What do you propose?"*

"There are nearly forty thousand men, women, and children here. Guarding or taking that potentially hostile population into custody is a formidable task."

"'Potentially' hostile?" Thorne spat out the words. *"Al-Hurra's people have raided cargo, stolen ships, murdered civilians and military alike for decades—"*

"Which begs the question," Eva said, "why you haven't moved on them in force before."

Thorne's eyes flattened. *"Had it been Fleet's decision to make, there'd be no question at all."*

"Ah. You're insinuating the politicians are to blame."

"They usually are," Thorne said dryly.

Al-Hurra snorted. "On that, at least, we agree."

"Oh, look," Eva said, indulging herself for a moment, "mediation is already bearing fruit."

"We'll be in orbit in less than half an hour," Thorne said. *"Again, what do you propose?"*

"The pirates will stand down any armed resistance," she stated. "You will land your Marines—but *only* your Marines—and take operational control of the colony."

"Wait, what?" This from al-Hurra, who was staring at her in shock.

"Weapons cold," Eva continued. Thorne's blooming expression of triumph withered. "All parties will retain their arms.

Anyone that breaks the armistice will be held accountable by the Bragg Administration."

"*Unacceptable,*" Thorne said. "*Civilian oversight is one thing, but this is a time of war. Casualties are inevitable. And these people are outlaws! I won't have my personnel subject to—*"

"And we'll never agree to that." Al-Hurra was adamant. "We won't simply hand over—"

"What choice do you have?" Eva said. "Admiral Thorne has enough firepower and a distinct technological advantage. Hold on to your pride, Commander al-Hurra, and it's likely to be all you have left. Ask that mother who lost her infant which is more important: life or pride."

Al-Hurra's silence in return masked a simmering anger.

Thorne was nodding and whispering to someone off-screen. "*Our fighters are closing on that ship, al-Hurra. Soon we'll have it secured.*"

"Good luck with that," al-Hurra muttered where only Eva could hear.

"*We're tracking your other launches as well, even in the Triangle. Unconditional surrender is your only option here.*"

"It's not, actually," Eva maintained.

Thorne regarded her a moment. "*Miss Park, whose side are you on exactly?*" he asked.

"I'm on the side of victory over the Arcœnum!" she shouted. Then, more restrained and slyly, "You know—President Bragg's side. How about you?"

The admiral's jaw flexed. "*I can't hamstring AGF Marines by telling them they can't defend themselves.*"

Al-Hurra said, "Nor will I tell my people they can't shoot back if provoked."

Good, Eva thought. *They're ganging up on me. Together.* And they likely hadn't noticed how doing so had put them, at least in their opposition to her, on the same side if only for the moment.

"I never said they couldn't. But whoever starts shooting—pirates or Marines—will be held to account." When neither of them spoke, Eva pushed further. "Gentlemen, would you rather endure a shooting war? Commander al-Hurra, you *will* lose that war. Everything you've built here will be destroyed. Everyone who lives here will suffer, directly or indirectly. Any dreams the people of New Nassau might have had—" She stared hard at al-Hurra. "—*any* dreams ... will be lost." Eva now turned her analysis on Thorne. "Think you can keep hundreds of civilian deaths out of the media, Admiral? I don't, and I'm a little more expert in that arena than you are. And do you really want to tie up ships to guard tens of thousands of angry pirates, all bent on revenge for what they perceive to be your atrocities? Bombing and shooting these people into pulp will only hand the Arcœnum a moral victory. And quite possibly a strategic one as well, if public reaction goes badly for the president. You really want to risk all that?"

Thorne adjusted himself in his chair. *"I'll agree to the spirit of the terms you've outlined. But the AGF Marines will have complete operational control of the colony. All ship launches will cease immediately, and their crews will stand down. Everyone will return to their personal quarters until further notice. Every citizen of the colony should consider themselves under house arrest. Martial law will be implemented the moment my Marines touch down."*

Eva turned her head so Thorne wouldn't see the tick of her cheek. It would be too much for al-Hurra to surrender complete control of his citizenry to the good graces of Malcolm Thorne. It was with astonishment, therefore, that she absorbed the colony commander's next words.

"You can't simply say no one can move about the colony," al-

Hurra said in measured tones. "People need supplies. We have citizens here with significant medical conditions. They'll have to have access to care."

"We can work out those details," Eva stated quickly, seizing the moment. "Escorts and such, maybe provided by Marshal Gauss? Commander, help me here. Help me avoid the calamity that armed resistance would most certainly cause."

Al-Hurra turned to her with a long, appraising look. To Thorne, he said, "We need to work out the details of occupation before you land a single Marine. And you'll only land one battalion. I'll guarantee the conduct of my people."

"And you'll hand over all ship manifests and logs for every incoming and outgoing vessel for the last month, no matter how innocuous," Thorne said. *"I don't care if you launched a garbage scow to dump the colony's biowaste. I want its log and manifest."*

"Very well," al-Hurra said.

"I'll have my people draw up the articles of occupation for your review," Thorne said.

Eva exhaled relief. She hadn't known she'd been holding her breath. "Thank you, Admiral. I appreciate—"

The feed from the *Monolith* dropped.

In the C&C, there were murmurings among al-Hurra's staff. Disbelieving gasps. Angry expletives. But those folks, no matter how loyal, didn't carry responsibility for the fate of New Nassau on their shoulders. Al-Hurra did. He'd had to make the tough call. They hadn't.

"I know that was difficult—" she began.

"Actually," al-Hurra said, "it was one of the easiest decisions I've ever had to make. But I had to make it look good. For Thorne. So he felt like a winner. So the terms weren't worse."

Eva regarded him, understanding coalescing in her mind. Not for the first time, al-Hurra had surprised her. Unlike Thorne, Bragg, and pretty much any other man but Leo she'd known, al-Hurra seemed undriven by ego. A rare trait in any leader, much less one who led the infamous pirates of the Malvian Triangle.

"You were right, Miss Park, in what you said. It would have been a bloodbath. Might still be. But for now, at least, my people are safe. Thank you for facilitating that."

"You're welcome," Eva said, a little surprised that she meant it. "Perhaps their dreams of reconciliation are even still possible."

Al-Hurra offered her a weak smile. "Perhaps."

The docks were nearly deserted except for Hadrian al-Hurra, his senior staff, and Eva Park. They were assembled to formally welcome, if that was the right word, Lieutenant Colonel Bathsheba Toma and her company commanders. The rest of the 214th Battalion, First Drop Division, Alliance Ground Forces, would follow once symbolism was satisfied.

The Fleet dropship descended, languid and graceful, into the cavernous asteroid, its engines an unfamiliar purr of modern refinement in a space Eva associated with the rattle and hum of ships under constant maintenance. Her peripheral vision caught movement off to her left—Sayyida al-Hurra walking toward the receiving pad. She reached them as the dropship settled onto its landing struts.

"Father," she said. "Miss Park."

"Miss al-Hurra," Eva acknowledged. Sayyida hadn't been invited to receive the Marines but had clearly seen fit to attend anyway. Maybe that was for the better. Any dissension on display between father and daughter would surely be exploited by Thorne and Toma. Sometimes Eva hated her inability to turn off the compulsion to think through the political outcomes of a given situation. Hazards of the job.

"I'm glad you could join us," al-Hurra said to his daughter with genuine warmth. Sayyida nodded formally in return. While Eva would never call Hadrian al-Hurra naïve, she had to wonder at his daughter's agenda. Sayyida had one. Eva was sure of it.

The ramp of the dropship breached and descended. There was the heavy tread of armored boots, and Eva recognized Bathsheba Toma leading the contingent of Marine officers. They were dressed in their battlesuits minus the helmets, which they had tucked formally under one arm. Toma's face was flinty with purpose. Her rifle, slung. Five others, her company commanders Eva assumed, followed at a respectful distance.

"Miss Park," Toma said formally, "good to see you again."

"And you, Colonel."

It'd been a slight, though perhaps an inadvertent one by Toma. She was new to the political aspects of being a military leader, Eva knew. She should have addressed al-Hurra first. The stumble surprised Eva. Toma, she remembered, was a stickler for correctness and accuracy. But if al-Hurra cared, he seemed to shrug it off and stepped forward.

"Lieutenant Colonel Toma, I'm Hadrian al-Hurra. Commander, New Nassau Colony."

Toma nodded. "Commander, I am here to legally assume operational control of your settlement.

"By the protocols you agreed to," she went on formally, "your command staff will be replaced by Fleet personnel. However, I'd like you to shadow me in the C&C until I get the lay of the land. Under martial law, strict adherence to the curfew is expected and will be enforced. Violations will be prosecuted to the fullest extent of Fleet regulations and the Uniform

Code of Military Conduct. Are we clear on the basics, Commander?"

Stickler was too loose a word for Toma, Eva decided.

"We are," al-Hurra said in a compliant monotone.

"Colonel, I'm Sayyida al-Hurra." The young woman stepped forward to stand beside her father. "The commander's daughter."

Toma regarded her curiously. "Nice to meet you." The greeting sounded like a question.

"I'd like to talk if you have a minute. Someplace private."

Eva's hackles rose.

"I'm very busy at the moment, Miss al-Hurra, but if you—"

"It's important. You'll want to hear what I have to say."

"Sayyida…" al-Hurra said, "it's important to maintain *one* point of contact to avoid—"

"No," Toma said, her curiosity piqued. The dissension was palpable, and she'd sensed it. Tactically, Eva judged, Toma might consider herself derelict in her duty if she didn't talk to Sayyida. "This way, miss," the Marine said, gesturing away from Eva and al-Hurra. To her company commanders she said, "Ladies and gentlemen, you have your assignments. Begin debarking your troops and securing strategic objectives immediately."

A chorus of snap-to acknowledgments followed.

Toma and Sayyida stepped away, out of earshot.

Hadrian al-Hurra turned to Eva with a worried expression.

Oh, no.

38
YES RETREAT, NO SURRENDER

THERE WERE RAISED voices coming from the front of the ship, and even louder complaints from the back. Strapped in for safety, Alice felt useless in the current crisis and, worse than that, helpless. Her left hand pulsed with indistinct memory, though now there was only a dim scar lining the palm. Her entire time in New Nassau, Alice hadn't been tempted to re-carve the bloody wound, not once. Now, frustrated at her own inability to help Cinnamon and the others, the temptation tickled at the back of her conscious mind.

Cursing erupted from the rear of the ship. Cinnamon Gauss at the top of her lungs, and an apologetic Moze trying to soothe her, which only seemed to make the *Dog*'s captain swear louder. The conflict was being played out shipwide on comms, with increasingly anxious calls from the cockpit suggesting that having a working translight drive sooner rather than later would be a good thing.

Her sublight engines straining, the *Junkyard Dog* rattled along, using the Malvian Triangle to obstruct her pursuers. Darting between space debris, keeping it between her and the pursuing fighters whenever possible. Cutting her engines and hugging larger asteroidal bodies to slingshot around them using their gravity for speed while the Triangle's natural interference muddied the sensor wake of her passing. Alice could feel the *Dog* working hard for her. The ship's grind and growl droned along her hull and came straight up through Alice's poorly padded seat.

The Arcœnum called Louie sat across from her in the compartment, calm and still as always. Maybe it was just her boredom, but Alice was perversely curious about the alien. She wondered what it would be like to share thoughts with him. A childhood memory bubbled up, something about saying "Bless you" to prevent a demon infiltrating your body following a sneeze. She'd never really understood that and always thought it silly. Why would a demon choose the breath after a sneeze to hop aboard in the first place? Now, as she stared at the large Arcœnum with its multiple, gangly limbs, the silly ritual seemed almost sage advice. And yet, part of Alice burned with curiosity about what the experience would be like. To share consciousness with another being so totally foreign to herself—an *alien*. To know their most intimate thoughts and be unafraid to share your own. Fearless of judgment. Hopeful for understanding.

"Penny for your thoughts."

She set aside her musing to find Torque reentering the middle compartment from engineering. Cinnamon-branded swearing seemed to press her forward like a stern wind.

"What?" Alice replied, her eyes lingering on Louie. "You don't have to pay me to—"

Torque laughed lightly and sat down next to her. Sighing with the load off her feet, she strapped in.

"Old Earth saying," Torque explained. "It means, whatcha thinkin' 'bout?"

"Oh."

"Well?"

Alice shrugged.

"Yeah, right. Never kid a kidder, kid."

The teenager bunched her shoulders again, staring at her left palm with its crossroads lifeline. "I'm sorry for all this, I guess."

"Sorry for what?"

"This," she said, jabbing her temple toward the four-letter stream-of-consciousness flowing nonstop from engineering. "This is all because of me. That fleet coming. What's happening in New Nassau. You guys risking your lives." She shrugged again. "Everything."

"Hey now, little sister, that's not true," Torque said. But she paused, and they were both acutely aware that Torque's good intentions to make Alice feel better had run a little astray of reality.

"It kinda is," Alice said gently.

Torque considered her next words more carefully. "Look, maybe it is—*kinda*. If you factor out everything else."

"*Try that!*" Cinnamon Gauss's voice filtered back to them from the cockpit, crackling over comms in an echo of her shout from astern.

"What do you mean?" Alice said.

Torque placed one large hand on Alice's arm. "Maybe it's true that the scats finally moving in is cuz they're looking for you. Then again, maybe they just decided it was time to clean us out. They're facing a war. Maybe they finally decided to get rid of the pirate menace in their own backyard. One less thing to worry about."

"Scats? Like animal—"

"Space cadets," Torque snorted. "Fleeters."

"Oh."

"So yeah, exactly like animal sh—dung." The ship's bouncer clucked her tongue. "Either way, it doesn't matter. Cinnamon would never let them take you. None of us would."

Her heart swelling with guilt-laden gratitude, Alice asked, "Why?"

"Because we have a code." As if that explained it, Torque sat back in her seat.

"What code?"

"A pirate code!" Torque flared her fingers dramatically like a magician, the way Cinnamon liked to. "If we don't hang together, we shall surely hang separately. Another old Earth saying. It means we stick together and look out for one another, so we all make it through."

Alice nodded. That she understood. And she was cheered by the weighty kinship she saw in Torque's eyes, the absolute support she felt from the tough woman sitting beside her. From all of them, really, Cinnamon's whole sisterhood of a crew. She felt closest to Cinnamon herself for some reason Alice couldn't quite put her finger on. She'd promised herself after Zoey and Ian shunned her that she'd never let herself get close to anyone again. She didn't want to be hurt anymore. But she didn't want to feel alone either. Or worse, abandoned by someone she'd come to rely on to be there.

Then along came the *Junkyard Dog* and her colorful crew in the Blind Passage. Alice had been instantly drawn to Cinnamon's shameless humor, Torque's quiet strength. To Gal's funny fixation on men, and Moze's unassuming genius with all things mechanical. Those three followed Cinnamon without question, as if doing so were a universal law. Alice had soon found herself recruited to the faithful. And all of them, led by Cinn in this too, looked after her. Called her little sister. It was nice to be part of a family again. She was grateful, and maybe that's why she felt so bad about putting them in danger. Whether by circumstance or conscious choice, it felt to Alice like she was, plain and simple, asking too much.

"*Try that!*"

"Something's gotta work eventually," Torque said with a wink. "Law of averages, y'know?"

She and Alice listened to see if the latest adjustment had done any good.

"*Sorry, Cap,*" Gal muttered over shipwide.

"*Son of a pock-marked, worm-riddled, scabby-skinned whore!*"

Alice shared an amused smile with Torque, who too loved Cinnamon Gauss. Maybe not *love* loved—or maybe so, it was hard to tell sometimes—but held her in the highest esteem with a fierceness equaled only by her physical presence.

"You're a lot like her, you know," Torque said.

"Who?"

"Cinn."

The notion astonished Alice. "We couldn't be more different," she said with a nervous giggle.

"I didn't mean on the outside."

Alice clamped her mouth shut, stubbornly refusing to play.

"Cinn's the kind of person who can be lonely in a roomful of people," Torque said. She hesitated, as if reluctant to share a confidence. "She lost her family too, you know."

And there it was. The indefinable quality, the covert but irresistible force attracting Alice to Cinnamon's bright, burning light. A subconscious quality that branded someone as broken, and obvious as lines on a face. Something moved inside Alice's chest.

"How?" she whispered.

"Disease. Something endemic to New Nassau's asteroid. Random, alien bacteria. It took whole families twenty years ago, with the odd member, like Cinn, being naturally immune. The air recyclers filter for it now, and no one knows why it appeared when it did. Some form of the colony's been there for fifty years, you know? Maybe some miner released the bacteria when he cracked open a rock. Anyway, she lost her parents and younger sister. She was eight when they died."

Jesus. So, they had that in common. Yet, Cinnamon Gauss was so different. So *loud.*

"Her granddad raised her," Torque said. "The marshal. A hard man with a good heart, which he doesn't show that often. Can't, really, being the head lawman of the colony."

"Yeah."

"She's a good friend to have." Torque's voice became personal, introspective. "She's fiercely protective of those she cares for."

"Yeah."

The ship rocked. Her hull sang with a dull, static sound.

"Hold on!" Gal yelled over shipwide.

The *Junkyard Dog* banked hard to starboard, the g-force of the sudden turn briefly besting the ship's centrifugal compensators.

"What the hell!" Gauss demanded over comms.

"Sorry, Cap," Gal said. *"We just passed into their weapons range. And I need someone up here willing to shoot back."*

Torque flipped the comm switch on the wall behind her head. "On my way." To Alice, she said, "Stay here. Stay strapped in."

"Okay."

"And don't worry," Torque said, popping her restraint buckle. "We'll be fine. Cinn has the devil's luck."

She rushed toward the cockpit, leaving Alice alone again and staring at Louie. Not even a sudden turn could shake him awake. A scowling Ben Stone stalked into the compartment from up front and dropped into the seat next to her, mumbling to himself.

"What's wrong?" Alice asked.

"Nothing!"

She flinched from his anger and let out a brief yelp when the *Dog* maneuvered sharply a second time. Ben reached out a hand to touch her knee.

"Sorry," he said. "I just got kicked out of the cockpit. For refusing to shoot Fleeters." His gaze wandered from hers to the alien passenger across from them. "Everything's upside down. Protecting Archies. Shooting down Fleeters."

Rapid blasts sizzled the *Dog*'s hull. Another turn by their pilot, another somersault of Alice's stomach.

"Aft-port shield minimal," Gal reported to the ship.

"Thanks for the motivation!" Gauss shouted from engineering.

"Transferring power from forward shield." Torque's calm recitation was a counterpoint to her shipmates.

Alice took a breath and popped the buckle of her harness.

"What are you doing?" Ben asked.

She moved closer to him.

"Oh." Ben folded his arms around her as she pressed into him, head against his chest. "Not a good idea," he said unconvincingly. "To be safe, you should strap back in. If the AG fails—"

"I don't care," Alice said. "I feel safe here."

She could feel the bob of his Adam's apple against the crown of her head.

"Okay," he said.

A series of thick, fast drumbeats pounded up through the

bottom of the ship. Alice counted four before they were repeated, this time from the *Dog*'s upper hull.

"What's that?" she said.

"AFGs," Ben said. "Anti-fighter guns."

The thumping pulses came again, only in reverse, traveling from topside to the ship's underbelly.

She pressed closer against him. His scent was familiar and soothing. It made her think of the moment beneath Drake's World when they both thought they were about to die. Ben had protected her with his body from the avalanche of falling rock, a valiant if vain gesture. Then she'd protected them both, deflecting the falling rocks with her ability. As then, Ben's closeness reassured her now. Made her feel safe. Made her feel *alive*. The way the heroines in the romance stories always seemed to feel in the arms of their heroes.

The *Dog* heaved over to port, and the guns cycled again from up top and below. The ship rocked violently under return fire.

"One less scat to worry about," Torque announced.

"Keep at it!" Cinnamon sounded relieved. *"Engines almost there..."*

The banter reassured Alice, made her almost believe they'd make it.

Another *whoop!* of triumph from the cockpit, this time from Gal.

Ben blew out a breath. *This must be hard for him*, Alice thought. If it weren't for her, he might very well be on the other side. It could be his friends dying out there.

She hugged him tighter.

"I can't breathe, Alice," he said. It sounded almost resentful.

Alice released him and shuffled back to her seat.

"It's not you," he said quickly. "It's—"

"I know," she answered, buckling back in. "I get it."

Cinnamon Gauss sprinted by without a word. Excited voices from the cockpit greeted her.

Ben popped his harness loose. "Stay here." He followed Cinnamon forward.

But Alice was tired of sitting and staring at the seemingly comatose Louie. She released her safety belt and dashed after Ben. But there was nowhere to sit now that Cinnamon had reoccupied the co-pilot's seat. Cinnamon barely spared them a glance as they wedged themselves into the doorway.

"Both of you," Cinnamon said, "get the hell back to your seats. And strap in!"

"Moze, ETA?" Gal said. "And don't give me the estimate from the manual, either."

"Cold firing a TLD in the middle of a space battle—"

"Moze!" shouted the captain.

There was a pause that suggested a likely ethical debate between an engineer's fondness for safety margins and their current need for speed. *"Two minutes."*

"Half it!" Cinnamon said.

"The two fighters left out there are regrouping," Torque reported. "Gal, see that proto-planet? Can you tuck us in behind it? Cut the sublights, sling us around like earlier? Maybe buy us enough time so we don't have to—"

"On it," the navigator said.

The *Dog*'s icon swept toward the nascent planetoid on the navigation display. It wasn't long before Alice felt the familiar queasiness of the ship's artificial gravity dancing with the natural pull from the proto-planet. Gal cut the engines, relying on thrusters to guide them in close without allowing the gravity of the planetoid to take over. Alice squinted through the forward window. But the haze of the Triangle prevented her human eyes from seeing what the sensors insisted was out there.

"You're getting too close," Ben said.

"Quiet, poster boy," Gauss said. "And get back to your seat!"

Two vertical columns lit up on Gal's navigation console. The red at the bottom began to rise toward the mid-range, yellow part of each column.

"Translight drive coming online," Gal announced.

"If you try to jump too close to the planetoid's gravity well, you'll rip this bucket of bolts apart," Ben said.

"Torque! Escort our guests rearward."

Torque grumbled, "I'm a little busy here."

"You need to pull up!" Ben insisted.

"Fifty percent," Gal reported. The columns were halfway into the yellow. The higher they rose, the slower they seemed to move. Or maybe Alice's mind was just playing tricks on her.

"Where are those fighters?" Cinnamon said.

"Just cutting across our displacement wake," Torque informed her. "They must still have us on their scopes, though."

"Seventy percent," Gal said.

"Pull up!" Ben moved forward as if to yank Gauss from her seat and take control.

In half a heartbeat, three pistols were out and pointing at him from the *Dog*'s cockpit crew.

"Keep backseat flying, and you'll distract me enough to get us all killed," Gauss snarled. "Now, shut ... up!"

Ben closed his mouth with clenched jaws.

"They've definitely got our trail," Torque said. "Cannons recharged."

"Eight-five percent." Gal's voice dripped with eagerness.

"Hold on!" Cinnamon yelled.

Alice groaned as the captain pulled the *Dog* up hard and away from the proto-planet. Tracer fire from the pursuing fighters crackled against the hull.

"They're closing," Torque said.

"Gal, get us out of here," Cinnamon ordered. To engineering, "Moze, hold on!"

Gal engaged the translight drive, and for the briefest of moments, nothing happened. Again. After what felt like an eternity, the ship's translight drive overcame the hard boundary of Einsteinian physics.

The *Junkyard Dog* jumped away.

39
TOWER'S FALL

EIGHT HOURS LATER, they'd covered more than half the distance to Tower's Fall.

With the escape behind them, the crew of the *Junkyard Dog* had settled back into some semblance of normalcy. Cinnamon, cutting with her knife's-edge wit. Torque, Zen-like, chatting up Alice and even Ben to pass the time. Gal and Moze, comparing notes on the men they'd had and the ones they intended to. And Light Without Shadow, serenely stoic as ever.

But then news of New Nassau's surrender came through. The easy respite disappeared. The collective mood of the ship turned bleak.

"We're about six hours out," Torque told her when boredom sent Alice's feet ranging forward to the cockpit. Gal at the helm as usual. Cinnamon was in her quarters below, catching up on much-needed sleep.

"What's it like, Tower's Fall?" Alice asked.

"It's a shithole," Gal answered.

"Come on," Torque said, "it's not that bad."

"You're right, it's worse. Other shitholes take offense when you call the Fall a shithole."

"Don't let the captain hear you say that. She loves the place." Torque arched her chin up to Alice, who was standing behind her tactical station. "It's an extensive asteroid field with one large asteroid at its outer edge, where the cove is hidden. The Fall is part of a delicate balance of gravitational fields that forms the Triangle. And it's not that bad."

"My advice," Gal said, "is to stock up on antibiotics."

Alice smiled at the banter because, after hearing about New Nassau, it was nice to hear some levity, even dark humor. She took her leave and walked back to the passenger compartment where Ben lay snoozing across several seats. His pistol was strapped in its holster. Cinnamon had let him keep it after Ben made it clear she'd have to take it from him. Alice stood and watched the rhythm of his chest rising and falling. Gal had offered him her rack while she was on duty—and off—but he'd declined, preferring to sleep in the common area for some reason known only to him. Alice sat down, trying to be quiet, but the seat creaked.

"I'm not asleep," Ben mumbled.

"Sorry."

"Don't be." He sighed, took a deep breath, and sat up. "It's impossible for me to sleep on this rattle-trap."

"Why?" she asked. Alice had suffered a bad dream or two, but she'd been able to sleep aboard the ship just fine. True, she'd been below in the luxurious expanse of Torque's oversized but surprisingly soft bed.

Rack, she reminded herself. *They call them racks.*

"I don't trust *her*. Gauss. I don't trust any of them, Alice. I don't even trust this ship to stay in one piece. Makes it kinda hard to relax, y'know?"

Being uncomfortable in one's surroundings, distrusting those in charge of one's welfare—those were obstacles to a good night's sleep Alice could appreciate. Still...

"You can trust Cinnamon," she said. "I mean, look at all the trouble we've been through—and she's gotten us through it."

Ben hacked something up and swallowed it again. It sounded like disagreement. "Half that trouble was her doing. She's reckless. She doesn't think first. She just charges in."

Alice held her tongue, though her impulse was to defend Cinnamon. She liked Ben—a *lot*—but she liked Cinn, too. And Ben seemed to be making judgments based on who he thought Cinnamon Gauss was, not who she'd proven herself to be. To Alice, at least.

"You should give her a chance. I was a little afraid of her too, at first, after they took me off the *Archimedes*."

"Who says I'm afraid of her?"

"People are always afraid of what they don't understand," Alice said.

Ben regarded her briefly. "Yeah, well, I'm not afraid of Cinnamon Gauss."

They stopped speaking. The air of the passenger compartment droned with the *Dog*'s engines. The silence between them stretched uncomfortably long. Trying to lighten the mood again, Alice said, "What about Torque? Afraid of her?"

Ben offered a tired grin. "No comment."

Alice laughed. "I was too, at first. I mean, she's big! But soft on the inside, I think."

Ben grunted a sound of noncommittal tolerance. "What happened, by the way?"

"When?"

"After you left Tarsus Station. After Korsakov. We never got to that part of the story."

Right. She'd told him all about her time at Tarsus and why she'd left, but nothing about the journey itself. Maybe those details would help him warm up to Cinnamon and her crew.

"Well, I was very bored," she said. "But I found things to

do." Alice ignored the pulse of memory in her palm. "Ian programmed the ship to fly me into the Blind Passage, where Cinnamon picked me up."

"You said something about a deal?"

Alice nodded. "I don't know the details. But sometimes the pirates trade with Korsakov's station, supplies for tech."

"There's a lot of that going around," Ben said, flashing the fisheye at Louie.

"They promised to get me to Sylvan Novus using their trade network," she said. "After the war started, I was stuck in New Nassau. Cinn said they'd keep their part of the bargain after things settled down."

"Black markets always thrive in wartime," Ben said. He took a moment to digest the information. "But they've treated you okay?"

"Oh, yes!" Alice exclaimed. "Ben, Cinn is so awesome! And Torque. All of them!"

Ben appeared unconvinced. "What happened to the ship? The *Shelley* something?"

"*Shelley's Fever Dream*," Alice corrected. "But that was just the fake name. It was really called the *Archimedes*."

"This Ian certainly covered all the bases, didn't he?"

Was that resentment? Or something else she heard in Ben's voice?

"So, what happened to the ship?" he asked.

"They drilled through the hull to make it look like a typical pirate raid. Left it adrift. If anyone found it, Cinn said, they'd just assume I was another victim of the Triangle. One person, small ship. Would probably be ignored, Cinn said, especially since the war—"

"Looks like they were wrong about that," he said.

Alice sighed. "Ben, they've been really good to me. They care about me. They've looked out for me."

He considered that but still sounded suspicious. "As long as they get their tech from Ian, right?"

"No, it's more than that." She was beginning to get annoyed. "I hear it every time Cinn or one of the others calls me 'little sister.'" That nickname meant even more to her now that she knew Cinnamon's story. Alice felt even more loved. And increasingly irritated with Ben's constantly questioning and insulting her new friends.

He laid his head back. "Maybe." There were dark circles under his eyes. They'd manifested over the last twenty-four hours, and they made him look much more like his grandfather. They made look tired. Old. "Maybe she's got some flying ability," he allowed. "She thinks on her feet. Maybe she's even a good soldier in that way." He cracked his eyes to slits and peered at Alice. "But don't tell her I said that."

Her frustration drained away with a smile. Ben just needed time to adjust, the same way she had. He yawned, and nature forced Alice to answer in kind. She moved closer and folded her body against his. Being next to him like this was beginning to feel normal. Needed.

"Do you mind?" she asked him sleepily. "I feel safe here."

"So you've said," he said.

He didn't sound resentful. Just ... unsure. Of what? She could hear his heartbeat, masked by his rough smartfatigues. She began to count the beats. It sounded like fast-leaping sheep just dropping from a gallop to a canter. The dull thrum of the *Dog*'s engines lulled them both.

"Sure," Ben said lazily. "I mean, no, I don't mind."

"'kay."

There was another long period of silence. After a while, Ben said something else, but it was distant and dreamy and inconsequential. Alice gave in to sleep, safe in the arms of the man who'd rescued her from the dungeon beneath the Terror

Planet. And in that particular moment, nothing was more important.

———

"Wakey wakey, eggs and bakey."

Cinnamon Gauss trilled over shipwide. Alice woke to find herself alone and lying on her side. When she lifted her head, her cheek peeled away from the seat, slick with sleep drool. She wiped it clean, then polished the plastinium with her sleeve. Louie, the only other occupant in the compartment, didn't seem to notice her embarrassment.

"Ben?" she mumbled sleepily.

She couldn't move. "Oh." At some point, he'd laid her down across the seats and strapped her in. Alice popped the buckles loose and sat up. There was the stamp of boots on the deck, and she rubbed her eyes clear to find Ben approaching from forward.

"Sleep okay?" he asked.

The rings around his eyes seemed darker. It was apparent that he hadn't.

"Yeah, I guess. What's going on? Where'd you go?"

"We've entered Tower's Fall space," he said. "Gauss needed someone at tactical to help steer in the asteroid field. The others are sleeping below."

"Were," Torque corrected as her head popped up from the well that led to the crew quarters. She stepped off the ladder and stretched. Her joints cracked like popcorn. Gal followed next, then Moze. Alice wiped her cheek again as Gal heaved a back-to-the-salt-mines sigh and headed forward.

Moze nodded to Ben. "Don't think we've been formally introduced. Serena Mozart. Engineer. But I guess you probably figured that part out."

"Ben Stone." He took her proffered hand. "Captive."

"Good one, Stone." Torque guffawed, following Gal. "I don't care what people say. You're not a total asshole."

"I wasn't kidding," Ben murmured to her back.

As if sharing a secret, Moze said to Ben, "It's the charisma."

"What? What is?"

"The cap's charisma. It kinda captures everyone. Very heavy-g," she said and proceeded to engineering.

Cinnamon came on shipwide again. *"Strap in! There's pretty heavy traffic."*

Ben shared a conspiratorial look with Alice, who smirked, and they wandered forward.

"Didn't you hear me?" Gauss said.

"Yes," Ben and Alice answered together. They smiled wickedly at each other, co-mutineers against their pirate captain. Ben braced against one side of the doorframe, Alice the other.

"Fine, have it your way," Gauss said. "But I warned you. Hope you haven't had anything to eat in the last hour..."

The space ahead of them seemed stuffed with starships, each vectoring in a different direction. The *Junkyard Dog* approached an extensive asteroidal formation that appeared to lean to the left. Alice knew that in space, terms like top, bottom, and side had only relative meaning. But their present approach made it seem as if a series of smaller asteroids had been chipped away from the larger body dominating the screen. She now understood where the region's name came from. The long, tall space rock and its scattered children looked every bit the castle tower, newly breached and about to suffer final collapse.

The lights of a colony appeared like a smaller stepchild of New Nassau, twinkling against the slate-gray crags of its host asteroid. Starships maneuvered in a dangerous dance of approaches and departures. Gal issued a hail, requesting permission to dock.

"The Fall is one of six coves Commander al-Hurra's father founded years ago as reserve positions," Torque explained from the tactical station. "Places to retreat to, should New Nassau fall."

"It hasn't fallen," Gauss corrected her. "It's only surrendered."

Torque paused before giving her response to that odd distinction. "Right," she finally acknowledged.

The *Dog* angled downward sharply, and Alice found herself grabbing on to Ben to keep her feet. Another vessel passed close and overhead, veering upward and away.

"Watch where you're going, asshole!" Gal yelled after the ship. To her fellow passengers, she said, "Sorry about that."

"Like I said, heavy traffic," Gauss allowed. "Dock ops is a little strained."

Lights blinked in the distance, framing an entry port large enough for a starship three times their size. Gal lined up the *Dog*, using thrusters to slow their approach.

"This place looks like a dump," Ben said. "Is it safe?"

"Don't worry," Gauss answered. "I'm practically royalty here."

Alice elbowed Ben in the ribs before he could comment.

"She's coming with me."

"Why?" Ben demanded. "She's safer here."

Cinnamon strapped on a second pistol to her left side. It was the first time Alice had ever seen her wear more than one sidearm. "She's safest with me."

"Says you."

"Yep! And I'm in charge here." She moved past Ben, nudging him lightly aside with one shoulder. Torque, Gal, and

Moze had assembled in the passenger compartment. "Torque, with me. As for you two, no whores! I don't care how *packaged* they are. Stay with the ship and make sure that damned TLD stays reliable. Soon as we have some intel, we'll be out of here."

Gal and Moze acknowledged their orders. Torque nodded, slipping a double-barreled scattergun into a leather sleeve on her back.

"Grease up, poster boy," Cinnamon said, handing Ben a small pot of hydraulic grease. "And put that eyepatch on. Goes with the rest of the outfit—and remember, you're a mechanic. Who's *mute*. And try to lumber."

Ben applied the grease to obscure his face, then put on an oversized flight jacket and wiped his hands clean on it. "This is a bad idea," he growled.

Drawing herself up, Cinnamon was suddenly calm. "You're the one who insists on going. You do it my way or no way. Alice, put on that helmet. Tuck your hair up inside. You shouldn't speak either. The less attention you draw to yourself, the better." She punched the release button with the side of her fist, and the ramp began to lower. "You'll be fine."

"What about him?" Ben asked, indicating Louie.

"He'll be fine too! Now, move out, Marine."

40

LEAP OF FATE

THEY MADE their way across a dock alive with activity. Maintenance teams darted between vessels, exchanging tools and tech and working to repair ships. Every one of the dock's half-dozen berths was filled with waiting vessels. Anxious residents scurried back and forth or stood in long lines for supplies.

"Cinnamon Gauss! As I live and breathe!"

The four halted as a tall, animated man opened wide his bony arms.

Cinnamon shouted "Val Pelles!" before surrendering to his hug.

"Good to see you! Even if it is under such doomsday circumstances."

"Likewise." She pulled away and beamed up at him before turning serious. "Seems like the Fall is handling Operation Exodus pretty well?"

"Best we can," he nodded.

"My crew," she said, gesturing. "You know Torque. This is Meris, navigator's apprentice. One of my nieces on my mother's side. And square jaw here is Rhysio. A recruit of Moze's. Mechanic, second class."

"Kinda young, ain't she?" Pelles said, indicating 'Meris.'

"Gotta learn sometime."

"Right. We could use you, Rhysio," Pelles said. He gestured at the busy dockyard. "We're running double shifts trying to get folks outfitted for the Long Night."

"Long Night?" Cinnamon said.

"It's what we're calling it," Pelles said soberly. "These folks might be on the run for a while. A friendly port could be a long time in the future for some of them."

"Ah, right," Cinnamon said. "I'd love to help, but I can't spare him." She leaned in closer and kept her voice low. "Mission for the marshal."

"Mmm," Pelles said. "Well, if your grandpappy says it's priority, who am I to argue?"

"That's usually wise," Torque observed.

"Who was your last captain?" Pelles asked Ben.

Ben glanced from Pelles to Cinnamon and back again.

"He won't answer," Cinnamon told Pelles. "He can't. Mute." In a loud whisper, she added, "Birth defect."

"Oh," Pelles said. "Too bad."

"Kinda touched, too," Torque said, tapping her temple.

"But a goddamned savant with tools," Cinnamon added. "He was one of Sandoval's crew."

"Lucky he escaped then," Pelles said sympathetically. "And you're luckier you hooked up with the Queen of Thieves here, Rhysio. Just don't stand too close to her in a fight. You'll take the bullet instead of her, every time!"

Ben nodded with a simple expression.

"Captain Pelles!" A woman walked quickly toward them. "It's—"

"Again?" Pelles said.

Exasperated, she said, "I'm afraid so, sir."

Pelles clapped Cinnamon on the shoulder. "Duty calls.

Check in before you leave again?"

"You got it," she said, but he was already walking away with the woman.

"This is a bad idea," Ben breathed.

Cinnamon walked past him. "Shut up, mute."

"Where we headed?" Torque called ahead to her captain.

"Where do you think?" Cinnamon tossed over her shoulder. "The center of all knowledge in the Fall, of course."

"Swashbuckler's Leap?"

"Swashbuckler's Leap."

"Gal was right," Ben said. "This cove is a shithole. And this particular hole is where all the other shit flows into."

They stood in the entryway of a brothel-bar called, according to the half-functional neon sign out front, The Swashbuckler's Leap. The Leap was noisy with slurred speech and loud bragging and smelled like a devil's den of recent sex and yesterday's overindulgence in alcohol.

"Elitist," Gauss snapped, leading them in.

They navigated the crowded tables, trying not to jostle the patrons or otherwise draw attention to themselves. Torque muttered, "There's Norman."

She bobbed her head at a table where two women and two men sat. One of the men lifted a carafe of orange liquid with a muscular arm, refilling the women's glasses. He was dressed in loose, open clothing that was too tight at its tapered waist. The woman nearest him nearly choked on her freshened drink when he whispered something into her ear.

"Don't tell Gal," Gauss warned. "She got paid recently."

Ben groused, "That is one oversexed woman."

"Said the playboy." Torque animated her eyebrows for emphasis.

Staying close by his side, Alice giggled, red-faced. Ben halted in his tracks so quickly she ran into him.

An Arcœnum stood behind the bar, tending to customers. Gauss let the others pass, then doubled back and stretched upward to whisper in Ben's ear.

"You're attracting attention." Gauss wore a serpent's smile meant for anyone watching and indicated a table in one of the darker corners. Torque was leading Alice toward it. Ben held his ground a moment, then let the short pirate move him. He never took his eyes off the Archie behind the bar.

"What better job for him," Gauss whispered as they walked. "Archies make the best bartenders."

Ben eyed the alien, who seemed to anticipate his current customer's needs without their even flicking a finger for a refill.

"Hard to lie to a mind-reader," Torque added as Ben and Gauss joined them at the table.

"Why are we here?" Ben asked.

"Information," Gauss answered simply. "Find out which routes are safe, which are cut off. The war's changed things. Made old, reliable routes too dangerous. Thorne's invasion of the Triangle just upped that ante."

"Couldn't you have gotten your intel over an encrypted channel?"

"I like speaking face-to-face."

Ben released a breath of frustration. "You're putting Alice at risk because you—"

"Don't start in again," Gauss rumbled. Her demeanor abruptly changed, and she offered a welcoming smile to a woman approaching with a tray balanced on one hand.

"What's your poison?" the woman asked, placing a carafe and four glasses on the table.

"The water's fine for now," Gauss said.

"GC won't like that," the waitress cautioned. "Times are tough. Chairs are money."

Gauss widened her smile. "Oh, Gotz and I have an understanding."

Shrugging, the woman wandered back toward the bar.

"It's good she didn't recognize you," Torque said. "Best to keep a low profile in here."

"That won't last," Gauss said.

"Why not?" Alice wondered.

"She's Cinnamon Gauss!" Torque enthused in a melodramatic whisper. Adding, with an exaggerated leer: "A more famouser pirate ye'll never see!"

Alice laughed.

Ben scanned the room. Most of the patrons were older. Their relaxed manner suggested they were regulars. Day drinkers, maybe. The fright of the residents rushing to leave New Nassau—even the anxious eagerness infesting the docks of Tower's Fall—wasn't to be seen here. These people seemed content to squat in this bar and die inebriated and sexually sated. Which, Ben had to admit, was the way he'd want to go.

His gaze lit on their disappointed waitress standing at the bar. She was talking to a man half as wide as he was tall. He moved his attention to their party. Gauss noticed too.

"See, I told you," she said. "Didn't last."

The large man headed their way. His eyes never left Gauss as he walked between tables, smiling and nodding at folks like they were old friends as he passed.

"Hey Tank," he said, addressing Torque. "How's it hangin'?"

"Lower in real gravity. You?"

"Same," he replied, patting his prodigious belly. "And

gravity seems to get stronger every birthday. Up for another bout?"

Torque blew out a breath. "I'd think you'd be a little more wary of getting your ass kicked after last time."

"I slipped."

"Twice, as I recall."

"Bah. You're no fun." He took stock of those at the table before settling once again on Gauss. "Who're your friends?"

"New crew," she answered, then took a sip of water. "Showing them the good life."

"And you brought them here? Well, ain't you the sweet-talkin' salvage wench." Shoving Ben aside with one meaty shoulder to make room, he pulled up a chair and sat astride it.

"Don't mind the one-eye. He don't talk." To Ben and Alice, Gauss said, "This is Gotz Connor. He owns the Leap."

"Folks," Connor said, acknowledging and dismissing them with one word. His smile dropped as he sat forward and dipped his head. "Time's short, Cinn. Listen up."

"I'm all ears," she said.

"Sayyida al-Hurra called ahead. Everyone knew you were coming here. Her people are actively looking for you."

Gauss shot a look to Torque. "I thought we'd have a *little* time, anyway."

"You don't," Connor said.

"Shit.

"It gets worse."

"It usually does."

"Val's in her pocket."

"Pelles?" Torque said, disbelieving. "He always seemed like a straight shooter."

"And a friend," Gauss added, her mood going south.

"Yeah, well—the vote for reconciliation plus Thorne's incursion forced Val to choose sides. Anyway, the word's out—

Sayyida wants the girl." He looked over the two newcomers at the table, his eye lingering on Alice. To Ben, he said, "You're not fooling anyone with the eyepatch and axle grease, sonny boy."

Ben grumbled. "I told you this was a bad idea."

"Shut up," barked Gauss. She took a breath and looked at Connor. "How long do we have?"

"Not long, boss." Torque rapped her knuckles lightly on the table. "Eleven o'clock—four ne'er-do-wells."

"How can you tell?" Ben muttered.

"Don't look!" Gauss said, then looked. So did Ben. Four men stood in the entryway. Atypical of the clientele—younger, sober, armed. Reconning the dense crowd.

"Shit."

"You're looking for the green, I assume," Connor said.

"Yep." Gauss kept a watch on the four hunters. "Any route that ain't compromised."

"The Shallows are still your best bet," Connor said, stating a truism. "And I don't have to tell you, stay away from New Nassau. It's now under full occupation."

"We know," Torque said.

"But your grandfather's okay," he assured Gauss. "There wasn't a battle. Al-Hurra surrendered."

"We heard," Gauss said.

"Seems to be what you pirates do best," Ben said.

"I said, shut up!" hissed Gauss.

The four hunters spotted them. One of the men loosened his pistol in its holster but didn't draw.

"We need to go," Ben said.

Connor produced a scrap of paper and scribbled quickly. "I don't trust the network. Here's the latest on safe routes. Could already be out of date."

Torque palmed the paper.

"Thanks, GC," Gauss said. "Nice to know you can count on *somebody*."

"Head out the back. Use the keg door." He stood up and shuffled away. "Folks! Patrons! The best customers in the Triangle!"

The four hunters were pushing their way through the crowd. When Connor repeated his call for attention, the buzz of boasting and negotiation began to wane.

"Follow me," Gauss said.

"Given current circumstances," Connor shouted, "I can't think of a better time for a free drink!"

His customers roared approval.

The itchy hunter pulled his pistol and prompted his mates to do the same. Drunks began to make way for the armed men. Seeing their quarry melt away, the men elbowed their way forward through the crowd.

"That's not all!" Connor declared. "First one to the bar gets three!"

Chairs screeched on the floor. Prostitutes fell on their butts. Friends and acquaintances pushed one another aside. A mad scramble surged for the bar, sweeping the cursing hunters along with it.

"I like that guy," Ben said as they ducked through the back door.

"Frying pan and fire," Torque observed. She reached over her shoulder and drew her scattergun.

"—just get ready for dust off!" Gauss was shouting into comms.

Ben exited the Leap into a high overhang of tunnel rock with Alice close behind. The alley was long, dark, and dank.

And not quite deserted. At the far end stood three pirates obstructing their escape route. They'd seen Gauss and company barrel out of the Leap and drew their weapons.

"Up!" Torque shouted. Grabbing the ladder hanging on the wall, she hauled it down with her weight. "Go, Stone!"

"Alice, hurry," Ben said, pulling his pistol. She climbed surprisingly fast for a Centaurian. He tossed shots down the alley, and the ambushers dove for cover. Gauss rolled behind a stack of empty kegs, firing both her pistols. Ben scrambled clumsily up the ladder one-handed while Torque blocked the keg door with her body to stymie any pursuit from inside.

Alice reached the roof. Torque roared below, unloading both barrels of her shotgun. She thrust the weapon into its back holster and grabbed up an empty beer keg. Thundering a challenge, Torque heaved the keg down the alley like a bowling ball looking for pins to mow down. It cracked the stone alleyway as it bounced, echoing like hammer strikes off the hard rock walls.

"What's—" Alice began.

"Quiet!" Ben said, levering himself over the lip of the roof. "And stay down!"

More feet on the ladder, and Ben found Gauss climbing as he had with one hand and shooting with the other. From the high ground, he could see heels and elbows of the enemy behind cover, waiting for a lull in Torque's tirade to shoot her down. One stood up and drew a bead as she hefted another keg. Ben aimed, exhaled, and squeezed the trigger. The pirate jerked once and went down. Gauss tumbled onto the roof beside him.

"Are you okay?" Alice asked her.

"Fine," She thrust her back against the short wall and caught her breath.

"I told you," Ben began, "this was a—"

"Go ahead," Gauss said, cocking both pistols, "finish that sentence."

"Never mind."

"A little help down here!" Torque shouted. "I'm running out of kegs!"

Ben eyeballed the tactical situation below. One dead pirate had inspired caution in his luckier mates. It wouldn't be long before the two in hiding were joined by the four from inside. Torque was running out of time. "We provide cover," he said, "she climbs up."

"Wow," Gauss said, "you *are* a military genius."

She stood up, yipped like a banshee dog, and threw bullets from both barrels onto the heads of the cowering duo. Her pistols dry clicked, empty, and she dropped again beside Ben to reload. Two more blasts of buckshot thundered the alleyway before Torque's heavy weight began gonging on the rungs of the ladder. Less brash and more surgical than Gauss had been, Ben knelt on overwatch and waited. One of the pirates offered himself up, and Ben fired twice but missed. The brave man became discrete again.

"Guys!" Alice said.

"Not now, little sister," Gauss said, thumbing slugs.

Reloaded, she stood again with a boldness Ben could only admire as stupidly optimistic.

"But—"

Whatever Alice was about to say was drowned out by the rapid fire of Gauss's dual hand cannons. One big hand, then another reached over the lip of the half-wall. Torque heaved herself up to crash shoulder-first onto the roof. Her grunt of pain meant she hadn't stuck the landing.

Gunshots pinged the brick next to Ben's leg. A shard of rocky shrapnel wedged into the knee of his smartfatigues.

Not from the alleyway...

"Ben!" Alice warned.

He turned to find two of the four hunters from the bar below dashing through the roof's access door.

"Gauss!"

Grabbing Alice, Ben dove for the housing of an air processing unit between them and the latest threat. He lined up on the fourth pirate passing through the door and fired. The man went down wailing. His three comrades dropped and belly crawled, seeking cover.

"What I wouldn't give for Desi right now," Ben said.

Gauss sidled into the narrow space behind the exhaust unit. There was no room for Torque, who crawled in as close as she could and lay prostrate in the grime.

"Who's Desi?" Alice asked.

"Not who, what," he said. "She's the AI of my combat armor. Named her ... well, Desi."

A brace of rifle fire peppered the housing from the doorway.

"Aboard the *Dog*," Gauss said, glancing around a corner of their low metal cover. She thrust a pistol backward over her head and squeezed off a few rounds meant to inspire caution. "And I'm almost out."

"What?" Ben said.

"I said, I'm almost out!"

"No, what'd you say about Desi?"

"Your armor! It's in the *Dog*'s lower hold."

Ben stared, thinking he hadn't heard right. "You took my armor from the *Terre*?"

Another round of rifle fire made them all cringe to be smaller. The metal of the exhaust unit was getting chewed up and spat out.

"Hello!" Gauss waved her pistols. "Pirates!"

"So, I was thinking," Torque said from the fetal ball she'd become, "maybe we should get the hell out of here!"

"We're too deep into the cove," Gauss said. "*Dog*'s too big."

"The skiff, maybe—" Torque said.

"Cover us!" Ben said.

"What do you think I've been doing, poster boy?" Gauss answered before popping off a few more rounds.

Hoping there wouldn't be too much interference from the dense iron-nickel asteroid, Ben pinged the *Junkyard Dog* with his NFC. He sent a pairing request to Desi, and there she was, passively listening and powered down in the ship's cargo hold.

At his command, Desi powered up his battlesuit.

41

THEM

"YOU'D BETTER WARN YOUR PEOPLE," Ben said to Gauss. "Desi's awake."

"Warn them about? ... ah."

"Hey, Cinnamon!" A voice called from the doorway. "Weapons cold, yeah? Parlay?"

Gauss cursed. After sending a heads-up to her crew aboard the *Dog*, she said to the others, "Use this time to reload. Torque, here." She handed the big woman a pistol and her last handful of slugs. "Any more in that scattergun?"

Torque looked sheepish. "I didn't think there'd be this much trouble."

For once, Gauss didn't bark. "Neither did I."

"Y'all still alive over there?" wondered the voice.

"How long, Stone?" Gauss asked.

"ETA: two mikes."

"Fast-mover," Torque said.

Ben shrugged. "That's kinda the point."

"Stand up, Val?" Gauss shouted over the top of the housing.

"Sure! We got no beef with you, Cinn, you know that. All we want is the girl."

"If they clip me," Gauss growled, "kill Pelles first."

"Wait, Cinnamon!—" Alice said, but the pirate captain stood up straight.

"No man's land rules," Gauss called across the distance.

"Agreed," Pelles answered, emerging from the doorway. His hands were up, his rifle pointed at the cavern roof. He gave the weapon to one of his cronies, who slung it barrel down. Pelles walked slowly forward. Gauss mirrored him, step for step. They halted within arm's length of one another, halfway between the two groups. Three men, not quite as bold as their leader, stepped partially out of cover.

"I'm disappointed, Val," Gauss said. "I thought you were a team player."

"Oh, I am," answered the de facto ruler of Tower's Fall. "But I'm playing for the long term. Sayyida's next in line for al-Hurra's job."

"That's a big assumption. And it's King Hadrian to you."

"See, that's always been your problem, Cinn. You're a romantic. Now, me? I'm a pragmatist."

Ben cast a furtive eye over the housing. Gauss stood in her cocky manner, left hip out, a pistol in the holster hanging on it. The other holster hung empty, its former occupant now in Torque's possession. Pelles was relaxed, his thumbs in his lanky beltline.

"Handing Alice Keller to Sayyida as a bargaining chip isn't pragmatic. It's betrayal. How many times did you spit on the Alliance for the same thing back in the day?"

"Times are different now."

"Principles aren't," Gauss snapped.

Pelles straightened up. "This isn't much of a parlay."

"I'm waiting on your offer."

Pelles squinted and said, "I'd have thought my offer was obvious. Give us the girl, you and yours walk away."

Ben could feel it through the thin roof. The subtle, pulsing vibration.

"Oh, my mistake," Gauss said to Pelles. "I thought you were here to offer us free passage as a patriot of the pirate code."

The man's expression hardened. "I'll even throw in Stone. That oughta sweeten the deal."

Gauss made a sound of amusement. Hacked and spat on the rooftop.

"You obviously don't know Stone."

Pelles regarded her a moment. "You're stalling," he said.

"For what? It's not like Gal can get the *Dog* into this narrow cavern. I'm at your mercy here, Val."

There came the whir of mechanical servos and the percussive rhythm of heavy footfalls. The shrieking of disbelief in the distance—the remaining two pirates in the alley, yelling in shock and surprise.

Pelles heard it too. "Keep your eyes open!" he called to his crew. To Gauss, "What are you up to?"

"About five-four," she said. "Five-five when I'm feeling good about myself."

The weight of a thousand pounds of combat armor hammered the alleyway below.

The eyes of the thin man narrowed. Then widened to saucers when he saw the battlesuit leap up and over the lip of the wall to smash the rooftop like a dropping anvil. Shards of rock erupted around the impact of its heavy metal feet.

"What the..." Pelles backed away. The suit drew itself up to its full height and deployed twin Gatling cannons from its wrist gauntlets. They spun up with a mechanical whine.

Ben's voice projected from Desi's mouth port as he stood up. *"Throw down your weapons."*

No one did.

"Do it," Ben said. His voice was eerie and metallic amplified by the suit's vocal emulator. *"Or die."*

Gauss dove flat against the roof.

"Ember!" Pelles shouted. "Ember!"

One of the pirates tossed something, and Pelles caught and redirected it in flight straight at Ben's battlesuit. It clamped magnetically to the chest piece. Three short beeps sounded, and the device went off. Blue lightning arced across the armored exterior. The empty battlesuit collapsed to its knees, then crashed visor-first to the rooftop.

"What happened?" Alice said.

"Ember grenade," Ben said, shocked. Once again, decades-old tech had subverted the latest in Alliance military capability. "Shorted out the electrical system."

"Seems like *they* thought there'd be this much trouble," Torque mumbled.

A newly heartened Val Pelles stood up straight from the duck-and-cover posture he'd fallen into. His men came forward, bringing their weapons up. "Nicely played," he said, moving to stand over Gauss. "But I win."

The pirate captain rose to her hands and knees and stared hard at Ben. He was surprised at how much her helplessness disturbed him. But Desi had been his final card, and Gauss knew it, too. Something passed between them—the captain of Marines and pirate queen—a shared acknowledgment that they were out of options.

But the armor had other ideas.

It began to move. Jerkily, at first. Like a human, discovering how muscles worked for the first time.

Pelles took a half-step back. His men leveled their weapons and pulled their triggers. The rapid fire of slugs was deafening. The shots ricocheted off the battlesuit as it climbed to its knees.

Cautiously, like its joints were learning to lever weight again. Its armored legs, remembering how to stand.

"That's impossible," Ben said. "She's shorted out!" It was then he felt Alice beside him. Ben looked over to find her standing, her hands manipulating in the empty air.

Controlling.

The battlesuit stood to its full height and put one heavy foot forward. The grainy muck of the rooftop squelched beneath the ton of polysteel armor.

A second step. Slowly, almost as if the mindless metal were being deliberate, counting. Each step a kind of victory in its own right.

Alice concentrated, crinkling the corners of her eyes into crow's feet. The roof was unnaturally quiet now after the hailstorm of bullets mere moments earlier. The only sound being Alice's labored breathing.

"Shoot them," Ben urged her.

"No," she hissed back.

"What?" Their window was closing. They had the advantage. "Shoot them, Alice!" he shouted.

Pelles's crew dropped their weapons.

"No," she whispered. "I can't."

Instead, Alice spun up the Gatling cannons as she'd seen Desi do before. They filled the roof with the deadly promise of well-maintained military hardware.

Pelles stumbled over his own feet as he turned to flee. His pirates broke and ran first, leading their leader through the access doorway, their weapons forgotten behind them.

As the battlesuit's cannons began to slow their rotation, Ben, Alice, and the others quickly found themselves alone on the roof. Her shoulders slumping, Alice released a long exhale of relief.

Over the lip of the short brick wall behind them, a small skiff rose.

"Hey, Cap!" Gal called as she worked the controls. "Need a lift?"

Ben caught Gauss's eye. *Can you believe we were this lucky?* She showed him a slight smirk of triumph before the cynic's mask descended again.

"About time!" she complained, hopping to her feet.

Gal grinned. "All aboard!"

"Can you get Desi on there?" Ben asked Alice.

Alice was sweating. She looked almost in pain. But she straightened up again and closed her eyes and worked her fingers. The armor turned slowly toward them as if presenting itself for inspection.

Ben touched Alice lightly on the shoulder. "You might want to lower those gauntlets."

Everyone crowded into the cockpit of the *Junkyard Dog*, much to her captain's annoyance. But she let it slide. The occupation of Tower's Fall was unfolding, and it was a fascinating if disheartening process to watch. Gal had parked them behind the heavy nickel-iron body of one of the Fall's smaller children, where they waited on their opportunity to make a run for it. To where—well, that was still an open question.

"Never thought I'd see the day," Gal said, slumped in the co-pilot's seat.

Gauss grunted something foul from the back of her throat.

"Stone," Torque said, curious, "your suit just pinged."

Ben pried his eyes away from the drama at the cove. "What?"

"Tightbeam transmission," she said. "From one of those ships over there. The troop carrier."

That got Gauss's attention. "What? Shut it down! They can track it."

"Not out here," Torque said. "Too much interference. And it's a short-range transponder, for keeping units cohesive."

"Shut it down anyway," Gauss said, eyeing Ben with suspicion.

"A message?" Moze asked.

Torque grunted. "Seems like."

"You playing both sides, Stone?" Gauss wondered aloud. "Like Pelles?"

"Someone needs to turn it off," Gal reminded them.

"Desi must have rebooted. I'll have to do shut down the link manually," Ben said, holding Gauss's gaze. "Someone severed my connection when we got back aboard."

"Why don't we all go," Gauss said, climbing out of the pilot's seat after him. "Nothing to see worth seeing, that's for sure."

Everyone, save Gal who stayed at the helm, followed Ben to the middle compartment.

The combat armor lay cockeyed on the deck where Alice had released it from her control. Ben opened a panel on the back of the battlesuit, and the AI righted the suit to a sitting position. Gauss pulled a pistol and aimed it casually at the armor, then turned the barrel on Ben.

"Won't make a dent on your girlfriend," Gauss said, "but it'll sure dent you."

"Cinnamon!" Alice said.

Light Without Shadow sat in his fixed position, observing all impassively.

"There's no need for that," Ben said. "I just need to—"

"Don't turn it off," Gauss said without holstering her

sidearm. "I want to see that message. External display. Now, Stone."

He held her eyes a moment, then flashed a sarcastic leer. "Aye-aye, Cap'n."

Ben queued up the message. The air in front of the battle-suit shimmered. Bathsheba Toma's upper torso appeared in full combat armor. Behind her was the docking facility at Tower's Fall. Her face was grim as the grave, Ben thought.

"This message is for Captain Ben Stone," she said. *"I'm breaking protocol by sending it, and I'm quite sure he won't be the only one to see it. But, desperate times..."*

"A bit dramatic isn't she?" Gauss said.

"Not usually," Ben replied. "And now it's your turn to shut up."

"You have to know you're in deep shit, Captain. Admiral Thorne has issued a warrant for your arrest. You're lucky he hasn't ordered you shot on sight. But more pressing matters have taken priority." She cleared her throat. Her face appeared to blanch. Or maybe it was just the poor signal. *"A massive Archie fleet is heading toward Alliance space from Sirius C."* She paused again to let that sink in.

"Hold that," Gauss ordered.

Ben paused the playback.

"Could be a mislead?" Moze ventured. "She said herself she knows others will hear this message. Maybe trying to scare us? Flush us out?"

"Maybe," Gauss allowed. "Stone, how well do you know that officer? How good an actress is she? And don't lie." She moved her pistol around to motivate him toward a truthful response.

"Well enough to know that she's not that good an actress."

Gauss made a noncommittal noise. "Play the rest of it."

"We've begun tracking the fleet's progress via subspace relay stations," Toma said.

On-screen the image shifted from a tight focus on Toma to long-range subspace scanner returns. First one, then a dozen, then scores of ships appeared. Close formation, all burning hard on their course. The fleet composition was a miscellany of ship designs, reminding Ben of the left-behind Archie's tech in the cave on Canis III. Or al-Hurra's corridors in New Nassau with their jerry-rigged conduits. Arcœnum ships and old-style Alliance ships flew side by side. It looked like archival footage from the Specter War, when the Arcœnum had supplemented their own fleet with human vessels.

Toma reappeared. She took a breath, as if double-checking her facts before speaking. Ben had no doubt that was exactly what she was doing. But her next words had another quality to them. For the first time in all the time Ben had known her, Bathsheba Toma sounded scared to death.

"Stone," she said, *"they're invading."*

Light Without Shadow moved subtly, unfolding himself with an elegance belying the time he'd spent sitting in one position. Ben saw and, drawing his pistol, backed up a step. Gauss saw too and steadied her own weapon on the Marine captain. A large, restraining fist wrapped around the gun in Ben's hand.

"Louie's not the enemy," Torque said.

"The hell he's not," Ben said. "You heard what Sheba just said."

"Stone, drop it!" Gauss warned.

Louie stepped closer to Toma's image, his four arms waving. He seemed to be in distress.

"Ben, please," Alice said.

"Something's wrong, Ben," Torque said, watching Louie closely. "He's upset. Trust us, here. Trust *me*." She squeezed his hand lightly. Reassuringly. But she didn't take his weapon this time.

Ben lowered his gun hand.

The Arcœnum touched a control on his exoskeleton. A second projection appeared beside Toma's message.

"What is that?" Alice asked.

"Trade window," Torque said. "It's what we use to communicate for bartering."

"Translates metaphorical images from the Arcœnum so we can understand them," Moze added. "Translates our speech back into images for them. Crude, but gets the job done."

In Louie's projection, the Archie fleet from Toma's message was recreated with its dozens of ships. Old Alliance vessels from the Specter War. More angelic, Arcœnum-designed super ships flew in formation with them as they had in Toma's transmission. And other, less elegant vessels. Bulky and boxy. They looked like transports to Ben, or freighters maybe.

The image changed. Humans, hundreds of them—thousands—escaping the outskirts of a human city in flames. Crying, scared, shock on their faces. A thermonuclear detonation incinerated the city behind them.

"Not an enemy?" snapped Ben. "The sonofabitch is threatening us. Showing us what they'll—"

"Wait," Torque said.

The image changed. Animals—a mixture of human species and exotic, alien creatures—fleeing a dense forest. Wildfires raged behind them, driving them onward and outward. Flushing them from their homes.

Louie's arms became animated again.

The image changed. The perspective leapt from the stern of the last ship in the Archie fleet and zoomed across lightyears before approaching a second fleet of black ships. Barely visible against the velvet darkness of deep space, dead starlight formed halos around their monstrous, spherical hulls. Branches jutted outward from the primary hulls like legs. Pinpoints of vibrant, violet light shone like eyes from within the arachnoid super-structures.

Alice caught her breath and clutched fiercely at Ben's arm.

"Alice?"

Light Without Shadow made a mewling sound. Regardless of species, regardless of language, his distress was clear.

With certainty, Gauss said, "The Arcœnum aren't invading."

"They're running," Torque whispered.

Alice began to tremble against Ben. He put his arm around her and held her close.

"Alice, what is it?"

"It's them," she whispered, her voice trembling. "*Shadow-spiders.*"

The adventure concludes in
INVASION
Book 3 of War for Empire

THANK YOU FOR READING WARPATH!

WE HOPE you enjoyed it as much as we enjoyed bringing it to you. We just wanted to take a moment to encourage you to review the book. Follow this link: Warpath to be directed to the book's Amazon product page to leave your review.

Every review helps further the author's reach and, ultimately, helps them continue writing fantastic books for us all to enjoy.

You can also join our non-spam mailing list by visiting www.subscribepage.com/AethonReadersGroup and never miss out on future releases. You'll also receive three full books completely Free as our thanks to you.

Facebook | Instagram | Twitter | Website

Want to discuss our books with other readers and even the authors? Join our Discord server today and be a part of the Aethon community.

Also in series:

War for Empire
Legacy
Warpath
Invasion

Looking for more great Science Fiction?

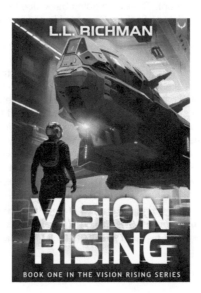

A lone soldier is gifted the power to save humanity. When a training exercise at a classified research facility goes awry, Joe Kovacs loses much more than his eyesight. He loses his career. He can't lead one of the military's top spec-ops teams if he can't see. A decision with consequences. Joe's only shot at getting his life back lies in the hands of an anonymous 'shadow' scientist. The offer is risky, an experimental implant that may or may not work. He jumps at the chance, but quickly learns the device does more than restore his sight. Much more. There's no going back. Joe begins seeing strange flashes. Ghosts of images, overlaid atop his own vision. Actions he could have taken but didn't. Worse, the visions are increasing in scope and frequency. Believing he's going mad, he confronts the scientist, only to discover the implant's shocking origin. Nothing is as it seems, and all the possible futures Joe can now see point to a system-wide conspiracy that will shift the balance of power for hundreds of years. Joe's visions hold the key to stopping it... if he can learn to control them in time. **Don't miss this exciting new Military Science Fiction Series that will make you not only question just what it means to be human, but also if there is ever a "right" side. It's perfect for fans of Halo, Rick Partlow (Drop Trooper), Jeffery H. Haskell (Grimm's War), and Joshua Dalzelle (Black Fleet Saga).**

Get Vision Rising Now!

A colony cut-off. A mysterious alien wormhole. A Captain with nothing to lose... Contact with Earth has been lost for generations and mysterious waves of disappearing colonists have been shaking the five moons of the Archimedes System for decades. When suddenly a wormhole appears in the middle of the system, the Union Navy faces an ancient danger from the darkness of deep space. A merciless war erupts, and Jeremy Brandt, Captain of the UNS Concordia, is sent through the wormhole to confront the mysterious enemy. **Pick up your copy of this new Military Science Fiction adventure from bestseller Joshua T. Calvert. Aliens, War, and a Captain who will stop at nothing to defend his people, this is Sci-Fi the way it's meant to be!**

Get Behemoth Now!

For all our Sci-Fi books, visit our website.

Made in United States
Troutdale, OR
06/04/2023

10447289R00260